"Bright and funny and remarkably poised."

—*The Boston Globe*

"A cool, funny, stylish, and very original look at life and love in Manhattan, by a remarkable new writer."

—ALISON LURIE

"*Till the Fat Lady Sings* is an engrossing satire of the New York female intelligentsia."

—NAOMI WOLF

"An immensely poised and well-crafted performance, which kept me smiling to myself throughout."

—PHILLIP LOPATE

FLIRTING IN CARS

"This exciting tease of a novel will set your heart pounding like the best love affair. Smart, funny, sexy—I loved it!"

—PAMELA REDMOND SATRAN,
author of *The Man I Should Have Married*
and *Suburbanistas*

"*Flirting in Cars* is a modern-day fairy tale about finding happily-ever-after where you least expect it. I couldn't put it down."

—KAREN QUINN,
author of *The Ivy Chronicles* and *Wife in the Fast Lane*

"Alisa Kwitney's cross-cultural love story is intelligent, funny, and sexy." —THELMA ADAMS, *US Weekly*

SEX AS A SECOND LANGUAGE

"The romance between Kat and Magnus is . . . true-to-life and achingly bittersweet . . . with one of the sexiest scenes involving two forty-somethings since *The Thomas Crown Affair*." —DEBRA PICKETT of the *Chicago Sun-Times*

"An engaging and intelligently written comedy—with a few genuinely titillating sex scenes."

—*Publishers Weekly*

"*Sex as a Second Language,* Alisa Kwitney's smart, sassy, sexy tale of the single mom who brings in a spy from the cold and warms him up, is funny and emotionally true, a great read!"

—JENNIFER CRUSIE, bestselling author of *Bet Me*

ON THE COUCH

"A teasingly good read. Sexy, sassy and a little kinky. A different take on Manhattan life—more handcuffs than cocktails."

—CAROLE MATTHEWS, *USA Today* bestselling author

DOES SHE OR DOESN'T SHE?

"Alisa Kwitney is my guilty pleasure."

—NEIL GAIMAN,
Hugo Award–winning author of *American Gods* and
New York Times bestselling author of *Coraline*

"Witty, charming, funny and real, Alisa Kwitney brings a fresh voice to chick-lit and romance!"

—CARLY PHILLIPS, *New York Times* bestselling author

"Sharp, sassy, and sexy."

—JENNIFER CRUISIE, *New York Times* bestselling author

THE DOMINANT BLONDE

"Her search for the perfect boyfriend and the perfect hair color is delightful. It belongs right up there with all the legally and naturally blonde bombshells of our time."

—LIZ SMITH, nationally syndicated columnist

ALSO BY ALISA SHECKLEY

The Better to Hold You

BY ALISA SHECKLEY WRITING AS ALISA KWITNEY

Flirting in Cars
Sex as a Second Language
On the Couch
Does She or Doesn't She?
The Dominant Blonde
Till the Fat Lady Sings

Sandman: King of Dreams
Destiny: A Chronicle of Deaths Foretold
Vertigo Visions: Art from the Cutting Edge of Comics
Token

MOON BURN

ALISA SHECKLEY

BALLANTINE BOOKS • NEW YORK

A Del Rey Mass Market Original

Copyright © 2009 by Alisa Sheckley

Published in the United States by Del Rey, an imprint of The Random House Publishing Group, a division of Random House, Inc., New York.

DEL REY is a registered trademark and the Del Rey colophon is a trademark of Random House, Inc.

ISBN 978-0-345-50588-0

Printed in the United States of America

www.delreybooks.com

OPM   9   8   7   6   5   4   3   2   1

To Ted Wolner, a.k.a. Dr. Grinch,
who taught me everything I know about
Bach, algebra, jump shots, and loyalty

ACKNOWLEDGMENTS

I raise my martini to my editor, Liz Scheier, who is a rare combination of book smart, market smart, and people smart, and knew just what to say to guide and encourage me and keep me on the right side of the bestiality laws; and I owe a martini to assistant editor Kaitlin Heller, who has been amazingly efficient and incredibly kind during this unusually unsettled time. Shauna Summers and Jessica Sebor, thanks for taking such good care of me. My husband, Mark, son, Matthew, and daughter, Elinor, were wonderfully tolerant as I spent two or three months (the days blurred) in a caffeine-fueled writing frenzy, and my mother, Ziva, spent a week going over the manuscript and spotting the awkward, the inadvisable, and the downright inexplicable. Last but never least, thanks to Meg Ruley, my agent, for being both wise and clever, and helping me take this walk on the wild side.

◑ ◯ ◯ ◯ ◑

PART ONE

"You were once wild here. Don't let them tame you."
—Isadora Duncan

ONE

◐○○   Manhattan is not the center of the universe. It only feels that way. But outside of the immense gravitational pull of that small island, there are whole other realms of existence.

For the past year, I've been living in the town of Northside, which is two hours from the city but subscribes to an alternate reality. Winter arrives earlier and tests your resourcefulness. The moon is more of a presence. Your regular waitress not only knows exactly what you're going to order, she also knows how much money you have in the local bank, the status of your divorce negotiations, and your entire medical history, down to the name of the prescription cream you just called in to the pharmacy.

Yet there are also secrets that are easier to conceal here, buffered by trees and mountains and distance. The city may offer a kind of intimate anonymity, but the country permits other freedoms.

The freedom to run around naked in the woods, for example. Which I do about three days a month, when the moon is at its fullest. Having lycanthropy, like having children, forces you to reevaluate the advantages and disadvantages of apartment living. Of course, I'm not talking from personal experience here—I don't have children.

But even though I accept that I'm better off in the country, it's been a bit of an adjustment. Before I moved out here, trying to save my doomed marriage, I'd had a coveted slot as a veterinary intern at the Animal Medical Institute on the Upper East Side. And while the education I got there was top of the line, I've had to unlearn a fair chunk of it.

In the city, people don't purchase pets, they adopt substitute children to carry around in big handbags, or rescue surrogate soul mates who will wait uncomplainingly at home all day, then greet each homecoming with frenzied affection. If Basil the basset hound gets cancer, nobody blinks an eyelash at spending thousands of dollars on medical care, physical therapy, a specially designed prosthesis.

Around here, it's a different story.

Northside dogs are considered animals, and they spend much of their day outside and unattended, having adventures that their humans know nothing about. There are exceptions, of course, but in general, country people love their dogs, though they don't regard them as quasi-humans covered in fur. Northsiders acknowledge the wolf that resides within the breast of every canine, no matter how outwardly domesticated. "It's no kind of life for a dog" is the verdict for most serious illness.

Looking at the massive, gore-spattered rottweiler stinking up my examining room, I had to wonder who had it better: the beloved city pets who received constant attention and care, or their country counterparts, who had the freedom to follow their instincts and roll in decomposing deer entrails.

"I don't see or feel any cuts or abrasions," I told the dog's owner, a lean woman with work-roughened hands, leathery skin, and brittle, teased black hair. Her name was Marlene Krauss and she ran a hair salon out of her home. I could feel her sizing up my long brown braid the way a lumberjack sizes up a redwood.

"In fact," I said, double checking the pads of the rottweiler's large paws, "I don't think this is her blood at all. Queenie's probably just been frolicking in something dead."

"Oh, I don't care about that," said Marlene. "She's always getting into something." When she moved, I caught a whiff of stale cigarette smoke and some drugstore version of Chanel No. 5. If I'd been completely human, the combination would have been strong enough to mask the usual vet's office odors of cat urine, bleach, rubbing alcohol, and frightened dog. If I'd been completely wolf, I wouldn't have made any olfactory value judgments. As it was, I was smack in the middle of my monthly cycle, which meant that the scent of Marlene was getting up my nose and on my nerves.

"So what was the reason you brought Queenie in today?"

Marlene tapped her manicured fingers impatiently on the steel operating table. "Because I think she's pregnant."

"Oh," I said, momentarily nonplussed. There I was again, making urban assumptions. In Manhattan, most people didn't know that most dogs' dearest wish is to roll in a putrid corpse. The experts theorize that dogs do it to disguise their own predator's scent from potential prey, but watching dogs, you can see that there's a wild, abandoned joy to be had from rolling around in something truly rank.

Of course, I knew this from personal experience as well. But I try not to think about that part of my life during my working day. Compartmentalize, that's the trick.

"Well? Aren't you going to check her?" Her voice sounded like it had been fed a steady diet of cigarettes and broken glass.

"Of course." Crouching back down, I looked at Queenie, who instantly licked me on the lips. Maneuvering my face so it was out of tongue range, I put my hand on the dog's abdomen and palpated. Her mammary glands were swollen. "Were you trying to breed her?"

"Not to a damn coyote."

"You think she was bred by a coyote?"

"I could hear them howling, and when I went out to bring Queenie in, I found her rope had been bitten clear through." Marlene went on to explain how she had just shelled out good money to fix Queenie up with a pureblood rotty male, and the stud fee wasn't refundable just because Queenie had hooked up with a no-good-thieving lowlife who wasn't even from the same subspecies. I had to bite the inside of my cheek to keep from laughing, because I wasn't sure whether Marlene was talking to me or her dog, or both.

And then it wasn't amusing anymore, because Queenie started to whimper. She gave Marlene a particularly pathetic look, equal parts hurt and confusion. It probably affected me more than it should have, because I'd worn that look myself for the better part of a year, while my ex-husband criticized and cheated and infected me with a little something he'd picked up in the Carpathian mountains.

I suppose I hadn't been much savvier than Queenie, who didn't understand what she'd done wrong by following her instincts, and certainly couldn't make the connection between that long-forgotten afternoon with Mr. Wile E. Coyote and her owner's current cold disapproval. I ran my hand over the short, filthy black fur on Queenie's thick neck. It struck me that a woman who had time to apply little flower decals to the back of each nail ought to be able to hose off her dog before bringing her into the vet. I wondered if Marlene had been neglecting her dog in other ways as well.

I was still crouched down next to Queenie, but I'd stopped petting her for a moment. She nudged me with her tan and black muzzle, then pressed her full weight against my shoulder and arm, knocking me back on my heels. Like a lot of big dogs, rottweilers have an inbred desire to lean on the unwary. "You're a good girl," I told her.

Then, before Marlene could disagree with this diagnosis, I added my medical opinion: "She feels like she's about two months along."

"Damn. I'd meant to come by a few weeks ago, but I just couldn't find the time. Well, nothing else for it. How long will it take for you to clean her out?"

I straightened up so that I could look Marlene in the eye, trying to decide how to respond. I had terminated animal pregnancies before, usually with a morning-after pill or hormone injection. Sometimes the mother is too small or too young to whelp a litter successfully. At other times, I had performed the procedure because there were too many unwanted puppies and kittens in the world, and the world isn't kind to the unwanted. Nobody picketed the clinic or called me a killer: When it comes to veterinary medicine, the controversial is commonplace.

But like most vets, I have my own moral code. I don't believe in performing euthanasia on animals that aren't incurable and in pain. I'm sorry you're moving and can't find a good home for Captain, but that's not really sufficient cause to kill a perfectly good young dog whose only crime is being too big for your new apartment.

I don't dock the ears or tails of puppies, because I consider it mutilation, pure and simple. I don't declaw cats until I explain that I'm basically amputating finger bones. And I do not abort puppies that are already viable outside the womb.

"The problem here," I said, "is that a dog's gesta-

tional period is usually around sixty-three days . . ." I
trailed off, managing not to add *as you should know,
since you were planning on breeding Queenie.*

"Yeah? So?"

"Well, it's just a bit late to do it now. Queenie's due in
about a week."

Marlene gave an exasperated huff. "Damn it."

"I'm sorry, but if you need help with the whelping or
placing the puppies in good homes . . ."

"That won't be necessary." Marlene snapped a leash
onto Queenie's collar. "How much do I owe you?"

I looked back over at Queenie, who had the kind of
broad, large-muzzled face that a lot of people consider
frightening, but who struck me as a big, genial barmaid
of a girl. "What are you planning on doing with the litter?"

Marlene gave me a cold, hard look. "Since you won't
help, I'll have to deal with it on my own, won't I?"

Queenie gave two quick thumps with her blunt stub
of a tail, probably eager to be on her way outside, where
the air was cool and the newly melted snow had left the
ground covered with a smorgasbord of fascinating
scents. I imagined the good-natured rottweiler giving
birth, then lying back trustingly as her pups were taken
from her one by one. Marlene would probably worry
more about damaging her nails than any possible suffering as she dropped the pups into a sack and then deposited them in a Dumpster.

I took a deep breath. "Wait a second, Marlene." She
paused in the act of rummaging through her purse, looking up with fake eyelashes and real animosity. But then I
didn't know how to continue.

Back at the Animal Medical Institute, I had a
coworker named Lilliana who could gently steer a person toward a different decision. I lack that kind of fi-
nesse. I was aware that I was probably giving Marlene

what my mother calls my disapproving librarian glare, and I tried to imagine what Lilliana would have said.

"Are you possibly considering . . . disposing of the puppies yourself? Because I need to tell you that it's illegal to kill them." Oh, yes, that was wonderfully diplomatic.

Marlene's lip curled. "Weren't you listening to me? She's going to have a litter of coydogs. They'll be bigger and stronger than coyotes, and they won't be scared of people. But they'll have all their father's sneaky hunting instincts. You can't give a coydog up for adoption." Marlene snapped her purse shut, clearly deciding I had not provided satisfactory service and was therefore not deserving of remuneration. "You want to adopt out an enormous half-breed coyote so he can chew up some unsuspecting kid? Fine. But I'm sure as hell not going to be a party to it."

The growl that rumbled out of my chest shocked all three of us. I saw Marlene's eyes widen as she clutched her purse with both hands, trying to back away. Gentle Queenie had gone stiff-legged in front of her owner, her muzzle wrinkling in warning.

I think I would have gotten myself under control then, but Marlene looked me up and down and said, "What are you, crazy? You some kind of rabid Animal Rights nut job?"

I opened my mouth to say something else, but wound up growling again as a wave of heat rose up from my toes to the top of my scalp, anger boiling up in me too thick for words. My skin prickled, all the tiny hairs bristling.

Oh, Jesus, not here. Not now. It was broad daylight and I was wearing jeans and a shirt and a lab coat—and it wasn't even the right time of month, goddamnit. Except that I'd never had regular menstrual periods back when I was normal, so maybe my fluctuating estrogen levels were activating the lycanthropy virus out of sequence.

Interesting basis for a study, I thought. Then another flash of heat had me gasping for air and pulling off my coat.

"Okay, lady, I can see you need some help," said Marlene, drawing my attention back to her. "So if you don't mind, I'll just be taking Queenie here before you . . ."

My growl cut her off in midinsult. Like hell you're taking that poor dog out of my sight, I thought, staring Marlene down. I didn't realize that I'd moved, backing my human client into a corner, until I heard another voice from behind me.

"Excuse me, Dr. Barrow—I heard something, do you need assistance?" I whirled, and there was Pia, our veterinary assistant in training. Like me, Pia had the lycanthropy virus. Unlike me, she'd started out life as a tame wolf. Malachy Knox, my boss, had been tinkering with the virus and experimented on her, and now she was more human than I was: Unlike me, Pia was unable to shift back into her original form.

Right now, I took in the fact of her surprise, her fear and alarm, without quite processing what it was that was causing her reaction. "Dr. Barrow, are you all right?" Her soft, brown, pixie-cut hair stood out like the fur of an anxious dog.

I gave a little growl of irritation and Pia licked her lips nervously. "Dr. Barrow?" For a moment, I was so annoyed by that tentative voice and posture that I just wanted to take her down. Next thing I knew, I was weaving on my feet, light-headed and confused. Pia was behind me, whimpering anxiously in the back of her throat as she tried to prop me up.

"Stop whining, I'm perfectly all right," I said, and then everything went black.

TWO

◐○○ I woke up on the abused couch that had taken shelter in our back office, the stink of ammonia burning my nostrils.

"Better now?" My boss was capping the glass vial of smelling salts which he'd been waving under my nose. Trust Malachy to have the appropriate Edwardian remedy on hand. I rubbed my nose, trying to get rid of the pungent residue of the ammonia fumes.

"I'm awake."

"I'd call that better." Malachy passed the smelling salts to Pia, who was standing behind him. I had a vague sense that they'd been discussing me a moment ago, and that I'd just missed some crucial bit of information.

Reflexively, I touched my face, checking for my glasses. Still on my face, although everything was a bit blurry. "What happened?"

"You passed out in the examining room. How do you feel?"

I took stock of myself: All my clothes were still on and I felt more or less human, though none too pleased with myself. My vision had cleared, though.

"I'm good now," I said, trying to sit up. "Whoa, head rush."

"You might want to take it slowly," said Malachy. "You gave yourself a bit of a knock on the head going down." He had a clipped, Home Counties accent, the patrician features of a Roman senator, and the unruly tangled black curls of a Portuguese water dog. Some of our female clients wondered why he didn't cut it, and I explained that a certain amount of ostentatious eccentricity is the hallmark of the British upper classes.

"How about giving me a hand, then?"

I felt his bony arm come around my back, and wondered who had gotten me onto the couch. I had about three inches and twenty pounds on Pia, and while Dr. Malachy Knox was a lot of impressive things, physically, he wasn't up to lifting anything larger than a Siamese.

"Okay," said Pia, cheerleading from the sidelines, "swing your feet over, Dr. Barrow. Great. How's that feel?"

"I'll let you know when the room stops spinning." For someone who'd been human for less than a year, Pia had adapted amazingly well to life on two feet. I still had trouble believing that the shy young wolf I'd met last October was now a high-functioning young woman. Granted, Pia still didn't understand why most women colored their lips and eyelashes, and her approach to food was to consume it as rapidly as possible. Still, this made her seem more like a recent immigrant from some impoverished traditional society rather than a recent convert to our species. Part of the credit for Pia's transition went to Jackie, her former owner, who had worked intensively to train Pia to sit at the table, and not under it.

Jackie, for her part, refused to acknowledge her role in Pia's transformation. "You'd be surprised how little I had to teach her," Jackie had said. It seems our canine companions understand more about human language and culture than we imagine.

What Jackie had never expressed overtly was how

much she disapproved of what Malachy had done to her favorite wolf. Like my mother, Jackie didn't particularly care for Homo sapiens. Nobody knew what Pia thought about the enormous changes in her life—she wasn't offering her opinion, and I, for one, was a little afraid to ask her.

I realized that I had been sitting up for a full minute now, and my head had stopped spinning. "I do feel better," I told Pia. "Thanks." I tried to look the younger woman in the eye, but she kept averting her gaze. Now why was she acting so strangely around me all of a sudden? Most of the time it was Malachy who had her running scared.

Pia cleared her throat. "Can I get you something, Dr. Barrow? Water?"

"No, I'm fine. And what's with the doctor business? I've said you can call me Abra."

"Sure . . . Abra." She gave me a poor excuse for a smile, and I had to fight the urge to shout, Stop that cringing, woman!

"Well, I'll just be going now," said Pia, inching toward the door. "Unless you did want some water?"

Belatedly, I felt guilt kicking in, replacing all my previous annoyance. The bad dog owners of this world deserved my anger. Pia did not. "No, I'm really fine. But thanks for all your help back there. Oh, hey, one question: How the heck did you guys shlep me all the way over here?"

Pia ducked her head, embarrassed. "Oh, you know . . . Dr. Knox and I just sort of managed."

Malachy snorted derisively. "Don't try to spare my feelings, Pia. I was of no use whatsoever. It's a good thing you're stronger than you appear."

"Oh, I'm not so strong. You can lift a lot of weight when you have an adrenaline rush."

"Gee," I said, "thanks a lot." It took Pia a moment,

but when Mal threw back his head and gave a short bark of laughter, she realized what she'd implied.

"I . . . I didn't mean to say . . ."

"Never mind, I was just teasing." Pia smiled a little uncertainly. To her, teasing was like play fighting—a relatively gentle way of testing where you ranked in the pack hierarchy.

"I really don't think you're overweight, Doctor . . . Abra."

"Pia," said Malachy, "stop worrying. She knows she's not fat."

This was true. I could probably lose a couple of pounds around my midsection, but it wasn't swimsuit season, so I didn't care that much.

"Now, why don't you go on out and see to the clients before they stage a revolt?"

"Oh, gosh, of course, sorry, Doctor." Pia scrambled out the door and Malachy swiveled around in his chair to face me. "All right," he said, "look at the wall behind me." I tried not to blink while he shined his penlight into my eyes.

"Good." Malachy took my pulse, shushing me when I tried to speak. "So. Blood pressure and pupil response is normal, but I think the next logical step is to do an MRI."

"Oh, I don't think that's necessary."

"Any particular reason?"

Pulling the tip of my braid over my shoulder, I tried to think of a polite way to answer. Malachy knew about my disorder, and for a while, he had even supplied me with a noxious cocktail that suppressed the change. But even if he was the closest thing to a medical expert on lycanthropy, I never knew whether he viewed me as a patient or as an experimental subject.

"I don't need an expensive brain scan to tell me what happened. It was just low blood sugar. I forgot to eat breakfast."

Malachy raised one eyebrow. "That would explain the loss of consciousness, but not the growling." He paused. "Another possibility is that you've experienced a seizure of some sort. That being the case, an MRI would seem the next logical step." He paused again, steepling his fingers and clearly waiting for my response. On the wall over his head there was a Wegman poster of a Weimaraner sitting in the same pose and smoking a pipe, my personal contribution to the back office decor.

"I was just irritated. And I didn't growl. I made an inadvertent sound of disgust, which I realize was unprofessional, but she wanted me to terminate her dog's pregnancy, and the puppies are due in less than a week!" I rubbed my right temple, trying to stave off the onset of a monster headache. God, I hated my hormones. I used to have irregular menstrual periods. Now I appeared to be suffering from irregular wolf cycles.

Malachy took my chin in his hand. "I was tempted to snarl at her myself, but, and here is the critical difference, I restrained myself." He took his penlight back out of his lab coat pocket.

"Hey, cut it out. We did this already."

"You're squinting. Is the light bothering you now?"

"I'm not loving it."

"And your head is hurting. All right, you say you're suffering from low blood sugar . . . how about something to eat?" Malachy reached over for a box of powdered doughnuts that Pia kept by the computer.

Unfortunately, I couldn't eat this close to a change. About an hour before or after, I went on crazy protein binges, but something about having your bones rearrange is a real appetite suppressant. "Not just now, thanks."

Malachy replaced the doughnuts on Pia's desk. "Abra, when you stopped taking the suppressants, you agreed to let me know if you started experiencing any new symptoms."

I looked into Malachy's lean, clever, weathered face, figuring out how much to reveal. "The thing is," I said, "this has happened before."

"Ah."

"I usually have it under control." By which I meant, Red was around to make sure I didn't wake up with any vague memories of doing something unspeakable, or didn't wake up at all. Unlike Hunter, my ex, and Magda, his Romanian import, Red was a shapeshifter by birth, which gave him a greater degree of control over going lupine.

Although his long, bony body was still slouched in his chair, Malachy had dropped his habitual pose of detached amusement, and was regarding me with an almost predatory sharpness. "So you've begun to experience preliminary shifting between lunar cycles?"

"Just the odd cramp, or a little tetchiness. Last month I accidentally ate a raw hamburger. To be honest, I thought it was just premenstrual syndrome," I added. "At least, until today."

Malachy didn't respond, and I waited him out. An absurd image popped into my head: a Wegmanesque wolf in lab coat and glasses. But as the moments ticked by, I became increasingly conscious of all the clients out in the waiting room, wondering what the two veterinarians were doing. "You know, we're getting all backed up." Our practice was surprisingly busy, considering the fact that we were the second, and decidedly less prestigious, veterinary practice in town. The Northside Animal Practice, located on Main Street, was where most everyone in the area went first. Our clinic, hidden on a side street, got the clients who couldn't afford Dr. Mortimer, or whom he no longer wished to see. Naturally, we also got our share of unsavory types, both human and animal.

Which reminded me: People were still waiting for their animals' appointments.

"Mal," I said, "if you have something to say, say it. Because there are people out there who are going to walk out the door and not come back if we keep hiding back here."

The crease between my boss's dark brows deepened, but he didn't respond. I still wasn't completely sure I knew how to read Malachy, though. Back when he'd been my instructor at the Animal Medical Institute, Malachy had given me the impression that he'd selected me for his group because of my husband's interest in lycanthropy. Mal had led me to believe that he saw me as a sturdy, industrious, hardworking type—the straight A student who spends her life in the library. It shouldn't have hurt my feelings as much as it did, but I'd always accepted that I wasn't beautiful or charismatic, like my mother. I guess I'd convinced myself that I possessed a knockout intelligence, until Mal set me straight.

On the other hand, his own brand of wild brilliance had lost him a research grant, gotten him kicked out of the Institute, and landed him here in Northside, working alongside me. Partially, I knew, he was attracted to the location; something in the air or water of the town seems to have an amplifying effect on certain conditions, such as lycanthropy.

I didn't know what impact Northside was having on Malachy's own health. It wasn't something we discussed, but I was aware that my boss must have infected himself with some genetically manipulated form of the virus. At forty-two, he looked as though he'd spent a good stretch of time in the French foreign legion, or a dungeon, or both. He wasn't unattractive, exactly, but his skin seemed to be stretched too tightly over the bones of his face, and there were days when he looked more than just unwell, he looked terminal.

As if he were reading my mind, Malachy said, "You know, we can't really run this practice if we're not honest with each other. I have to tell you if I'm coming down with something. And you have to tell me."

"I promise you," I said, hoping this would break the impasse. "If my problem starts to get worse, I'll let you know."

Malachy looked at me for another moment, then glanced over at Padisha, the obese office cat, who was padding into the room, his flabby white belly wobbling beneath him. Padisha paused, staring at me intently with startled green eyes, his back beginning to arch. I stared back at him, willing him to act normally. After a moment, Padisha visibly relaxed, leaping up onto the table with surprising agility and then slinging himself over the top of the computer.

"All right then," said Malachy. "We'll forgo the brain scan."

I was surprised he'd given in so easily, and then recalled that some cats are able to predict seizures. I seemed to be passing the cat scan: Padisha was dozing peacefully, his hind leg and part of his stomach hanging over the side of the computer.

"Excellent." I stood up. "Then I can go back to work now."

The cat opened one green eye, as if curious to hear Malachy's response. "I can handle it today, Abra. Can you call Red and have him drive you home?"

I felt a wave of annoyance and started to say, I don't need my damn boyfriend to come get me, but stopped when I saw a blur of striped gray fur as a hissing Padisha jumped off the desk and streaked out the door.

Malachy raised one eyebrow, but refrained from making any comment.

"Fine," I said. "I'll call Red."

THREE

◐○○ "I'm so sorry to put you out," I said for the third time, addressing my boss's profile.

"Well, stop being so sorry," Malachy snapped, not taking his eyes off the road. "It's nervy."

I resisted the urge to apologize for that, as well. Ordinarily, I would have snapped back at Malachy—from the start, we had established that mildly barbed bantering would be our standard mode of communication. But right at the moment, I was feeling a bit vulnerable. We hadn't been able to reach Red on his cell phone. Either he was out of signal range, removing vermin from somebody's attic, or he was off at Moondoggie's enjoying a beer. Then again, it was also possible that he'd left his phone along with his clothes while he ran around with the coyote who'd gotten Queenie knocked up. That was the thing about shacking up with a shapeshifter: There was a high degree of unpredictability.

It wasn't the kind of unpredictability that my ex-husband had taught me to expect, the kind that had me vacillating between yearning and pain, but it was inconvenient, nevertheless. Besides, I didn't like having Malachy drive me home. It made me uncomfortable, and not entirely because he insisted on driving an English car with the steering wheel still on the right.

A truck roared past, making me squeak.

"Stop fussing. We were nowhere near him."

"It's just a little weird, having you on my right."
Malachy took a blind corner with a cool aggressiveness
that had me sucking in my breath.

"You're being nervy again."

"Does nervy mean nervous, annoying, or some combination of both?"

"The latter. Is this your turning up ahead?"

I glanced at the long driveway that led up to my ex-
husband's grand ruin of a house. "No, that's Hunter's.
The next one's mine." The trees were all bare now, but
in the autumn, the maples that lined the long driveway
turned bright crimson and yellow. It had been October
when we'd moved up here from the city. There ought to
be a law against moving when the fall foliage is at its
peak, and everything is infused with a witchy glamour.
Then the spell breaks, the leaves fall off the trees, and
you discover that your husband doesn't love you any
better in the country than he did in Manhattan. In fact,
he loves you less. Or maybe you just notice it more.

"Do you mind him living so close?"

I was so startled, I didn't know how to respond. "Isn't
that a personal question? I thought you disliked personal questions."

"I take that as an affirmative."

I glanced at Malachy, mildly irritated. "I keep telling
myself that we have ten acres between us. In the city,
that wouldn't even mean the same zip code."

"But you're not in the city."

"True." And considering how close we all came to
killing each other last year, I'd probably have felt
crowded even if Hunter were on the other side of the
state. But Red wasn't about to sell the cabin, because it
was situated on some kind of crucial supernatural fault
line. According to Red, the town of Northside was an
ancient crossroads between worlds, which meant that a

lot of old magics had soaked into the earth and stones. Not everyone in Northside was of the supernatural persuasion, just as not everyone in the Hamptons was a movie star, but this was one of the few places where a seven-foot sheriff with strange tattoos on his forehead could walk around without generating comment. And Northsiders treated supernaturals the way Hamptonites treated movie stars—with a sort of studied nonchalance.

Of course, you were more likely to spot the strangeness in some parts of town than you were in others. Red's cabin formed the point of a triangle between Old Scolder Mountain and a cavern that ran underneath the cornfield on the east side of town. If a preternatural pest were to sneak into Northside, Red was the guy who was going to stop it before it became a real menace.

So if I wanted to stay with Red, I had to put up with living next to Hunter and Magda.

"Turn here?" Malachy's question took me by surprise, and it took me a moment to realize that we had reached the road that leads to our house. I nodded and Malachy turned his ancient Jaguar onto an unpaved driveway that looked pretty much identical to Hunter's. Except there was a fantastic, dilapidated old Gormen-ghastly mansion at the end of his dirt road, and a log cabin with an outhouse at the end of mine. I half expected a snarky comment, but Malachy didn't say anything as he turned off the ignition.

I tried to tell myself that I had no reason to feel embarrassed. After all, the outhouse had a hand-carved toilet seat, and we did have an indoor toilet for blizzards and emergencies. Besides, the cabin was only temporary. Red and I were still working on the plans for our new home, which was going to be a shapeshifter dream house, intended to accommodate both our human and canid forms. Red intended to build it himself as well, as soon as he had the spare time. And I knew Red meant what he said. Unlike my former husband, he didn't specialize in saying what people wanted to hear and then doing whatever the hell he pleased.

Still, for the time being, I was living in a log cabin with no electricity, and sharing the space with various rescued wildlife, including a half-blind red-tailed hawk, a bat with a broken wing, and a raccoon kit with an eating disorder.

Malachy pulled the key out of the ignition. "Are you finished contemplating the view? Can we go inside now?"

"You don't need to see me in."

He paused. "Actually, I thought I'd wait for Red."

"Come on, Mal. There's no telling when he'll be home. Leave. I'll be fine."

"I need to speak to him about another matter." Malachy opened the car door and started heading toward the cabin. From the back, he looked like an emaciated thoroughbred. His shoulders and chest had been designed to carry more flesh and muscle, and the thick Irish cable-knit sweater and loose corduroy trousers hung on his rangy frame. I wondered, not for the first time, what was wrong with him.

"Are you coming, or do you require assistance?" Malachy paused, ostensibly in annoyance, but I could see the puffs of his breath on the cold air.

"I just wanted to watch your ass move," I said, grabbing my handbag.

Malachy ignored me, making me wonder if my last comment had been too crass. He had that odd English quality of being dignified when an American would have been easy, and then saying something so crude no American would have dared mention it in public. Once he and Red had gotten into a discussion about the difference between bear dung and human feces that had turned personal enough to make me leave the table. But sex wasn't something that Malachy talked about, so maybe I'd stepped over some line.

"I'm sorry if I offended you," I said. "The truth is, as far as I can tell, you don't even have an ass."

"You're being unusually tiresome. Is there anything in particular that has you on edge?"

As soon as he asked the question, I realized that I'd been baiting him. This wasn't our typical mode of teasing; I'd been spoiling for a fight. "I'm not sure why I'm so cranky," I admitted, taking a deep breath. There was a sliver of moon in the sky, a wink of light between two half-bare birches. Something cramped low in the left side of my abdomen, and I wondered if I was ovulating.

"Hang on a moment."

"Are you feeling dizzy?"

I tried to shake my head no, but got stabbed by another cramp. Malachy grabbed my arm, right above my elbow, and with his touch my head really did begin to spin. It made no sense. This wasn't even close to the full moon, and it was still broad daylight. My throat was parched. I couldn't swallow. I thought of losing control in front of my boss and something clogged in my chest, making it hard to breathe. Reaching for the high neck of my turtleneck, I tried to pull it away from my skin.

"All right, Abra, hang on, let's get you inside." I felt one of Malachy's arms come around my shoulders, the other around my waist. He'll never be able to support me, I thought, but I couldn't seem to keep my weight from leaning into him. I tried to tell him just to let me sit down, but my voice seemed a long way away. I managed to get my foot onto the front step, then sagged more against his arms. We both went down hard, and I banged my head against something, a rock or a tree. The ground was cold and slightly damp.

"Bugger," I heard Malachy say. "All right, let me up, I'll get my bag from the car. Abra? Abra?"

But as I tried to get up, I found that I couldn't breathe. I wrestled with my turtleneck again, trying to tear it off me, but found my wrist pinned to the floor.

"Abra? Look at me. Try to focus. Abra!" My boss's sharp voice brought me back and I stared up at his craggy face. He looks different from this angle, I thought woozily. Then it struck me that I was belly up to him, submissive. That wasn't right; I always argued back with Malachy, I never just rolled over. Tightening my wrists, I was about to break his grip and flip him over when my boss narrowed his eyes and leaned more of his weight into me. "Stop that," he said, and there was no doubt in his voice. "Stay still!"

I obeyed him without thinking. He was lying on top of me, which should have made it harder to breathe, but instead I felt comforted by the pressure of him weighing me down. "Do you know where you are?" He was still pinning my wrists. I nodded, coming back to myself enough to feel embarrassed, then tucked my chin so that my nose was close to the armpit of his sweater. I caught a hint of his scent in the wool, faint and muted but still discernible. But underneath the familiar smell of the man there was a trace of something unusual. It was an illness, but not one I recognized. Not the warm, deep musk of a lycanthrope, but not a conventional disease, either. I couldn't detect any of the putrid sweet tang of cancer or diabetes, or the acrid, singed edge of some of the neural disorders.

From this distance, I could see the strands of silver woven into Mal's tangle of dark, unruly curls. Without thinking, I dipped my nose closer, trying to isolate that last layer of scent.

"Stop that!" A hand, clenched in my hair, tugged my head back. I stared back at him, noticing for the first time that his eyes were the pale green of early spring, when everything is bright with untapped potential. I could feel how close I was to the change, but he was holding me back by sheer force of will. Even with natural wolves, it is not always the strongest male who leads the pack.

"Sorry," Malachy said, a moment later. His hand eased its grip on my hair. "Did I hurt you?"

I just continued gazing up at him, passive, waiting. For a moment, I had a dazed impression of him as an ancient tree, his outer layers gnarled and ailing, his inner channels still filled with sap and the possibility of life. A tremor went through Malachy, not muscle fatigue but something that rippled through him like the change that transformed me from woman to wolf.

His knuckles were white with strain, but I was no longer struggling. I didn't know what Malachy was holding back by sheer force of will, but it wasn't me. His arms shook with another spasm, and the long muscles of his thighs contracted where they pressed against mine, hardening until my own body yielded in response. His eyes began to glow with an uncanny light. It called to me like the moon, and I could feel the dull ache of my bones as they began to shift under him.

Just as I could feel something shifting in him. Not a wolf; something else, monstrous and strange, that tore at him as it tried to emerge. His face turned white. "No," he whispered through clenched teeth, a muscle jumping in his jaw. "No."

Lower down, the change didn't seem to be paining him.

Arching as my muscles rippled convulsively, I threw my head back, staring up at the blue sky, the crescent moon, the tops of the trees . . . and Red, frowning down at us.

FOUR

◐ ○ ○   I was caught in some bizarre redneck version of a French bedroom farce. There we all were, seated around the kitchen table, trying to act as though two of us hadn't just had a close encounter of the ambiguous kind. The one-eyed hawk, a female, was perched on top of a high kitchen shelf, where she'd made a nest out of paper towels, twigs, and a fair amount of hair, most of it mine. She was watching me with one unblinking golden eye, like a hostess who suspects you might make off with the silverware, or the host. Our other fosterling, Rocky the raccoon, was curled up catlike on the hammock chair that hung from the ceiling. The bat, who had no name, was hanging upside down from the dream catcher beside the bed.

I wouldn't have minded escaping into sleep myself.

Red and Mal and I were being awfully polite to one another, but there was a peculiar undercurrent in the room, a low level hum from the conversation we weren't having.

At least, Mal was clearly too sick to have been doing anything carnal to me. And it hadn't been carnal. At least, I didn't think it had been.

Mal had explained that I had nearly fainted, and I'd just finished telling Red about my earlier encounter with Marlene. It seemed like the safest subject at the moment—

well, the safest for me, at any rate. I was pretty sure Red wouldn't be paying Marlene any house calls, even if she found a timber rattler in her basement.

Red winced when I got to the part where Marlene told me she'd have to take care of the problem herself. "No wonder you wanted to bite her. What made that fool woman think her dog had been bred by a coyote, anyway?"

"She said she heard coyotes howling," I said. "I guess she just assumed."

Red shook his head in an almost canid gesture of bafflement. "I hear it all the damn time. People see a stray dog, start insisting I come by because it looks like a coyote. So I show up and take a look, and it's some poor mutt that got left by the side of the road. But no one ever believes me. 'It must be a coydog,' they say. 'Kill it before it eats my babies.' I tell them it's more likely to be a wolf hybrid than a coydog, but no one ever listens." Red stood up and took a Budweiser out of the icebox. "Either of you want one?"

I started to say something about it being a little early for drinks, but then realized that the winter sun was already dipping below the horizon. It had been so warm lately that I'd forgotten it was January, the dark month when the ancients used to light candles and look for omens, and modern folk plan tropical vacations.

"I'll stick with my tea, thanks." Malachy was frowning. "Tell me, why is it so unlikely that a coyote male might breed a domesticated bitch in heat?"

Red popped the top of his bottle. "Because the coyote male would have to be in season, too." Almost as an afterthought, he added, "Folks always seem to think that wolves mate for life, and coyotes don't, but they're wrong."

I busied myself examining my nails and realized that, once again, I'd forgotten to wear the golden topaz engagement ring Red had given me last year. I hoped he didn't think it was symbolic; the ring just wasn't practical with latex gloves, and besides, my divorce still wasn't final. We'd decided it was a friendship ring for now.

"Fascinating," said Malachy, stirring sugar into his tea. "So coyotes do mate for life?"

"Sometimes." Red took a swig of his beer. "But sometimes wolves lose a mate and then take another. They don't all just pine away."

Still, wolves were a hell of a lot more faithful than people. After all, wolves didn't wake up one morning and decide they were bored with their old mates. You didn't get packs splitting apart because the alpha male had decided that the alpha female just didn't do it for him anymore. Werewolves, on the other hand, were as monstrous as humans when it came to fidelity. Or maybe it was just my former husband who was monstrous, in either form.

I stood up and checked on our European-style coffeemaker. It didn't require electricity, and Red swore it made a better brew, but I had yet to taste the evidence.

"Don't be so impatient," said Malachy as I started to press down on the plunger. "It's not ready yet."

I sat back down, feeling petulant. "I hate this coffeemaker. It makes weak brown water with grounds."

"It needs to steep, and then you have to press down slowly." Malachy sounded his usual autocratic self, but I noticed the tremble in his hands as he tried to lift his mug of tea. His face was even more pallid than usual, and perspiration beaded his upper lip.

Red took the water pitcher out of the icebox and poured him a glass, then said nothing as Mal reached into his pocket and extracted a pill container. "Here," he said, as Malachy tried for the third time to open the top, "let me."

"Thanks." I couldn't help but notice that the container had no label, and the pills were capsules, without any markings. I didn't ask what they were; Mal took three, his hand shaking as he lifted the glass of water to his mouth.

Without my noticing, it had grown darker in the cabin, and Red began walking around the room, lighting the good oil lamps, the ones from the antiques store. We also had a few Coleman lanterns stashed around the cabin, which were easier to use but not as pretty. We did have an indoor bathroom as well as an outhouse, but since we were off the grid, the toilet had to be flushed mechanically by pouring in a bucket of water.

Sometimes I felt like I was on a very long camping holiday. And like I was living somebody else's life, to boot. It had never been my ambition to have the smallest carbon footprint in town, and I had to keep reminding myself that this was only a temporary arrangement, until Red could build our permanent home.

The little brown bat had begun to flit around the room, and Red caught her and put her in the bedroom; in a confined space, bats really can get tangled in your hair.

As Red returned, he passed by the hawk, who jumped down onto his shoulder, reaching for a strand of his hair. "Easy, girl, you've got to leave me a few."

"You have plenty of hair," I protested. "You just need to let it grow out more."

"I leave the Tarzan look to my friend here," said Red, indicating Malachy's woolly mane. Removing the hawk's sharp talons from his shoulder, Red transferred her to his forearm. "Hey, Ladyhawke, why don't you pick on him? He could use the pruning."

Mal fixed the bird with a hawklike stare of his own. "I wouldn't advise it. Say, isn't it a bit early for her to be nesting? I thought red-tailed hawks' breeding season was in the spring."

"She's young," said Red. "And confused by the artificial heat inside." He set the bird back on her perch.

"She also appears to consider you a prospective mate."

Red's smile was subdued. "You overestimate my charms."

"No, she does. Didn't you see, she was attempting to preen you—see, look at her, grooming herself like a teenager preparing for a date."

Sure enough, the hawk was fluffing her feathers and cocking her head in what I now perceived as a flirtatious manner. "So why does she keep trying to pull *my* hair out? Does she have a crush on me, too?"

Malachy took another sip of water. "Doubtful. Perhaps she's trying to drive you away. On the other hand, it might just be general bloody-mindedness. It's very common to find females displaying higher levels of irritability and stress just prior to choosing a mate. Often, she'll alternate between inviting and rebuffing various males until she chooses."

"I never realized the term 'cock tease' had avian origins."

Malachy didn't acknowledge my pun, making me feel slightly foolish. "As I recall, Red, you had the same effect on a young great horned owl a year or so ago."

"Yeah, that's me, the ladykiller. I think your coffee's about ready, Doc." Red reached up into a cabinet for a coffee cup and the hawk made another unsuccessful attempt at his head.

There was a loud, clinking sound as Red knocked the mug he was bringing down, which surprised me. Usually, he managed to move around the confined cabin space without bumping into anything, a trick I had yet to master. There were so many things to admire about

Red: his many practical skills; his calm, efficient manner; his wry sense of humor; and above all, his basic goodness and decency.

So why was I feeling so testy with him these days? I knew it was superficial, but part of it was his lack of care in his own appearance. When I'd first met Red, I'd thought he looked scruffy and a little disreputable, like one of those marginal men who do odd jobs and rent their rooms by the week. It didn't take me long to see behind the local yokel disguise and discover how attractive he really was, lean and high-cheekboned, with steady, clear, light hazel eyes that took in more than they let on.

But now, as Red poured me a cup of coffee, I found myself wishing that he'd make a bit more of an effort. As soon as Red's silver-flecked auburn hair grew long enough to soften his sharp features, he went to see our local Sweeney Todd to have it all mowed off again. And then there were those burlap-tough Carhartt coveralls, with "Red Mallin, Wildlife Removal Expert" stitched over his right pocket. I was never one of those women who drooled over men in Armani jackets, but still, you didn't catch me wearing my bloodstained lab coat to the kitchen table.

"Honey," I said, taking a grateful sip of my coffee, "you've got some kind of gunk on your . . . no, not that side, yes, right there."

Red flicked at his overalls, and something flaked off into the sink, making me wish I hadn't said anything. "That better?"

"Actually, there's another patch of blood or something. Would you mind changing out of that?"

Red hesitated, then turned his back and unzipped the coveralls. At first, I took the stiffness of his movements to be annoyance at my request, but then I caught the way Malachy was watching Red. "Simple puncture wound, or was there some laceration as well?"

Red gave a noncommittal shrug. "It's just a little love bite. Some of the blood's dried, is all. I was just going to leave this for later."

Now I really felt like the world's worst girlfriend. "Oh, God, why didn't you say something?"

" 'Cause it's not a big deal, Doc."

"Let me see."

With obvious reluctance, Red peeled off the coveralls, wincing a little as he extracted his right arm from its sleeve, revealing a series of small, reddened puncture wounds.

I sucked in my breath when I examined his arm, which was swollen and clearly sore. "Jesus, Red. You're going to need rabies shots." I realized that wasn't the most professional tone to take, but I was a little shocked. In all the time I'd known him, Red had never once been bitten by any of the wild animals he removed from their lairs. Something must have gone very wrong.

"The critter that got me didn't have rabies." As if on cue, there was a high-pitched squeal of distress and then a flash as something dark plummeted from the ceiling to the floor. For one startled moment, I thought it was a bat, then I remembered that Red had locked her in the bedroom.

"Jesus," said Malachy, "what the hell is that?"

"It's Rocky," I said in surprise, kneeling down beside the adolescent raccoon. Red had rescued Rocky last summer, when he had been cute and small and badly injured by a car. At nearly a year old and almost twenty-five pounds, our raccoon was now hale and hearty and more than old enough to be living on his own, but the call of the wild had been trumped by the call of our kitchen. Rocky was a raccoon who liked his carbohydrates complex.

At the moment, he was lying on the floor, clearly stunned, looking almost comical as he touched his little black paws to his face. I glanced up to see where he'd fallen from and realized that he must have been hanging on to the chain that holds the largest lamp over the center of the living room. I had no idea how he'd gotten there without us spotting him, but I wasn't entirely surprised. Raccoons may look adorable, but that bandit mask is no costume. They are wild things, and second to none in making a rumpus.

I ran my hands over Rocky's dense salt and pepper fur, checking for injuries. Luckily, he was well padded with fat, the result of constant thieving. "What were you doing up there, you idiot?"

Rising up on his hind legs, Rocky looked straight at Red and gave a series of low grunts, for all the world as if he were giving his foster father a lecture. This wasn't unusual; unlike Ladyhawke, Rocky didn't actively dislike me, but like all the forest creatures Red rescued, the raccoon displayed a marked preference for Red. I suppose the animals tended to associate me with shots and stitches, while Red fed them and soothed them.

Red said something, a soft, long, liquid string of sounds that might have been a sentence or a word, and seemed to calm the raccoon down. Red reached out one hand and scratched the side of Rocky's masked face, as he might have done a cat, and said something else that meant nothing to me but evidently had an almost magical effect on Rocky. With a soft churring noise, the raccoon shuffled over to the bureau, climbed up to a partially opened drawer, and hopped in.

"You've trained him well," said Malachy, watching as Rocky settled himself among Red's woolen winter socks. Red's socks all had holes now, thanks to the raccoon's sharp little claws, but I think Rocky knew what I would do to him if he tried to get into my underwear drawer.

"I haven't trained him at all," Red corrected him. "We

just have an understanding." Rocky settled himself in the drawer, snout just hanging over the side so he could watch us, bright black eyes glittering. Red watched him, unthinkingly flexing his injured arm as if it were hurting him.

In all the excitement, I'd momentarily forgotten about Red's injury. "Come sit over here," I told him, "and let me see what you've done to yourself."

Red didn't protest when I took his arm and inspected the bite. Whatever had sunk its teeth into him hadn't crushed down or shaken its head, like a dog, so the puncture wounds were small and neat and already showing signs of inflammation and infection. "So, tell me what kind of animal does this and isn't a potential carrier of rabies." Shapeshifters, like lycanthropes, are rapid healers, but I figured some viruses and bacteria could overtax even the best immunological defense system.

Red tensed almost imperceptibly as·I pressed around the site of the wound. "Manitou."

From his drawer, Rocky snarled softly, but this time, Red just ignored him.

"Don't those things live in Florida swamps, chewing on seaweed and getting scarred by motorboats?" I paused. "Hang on, I need my supplies."

I went into the bathroom and gathered my little first-aid kit, which contained sterile saline solution, iodine, antibiotic ointment, a roll of gauze and medical tape, and some other odds and ends that came in handy when your man liked to bring home injured wildlife on a regular basis. When I came back to the living room, I heard Malachy say something that made Red laugh, then stop abruptly.

"What did I miss?" I guided Red to the bench while Malachy readjusted the lamp.

"Red, manfully trying not to moan with pain."

"Mal was just saying that you're thinking of mana-tees," said Red. "Not manitou."

I wondered if that was the entire truth. When the moon was nearly full, I did find some enhancement in my sense of smell and hearing, but nothing like what they showed in the movies. It would have been nice to have canid hearing while in human form, but as long as my ears were situated on the sides of my head, there was a limit to my capabilities.

As I irrigated Red's wound, I asked, "How long ago did this happen?"

"Few hours."

"And you're sure that in addition to not getting rabies, these manitous don't have nematode worms and won't give you trichinosis? Because from where I'm sitting, this looks like your garden variety small mammal bite." Having finished with the iodine, I applied a layer of antibiotic ointment and began wrapping Red's arm in gauze.

Red chuckled. "I'm sure. It's not some fancy new word for a possum, Doc. These days, people translate 'manitou' as a spirit, the force that flows through all things. But my grandfather used to say that was the tourist version. He said that in the old legends, when they say Raven went to Beaver's house, and they half acted like animals and half like folks, those were the manitou."

"I believe the word's Algonquian in origin," said Malachy. "Correct me if I'm mistaken, but didn't you say that your grandfather was of the Mohawk tribe, Red? I believe they were part of the Iroquois nation."

I secured the gauze with a piece of medical tape and looked over my shoulder at Malachy. "You know, Boss, you're being even more pedantic than usual."

Malachy caught my eye and raised one sardonic eyebrow. "Am I? Well, forgive me. I'm always intrigued by the origin of words."

"Well, first off, the name Iroquois is a kind of insult. And as for manitous, that was the word my grandfather used," Red said mildly. "I never asked him where he picked it up." For a moment I thought Red had finished speaking, but then he added, "I only ever saw one once before, when I fasted for a week and went out into the desert."

"Here," I told Red, "try to elevate that as much as possible." I took another sip of coffee and discovered it had gone cold. Setting the cup down, I added, "A week of fasting, huh? I imagine you can see a lot of things in that state."

"Some things exist on the borders between sleeping and waking, between this world and the next," said Red, very evenly. I wasn't sure if he knew I'd been teasing him. "You see them better out of the corners of your eyes than you do straight on."

I wondered how Malachy was taking all this. To my surprise, Mal indicated Red's bandaged arm. "That looks pretty bloody straight on to me."

I must have given Malachy a strange look, because he raised his eyebrows. "What?"

"I was expecting a different response. More along the lines of, harrumph, Indian legends, balderdash." Northsiders might be blasé about the supernatural, but my boss was a recent transplant.

Malachy gave me his exasperated professor look. "My dear girl, do you have any idea how many supposedly mythic and extinct animals have subsequently been discovered by scientists?"

"Are you talking about people finding dinosaur bones and thinking they're dragons?" Reflexively, I inflected my question with the faintest hint of impatience. Mal-

achy and I tended to spice our conversations with a bit
of conflict.

Malachy made a little *tsk* of annoyance. "No, no, I'm
not talking about fossils. There are living examples, like
the tuatara of New Zealand, with a vestigial third eye on
the top of its head."

"I saw one of those, once," said Red, reminding us
that he was in the room. "The Maori tohunga I knew
told me they were damn smart—lived in packs, not like
lizards or iguanas. Breed even when they're a hundred
and fifty years old."

"I didn't know you'd been to New Zealand." I knew
that Red had been raised in foster homes in Texas before
learning that he had a grandfather in Canada, but I'd
had no idea that he'd traveled to the other side of the
world.

Red gave me a wry smile. "Hell, you can't learn all
about me in one year. I have hidden depths, darlin'."

"So tell us about this meeting with the manitou, already."

There was a scrabbling sound as Rocky rearranged
himself in Red's sock drawer, and I could have sworn
that the young raccoon flashed his foster father a look of
warning as he settled back down.

Red stood up. "You know what? I think we could all
use a change of scene." Gesturing down at his half undone coveralls, he said, "What do you say I get cleaned
up and we all go out for a bite to eat?"

Rocky and Ladyhawke watched us leave, and I had
the bizarre impression that the two disapproving teen-
agers would be discussing us when we were gone.

FIVE

◐○○ Northside didn't offer much choice when it came to dining out. There was the Belle Savage Cafe, named for a local Pocahontas and run by the three ancient Grey sisters, Dana, Enid, and Penny. The sisters served up delicious pastries, soups, and coffee. Unfortunately, they didn't do dinners—the cafe shut up shop the moment the first streaks of sunset crossed the sky.

If you wanted an evening meal, our town boasted only two options. The more upscale establishment was called the Stagecoach Tavern and Inn. The Stagecoach had been around since the seventeen hundreds, when the stagecoach had brought customers in from Albany and New York City. These days, the chef was a recent graduate of the Culinary Academy, and I really hoped he would last. The odds, however, were against him. There had been a succession of different owners and chefs at the Stagecoach, none of whom had lasted more than a year. Supposedly the place was haunted by an ever-increasing number of ghosts, from the two-hundred-year-old spirit of a scullery wench who'd perished in a kitchen fire, to the revenant of Pascal Lecroix, the famed Manhattan chef who had ended his career and his life two years earlier, after a customer had complained about his veal.

Red, however, preferred Moondoggie's, which was

the restaurant the locals tended to frequent. Moondoggie's was the place to hear local bands while chewing on large hunks of meat or massive heaps of lasagna. It had two sections, one for people with small children, the other for people who rode in flatbed trucks or roared in on Harleys. Moondoggie's was nothing if not tolerant of a little noise and high spirits. If, on occasion, one of the Calder children held his breath and floated up to the ceiling, the waitresses knew how to bring him down. And if one of the bikers became a little too vocal in his appreciation of a band, a plate of hot salsa and chips would magically appear, and the biker would find himself compelled to eat chip after chip until the entire musical set was over. I had nothing against the place, other than the fact that Hunter had sampled the pretty blond barmaid, Kayla. My only consolation was that she now disliked Hunter as much as I did, and she worked on the other side of the restaurant.

Naturally, we all wound up going to Moondoggie's.

"What I don't understand," Malachy was saying as he frowned down at his chilled mug of Guinness, "is why Americans want to treat beer as though it were soda."

Red looked around for the busboy who had brought us our drinks. The place was packed, and there was a lot of wandering back and forth as people spotted friends across the room and went over to join them. The wait-staff looked exhausted and a little unnerved, and I suspected that one of the cooks had gone off for a smoke.

"If it's Kayla tending bar, you're lucky she didn't send it over with a straw," I told Mal.

"Aren't you being a bit hard on her?" Red leaned back in his chair, visibly more relaxed now that he'd gotten out of our cabin. The bandage on his right arm was covered by a dark navy sweater and he had taken the time to put on a subtle, woodsy aftershave.

I was about to make a biting comment, when I inhaled another lungful of his fragrance. He'd never worn a scent before, but I liked this; whatever it was, it made me want to stick my nose into the bare skin of his neck and inhale.

"What's wrong now?" Red asked, a touch of impatience in his voice. "You're looking at me funny. I got more blood on me somewhere?"

"Not at all. I'm thinking that I like that new after-shave you have on."

Red gave me a quizzical look. "Darlin', you know I don't wear chemicals."

"But there's definitely something different. Mal, can you smell it?"

Malachy raised one eyebrow a fraction. "Surely you are not suggesting that I sniff Red to ascertain if his aroma has changed? No, I thought not. Red, do carry on with the story of your manitou encounter."

Red hooked his arm across the back of my chair. "Well, I went to this fellow's house to remove whatever was skittering around in his walls. City fellow, late forties, big-shot executive, bought himself a bit of forest around Old Scolder Mountain."

He injected a fair dose of venom into that last sentence. Back in the summer, the developer J. B. Malveaux had convinced the town that a few dozen McMansions planted around the town's tallest mountain wouldn't spoil its natural beauty. At the time, Red had been extremely vocal in his disapproval, showing up at town meetings and talking about the possible impact on local wildlife.

But the town mayor had decided that he didn't need no stinking environmental impact statement; as he put it, "We got more than enough trees in Northside." So the deal had gone through, and Red had packed up a small rucksack and spent a week on the top of the mountain. He'd come back home with Rocky, who had been hit by Malveaux's Land Rover on the site of one of the first houses.

"I thought you said you weren't going to work for anyone who moved into the Old Scolder development."

"You mean Mountain View Lanes," Red said, giving me an ironic toast with his Budweiser bottle. "And, yeah, I know what I said, but if I don't help those rich assholes, they'll go hire someone to spread a load of rat poison around."

Opal, our usual waitress, sailed by our table with a platter of trays, and I tried to catch her eye. "Sorry, guys, you're not my station tonight. Your waitress should be by to take your order in a minute," she said.

"We should have gone to the Stagecoach," muttered Malachy.

"Yeah, well, if you don't mind your steak stinking of specters and ectoplasm," replied Red facetiously. At least, I thought he was being facetious. "So anyway, this city guy built himself some big *Architectural Digest* house. Naturally, the weather gets colder, and various critters move into the house."

It never ceased to amaze me how intelligent people didn't understand that wilderness and pertinacious vermin were a package deal.

"Okay, guys, I'm here," said Kayla, dressed in tight black jeans and a white buttoned-down shirt that barely closed over her generous bosom.

"Hey, you're waitressing now," said Red approvingly.

"I wanted to get away from the roughnecks. Hi, Abra."

I nodded and busied myself with the menu, as if I hadn't memorized it. With her strawberry blond hair pulled back in a high ponytail, Kayla looked older and heavier than she had last year. Then, I'd thought she had the bright, hard prettiness of a beauty contestant. Now, she'd gained at least twenty pounds, and although she was still pretty, it was in a softer, more matronly fashion, and her sparkly green eyes were shadowed with experience. My creep of an ex-husband had been the one to add those shadows, so I supposed I ought to feel a certain kinship with her.

I didn't. Last year she'd confronted me in the street, glaring at me as though I'd done her some injury and telling me that Hunter was stalking her. She'd let me know that some guy named Dan—a boyfriend or a husband, I didn't know or care—had left her because of it. Call me hard-hearted, but this did not evoke any feelings of compassion. For her, that is. I felt plenty sorry for Dan, whoever he was.

I gave my order without looking at Kayla, and she left without her usual display of dimples and cleavage.

"You know, she feels real bad about how she was with you," Red said. "She told me to tell you that."

"Go on with your other story," I replied, stone-faced.

"People can change, you know."

I glared at him. "Not for the better."

Red rolled his shoulders as if he'd taken a punch, but he didn't argue. "So," he said, "I head on over to this big-ass house and the owner's shaking all over, telling me about something huge living down in his basement, going on and on about how he keeps hearing these terrible scraping sounds and once he saw these red glowing eyes."

"And you go down and find a squirrel," said a heavy-set, bearded man sitting at the next table. In his red-checked flannel shirt, Jerome looked like the genial next-door neighbor from *Little House on the Prairie,* a look he cultivated; he had been a Wall Street big shot back in Manhattan. "Sorry, Red," he said, "couldn't help but overhear. It was a squirrel, right?"

"No, Jerome, but you're right, I was expecting to find

a squirrel. Maybe a raccoon—they're a lot bigger than most city folk expect."

Like so many converts, Jerome was extremely prejudiced against the group he had left. A lot of people, I had learned, came to Northside completely unaware that it was to the realm of the supernatural what Saratoga Springs was to the world of horse racing. But after a few years in Northside, even nonmagical people soaked up some of the local culture. "So," Jerome said, hooking his fingers into the loops of his belt, "what did you find in the guy's basement, Red?"

"Well, I head downstairs to check out the crawl space in the basement, and sure enough, there was something in the shadows, staring out at me with glowing red eyes. I knew straight off that it was an Old One. Still on the small side, and more shadow than substance, but old as the hills and twice as powerful."

I tore a bread roll in half, feeling a bit awkward having this discussion in front of Jerome and Malachy. This wasn't the first time Red had encountered the kind of beastie that you don't find in a field guide, but up until now, he had only acknowledged this aspect of his work with me and Jackie, his ex-girlfriend, who lived in a trailer some two miles farther up the road. Malachy might be prepared to believe in bizarre viruses and three-eyed reptiles, but those were basically scientific phenomena disguised as myth. As for Jerome, well, he probably just thought his adopted town was a little weird. But what Red was talking about was weird in the original sense of the word—uncanny, preternatural, not of this world.

Yet to my complete surprise, neither man blinked an eyelash.

"You know, I thought I saw something peculiar running across my front lawn just the other night," Jerome said. "Thought I was losing my mind, because I couldn't figure if it was human or animal."

"Surely, that could just have been a therian," said Malachy to the older man. Red raised his eyebrows inquiringly, so Mal elaborated, "a shapeshifter?"

Jerome pulled himself up in his chair. "Don't you think I know what a shapeshifter looks like? What am I, a greenhorn? It wasn't one thing or the other." Kayla came by with his check and he pulled out his wallet.

"Shifters and wereanimals have a fair amount of human in them. I don't think that what I saw had much human about it," Red said. "But I do think it was dual-natured. Like one of those inkblots you look at, and one way it's a fox, and the other way it's a man."

"Like a Rorschach test? But if it was a spirit shadow thing, how did it do this?" I pointed at the wound I'd just bandaged shut, and Red hesitated.

"It's only a spirit thing in the spirit world," said Red. "It's in our world now." Red absently peeled the label off his beer. "And there's a lot more where that one came from."

I leaned forward. "What do you mean?"

"Those new houses up on Old Scolder Mountain cut across a sacred hunting ground. For as long as anyone can remember, there's been no man-made roads up there—only animal trails, and spirit pathways. You know what happens when you build a road over a corridor that animals use on their migrations?"

Jerome stood up and put Kayla's tip on the table. "Sure. You get a lot of moose and bear coming into town."

"Yeah, well, that's what we're going to get. Except it won't be a moose. It'll be the great-granddaddy of all mooses."

I resisted the urge to tell him that the correct plural of moose is moose. At that moment, Jerome said good-bye and Kayla arrived with our dinners, and there was a pause in the conversation as she served each of us.

"Just let me know if there's anything you want," she said, looking at me.

Red reassured her that we would and she finally left us in peace.

"You know, Doc, that girl wants to be your friend," he said, picking up his burger.

"Don't even go there." I stabbed a piece of pasta, and looked up. "And don't make this about me being the bad guy."

"Of course you aren't the bad guy, but what I can't figure is why you seem more riled up about her than about Magda. I mean—" He broke off when I pointed the tines of my fork at him.

"Red? Drop it. Unless you have some special reason for caring about Kayla so much." There was no way I could explain my antipathy for Kayla. Maybe the problem was that she reminded me of every popular girl who had ever made my life hell back in high school and college. Or possibly it was just safer to dislike her than it was Magda, since she didn't have the ability to tear my throat out. In any case, I didn't feel like examining it too closely.

"Hang on a moment, Doc, all I was saying was—"

"I suggest you do as Abra suggests," Malachy interrupted, "or you'll wind up with a set of fork punctures to go with your bite marks." Taking out his little vial of mystery pills, Mal reached for a glass of water. "Now, you said before that the animals in the old Native American stories were really manitous, correct?"

"Uh huh."

"Well, as I recall, Raven and Bear and Coyote and the others were always hungry." Malachy shook two capsules out onto his palm. "If that turns out to be accurate, then what do spiritual beings eat when they visit the physical world?"

I didn't know the answer to that, but Red did. "Sacrifice," he said simply.

Sometimes I forget that Red isn't just a simple, good old boy—that's one of his guises, but not the only one.

None of us was terribly hungry after that. Kayla asked us if anything was wrong when she took our plates away, and I let Red assure her that the food had been delicious.

I did give her my best attempt at a smile, however, and added an extra five percent to the tip to make up for wishing that she'd break out in boils.

SIX

◐○○   Before I moved to the country, I used to think there were man-made things, like skyscrapers and cars and paved roads, and there was nature, which basically meant anyplace that had grass and a few trees. Red's ex-girlfriend, Jackie, was the one who had set me straight.

"This country around here's about as natural as my hair," she'd explained, pointing at her poor, frazzled, overprocessed blond head. "It's been used and abused by people for the past four hundred years or so, and now the only thing it needs is about four hundred years to recover. Like my hair."

But nature can reclaim a landscape, if left to her own devices. And that was what Jackie was doing with her land—leaving it to grow wild and unruly. Which is why I was muttering a little prayer as I changed into first gear for the long, steep drive up Jackie's unpaved road. About three quarters of the way up, the dirt turned to ice; at this elevation, the ice and snow never melted completely until late April or early May.

By the time I got to the top of the mountain, Jackie's mixed breed wolfdogs had gathered into a growling, snarling pack around her trailer's front door. They didn't bark—there was too much wolf in them for that. And they wouldn't attack me, because although I wasn't quite pack, I wasn't a complete stranger, either.

"You planning on staying in there all day?" Jackie grinned at my startled reaction, resting her handax on her shoulder. She was dressed in a down parka and Wrangler jeans, and her windblown blond hair had oxidized to an unfortunate shade of apricot that clashed with her chapped, red cheeks. The wolfdogs gathered around her as if she were their queen.

"I like for you to be around before I go walking up to their den," I said, honestly. As I stepped out of the car, I caught the smell of wood smoke and resin.

Jackie propped the ax against a respectable woodpile. "That's a bit chickenshit, considering that you can change into a wolf."

"It's not my time of the month. Besides, I only turn into one wolf, so I'd still be outnumbered." Jackie had known about my lycanthropy for longer than I had; Red had confided his suspicions to her from the beginning. She had a kind of easy, pragmatic acceptance of all things supernatural, as if shapeshifters and werewolves were no stranger than horoscopes and lucky numbers. She believed in those as well.

"You don't need to worry. My babies aren't vicious to people or dogs," Jackie said.

"I know." I held out my gloved hands so Jackie's wolf hybrids could sniff me. One or two, the ones with more dog in them, warily wagged a tail. The others, more skittish, danced away from me every time I moved. People buy wolf hybrids expecting some kind of savage über-dog. What they get, nine times out of ten, is an animal as timid and wary as a rabbit. Wolves don't survive in the wild by being indiscriminately savage. They survive by being cautious and fierce. Of course, the distinction can seem moot if the animal winds up clamping its teeth on your forearm.

"So," Jackie said, "how's my girl doing at work?" Before Malachy had turned her human, Pia had been

Jackie's favorite, her furry daughter, allowed in the house and on the bed. As a young woman, Pia still lived with Jackie, but these days, she doted on Malachy.

"Pia's great," I said. "When does she get home?"

Jackie checked her watch. "In an hour or so. The loop bus drops her off at the base of the mountain, and she hikes the rest of the way." Jackie paused a moment. "But these days, she's leaving work later and later. I think she's angling for Malachy to give her a ride home—or better yet, to let her stay over at his place."

Malachy lived in an apartment over the offices. "Really? That's funny, because she's so jumpy when he's around. I was under the impression that he intimidated her a bit."

Jackie looked at me as if I were a little slow, then gathered up an armful of wood. "Don't try to tell me you don't know that my girl has a woman-sized crush on that old stick of a boss." Carrying the wood over to the side of the trailer, she dropped it in a large metal basket, then crouched to stack the wood more evenly. "Good lord," Jackie said, as I added a much smaller armful of wood to her pile, "you're as bad as she is. Pia's missed out on about twenty-eight years of human courting etiquette, so it's all I can do to stop her from lying on her back and waving all four legs in the air. And you haven't noticed?"

I shrugged, embarrassed by my lack of social acumen. "If it's any consolation, I don't think Malachy's noticed, either. He thinks of her as a kid."

"Does he?" Jackie's eyes were shrewd. "I wonder."

I went back for another load of logs; Jackie was the sort of person you impressed with actions, not words. Besides, there was something satisfying about performing a basic, physical task like gathering wood. I could feel the cold through my leather gloves, and my fingertips would probably be numb when I went inside, but for now I was enjoying the soft rose glow of the sunset between the bare trees in the west, the shadowing of the valley below into soft mauve and indigo, the smell of wood smoke. A few of Jackie's wolfdogs were trotting by my heels, but when I looked at them they broke away, loping toward the forest. At the edge of the clearing, they sat and whined, and one or two pointed their noses to the tree line and sang out a soft howl of greeting.

Pia came out of the forest wearing a gray sweatshirt, a down vest, jeans, and sneakers, and unless you looked closely, you might have mistaken her for a high school boy. Except that she wasn't carrying a backpack; Pia had never gotten into the human habit of carrying things with her. As she came closer, I saw that her cheeks were flushed, and I noticed that she hadn't taken the path up the mountain.

The other dogs whined and laid their ears flat as she walked up to them, beating their tails slowly from side to side. Clearly, they loved her, but there was something confused and tentative about their posture. Pia looked miserable as she crouched down to bump noses with them.

"Pia," Jackie said, "I wasn't expecting you for another hour."

Pia rested her head against one of the other dogs; Patsy, I think. "Malachy said I should go before it got dark." Pia was attempting to sound matter-of-fact, but she looked as though she were reciting a list of casualties of war. She stood up, blinking back tears as she added, "He says my hours have to change until it's spring."

Jackie put her arm around her daughter's shoulders, and Pia cringed. Crossing another's body meant dominance to canines; Jackie still hadn't figured out how to touch a human child with wolfish instincts. Pulling back, Jackie sighed. "Ah, well, honey, he's looking out for your welfare." Then Jackie noticed her foster daughter's cold, bare hands. "Sweetheart, you forgot to wear mittens again."

"Did I?" Pia looked down at her fingers. "I didn't notice."

I was clearly the most clueless woman of all time. Now that I knew, it was painfully apparent that Pia was infatuated with our boss. After all, he was emotionally unavailable, autocratic, condescending, and critical. What woman could resist? "Hey, Pia," I said.

"Oh, hi, Dr. Barrow."

"Abra. Call me Abra."

Pia met my eyes with difficulty. She had been a submissive wolfdog, and now she was a diffident woman. "Sure . . . Abra." She attempted a smile, but it came out crooked.

"Why don't you go inside and grab a bite to eat?" Jackie smiled. "I bought some cookies, and you can help us give the other guys their shots."

Pia shook her head, looking at the other dogs. One or two whined, and then broke off and moved up alongside me. I patted one absently, wondering why I was suddenly so popular with Jackie's dogs.

Pia must have been wondering the same thing. Her soft gold eyes, so like Red's, filled with tears. "Actually," she said to Jackie, "if you don't mind, I'd rather just go for a quick run."

"It's getting dark, and I need to keep the others with me, to get their shots," Jackie said.

"That's all right. I'm used to being alone." With a short bark, Pia told her former packmates to stay. Then, with a glance at Jackie and me, she held up her palm. "Stay," she repeated in English. And then she broke off into an awkward run, as if she still had forgotten for a second that she couldn't just throw her body forward. With an embarrassed glance over her shoulder, Pia found her rhythm and then was swallowed up by the woods.

"Come back before full dark," Jackie called, then turned back to me. Still looking after her, she said, "Since you didn't know about her feelings about Malachy, you might not realize, but she's jealous of you."

"Of me? Why?" But as soon as the words were out of my mouth, I knew. "Oh, Christ on a crutch," I said, almost pleading with Jackie. "Malachy has no interest in me as a woman. As far as I know, he doesn't want anybody in that way."

"I know, I know," said Jackie, looking tired. "But you're his peer and he respects you, and she thinks you're the other woman." I had to wonder how much Jackie had to do with that misperception. "Come on, Abra, let's get on with tending the dogs."

I went back to my car and grabbed my medical bag, the male hybrids following me like an honor guard. The sun was lower on the horizon now, and shadows were chasing what remained of the light. It was still prime hunting time, though when I glanced down at the dogs, they were utterly focused on me. Two of them kept circling round and sniffing at my legs with rising levels of excitement. For a moment, I wondered if they were planning an attack. "Hey, Jackie? Just keep reminding them I'm an invited guest. Where do you want me to give them the vaccines?"

Jackie gestured at her trailer, which looked even more forlorn in the winter than it had in the autumn. "Set up on my kitchen table. I'll bring them in one by one." To my surprise, the dogs continued to follow me as I opened the trailer door.

"Come on, boys," Jackie said, pushing the dogs away from me. "Give her some room to move." As she opened the door, she said, "They're a bit nervous these days. Some city idiot is busy knocking down trees about a mile away. And there's another bulldozer starting in down that way." In a softer tone of voice, Jackie addressed the dogs who were scrambling to get in through the door in a giant, furry pack.

I laughed, because I'd never seen them so eager to be examined. "Jeez, one at a time, I can't even get in the door."

"Now, stop it, boys," Jackie said, a bit more sharply, "you can't all come in at once. I want the Doc to see Patsy's dewclaw first." Jackie shooed the dogs away, although one, a large husky mix, seemed intent on sticking his muzzle in my crotch. I managed to get myself over the threshold as Jackie stood in the doorway, berating her pack with mock sternness.

"Jeez, you guys, lay off her. And where's Patsy and Miyax? How come it's just you boys dogging her? Huh? Huh?" The wolfdogs whined and looked abashed.

I turned and looked for a place to set up my medical kit. There was a coffee cup filled with old cigarette ashes on the kitchen table, which I moved into the pile of dishes in the sink. The trailer stank of Marlboro Reds and wet dog, and by comparison, Red's cabin was roomy and luxurious.

Thumbtacked on the walls were various photographs of the wolves, along with a snapshot of a much younger Red, holding a wolf cub on his lap. There was also a picture of Red and Jackie together, on the back of a dogsled. Like everything else in the trailer, these were covered by a fine coating of dust. I wondered if Jackie had cleaned the place at all since the last time I'd been here. That had been last year, and I'd been hiking, miserable about the state of my marriage but still in denial about what was happening to Hunter. Jackie had told me that she knew that Red and I were going to get together, but even though she'd accepted it, it had been clear she wasn't exactly happy. It wasn't jealousy; at the time, they were no longer a couple. But Jackie had worried that I was going to end up bringing Red more pain than happiness.

In the end though, Red had walked me home, and somewhere along the way we'd taken an unexpected detour into intimacy.

"All right, I couldn't get Patsy, but here's Romulus, ready for his shot."

I jumped a little as Jackie brought the German shepherd mix in. Misinterpreting my guilty look, Jackie gave a rueful smile. "It's a mess in here, I know. But I spend all my time outside."

"You don't need to apologize to me, Jackie. I don't know how you find time for everything as it is." In addition to her work with the pack, most of whom had suffered in their former homes, Jackie was a wildlife rehabilitator. She took in many of the creatures Red removed, and also served as an unofficial nature warden, keeping tabs on the nests of endangered birds and turtles, and watching out for fire hazards in summer. Her only real source of income, as far as I could tell, came in the form of donations for the wolves, with a little extra from the sale of her homemade moonshine. Which reminded me, I had to bring Red back a bottle.

"Don't let me forget to buy some of your whiskey," I said as I removed my coat and gloves.

"You don't have to buy it, girl." Jackie bent down to pull a bottle out of a drawer, and I realized that she was stocky with muscle rather than fat.

"You have to let me pay, Jackie."

"How about you just loan me Red back for a night? Just kidding, Doc. Red and I are past all that nonsense. And he would never cheat, you know. He's a good man, and there's not too many of them going around."

I murmured something in agreement, then busied myself giving the shepherd mix his vaccines. As far as I could tell, Jackie's affection for Red was that of an old friend, and she certainly didn't act as though she were jealous or resentful of me. Still, it was clear that she saw me as the younger, more sophisticated woman who had bewitched her old boyfriend. It wasn't a role I was comfortable playing.

"So," I said, changing the subject with my usual lack of grace, "anything going on with the pack besides needing their rabies and Parvo boosters? You said Patsy had torn one of her dewclaws."

Jackie's eyes twinkled with amusement at my discomfort, but she followed my lead. "Let me think. Loki's gone and gotten into a fight with something. Banged up his tail pretty good. I bandaged it, but I wanted you to take a look while you were here."

"I didn't see him when I got here."

"He was there; he's just shy and easy to overlook. But he's my special boy, because when he warms up to you, he's one of the smartest, kindest dogs you'll ever meet. Reminds me of the way Pia used to be."

I suppose all parents must feel some shock when their sweet, smooth-skinned little boy or girl suddenly shoots up, sprouts hair, and breaks out in angry adolescent acne and opinions. But dogs and tame wolves exist in a kind of perpetual childhood, and Jackie had never expected her furry girl to rebel. I think Jackie was more shocked at Pia's emotional shift than she was by her physical transformation—after all, Jackie had known Red in more than one form.

Out loud, all I said was, "She still loves you, you know."

Jackie shook her head. "All she can see is the ways I don't quite measure up."

"I'm sorry, Jackie. I'm sure it'll pass." But I could see that for Jackie, a human daughter was a poor excuse for a dog.

In a way, meeting Pia had been the start of all the

changes in my life. Jackie had brought her into the Animal Medical Institute, mistakenly thinking that the services there were basically free. She'd also had some trouble with some of the local vets, who believed she was breeding wolf hybrids instead of rescuing them. But when Jackie had learned how expensive the Institute really was, she'd thought we wouldn't let her have Pia back, and had sent Red to do a little wildlife removal operation.

"You done with Romulus now? I'll take him out and bring Loki in."

I was done with Romulus, but he wasn't done with me. Whining and snuffling, he fought to stay inside with me as Jackie half coaxed, half dragged him back outside.

Jackie was back in a matter of moments, leading Loki on a loose leash. In a show of affection completely out of character for the shy animal, Loki jumped up and actually licked me on the face.

"Well, that's some hello," said Jackie, sounding mystified. Unlike dogs, wolves stop bonding with new people after about three months of age.

"Guess you really like me, boy." I ruffled Loki's brindled gray fur. For a moment, I actually thought he was going to stand and let me examine his tail, but then, right on cue, a chain saw fired up, making him jump and cower under the table. "God, Jackie, that's awful. I thought this whole area had been declared a wetlands preserve."

Jackie squinted out her small window in the direction of the offending noise. "Yeah, well, you know how that goes. Somebody offered somebody some money, and presto, an expert appeared who redrew the boundary lines." Jackie coaxed Loki out into the open, rubbing his ears until he looked up at her with a purely puppy look of devotion. She held him while I ran my hands up and down his tail. "My neighbor set up the lights so they can work after dark."

I was about to say something sympathetic when I felt Loki wince at my touch. "Jackie, is there any chance that Loki could have gotten into a fight with some of the other dogs?"

"Sure, there's always a chance. Why do you ask?"

I took out my tweezers and removed a claw from the thick, double coat of fur near Loki's tail. "Tell me. What do you make of that?"

Jackie took the claw in her palm. "That's not dog or wolf. That's a bear claw."

"I should show it to Red. He said he had a run-in with a bear. Well, not exactly a bear."

She paused. "Is he all right? And what's not exactly a bear?"

"There's a bit of a story there, and I think Red should probably be the one to tell it."

Jackie looked at the claw again. "You mean something supernatural," she said. "A regular old black bear would be hibernating this time of year."

I started to reply, but then the whine of the chain saw drowned out the possibility of easy conversation. Jackie's generous mouth tightened into an unhappy grimace. "Of course, who can sleep, with that racket going on?"

An hour later and we were done. We'd successfully vaccinated all eight of the wolfdogs, and I'd given Loki a shot of antibiotic and bandaged up Patsy's paw, and Jackie had loaded me up with two bottles of bourbon and one of home-tapped maple syrup from the previous spring.

As she walked me to my car, the wolfdogs swarmed around me again, but this time there was no mistaking their mood. Wagging their tails like excited puppies, Romulus and the husky mix jockeyed each other for the right to sniff, while the usually timid Loki kept worming his way between the other dogs' bodies so he could sidle up and lick my hand.

Jackie scratched her head as I tried, for the third time, to get my hand to the handle of the car door. "You put something extra in those injections of yours?"

"I guess I just have the magic touch."

"Guess you do." Jackie pushed the dogs off, allowing me to get into the car. "Leave her alone, boys, leave her alone! What are you trying to do, ride on home with her? I can't have all my boys leaving me for Abra, now."

Wincing a little, I lowered my window so I could say good-bye to Jackie. "We should meet up at Moondoggie's for dinner this week. I know Red would love to see you."

"Storm might be coming, but we'll see. Thanks for coming all the way out here," said Jackie, fishing a cigarette out of her pack and lighting it. As I drove slowly away down the icy drive, I caught her reflection in the rearview mirror, dragging on the Marlboro as if she'd been postponing this smoke for a long time. She looked off into the shadowy woods, searching for Pia. Who seemed to think I was standing in the way of her winning Malachy's affection.

I sighed, suddenly bone-tired. Somehow, Jackie must have inadvertently convinced her daughter that I was some kind of man-eater. And in a way, I supposed I was to her what Magda was to me. But I hadn't actually broken Red and Jackie up, and Magda was a crazy bitch. Still, I wished Jackie could find another man's photograph for her trailer wall.

As I backed into my parking space outside the animal clinic, I wondered if I should convince Jackie to come with me to a day spa one of these days. She couldn't be much more than thirty-eight, and there was really no reason for her to live alone with the dogs. She just needed a little fashion advice, a lot of moisturizer, and a good haircut, none of which were available in North-side.

As for Pia, it suddenly struck me that the other dogs hadn't greeted her as a submissive, and that she hadn't spoken to them as one. She was shy around Malachy and me, but maybe there was another side to Pia.

People thought wolves and dogs could be categorized as alphas, betas, or omegas, as leaders or followers. Some people even thought that was the way the human world worked. But the truth was more complex. Just as a woman could be a powerful manager at work and then a meek wife at home, or a man could be a tyrant at home and a milquetoast in the office, a wolf could be dominant in one pack, and submissive in another. Status was fairly fluid, and every wolf encounter was filled with nuance and negotiation.

I had just removed my key from the ignition when I heard a screech of tires as someone burned rubber pulling in beside me. I stepped out of my car, bracing for an animal emergency, and found myself face-to-face with Marlene. She was in acute distress, her face pale and wide-eyed, her coarse black hair still in curlers, and her pink chenille sweater stained with blood.

"You have to help Queenie! She's bleeding!"

I raced to the back of Marlene's cherry red pickup truck where I saw exactly what I'd been dreading: Queenie, staining a white towel scarlet.

I didn't worry about losing control of my temper; with a patient bleeding out in front of me, I snapped into professional mode. "Take the other end of the towel," I ordered Marlene, who had come up beside me and was staring, horrified, at Queenie. "On my count: one, two, three, now." As we lifted her I had a moment to think, I wish to hell Pia hadn't gone home. Then we were at the clinic steps, and I snapped, "Door, somebody get the door," but Malachy was already there, holding it open.

"Christ, let's get her into the operating room," he said, and I bit back a retort—where did he think I was going, anyway? Marlene's stringy arms were shaking as we lifted Queenie onto the table.

"I'll prepare the surgical tray," Mal said, brushing Marlene aside as he examined Queenie. "Scrub up, Abra." I was about to ask him why he didn't want to operate himself, but then I glanced over and saw my boss palm a pill from his pocket.

Marlene walked over to the sink as I put on an operating gown, her face old and oddly masculine without makeup. Her eyes did not meet mine. "Is she going to be all right?"

"I don't know," I said, scrubbing my nails, then shutting the faucet with my forearm. "But if she dies, we know who's to blame, don't we?"

"I asked you to take care of it! This is your fault! You think you were being responsible? Those weren't puppies, they were little monsters waiting to come out!"

I was dimly aware of my boss pushing Marlene out, murmuring something about waiting out in the other room, and I could feel Malachy watching me, but it didn't matter. All my attention was on Queenie now, and making sure she didn't lose her life along with her puppies.

SEVEN

◑ ◔ ○   I didn't want to wake up. There was a headache waiting for me when I opened my eyes—I could
feel it, knocking at my temples, wanting to get in. There
was a bad taste in the back of my throat, and a wave of
nausea chasing it. My muscles were aching, letting me
know that whatever it was I'd been doing last night, it
had been pushing my body to its limits. Or past them.

"Good morning, Doc."

I groaned, rolling over and pulling the covers over my
head. Red, who was clearly not suffering from whatever
was ailing me, was now kissing his way up my instep
and calf. I made a little flailing motion, trying to shake
him off, but it was a pretty weak effort.

"I know how to make you happy." Now Red was nipping his way toward the back of my knees. I made a sort
of convulsive hand and foot movement, trying to communicate the fact that I was in real distress here. The
nips were climbing my inner thigh, at almost the same
pace as the nausea was climbing my esophagus.

I curled up into a fetal ball before looking over my
shoulder. Red was looking feral and happy: He liked a
bit of a chase. He was wearing jeans and a shirt, and he
smelled of pine and sandalwood and smoke, with a faint
undertone of musk. It was that delicious woodsy aftershave again. Except that he had said he wasn't wearing

any fragrance. "What time is it?" My voice was hoarse, as though I'd been shouting at the top of my lungs. Or howling.

"Nearly eleven. Malachy said to let you sleep in. I told him you had to let off a bit of steam last night."

A bit of steam. I wasn't sure exactly what that had entailed. I had a vague memory of going to Moondoggie's, of drinking the Tuesday apple martini special, and not eating the chicken surprise. There might have been a second martini in there somewhere, but nothing to account for the class-five hangover that was steadily building in strength and intensity. "I need to get up."

"Mal said not to worry about coming in today." Red curled himself around me, his clothing rough against my bare skin. "You didn't want to talk about it last night, but I got the impression it was a pretty rough day at work."

Suddenly the musky scent of him felt overwhelming, and I grunted as the pain in my head battled for precedence with the bile in my throat. Funny to think that I'd once fantasized about having a man who would spoon with me and pay attention to my moods and feelings, back in the days when I'd been married to a narcissistic lout. Now all I wanted was some breathing space. And possibly some throwing-up space, as well.

"That was some run last night, huh?" Red lifted the hair off the back of my neck, which felt good, and then starting kissing my nape.

"We ran?"

"Oh, God, yeah. I couldn't keep up with you." He inhaled deeply, and I knew he was drawing in the scent of my hair and skin.

"Stop. I smell awful."

"Not to me. Not to any shifter, for that matter. And considering last night, I'm thinking we should be calling you a shifter, Girl."

I threw the covers off my head, needing cooler air. "What happened last night?"

"Yeah, good question. Let me think: dinner, drive home, something out of the ordinary, but what was it, again?"

I punched him. "Red, I'm not feeling up to this."

Red smiled at me, quizzical and fond. "You don't remember?"

"My head hurts. I'd like to throw up, but I'm worried that my head might split open. My body feels like I was hauling rocks, or maybe getting hit by them."

Red's smile faded. "You really don't remember."

I swung my legs over the side of the bed, then bumped my head on a lamp. "Oh, Jesus, I hate living in this damn cabin."

There was a momentary silence, like a vacuum of sound, as we both heard what I'd said. "Sorry, I'm just . . . I feel lousy, that's all."

"No, it's me who's sorry. Too caught up in my own good mood, I guess." I felt the bed dip as Red stood up. He walked away, opened the freezer, and came back with a bag of frozen peas. "Here, put that on your head."

"Thanks." I couldn't look at him, so I didn't try. "So, Red, what did happen last night?"

"You shifted."

Now I did turn to him, but he was looking away, measuring coffee into the pot. "I went furry before the moon was even half full?"

"Yep." I watched Red pour the water, all the excitement and pleasure gone from his face and posture. There was something else that had happened, I was sure of it, something that had revved him up and filled him with happiness. But before I could inquire further, the competition between pounding head and roiling stomach came to an abrupt conclusion. I bolted for the toilet with my hand clapped over my mouth.

*   *   *

The next day I decided that I couldn't put off talking to Red any longer. Nearly thirty hours had passed since my lost night, and we still hadn't discussed it, just as we hadn't discussed the strange moment with Malachy.

It was mainly my fault. Wanting to escape the tension at home, I'd taken two Alka-Seltzer and shambled off to work, where Malachy didn't ask me how I felt, or try to comfort me about Queenie. In return, I didn't confront him about his nameless illness. Neither of us acknowledged our strange moment of intimacy, which was a relief. Maybe if we pretended it hadn't happened, it would just go away.

To be honest, I didn't even like thinking about me lying underneath my boss on my front lawn in broad daylight. I wasn't sure what was worse: the knowledge that Malachy hadn't been interested in taking what I was offering, or the realization that I'd been offering. It wasn't that I'd just discovered a secret attraction to my boss—way, deep down, I knew I wasn't attracted. It was like having some sort of strange sex dream about some nerdy, bow-tied high school teacher you didn't even like. Which had happened to me, back in the tenth grade. Maybe in my wolf form I was still unformed and curious. Just what I needed, another adolescence to endure.

So, as much as I would have liked to tell Malachy about my latest episode, I decided that it was better to leave that Pandora's box unopened.

I had been steeling myself all day for a serious conversation with Red, but he'd been out when I got home. He must have come back after I'd gone to sleep, which was a relief, really. I'd figured we'd talk in the morning.

But when I'd just started waking up, Red had placed his hand on the curve of my hip, a question. Before I'd had a chance to think about it, I'd rolled away. A moment later, I had turned over to see him lying on his back, his hands under his head. His sharp cheekbones had cast dark shadows over his eyes, showing me the wolf in his face, and for a moment, I had wished for him to shift so there would be no need for words. That faint, delicious odor of forest and musk still clung to him—it might even have grown a shade more intense. If he had been in wolf form, I thought, he wouldn't have been so tentative and I'd have wanted to touch him.

But, a little voice intruded, you can't conduct an entire relationship out of just one aspect of yourself. As usual, the little voice sounded like my mother. I've never been sure, however, whether this is because, deep down, I recognize my mother's innate wisdom on such matters, or whether the sheer force of her personality has colored the tone of my conscience. In any case, I'm not at all sure that a B movie star turned animal rescuer is really the best source of relationship wisdom.

So I pushed aside my doubts. I loved Red, and I felt lousy about a bunch of things: yesterday's outburst, not noticing that he'd been injured, the whole rolling around on the ground with Malachy thing. So I did what most American women probably do when they want to please their men. I went shopping for steak.

Before my change, I'd been a vegetarian, and even now, I only ate meat at certain times of the month, and I preferred it to arrive on my plate fully cooked and sauced and as unlike a living, breathing cow as possible. At least, that's what I liked in my human form. When I was furry and four-legged, I would happily have torn a chunk out of a cow's chest, were the opportunity to arise.

But right now I was as human as I'd ever be, and shopping for raw meat, touching it and washing it and sloshing it around in marinade, well, that was a sacrifice I would have made only for love. I stared at the porterhouse, trying to remember if lots of little flabby white veins of fat running through the meat was desirable or not.

"Excuse me, but you're blocking the aisle."

I turned around, my muscles tightening at the sound of that familiar, sultry, accented voice. "Hello, Magda." I glared up at the woman who was living with my soon-to-be ex in the home we'd shared. She was wearing a fitted red wool coat and had a new, short haircut that showcased the dramatic streak of white in her dark hair. She had fifteen years on me, but I felt like a gnome standing beside her in unflattering jeans and a puffy vest from the Tractor Supply store.

"Oh, hello, Abra," said Magda, as if she hadn't known perfectly well it was me. Besides being a were-wolf, Magdalena Ionescu was a senior wolf researcher and an experienced tracker—not the type to let her mind drift while meandering around the supermarket. I had no idea why she was playing coy with me, but it was making me bristle. We weren't friends, and I saw no reason to pretend otherwise.

"Oh, don't these look delicious." Magda plucked the other four porterhouse steaks out of the display and smiled at me. "Are you taking that one, or not? I don't mean to seem greedy, but my brothers are coming to visit."

Belatedly, I comprehended that her fake friendliness was a form of aggression. If we'd been in wolf form, she'd have marched on over to sniff me before knocking me to the ground.

"I'm sorry, but I'm making a special dinner for Red." I threw the last porterhouse into my own wagon.

"You know, I'm very happy for the two of you," Magda murmured, leaning forward as if confiding in an intimate. "I know that you and Hunter were never right for each other, and I think it's marvelous that you've found someone who suits you. And I've always liked coyotes—they're very crafty, and they do make up in trickiness what they lack in size and strength."

I felt my right eyelid begin to twitch. "First of all, Red's not a coyote, he's a red wolf. Second of all, I don't remember asking for your opinion."

Magda gave a low, husky laugh. "My goodness, I seem to have hit a nerve. I'm sorry, I have nothing against Red being Coyote. In fact, considering that you can't have children, I think choosing someone from a different group makes a lot of sense."

Belatedly, I glanced around to see if anyone was listening to our conversation. Northsiders were experts at ignoring the supernatural weirdness all around them, and we were speaking very softly, but a small town is a small town: People care deeply about other people's business.

I waited till two women had pushed their shopping carts around a corner, then said, "What do you mean, since I can't have children? Just because I didn't get pregnant last time doesn't mean I can't have children."

Magda bared her teeth in a smile. "Poor Abra. You really don't have a clue, do you? And yet you are a veterinarian, so you must know about breeding cycles in wolves and dogs." In case I still hadn't made the connection, she said, "False pregnancies, my dear. A nondominant female hardly ever whelps a litter."

The moment she said it, I realized that I never really thought of myself as being half wolf. The way I saw it, I only moonlighted as a wolf; human was my day job.

But what Magda was implying was that I couldn't get pregnant because I wasn't assertive or alpha enough. In the wild, nondominant wolf females cycle with the alpha. Even if they don't breed, they go through the symptoms of pregnancy along with the lead bitch, and after the leader's pups are born, the other females produce milk, so they can nurse the pups when the mother is off on a hunt.

But even when lower-ranking females do become pregnant, they tend not to carry to term. It's not like a human miscarriage—there's no blood, no outward sign at all. Veterinarians don't really understand it, but the body seems to just reabsorb the pregnancy with no ill effects.

My face must have revealed some of what I was feeling, because Magda said, "Oh, now I've upset you." She leaned over the meat counter and absently pressed her finger into a package of liver so that blood pooled beneath the plastic. "But you wouldn't really want to start a family with someone like Red, would you, now?" Adding the liver to her cart, Magda met my eyes. "In Romania, we have two kinds of unwolf—vârcolac and pricolici. But Red, he says he is shapeshifter, yes? What is his word for it—Limmikin. He told me about it when I stayed with him."

Now that was rubbing salt in my wounds. I still hadn't gotten over the fact that Red had allowed Magda to stay at his cabin when she'd first arrived in Northside. Sure, he'd had his reasons—Hunter was new to his change, and Red had been scared that he'd tear me apart. Magda was supposed to step in as his mentor, helping him through the mindless violence of his early transformations. But part of mentoring him involved screwing his brains out, which was how he'd gotten infected with the virus in the first place.

So I wasn't exactly grateful to Red for putting Magda up. I wasn't actively angry, though—at least not unless I thought about it.

"I know all about the Limmikin," I said stiffly. "It's the Mohawk term for a shapeshifter."

"So you know that the term is not a complimentary one. Ah, I see you did not hear this. The Limmikin are—How do I explain this? They are like the gypsies of the human world. Thieves. Fortune-tellers. Con artists."

I gritted my teeth. "You forgot the part where they invented flamenco and suffered centuries of persecution. And before you say anything else, you should know that my father is Gitano. From Barcelona."

"How charming. Yet another thing you have in common with Red." Magda leaned down, emphasizing the difference in our heights. "But you should know that you are different kinds of therians. The strain you carry, the strain that comes from me, this is pricolici. There is also vârcolac," she added, making the motion of spitting over her left shoulder. "Those disgusting dabblers in dark arts. But at least we both have the sacred link to the moon. But your man, he is not lycanthrope at all. He is a lesser kind of thing, which is why I allow you to remain in our territory."

Sometimes I wondered if Magda had learned her English from my mother's old movies. "Lady, you have issues." I was aware of people openly watching us now, some of them clients, but the anger was pulsing through me now, pushing at my ribs, snapping my knuckles, making each hair on my head feel as if it were electric with fury.

Something flickered in Magdalena's dark almond eyes. "What are you doing?"

I took a step forward, shaking my finger in her face like an avenging nanny. "I have had just about enough of you today. What is it, you came here looking for a fight? Well, let's go for it, then."

Magda grabbed my right wrist. "Get control of yourself."

"Get your hands off me!"

"You are shifting, Abra. Look!" She thrust my hand in front of my face. The nails were darkening, lengthening, changing shape. And so were the bones.

Abruptly, Magda turned, putting her arm around me and turning me toward the freezer section. It must have looked as though she was comforting me, but she was effectively shielding me from the little audience we'd attracted. Looking over her shoulder, I spotted Marlene of the dragon lady nails and Jerome in his *Little House on the Prairie* shirt—two of the biggest gossips in the county. Oh, God, this was going to be all over town by tonight.

"Deep breath. That's it. Slow and steady." In teacher mode, Magda was almost reassuring. For the first time, I had a glimpse of what must have attracted Hunter back when Magda was a senior wolf researcher and he was a journalist chasing a story.

"Thank you." I took another breath and shuddered.

"You are all right now?" Her accent was more pronounced.

I nodded. "I'm sorry. I seem to have less control of my temper these days."

"Of your temper. And has your . . . cycle been irregular?"

I didn't need to respond.

"I see. And do you have any idea why this is happening now?"

I looked at Magda. Up close, there were fine lines visible between her brows, fanning out from the corners of her eyes. It made me like her better. "No."

The hand that had been loosely holding me across my shoulders tightened, and I winced. "The lycanthropy is progressing. I would never have expected it, but there it is. You are in season."

For a moment, I was so stuck on the first part of the sentence that I didn't understand the end. When I remained silent, Magda frowned and said, "Don't you get it? In season. In estrus. In heat."

EIGHT

●○○ According to my mother, every romantic relationship is a reaction to the one that came before it. Since my mother is Piper LeFevre, iconic sex symbol, her theories about romance carry some weight in the world. Women's magazines still quote her, usually with the picture from *Lucrezia Cyborgia* with my mother in that tight, clear plastic space suit.

The magazines might think twice about their sources if they knew that my mother renounced men about fifteen years ago. More recently she swore off women as well. Still, she did tell me that she'd always worried that Hunter didn't love me enough, and that being with him had turned me into a caricature of myself: the studious, earnest, geeky girl that's a staple of teen movies, complete with long hair, big glasses, and boxy wardrobe.

She'd been right about that. For all I knew, being celibate made her an objective oracle on love and romance.

After the very public scene with Magda in the Stop and Shop, I was willing to take a chance and pay Mom a visit. I'd be the first to admit that it was also a way to postpone having to talk with Red. So instead of a steak dinner, Red got a message on his cell phone: Had to run off to my mother's at the last minute.

I realized that leaving like this was the sort of thing Hunter used to do to me, but I couldn't help it. I recalled

Red's ebullient mood after my lost night, my feeling that there was something he had neglected to tell me. I didn't trust Magda, but I knew she was perfectly capable of telling the truth when it served her purpose.

Presumably she was as wrong about the Limmikin as she was about gypsies. What did a Romanian wolf researcher know about Native American shapeshifters, anyway? I tried to remember everything Red had told me about his family. Last year we'd meant to go north, to visit his surviving relatives in Canada. But then I'd gotten the position with Malachy and we'd postponed our trip.

But hang on a moment. It was Red who insisted that I go ahead and begin my new job immediately. Maybe he'd had second thoughts about my getting to know his people.

I may have had my reservations about my future with Red, but until this moment, I'd never questioned our past together. I'd always felt that I could depend on him to be open and honest. It was one of his chief attractions, after all of Hunter's secrets and subterfuges.

Now I wasn't so sure.

And even though I knew I could have called up my friend Lilliana for advice, I didn't feel up to exposing the fact that I was involved in yet another dicey romance.

So I threw the groceries in the back of the car and drove up to my mother's house, flipping around the radio dial until I found Natalie Merchant singing with bruised eloquence about jealousy. This was followed by yet another rendition of Faith Hill singing about how good she and her husband had it so I turned the radio off. The sky was overcast and gray, but as I approached Pleasantvale, the clouds and mist cleared and I caught a glimpse of the half moon, pale and almost translucent around the edges. The sight of it was a reminder, and I took stock of my body, but as far as I could tell, the change was still weeks away. Which was odd; usually, I felt a pang, like that of ovulation, in the middle of my cycle. Maybe changing last night with Red had used up the lycanthropic hormones. Which meant there might be a bright side to my having a complete memory blackout.

As I turned off the highway, all traces of snow and ice on the ground disappeared. My mother lived an hour and a half away, and seventy-five miles south the air was warmer, the houses larger and built more closely together.

In general, Pleasantvale was a very upscale community, although my childhood home was situated in the one remaining working-class enclave. It looked singularly out of place, surrounded by mixed-family units with names like Paradise Heights and small houses crammed together with mismatched fences and clashing holiday lights. When I was a kid, I'd thought that our neighbors' homes reminded me of strangers stuck sharing a table at a hotel banquet. Our own home was like a movie set. A movie set for a gothic romance, to be specific.

Modeled after El Greco's house in southern Spain, it was a fabulous, whimsical villa, and I have some hazy early memories of my parents entertaining other Hollywood types. There was always a cloud of cigarette smoke perfumed with women's eau de toilette and men's aftershave, and I could invariably find my father playing director behind his elaborate wet bar, while my mother passed around some fussy, fatty, now defunct appetizer: rumaki, or liver wrapped in bacon and doused in soy sauce, clams casino, pigs in blanket. The main course was often something gimmicky and low rent, like spice-your-own chili or stab-your-own cheese fondue. I remember sneaking into the living room in my pink flannel nightgown and fluffy slippers, risking third-degree burns to jab my skewered bread into the pot when no one was looking. When I was back in my bed, I could hear my parents, shouting with laughter late into the night. Being an adult, I remember thinking, was going to be a lot of fun.

Not long after came the realization that adult fun was paid for in blood. I stayed up listening to my parents shouting without laughter late into the night. The drinks no longer had names, and my diet of stolen appetizers was replaced by TV dinners. I used to read the product descriptions with great optimism: tender breast of chicken lightly breaded and fried, baby niblets of corn, crisp Idaho fries. I was aware that the reality was damp chicken, soggy potatoes and kernels of corn everywhere, but given a choice between fiction and reality, I went for fiction.

These days, my father owns a small hotel in Key West, and my mother has turned the house into Beast Castle, a not-for-profit refuge for abused animals. I admire my mother's decision, but it didn't make coming home a relaxing proposition.

"Thank God you're here," my mother said, as she opened the massive front door. She was wearing a purple caftan, just as she had in her hostessing days, and her dyed blond hair was pulled back with a barrette, revealing gray roots. She had lost weight, which I'd been nagging her to do for years. It made her look tired. And still, she was more beautiful than I would ever be.

"What's wrong, Mom?"

"I think the husky has an impacted tooth."

"I wish you'd said something when I called." Knowing her as I did, I'd brought a variety of medications, just in case, but I hated being taken for granted.

"I didn't know then. He just started acting funny when I gave him a bone."

I followed my mother as she swept down the hallway, the ragged hem of her purple caftan trailing behind her.

Like my mother, the house was looking a bit seedy, with antique chairs listing to one side, and all the couches and curtains bearing claw marks. The medieval suit of armor in the main hall looked as though it were rusting around the edges, and the tiled fountain under the domed skylight gave off a strong smell of feline urine.

"So, Mom, how is everything? Besides the husky, I mean."

"Oh, I'm going crazy. Two of the new girls never showed up for work today, and I'm expecting a new litter of kittens. And here's Snowboy, poor fellow, he was being kept in a closet all day." She pointed out the husky, who had his head between his paws and was regarding me with a baleful blue gaze. Like most wolfish dogs, he had a wider range of expression than smaller-faced breeds, but knew how to put on a poker face when he was in pain and strangers were watching. I held out my hand for him to sniff before rummaging in my large leather bag for my stethoscope. Hunter had given me the bag for my birthday, right before we'd left the city, and even though Red kept offering to buy me another, I still loved it too much to give it up.

I pulled the stethoscope out of my ears. "His heart sounds fine," I told my mother. "Will he let me check his mouth?" Some of her rescue animals had some unresolved issues about being touched by strangers.

"Sure. He's an angel, aren't you, Snowy?"

I put my hand beside his muzzle, and Snowy snapped his teeth together, barely missing two of my fingers. "Jesus, Mom!"

"Snowy, no. Abra wants to help you. Go on, try again."

I glared at my mother. "Mom, he's going to bite me. Let me give him a sedative first."

"Just for a little oral exam? You must be joking. Anyway, you're a werewolf, aren't you? You shouldn't need a sedative to control him." My mother had been more than understanding about the news that I'd become a lycanthrope. In fact, she'd been ecstatic, demanding that I give her the chance to experience the change as well. But all my nip had given her was a small abscess, and I refused to try again while in wolf form. Being a wolf was a bit like being a three-year-old; you were still you, but a much more elemental, less civilized version. A version that couldn't always remember why it wasn't a good idea to eat an entire package of Nutter Butter cookies. A version that didn't always know its own strength.

"Mom, it doesn't work like that."

"Why not? Don't you have some wolfdog language you can use to communicate? Just growl at him."

I rocked back on my heels. "First of all, there's different kinds of growling, and a lot depends on body language. There's I'm-scared-please-don't-attack-or-I'll-bite growling, and there's I'm-the-total-boss-of-you growling, just to name two. And as long as I'm a person and not a wolf, I'm not sure I wouldn't get the intonation wrong and tell Snowy here that I'm a total wuss."

"So why not go wolfy?"

"Because I can't!"

"Don't shout, Abra, you're making Snowy nervous." My mother petted the dog, who was looking back and forth between us, like a child caught in the middle of a parental argument.

"Okay, one more time. I'm not a shapeshifter, Mom. As I keep trying to explain to you, I don't have control over the change." I paused. "And lately, I've had even less control than usual."

My mother didn't blink. "Have you hurt anyone?" Her voice was utterly calm and businesslike. She was always at her best in a crisis, which was probably why she tried to create one at every opportunity. "Do you think you might have hurt someone?"

"No, no. It's nothing like that, it's just . . ." I let out my breath, unaware that I'd even been holding it. "I don't know where to begin. I met Magda in the super-market, and she told me something that got me upset. I don't know how much to trust her, but I also think Red might not be telling me something . . ." I shook my head. "I'm sorry. I should take care of Snowy first." I reached into my bag, and my mother put her hand on my shoulder.

"You know what? I think you need to come into the kitchen and let me take care of you first."

"But Snowboy's abscess . . ."

My mother, who never failed to surprise me, pulled me to my feet. "Come on, Abs. Let me make you— No, I don't have any human food in the house. Let me take you out for lunch, and you can tell me why you look more upset now than you did when you found out Hunter was cheating."

NINE

◐ ○ ○ An hour later, my mother and I were sitting at the local diner, polishing off our goat cheese and spinach omelets. I had told her everything—my outburst at Marlene, Malachy's unexpected scent, my feeling of unease with Red, Magda's pronouncement. For the first time in days, I was actually enjoying my food.

"So," I said, after the pretty, pierced waitress was out of earshot, "what do you think? An increase in hormones would explain the bursts of irritability and my starting to change when the moon isn't full." I cut a piece of omelet. "It would also explain that weird moment I had with Malachy. I mean, he's not someone I find attractive. But for a moment there, I kind of forgot that he was my snarky, unhealthy boss."

My mother took a sip of coffee. "Maybe you just don't realize that you're attracted."

"I'm not *that* repressed."

"Well, in that case, something's going on with you physically, and you need to have someone more reliable than Magda to ask."

"You mean Red."

"No, I don't. If Magda is telling the truth, then Red probably does know that you're in . . . estrus, I suppose. And then the question becomes, what would he have to gain by keeping this from you?" She buttered a crust of toast from my plate. "Why don't you ask that boss of yours? He seems very knowledgeable."

"He's probably the leading expert in lycanthropy."

My mother spread her hands in a sweeping theatrical gesture that knocked over a water glass. "So? Talk to him about your condition."

I mopped up the spilled water with my napkin. "Mom, he has no sense of ethics. I like to assume that Malachy would want to help me control my disease, but frankly, I don't know. In the eighties, he transplanted monkey heads—he had this scheme that eventually we could just remove healthy brains from failing bodies and implant them in animal hosts. I've also heard a rumor that he was involved in some scheme to artificially impregnate a female chimpanzee."

"Well, at least it was artificially. Was he going to use his own semen?"

"Mom!"

"Well, to my mind, it makes a difference. Using outside semen suggests scientific curiosity, using your own just sounds like pure male ego. By the way, Abra, I do hope you're being careful with birth control."

I stared, trying to make the connection. "Hello, Mom, what are you talking about?"

"What are you using, anyway? The pill? Condoms?"

"Excuse me, but I do not see why this concerns you."

"If you're using a diaphragm, make sure you hold it up to the light. Make sure there aren't any little pinholes in there."

"Why would there be— Are you suggesting that Red would stick pins in my diaphragm?"

My mother gave me a level glance out of eyes that had once seduced a generation of weedy young men. "Honey, that man would do anything to keep you. Lie, steal, cheat, kill, clean up after himself, and do laundry."

I recalled waking up next to Red, unable to remember

the events of the previous night while he had been effervescent with happiness.

Which suggested that either Magda had lied, and I could get pregnant and have a baby, or that Red didn't know as much about therian obstetrics as Magda did.

I explained all this to my mother, who had a fairly pithy response: "I think she's full of shit. She's trying to brainwash you into thinking you can't get pregnant, and you're falling for it."

"I don't think it's that simple, Mom. I mean, there is a precedent in wolves for what she's talking about."

My mother raised her coffee cup, and the waitress came by instantly to fill it. "I think you're dodging the real question, which is, do you really want to start a family with Red? Do you want to settle for him?"

"I thought you liked Red."

"He's very likable, Abra, but he's not exactly your intellectual equal. And I can't see him traveling with you or visiting museums or watching any film with subtitles. He's a small-town boy. If you need someone who can put a wounded deer out of its misery without using a gun and then butcher it up for barbecue, he's your man. He'll never cheat—he's got that primitive sense of loyalty you find in dogs and children—but if you ever stray with another man—oh, don't look at me like that, say you give Hunter one for old times' sake—a man like Red will never forgive you. I'm not saying he's a bad choice, just that you need to know what you're choosing. Is Red Mallin really the man you want to father your children, Abra? If you hadn't caught the lycanthropy virus, would you even have considered him—or would you have chosen someone more like this Malachy?"

That hit a little too close to home, so I came out swinging. "Okay, first of all, there is no chance in hell that I might 'give one to Hunter for old times' sake,' as you so charmingly phrase it. Second," I paused, thwarted by the return of the waitress. She cleared our plates so slowly it seemed almost sadistic, asking us repeatedly if we wanted anything else. Surely some amount of people-reading skill is required in your profession, I thought. Out loud, I said, "We'll let you know." My mother raised her eyebrows: I wasn't usually so assertive in her presence.

When we were alone again, I said, "You make Red sound like some cliché of a redneck. I wouldn't be with him if that's all he was."

"Honey, I'm not trying to put him down."

"Of course you are. I'm just not sure what your point is: that Hunter's really a better match for me, because he reads the *New Yorker* and likes early music? You hated Hunter, remember?"

"Abra." My mother reached across the table and took my hand. "You'll make whatever decision is best for you, and I'll support you no matter what. But I want you to be honest with yourself. Red's a lovely man, but I've seen a lot of women make compromises when they fall for men who aren't their equals. Yes," my mother insisted, tightening her grip on my fingers. "I am saying that Red isn't your equal. Professionally, culturally, economically, and from what you say, even physically in your wolf forms, you are the more powerful partner." She held my gaze, and I remembered that when she'd first met my father, she'd been something of a star, while my father had been a young replacement director, known in Barcelona but not in the States. "And I don't mind, if he's what you want, but I don't want you to relinquish your power to him. So many women shore up their husbands' egos by making themselves less. I don't want that for you, Abra."

"I think you underestimate Red, Mom. He's subtle, in surprising ways. Psychologically, he's way more perceptive than Hunter ever was."

"Hunter was a complete narcissist. I've encountered recorded messages that were more perceptive than Hunter. As far as I can tell, one of his chief attractions was that he allowed you to continue to play the role of the good, practical, put-upon Jane Austen–style heroine. Part of the problem with Red is that he's not playing to your script. He's got some kind of Mark Twain back-woodsman thing going on, which leaves you with a problem: What's your new role? Are you the snappish city girl to his laid-back lumberjack? Or are you the supportive little woman by his side?"

I pulled my hands free. "Mom, I'm not choosing my next role. This is my life."

"Darling, we are all constantly choosing our next role. And I think that once you really make up your mind what you want and take charge of your life, you'll be able to get pregnant. If that's what you want."

I knew better than to argue this point with my mother, who believed that meditation, positive thinking, and high colonics could cure almost any medical condition. "Okay, not getting sidetracked here. Forget the whole theater-of-life spiel for a moment. Let's concentrate on the meat. You've got me completely confused. First you say I can't trust Red, then you say I'm the more power-ful one in this relationship, and that I'm not as nice with him as I was with Hunter. So which is it?"

My mother took another bread crust from my plate and spread it with strawberry jam. "Both." She took a bite of the crust. "Which thought scares you more?" There was a speck of red jam on the corner of her mouth. For a moment, it looked like blood.

"Okay," I said to my mother, handing her a napkin and motioning to the left side of her face, "so what do you think I should do?"

"Figure it out for yourself."

"Are you kidding? You never stop giving me unsolicited advice. What to wear. Where to shop. How to make more friends. For once in my life, I'm actually asking for your opinion, so you tell me to go figure it out for myself?" I crossed my legs and folded my arms. "Typical."

"Abra, I'm not always going to be here."

"Oh, God, not the mortality lecture."

"I know you don't want to hear it, but it's true."

"Why do you always have to aim for maximum drama?" A horrible thought occurred to me. "You're not going to tell me you have cancer or something, are you? Because this would be a really shitty way of leading up to it."

My mother sighed. "No, I'm not going to tell you that I have cancer."

"So don't start in with the mortality thing. You know how I hate that. Hey, where are you going?" My mother had pushed her chair back, and was holding her hand to her mouth. "You're not going to be sick, are you?"

"No, no, I just have something stuck in my tooth."

I tapped my fingers on the table, wondering if my mother really might be keeping something from me. Nah, probably not. After all, this was the same woman who used to terrorize me with depressing lullabies. The worst was an old spiritual that went, "Hush little baby, don't you cry, you know your mama's bound to die, all my troubles soon be over." If I ever had a kid, I wasn't even going to sing about boughs breaking and cradles falling.

My mother came back to the table wearing fresh lipstick. "You know," she said as she sat back down in her chair, "while I was in the bathroom, I was just thinking about what an eerily intuitive child you were. From the time you were two until you turned twelve or so, I was convinced you had psychic powers, or were possessed by some ancient spirit. It was uncanny, the things you knew. Then you became this oddly mimsy little creature, constantly second-guessing yourself."

"So what am I supposed to do here, consult my navel? So far, it's been completely silent."

My mother was silent for a moment, resting her chin on her hands as she considered me. "The first thing you need to do is get in touch with your third eye."

"Can I use my finger?"

"I can see that's not the answer you wanted."

"If I wanted to consult a shaman, I have one at home, remember?" At least Red had the tribal background to make it sound authentic.

"You know, at your age, I'd gotten over the need for an authority figure to tell me what to do."

"Which explains why I used to have to wake you to get me ready for school." I motioned to the waitress for the check, and she bounced over immediately, silver eye-brow and nose gems twinkling. I half wondered if she'd been listening in. But then she turned to my mother with shining eyes, and I relaxed. Another fan of my mother's clever, campy oeuvre. "Excuse me," she said, "but aren't you Piper LeFevre? I loved your movies. When I was younger, I wanted to be just like you."

"You are so kind, but I'm with my daughter right now," my mother said, a little grandly. "She gets so jealous when I divide my attention during our times to-gether."

The waitress shot me a dirty look. I was ready to go back home.

TEN

◐ ○ ○ I may have had as much maternal contact as I could stomach in one dose, but my mother had not finished with me. By the time I had finished examining Snowboy's tooth, shaved a matted Persian, and de-wormed Pimpernel, the perpetually ailing Chihuahua, it was late in the afternoon, and the light was fading.

"You can always spend the night," my mother offered. She knew I hated driving in the dark and was probably hoping I could pull Snowboy's impacted tooth in the morning. But I didn't have a general anesthetic in my handbag, and the thought of spending a night and a morning trapped at my mother's held its own gnaw-off-your-own-paw terror.

"You know me. When I'm stressed, I can't sleep."

"So spend the night and don't sleep here. You can watch my old movies."

All through adolescence, images of my mother in various guises kept me company while my physical mother slept. "Thanks, Mom, but I really need to get back."

"As you like. Wait a second, let me give you something before you go."

I hoped it wouldn't be anything like my birthday gift, which had been a tooth-whitening kit, tweezers, a pot of facial wax, and a magnifying mirror—the deluxe criticism basket. I glanced at my watch. "Mom? Can't this wait? I really want to get on the road."

"Stop being so impatient, I'm coming." My mother ambled over as if she had all the time in the world and deposited something cold and metal into my hands. "Here. Put this on."

I held up the heavy silver chain, which supported a massive pale stone, its iridescent blues barely visible beneath the milky surface. As a whole, the piece was hideous—fussy and ostentatious and utterly at odds with the subtle beauty of the stone itself. "Thanks, Mom, but I don't really think it goes with anything in my wardrobe."

"Don't be ridiculous, Abra, you could do with a bit of decoration. And when are you going to get laser surgery? Nobody wears glasses anymore." She slipped the pendant into my hand; it felt like something used to secure prisoners.

"To be honest, I prefer delicate things."

"You prefer to disappear. Never mind about the style, Abra. Your father's mother gave it to me. She called it Las Lagrimas de la Luna, the tears of the moon."

I examined the stone again. To me, it looked more like drops of semen, but I refrained from saying so. "I think you should keep it, Mom."

"No." My mother's hand pressed down on mine. "According to your grandmother, this moonstone can increase a woman's powers of intuition. It can bring you true dreams. And it can help regulate your menstrual cycle."

"You should have given it to me fifteen years ago."

"Abuela said it was too powerful for you then." My mother placed the pendant over my neck. "You know, maybe if you didn't repress your thoughts and feelings so much, your wolf wouldn't keep trying to escape."

I put my hands on my hips, incensed. "You always

find a way to blame everything on my being inhibited. Maybe if you hadn't been so damn uninhibited during my childhood—" I broke off, because this was skirting dangerously close to a memory I did not want to drag out into the light.

My mother made a gesture with her hands that jangled various bracelets. "Abra, you know how terribly sorry I am about what happened that night. And if that's the event that shut you off from your intuitive, creative side, I'm even sorrier."

"I don't want to discuss it." I gave my mother a cursory kiss on the cheek and climbed into my car. When I reached the Taconic, a light snow began to fall, but it didn't seem like a problem until I turned off onto a side road near home.

Here, the snow was falling more heavily, and when I turned my headlights on high beam I was dazzled by what appeared to be a whirling geometric pattern. I switched back to low beam and crawled along the unplowed road, trying to look at the bright side. At least it wasn't rutting season for deer, and I didn't have to worry about slamming into some feckless ungulate racing headlong for sex and disaster. I turned on the radio for comfort, and found myself listening to Faith Hill again. This time, instead of boasting about her husband's stellar technique in the sack, she was singing about how fame hadn't changed her. You know, there ought to be a—

Dart of brown out of the corner of my eye. The antilock brakes shudder under my right foot. A sudden white bang, a smell of powder, a loud thump.

ELEVEN

◐○○ I woke and reflexively started licking myself, then pricked my ears, uncertain. There was a huffing sound, something breathing hard, in distress. I gathered myself in, tensing, the hair on the back of my neck rising in fear and alarm. I had a moment of self-awareness: I am a wolf. And then I realized that was not precisely so. I was somewhere in between wolf and woman, which was uncomfortable and sort of upsetting. I closed my eyes and panted, then felt my face with clumsy hands: No, I felt my muzzle with clumsy paws. I felt dizzy and light-headed, my nose hurt, and I seemed to have some kind of rope burn from the seat belt around my neck and chest. When I tried to release the belt, my paws wouldn't cooperate. *Great.* Wherever clothing constrained me, I was still human, for all the good that was going to do me. *Hands. I needed hands.* A sudden wave of nausea hit, and I swallowed hard, nearly gagging on the taste of goat cheese and spinach omelet. Were there any breath mints in my bag? My mouth tasted like sour peasant feet.

I was thinking like a human again.

The car must have hit something, I realized. There was a huge white bag on my lap and powder in the air: The air bag had deployed. I touched my sore nose again. Now I was using fingers, and it was a different nose, not as complex or sensitive, but it still hurt. I didn't think it was broken, though. Where were my glasses? I bent over to feel for them and was yanked back by the seat belt.

Okay, take this one step at a time. I released myself from the seat belt, rubbing my sore neck. It felt hot, and when I examined my skin in the rearview mirror, I saw the reason: The chain from my mother's necklace had left a red mark on my skin. *Thanks, Mom.* Still puzzling over how this had happened, I was trying to undo the clasp when I heard the outside sound again: labored breathing, an injured animal. I felt around frantically for my glasses and found them, twisted beyond repair.

Tossing my glasses onto the passenger seat, I grabbed the bag containing my stethoscope and other medical supplies, carefully opened the car door, and stepped out into the chill January evening. Through the steady fall of snowflakes, my headlights were illuminating a large, dark shape on the ground, and for a moment I thought I was looking at the bulk of an enormous man. I've killed someone, I thought, horror icing in my veins, but then I realized that this mammoth shape could not belong to a person. Just then the creature rocked, trying to right itself—whatever it was, I hadn't killed it. Yet.

Backing up, I watched the great body rippling with effort as it tried to roll itself over. I squinted, trying to focus my myopic vision. The beast looked over its shoulder at me with small, dark, furious eyes, and suddenly I knew what I was looking at. A golden brown bear, his long ears and narrow muzzle giving him an almost canine aspect; his huge, furry body deceptively clumsy. Larded with fat, this was still an animal that could run faster, swim longer, and climb higher than any human. "Easy, boy," I said, as he tried to roll again, his neck arching as he tried to get his huge paws underneath him.

Maybe I ought to get back in the car, I thought, but I hesitated, not sure how badly the bear was injured.

And then he was standing on all four paws, sniffing at the air. Flakes of snow dusted his head and shoulders, and I wondered why he wasn't hibernating. Jesus, he was big. Standing up on his hind legs, I guessed he'd be over seven feet, and as to how much he weighed, my estimate was the equivalent of two sumo wrestlers after a postmatch sashimi binge. I wondered if I looked like a last bedtime snack before settling in for the winter. The voice of common sense was saying, Get in the car, Abra. You're not a wolf now, you're a half-blind human, and this bear could take you out with one swipe of his paw.

But without my glasses on, the bear looked somehow hazy and unsubstantial, which was probably giving me a false sense of security. I stood there and watched him swipe at his face with one paw, and he was listing to one side, damaged by the impact from the car. As he came back down on all fours, he sprawled, as endearingly clumsy as a bruised puppy. I had done this to him, and the thought of just driving off and leaving him to a slow death went against everything I believed in.

And that was assuming the car and I were even capable of driving off. Damn, I wished I had Red with me. I felt for my vial of butorphinol, trying to recall how much of the sedative I had left. Enough for a couple of German shepherds, maybe, but would that suffice to calm a creature the size of a trailer home? I was about to find out.

"I'm not going to hurt you," I said, fishing inside my bag for my hypodermic. "I just need to look at you." Putting my stethoscope around my neck, I found my mother's necklace in the way. I took hold of the pendant, and then froze as the bear grunted, fixing me with a strange, almost imperious look. Then he rose up on his hind legs and the breath caught in my throat. My rational brain said he was just trying to get a better look at me. Something more primitive said, *this is the king of all bears, and he is going to eat me alive.* Mindlessly clutching the moonstone in my hand, I tried to remember everything I knew about bears. Red had told me something about how playing dead worked for grizzlies but not black bears, because black bears' attacks on humans tended to be predatory. That didn't help me much, because this bear looked like a black bear, even if his fur was a golden brown and he was as big as a grizzly.

The bear made a loud blowing sound like the wind rustling through dry leaves, then made a strange pulsing noise, nothing like the low, wolfish growl I'd heard bears make in the movies. I felt a wave of light-headedness. I remembered watching a nature documentary where a cougar stared at a deer for long moments before attacking. Red had said that his grandfather believed that the predator was asking permission of its prey, and wouldn't pounce until it was granted. Why would the prey acquiesce, I had wondered at the time. Now, I understood. There was an aura of power about the bear, a force so strong it was nearly tangible. I could see the lines of tension between the bear and myself, stretched out like the filaments of a metaphysical net. If I ran that way, he would catch me there. If I ran the other way, he would catch me in that direction. Wherever I looked, I saw myself caught. The bear and I were playing a chess game, and all that was left was for me to concede defeat.

Except defeat meant death, and I wasn't ready to die. My already blurred vision swam with tears, making the bear's outlines bleed. I blinked, and for a moment, he resembled a man, glowering at me out of slitted eyes.

The car crash, I thought. I've sustained a head injury, and this is a delayed reaction. I blinked to clear my eyes, but it didn't quite work the way I'd expected. Now I was definitely looking at a man in a rough black animal pelt coat. He had a stocky, muscular build, shaggy, golden brown hair, and a beard two shades darker. There was something about him that suggested rough whiskey and raw appetites, a score of hidden scars and blood under the fingernails.

Obviously, I'd hurt my head worse than I realized.

I rubbed my eyes, just like someone in a cartoon, but there he remained. I tried to say something, but nothing came out of my mouth.

Then he broke the silence. At first I thought the noise he made was a symptom of some sort—perforated airway, escaping blood. Then he repeated the sound and made another, and I realized that he was framing words. There was a "wh" sound that kept recurring, and a soft "sh" coupled with something guttural. It reminded me of an American Indian language I'd heard once in a linguistics class.

"I'm sorry, I don't understand," I said. "But I'm a veterinarian. I can help treat your injury." I swallowed hard, and moved in closer.

"Help me? You hurt me, woman." His voice was low, gruff, and had a French Canadian accent. Which fit perfectly. Straight from central casting, the lumberjack from hell.

"I d-didn't mean to," I stammered. "I didn't see you. I have medical supplies in my bag." I squinted, trying to make out the man's expression. I thought he was staring at me as though he were mulling my words over, syllable by syllable.

Then he snorted. "You want to help me, cherie? Then come, by all means, come, treat my injury." His Quebecois accent was thicker now. He smiled, revealing strong, white, even teeth, and spread his hands. I thought about the football player who had walked me home from a college party, then lunged at me in what he had claimed was play.

"I'm just going to examine you, all right?" Reaching into my bag, I closed my hand over the hypodermic filled with butorphinol as I came closer. From two feet away, the man gave off a powerful, musky animal odor, and his skin glittered. His nostrils flared as if he were scenting me, as well. Then something in his eyes changed. I knew that look. It was the look I got from my animal patients right before they attacked.

I whipped my hand out, trying to inject him with the hypodermic as he grabbed for my wrist. He was faster.

"Ah, what is this?" He shook my wrist and I yelped. "Is this what you call 'elp?"

"It's just a sedative, to help calm you before I look at the injury," I said, my teeth chattering. If only I'd had Telazol, I could have knocked him out completely. From now on, if there was a now on, I was going to carry Telazol. And a stun gun. And some tear gas. "Please, let me go."

"But you charged me," the man said. "You challenged me." Casually, as if part of an experiment, he ground the fragile bones of my wrist together under his fingers.

"I didn't mean to charge you! It was my car, I couldn't stop in time."

The man put his face close to mine. This close, I could see that his eyes were a blue so dark they seemed almost black, and that he had no visible pores. Instead, there was something glittering beneath his skin, as though there were flecks of gold dust embedded in his flesh. His breath stank of raw meat and berries. "Woman, if my claws tear your stomach open, am I responsible?" I stared at his hand, and now I could see the long, black claws at the ends of his blunt fingers. "If your car hits me, who is to blame?" I knew there was a counter-argument, but I could not seem to string the words together to defend myself. I felt a wave of fatigue, as I often did when I wasn't wearing my glasses. It was harder to clear my head when my vision made everything look soft and fuzzy. My captor paused, and whatever he saw in my eyes, it must have looked like concession. He opened his mouth, revealing massive canines.

"No!" I squeezed my eyes shut, trying to transform. I'd only attempted this once before, and I knew that it was like giving yourself over to something, like coordinating two different melodic lines, like singing one pattern while strumming another. But there had been a full moon that night, and a lot of pheromones zinging through the air, and tonight there was just me, alone with Ursa Major. For a moment, I thought I felt something, but then I realized that I was flat on my back, not a wolf, but a great whimpering girl. Great. The bear-man stared down at me.

"What are you?" I remained prostrate as he approached. My jeans and parka were not enough to protect me from the cold blanket of snow on the ground, but I forced myself not to move.

"What am I?" The man scratched his bearded chin as if the question intrigued him. "Maybe I am a ghost, eh? For a long time, I thought I was a ghost. But then, I was in a ghost-place. I forgot how it feels, to have skin and bones." He rubbed his hands up and down the rough fur of his greatcoat, then grinned, a flash of white in his bearded face. "Maybe I even forgive you for hitting me."

"I really didn't mean to," I said, adding, "I'm Abra. Do you have a name?" My friend Lilliana had once told me that a great way to diffuse hostility was to use people's names to establish rapport. Red had taught me that all names retained some of their owner's power, even false names and pseudonyms.

My companion smiled, as if he had caught me in a clumsy attempt at a trick. "You can call me Bruin, if you like. The pale humans called me that, back when they still told their stories about me."

Bruin—the name for bear in old French and English folktales. I dimly recalled a tale in which Snow White had a sister, Rose Red, who wound up marrying a bear who was really a prince. Well, that was encouraging; maybe he wasn't going to eat me, after all.

Bruin was still touching his hands as if he couldn't quite believe that he had them. He threw back his head and laughed, a deep, husky sound from deep in his chest. "*Sacre bleu,* it feels good to be— How do you say it? Incarnate?"

"You're manitou." I said it softly, suddenly recalling Red's wound. It occurred to me that I probably had heard some bastardized version of the Rose Red fairy tale, edited for children. The original story probably had a lot more blood in it.

Bruin looked pleased at the mention of the Algonquian word. "So we are not forgotten? There are so few of us left. I thought, perhaps, that your kind had stopped believing." He hunkered down beside me, and his coat gaped open; beneath it, he was all naked, hairy, muscular man. "Maybe you would like to worship me, little human?"

"I'm really not the worshipping type."

"I could change your mind."

In the blink of an eye, Bruin melted into bear form again, and the powerful ursine odor of his fur sent chills down my spine. The innate human desire to curl into a fetal ball was warring with the lupine urge to assume a submissive posture. Lupine had bought me bargaining time, so I was going with that. The bear put his long nose down to my neck and sniffed.

"Ah, not human, after all. Wolf woman," Bruin said. Or maybe he thought it; I didn't see his mouth move, and his muzzle wasn't shaped for human speech. "I have not met your kind in a long, long time." He sniffed me again, and I had a chilling recollection of a news story about a tame bear that had started licking its trainer's face and then, without warning, had torn out his throat. "But you are more woman than wolf, I think." I couldn't help it. I giggled. It was partly a result of fear and anxiety, and partly because this ancient spirit beast delivered his lines like a bad B-movie actor. And while I wasn't familiar with bears, I knew all about bad B-movie actors. "A very attractive wolf woman," he added, a giant, glossy brown bear with a Quebecois accent so thick you could have served it on toast. Unable to contain myself, I giggled.

"You laugh at me?"

I shook my head, but the whole thing was absurd, a bear glowering down at me and speaking like Klondike Sam. I laughed harder. My whole life, I have had an inappropriate impulse to laugh under duress. Hunter used to hate it. At the age of sixteen, I nearly got knifed by a mugger for chuckling nervously when he demanded my pocketbook. But of all the times in my life when it would be a really, really bad idea to laugh, this one topped the list.

The bear reared back, and for a moment I thought he was going to bite me. But instead, he became a man again, his nostrils flaring, and he pressed his enormous bulk down on me, crushing me into the earth. I could barely breathe, and my labored attempts brought his gaze to my chest. His heavy, irregular features took on a sensual cast. "I could make you stop laughing. I could make you worship me."

His mouth came down on mine, and he inhaled my breath. Dear God, he was going to rape me. The thought seemed to suck the strength out of my muscles, and with a jolt of panicked strength, I began to fight him, trying to wrestle my arms out from under him. He threw back his head and laughed, and I realized I was dizzy, as if I had just lost a great deal of blood. I looked into his dark eyes, which gleamed like obsidian, and I felt so small and insignificant that it seemed ridiculous that a being as powerful as this would waste his time on a creature like myself.

"Not laughing now, eh?" Bruin looked down at me as if I were his own personal picnic basket, and he was just deciding what to consume first.

He began to lower his head, and I held my breath, thinking, How can I possibly satisfy him? Not with something so trivial as sex. And then I knew. I could offer up my life for his pleasure. And it would be my pleasure, too, a pleasure so great that the sacrifice would be its own reward.

A second before his mouth touched mine, I realized: That wasn't my thought. And I remembered what Red had said the manitous would feed on. Sacrifice.

I gathered whatever saliva was left in my mouth and lobbed it at him.

Bruin twisted away with a hiss, as if my saliva had the power to repulse him physically. I spat again, and he gave a low bellow and fell back, which seemed like a victory until he fell on my leg, crushing it. I screamed and for a moment, I saw him standing there, blinking stupidly. For a frozen moment, I did something I hadn't done since early childhood. I deliberately let my eyes go out of focus, making the bear dissolve into the shadows around him. *If I refuse to see you, you're not there anymore.*

And then I heard an odd sound, like a high-frequency hum, and I focused again. Bruin appeared surprised by something. He looked down at his hands, and they began to blow away, as if an invisible wind were scattering him like dust. The hum grew subtly louder, and Bruin looked up at me, narrowing his eyes, as his arms and legs disintegrated, and then he was gone in a dark swirl, leaving me alone.

Or maybe I had been alone the whole time, hallucinating, in shock from the car accident.

Except I knew that I wasn't dreaming. You're a werewolf, my mother had said. Don't you believe in the supernatural? I did now. And I certainly believed in manitou.

I crawled toward my handbag, which was lying a few feet away, trying not to imagine the damage underneath my pants leg. My right foot felt loose and liquid and unutterably fragile. There was a moment of panic when I couldn't find my cell phone, and then my fingers closed around the smooth metal shape, and I murmured to myself, see, it's going to be fine, help is coming. I flipped the phone open, leaking tears of self-pity.

There was no signal. Fuck. I imagined the news report: and as she lay dying in a ditch, cars whizzed past her, never hearing her cries for help. *Stay calm. Find the car.* That would make a better story; the intrepid young woman, her foot badly broken, still managed to drive herself to safety. Assuming I could find the gas pedal with the airbag lying all over the place.

I looked around me, trying to get my bearings. It was hard to tell without my glasses, but it seemed to me that the trees were taller, thicker, older than I remembered. I dragged myself back toward my car, then stopped. My trusty Subaru wasn't there. And neither was the road. In its place, there was a small hill, no more than ten feet tall and some thirty feet around.

Okay, I was disoriented. I'd gone the wrong way. But if I climbed the hill, I'd be able to get my bearings. Assuming I could see that far without my glasses. *Don't analyze. Act.*

Fighting back waves of pain and fatigue, and trying not to picture what I was doing to the fractured bone, I pulled myself up the incline. I noticed the unnatural smoothness and symmetry of the earth under my hands, and thought: This isn't a natural hill, it's a burial mound, the kind some Native American tribes used to inter their dead.

Sweating profusely, my leg throbbing horribly, I reached the top. It took me a moment to catch my breath enough to sit upright, and when I did, I began to whimper. The road could not have been more than a few feet away, but it was nowhere to be seen. Instead, I seemed to be in the middle of a vast, primeval forest, filled with enormous oaks and chestnuts and elms, their bare branches interlocked like skeletal arms. As I watched, the trees budded, blossomed, and leafed up, a sudden and unnatural spring that filled the air with a fierce, almost overpowering sweetness. I recognized chestnut trees, but as far as I knew, no giant chestnuts had been seen in this country since the nineteen fifties.

Towering above them all was a cathedral of a tree, a giant chestnut almost a hundred feet high and some ten feet around. Its delicate, oblong, pale green leaves interspersed with creamy white blossoms, the tree looked like something out of a fairy tale.

And maybe it was a fairy tale, because as I had learned in school, these trees didn't exist anymore. And neither did the vast elms I could see. They almost all died out earlier in the century, the chestnuts from a blight brought in from Asia, the elms from Dutch elm disease. Once upon a time, animals had relied on chestnuts as a major food source, and Native Americans and colonists had kept from starving by peeling and eating the sweet nut. Their wood had been used to build this nation, and nowadays most people didn't even realize that they were gone.

I knew that the roots of the chestnut survived the blight, and from time to time, a small tree would emerge from the forest floor. But without another tree to cross pollinate with them, these young specimens were weak and unable to flower. Which meant the majestic trees I was looking at couldn't possibly be real.

And then I thought: Even if they are there, how can I see them? Without my glasses, I should only be able to make out what's right in front of my face.

More frightened now than I had been with the bear, I checked my cell phone, but it told me what I already knew: I was out of signal range. A memory intruded: me, twelve years old, stumbling into my mother's room. Mom, something's wrong with the floor. And my mother, laughing at first, then alarmed: You didn't eat those candy dots, did you?

Somehow I'd left reality behind again, and I was lost in a place where there were no rules and no logic and nothing to count on to keep me safe. And all around me, the snow fell in a steady rhythm that should have alarmed me more than anything else.

Instead, despite everything, it put me to sleep.

TWELVE

◑○○ "It's all right, she's coming around now."

I blinked, and for a minute I thought I was looking through the moonstone: everything was pale and hazy, with a faint blue shimmer around it. Then someone adjusted a hanging overhead light and I could see clearly. Red and Malachy were looking down at me. I was lying on an operating table. We were in one of the examining rooms, the one we used for the big dogs, mastiffs and wolfhounds.

"What happened?" I tried to sit up, and Red put his hand on my shoulder. "Easy, now. Don't try to move just yet."

"What's going on?" My right leg was throbbing steadily, the pain seeming to wake up along with the rest of me.

Red put his hand on my head. "You had some sort of accident on the way back from your mother's."

Oh, God, the forest. The bear. "How did you find me?"

Red smiled, but it didn't reach his eyes. "I tracked you down, of course."

Forget foreign films and in-depth literary analysis. Sometimes dating a man with backwoods skills was truly rewarding. "Did I pass out or something? The last thing I remember was climbing to the top of a mound and howling at the top of my lungs."

Red exchanged a look with Malachy, who was wearing his white coat and looking even thinner than usual. "You've been unconscious for a while, Doc. We haven't been able to wake you up, so Mal just shot you up with a little stimulant." Red put his hand on my forehead, smoothing my hair away from my face. "I'm so sorry it took me so long to find you. I didn't even know you were missing at first. Kind of thought you might be taking some time with your mom, and I didn't want to crowd you."

I tried to push my glasses up on my nose, then realized they were gone. "What are you talking about? How long did it take you to find me?"

Red looked over at Malachy again. "You've been missing a week, Doc."

"What?" I stared at his blurry face in shock.

"I didn't really worry till the end of the second day, and then Mal called to ask where you were."

"I've been in the woods for a week?"

Red reached for my hand. I had forgotten how calming his touch could be. "If you'd just been lost in the woods, I would have followed your scent as soon as we located your car. But there's old magic in the forest, and nothing messes with trail sign like old magic. You'd gone and wandered into the Liminal, so it was like all trace of your scent just stopped cold about six feet from your car. Even with the animals helping, all I could do for a long time was narrow down the search area." He nodded to something in the corner, and I saw that our red-tailed hawk was there, perched on top of a cat carrier, which the young raccoon was trying to unlock with his nimble little fingers.

My leg was really hurting now, but I knew that I was missing something important here. "The Liminal?"

"Strictly speaking, it refers to the threshold of consciousness," said Malachy, strapping a blood pressure cuff around my arm. "But Red uses it to refer to the boundary between realities." Malachy paused as the cuff tightened around my biceps, then released.

"Hang on a moment. How the hell did I wind up in a different reality? The last time I drove to Westchester, there was no sign that said last exit from this dimension." The rising note of hysteria in my voice kind of ruined the joke, but I couldn't help it. I'd had a longstanding fear of accidentally ingesting LSD, but at least with acid, the crazy things you saw and heard weren't real.

Red took my hand. "It's like I told you before, Doc. The boundary's breaking down. All those houses going up on Old Scolder Mountain that was sacred ground for generations. We've cut clean into their territory, and now they're moving in on ours."

I took a deep breath, trying to calm myself. It made no sense, panicking now, but panic was what I was feeling. "How did you guys even find me?"

Malachy stuck a thermometer in my ear. "I had nothing to do with it. Red went and sat cross-legged for an hour, then cut his arm and walked around, leaking blood until he found you. It took him about twenty minutes and a pint."

I recalled the burial mound, the thick, old growth forest that had seemed to go on forever. Then I noticed the bandage peeking out from the rolled-up sleeve of Red's work shirt. "What did you do?"

"Oh, this ain't nothing. Just a trick to get back."

The thermometer pinged and Malachy removed it. "He made a deal. That's how it works, I believe."

"Made a deal? With whom?"

Red flushed. I knew he hated how his redhead's complexion revealed everything. "Mal, you don't know what you're talking about."

"It's not my area of expertise, true. But because so much of my research hinges on the areas where myth and medicine intersect, I have done a fair amount of reading about various mythologies." Mal began to un-button my shirt, and I swatted at his hands. "You do it, then. I need to check your heart." Malachy's breath was cool and tinged with something faintly metallic as he leaned over me to press the stethoscope to my chest. His fingers were like ice on my skin. Either this was what he was like when he was up past his bedtime, or whatever was wrong with him was getting worse. He traced a line on my neck, and I shivered. "How long have you had this?"

At first I thought he meant the burn, but then I saw that he was lifting the moonstone pendant.

"My mother gave it to me. Why?"

Mal unfastened the chain and slipped it out from under my neck. "Because your skin is reacting adversely to the silver. Did you not realize you were allergic?"

I shook my head.

"Red should have told you."

I looked at Red, questioningly.

"Hell, Doc, I didn't know."

Malachy looked irritated. "Well, you should have done. Never mind," he said, cutting Red off. "How are you feeling, Abra? Any pain?"

"Not in my neck. What really hurts is my right leg. My shin."

"Scale of one to ten?"

"Eight or a nine. I was mauled by a bear." I glanced up at Red. "Except he wasn't a bear."

Red took my hand. "I saw his tracks." He smiled a lit-tle crookedly. "Both sets."

"I didn't believe you before. Not completely." I felt

tears sting my eyes. Right now, I didn't want to be on the outs with Red. I wanted him by my side, solid and steady.

Red squeezed my fingers. "Lot of new info to take in, Doc." His hazel eyes were level and knowing and just a little sad. I was just processing the implications of that look when Malachy took hold of my right ankle, and I stifled a scream.

"I need to cut away your jeans leg."

"Okay." I felt rather than saw Red move around to the head of the table, giving Malachy more room. I sucked in my breath as my calf was revealed. A piece of bone—tibia, probably—was protruding from a small hole. Open compound. "We're going to need an X-ray." Mal looked at me. "Ideally, a CAT scan would be in order, but we'll have to make do. I need to know if there's any possibility that you're pregnant before we proceed with the X-ray."

"I'm not pregnant," I said, a little bitterly. Red gave me a funny look, but I just ignored him as Mal cut through the waistband of my jeans, and parted the fabric, revealing my faded blue cotton underwear and winter white stomach. He inserted the scissors at the hem of my sweater, at which point I called a halt.

"Hey, what about a modesty drape?"

"Oh, good lord." Malachy sighed. "Red, see if you can reach up for one of those surgical drapes in that closet. No, that one, to the right. Thanks." As Mal draped the surgical cloth over me, he added, "Haven't you become casual about nudity, yet? I find most therians develop a more animal sense of their bodies."

"Well, I'm still more woman than canine, so give me a break. And I'd like some goddamn painkiller. When are you going to give me a shot of morphine?"

Malachy stared at me, then rubbed his temples. "I really do not have the time for this. What is the most common side effect of preoperative morphine on canines?"

"Vomiting," I said, beginning to understand. Mal's crack about therians being nudists hadn't just been another attempt to tease me. "What else do you know about my condition?" Because clearly, my boss knew a great deal more than I did.

"Oh, for crying out loud. Don't you know anything about your own condition?" Malachy turned to Red. "Haven't you taken the time to explain her disorder?"

Red flushed. "I'm the guy you call when you need to get rid of a pest, remember? I don't know what the hell is wrong with giving morphine. And since I'm not into the Guido look, I wasn't aware that there was anything wrong with wearing silver. I just thought it wasn't too healthy to have the stuff shot into your gut."

Malachy slid a photographic plate underneath my calf, which made me yelp. "Right. So, let's begin with the basics. You are aware that theremorphism is caused by a rare virus, the most common strain of which is lycanthropy. Most commonly, transmission occurs through the exchange of bodily fluids—blood and semen."

"Hang on a moment, Mal," said Red. "I think you're overgeneralizing, here."

"I'm trying to give an overview. But, yes, there is a genetic component, which determines who is affected and how much. In certain families, such as your own, Red, a specific strain can dominate, appearing in different individuals from early childhood on." Malachy lifted the X-ray camera and positioned it over my leg. "In early-onset lycanthropy, the children stabilize fairly rapidly and retain a fair amount of cognitive awareness in either form." Mal gave me a level look. "In cases such as yours, however, there tends to be a fair amount of disassociation between states."

I took a deep breath, pressing my palm to my chest.

"Meaning that I'm never going to be in control of my wolf?"

"Bullshit," said Red sharply, making me jump. "It's just practice, is what it is," he added in a more measured tone. "Give it a few more years, Doc, and you'll be planning your evening menu while you're out stalking rabbit."

"That is completely unsubstantiated conjecture," said Malachy, moving around the table. "What is established is that for anyone infected as an adult, the disease is progressive and, in the female, marked by neurological changes and greater divergence of lupine and human persona concordant with the onset of estrus." Malachy paused. "In the male, changes in brain chemistry are somewhat dependent on placement in a pack hierarchy. Sensitivity to silver is a common side effect in either gender, and there is a clear correlation between viral activity and the lunar cycle. I am intrigued by the effect that this town seems to have—I've been calling it the Northside factor in my notes." Malachy's voice trailed off and he bent his head, rubbing his temples as though a headache had come on suddenly.

"Are you all right?"

He made a grunting sound, then raked his hand through his tangled black curls, looking as though he would like to tear his hair out. "I'm fine." Malachy straightened up and filled a syringe with a blue liquid. "Unfortunately, the wider medical community has never had much time for my theories, or my research." He uncapped the needle. "Which is why I have been forced to conduct so many of my experiments in less than optimal conditions."

"Hang on a moment," I said, more than a little unsettled by these revelations. "What's in that hypodermic?"

"Don't worry, it's not for you." Without batting an eyelash, Malachy rolled up his sleeve and injected himself in the arm. After a moment, he sighed, then removed the sharps and disposed of them in the medical waste container. "Red, you need to release Abra's leg and stand behind this door whilst I take the X-rays."

"Actually," Red said, not looking at me, "you might want to hold off on that."

"Is there a reason why—ah." Malachy came back into the room and lifted the camera up and out of the way. "We'll have to work with a manual assessment, then."

I started to ask what Red meant, and then comprehension dawned. Any chance you might be pregnant, Malachy had asked. The standard query for any woman of childbearing age about to receive radiation. And there was that night that I didn't remember, when I'd woken up to find Red fairly glowing with happiness and excitement.

"No," I said firmly, not looking at Red, even though he was still holding my leg straight. "There's absolutely no reason why I can't have an X-ray."

"Yes, there is," said Red, which sent me over the edge.

"Funny, but it seems like neither of you know quite as much about my condition as Magda does. Or did you two just not care to mention that nonalpha females aren't fertile?"

The two men exchanged glances. For once, Malachy didn't launch into a scientific analysis, and Red didn't try to reassure me. Instead, everyone focused on small tasks, like getting the photographic plate under my leg and setting the switches.

The X-ray showed a compound fracture in the tibia, which was already fusing back together. Too bad lycanthropy didn't speed up the healing of emotional wounds.

THIRTEEN

◑○○ "Here you go, Doc, door to bed service." Red, who had insisted on carrying me into the cabin like a bride, deposited me gently on the couch. I scowled up at him as he handed me a flashlight.

"It's freezing in here." After Malachy had cut off my jeans, he'd offered to lend me something of his, but nothing had fit. So he and Red had wrapped me in horse blankets, which were itchy and did little to keep me warm.

"I'll take care of that in a sec." He went into the bedroom and brought back our quilt, which he draped over me. Then he headed back to the truck for the hawk and raccoon. Red had used the animals to help find me, flying the hawk during the daytime, and setting the raccoon out to help him explore the woods at night. I knew I should be grateful, but I was cold and unsettled, and when the door opened, letting in another blast of cold air, I had to bite back another complaint.

I hobbled into the bedroom, dragging the quilt behind me, and searched blindly in the drawer of the bedside table for my spare glasses. After a panicky moment, I found them, slightly scratched from the nail scissors I'd thrown in with them. Putting them on, I peered at myself in the mirror. My hair looked like it had been styled by harpies, and my rimless spare specs—all the rage when I'd bought them—did nothing to hide the dark shadows under my eyes. At least I could see again, even if I didn't like what I was seeing.

I limped back to the couch and huddled under the quilt, watching as Red settled the animals in their cages, speaking softly to them before taking his flashlight and heading over to the woodpile by the fireplace. As he hefted a great armful of lumber, I was reminded how deceptively strong his wiry body was, how competent he was in a nineteenth-century cabin.

Except my teeth were chattering, and I hadn't really ever planned on living in a nineteenth-century cabin.

"You doing okay there?" Red lit the oil lamps. Misinterpreting my pinched expression, Red said, "I could get you something for the pain."

"I'm not in the mood for drugs." I didn't have to add the reason why, because I'd had enough of altered consciousness. Red paused in the act of setting a match to a piece of kindling wood.

"I was thinking of a different kind of something." Lighting the kindling, Red arranged it under the larger logs in the fireplace. He listened until he was sure the fire had caught, then replaced the grate. "Let me see your leg." He was still facing away from me, gazing at the fire as if trying to remember something.

I pulled the quilt back from my leg, which was swollen underneath the Ace bandages. A human would have needed a cast. I kind of wished I'd had a cast. My leg looked awfully vulnerable like this.

Red approached me. "How bad does it hurt?"

"It's throbbing."

Red unwrapped the bandage, then stood up and brought back a mason jar filled with a pale yellow substance.

"What's that?"

"Special ointment. Granddad's own recipe." Red carefully lifted my injured leg, then sat down with my heel resting on his thighs. Scooping the ointment up in his fingers, he began rubbing it into my foot and ankle with long, slow, circular motions. The lotion smelled like lavender and mint, and my skin began to tingle pleasantly wherever Red was massaging it. He was murmuring something low, under his breath, and I realized it wasn't English. I leaned my head back, lulled by the touch and the chant, and as the pain in my calf eased, Red's fingers began to move upward, toward my thigh. A gentle warmth had begun to build, and I found myself wishing that Red would work on the other leg, as well. "Wow. That's good. Why didn't you use that on my burn last year?"

"I didn't have any left at the time."

I tried to keep my eyes open as Red took another dollop of grease and massaged it in. "So how come you didn't use it on yourself when the manitou got you?"

"It doesn't work the same way when you apply it yourself."

I stirred, curious. "And what's it made of?"

"Rendered bear fat."

I sat up straight. "Oh, yuck, please tell me you're joking."

"And some herbs and other powders."

"I think that's enough," I said, pushing his hands away and covering myself with the quilt. "I've had enough of bears touching me tonight."

Red didn't move for a moment, and I tried to ignore the residual warm tingling in my lower extremity. I had a feeling that this particular ointment might have some properties other than simple healing. "Is this some kind of aphrodisiac?"

Red gave a startled choke of a laugh. "No," he said, his eyes crinkling in amusement. "But it's nice to know

I've still got the touch." Underneath my heel, which was still on Red's lap, I could feel that he wasn't unaffected.

"I thought you could smell my response."

Red's eyes half closed for a moment, and I wondered what he was thinking, or what he was concealing. "You know I can."

"So I can't hide that from you."

Red studied me carefully. "Abra," he said. His voice was full of hope and desire. The urge to yield to him was almost overpowering. In one of her films, I can't remember which one, my mother said all women's virtue lay in resisting that first intimacy. Once the boundary of intimate touch had been breached, women were driven to yield themselves again and again.

I was on the verge of turning my head that small, critical distance, joining my mouth to Red's, but then his hand tightened on my injured leg, and the unexpected small jolt of pain brought me back to myself.

"But you have been hiding things from me, Red. Like the fact that I was going into heat."

Red drew in a sharp breath that turned into a long sigh. "I was going to tell you. I was just waiting to be sure. Even now, you're not in full heat."

"Jesus! I can't believe you're still lying to me. You were trying to get me pregnant. Just admit it." The last time we had discussed birth control, Red had insisted that we didn't need to worry about it when we were in canid form, since wolves only conceived when the female was in estrus. I couldn't take the pill—it gave me migraines. So Red and I used condoms or a diaphragm when we had opposable thumbs, and nothing when we went around on all fours. "You were trying to trick me into starting a family."

Red flinched a little at the word "trick" and I withdrew my leg as he stood up, walked over to one of the antique oil lamps, and lit the wick. When he replaced the top of the lamp, the tinted glass gave his face a warm cast, as if he were blushing. "Truth is, Abra, I never really expected . . ."

"You didn't expect that I'd go into heat at all? Or you didn't expect it so soon?"

"Most lycanthropes don't reproduce," Red said quietly. "I'd heard about it, sure, but it's pretty damn rare. Last year, when you thought you were pregnant by Hunter? That would only have been possible if you'd conceived before the virus took effect." Red hesitated. "Fact is, most women who've had the virus can't conceive a child in either form."

"And you didn't think I needed to know that? You didn't think I deserved to know that I might never be able to have a child at all!"

"Now, hang on a moment. Are you mad because I didn't tell you that you could get pregnant, or mad because I didn't tell you that you might not be able to get pregnant?"

"I'm mad at both, you idiot!" I started to cry, and Red drew me into his arms. Irrationally, I found myself punching at him, clumsy, ineffectual jabs at his hard stomach and arms that he absorbed for a moment before grabbing hold of my wrists. "Let go of me," I protested, as he drew me into his arms. I tried to hit him again, but he had pinned my arms and now my face was pushed into the warm flannel of his shirt and I was enveloped by the clean male scent of him, spiced with the fragrances of woods and winter.

"Easy, now, easy. I got you." It was the voice he used to gentle animals, but I didn't want to be gentled. I bit his chest, just hard enough to bring his hand up to my hair. "Ouch." He gave my hair a soft tug, but I wouldn't let go. I was fed up with partial truths and evasions, and I wanted to tear into Red's calm equanimity and rip it to shreds. As I clamped my jaw harder, Red's hand tightened on my hair, pulling harder. "Come on, baby, I don't want to hurt you."

"Maybe because you can't," I said, pulling away. I wasn't sure where this was coming from, but I couldn't seem to control myself. "We shift, and I'm bigger than you. Stronger."

Red raised his eyebrows. "That sounds like a challenge."

"Oh, so now you're going to turn it into a jo—" There was a blur of motion, and before I could finish the sentence, I was flat on my back, and Red was on top of me, pinning me to the bed.

"Looks like I won." Red looked down at me with a half smile.

"I said when we shifted!"

"You want to shift?"

"I can't just shift, as you very well know."

Red's eyes crinkled. "I suppose that's one advantage I've got over you."

I bucked under him, and suddenly we were kissing, harsh, hungry, rough kisses, and I tried to pull my arms free but Red caught my wrists, which made me thrash more fiercely against his grip. I needed to feel his strength; I wanted him to overpower me. His breathing grew harsher, I could feel him hard against my thigh, and I was about to throw the wrestling match when Red inadvertently shifted his weight onto my bad leg. I gasped, and Red scooted back as though he'd been scalded.

"Aw, shit, honey." Red was gently checking my leg, I was crying again, and this time even I knew I was riding a hormonal roller coaster, complete with twists, inversions, and sudden reversals. "C'mere," Red said, lying down and carefully spooning himself around me. "Care to tell me what's really going on in here?" He nuzzled my head with his chin.

"Magda says there's no way I can bring a baby to term." My voice was barely audible, but I knew he could hear me. "Even if I do get pregnant, she said I'd just wind up losing it."

Red had propped himself up on one elbow, and I glanced back over my shoulder so I could read his expression. "Well, that's just her opinion. I happen to hold a different position on the subject."

"So she's wrong? You're saying she just told me I was infertile to upset me?" I felt as if a more established doctor had just given me a second opinion: That's not cancer, it's a rash.

Red looked pensive as he formulated his response, and I felt such a burst of depression that I could barely force myself to listen. "It's not so much that she's wrong about the facts as wrong about the particulars. I mean, sure, in an extended family you're only going to have one breeding female, but even if she's sharing close territory, Magda's not exactly part of our pack. In the end, it all boils down to what you feel, deep inside."

I sat up, which made my leg throb. "So what exactly are you proposing? We just go ahead and try and if it's a false pregnancy, well, no harm, no foul, and if I do get pregnant and then just—whatever it is dogs do—reabsorb, then what?" My voice rose into the register of anger and fear. In the back of my mind, I was aware that I wasn't being completely fair, and that I was taking something out on Red. Give me an hour or two, and I'd be apologizing for my outburst. But not yet.

Red sat up and cupped my cheek in his work-roughened palm. His warm hazel eyes were kind and a little sad as he used his thumb to brush away my tears. "Everybody who tries to have a baby is taking some kind of gamble, Doc. You don't know how long it's going to take, or what might go wrong. You just go on faith and hope. And love," he added, his thumb stroking my cheek again.

I slapped his hand away. "Oh, no you don't. This isn't some typical situation here, and don't you go and try to whitewash it."

Red looked as though he were going to say something, and then must have thought better of it. "Tell you what. I can see you're awful upset right now. How about we take a break and I give you a nice cup of hot tea with honey?" He walked over to the gas range and filled the kettle with water.

"I don't want tea. I want us to face the fact that you clearly want to have a family. And the way it sounds to me, that's not going to happen."

Red looked at the kettle as if he'd forgotten what it was used for, and then put it down to face me. "I love you, Abra. I wouldn't trade being with you for anything. You . . . , you're my family. You're my pack."

"But you want me to have your baby."

Red looked straight at me then, his hazel eyes darker than I had ever seen them. Then he nodded slowly. "Yes," he said. "More than I ever wanted anything."

There was silence, as we both waited to hear what I said next. The flames in the fireplace crackled and an ember popped. "Does it all hinge on me, then? On how alpha I am?"

Red held my gaze. "No." And then, very simply, he added, "If the male is powerful enough, that can tip the balance."

And I thought back to the night that I couldn't remember, when Red had been so ebullient, and I had not understood why. I knew now what bothered me about it. It wasn't just that Red hadn't asked permission in words—mind if we risk knocking you up, sweetheart? It was that he'd felt that he had to trick me into getting pregnant.

I just blurted it out. "And are you powerful enough?"

Red hesitated. "I am if you believe I am." He said it bluntly, without embellishment, standing there like the very image of the salt-of-the-earth workingman.

I knew what I was supposed to say here: Of course I believe in you, you're my man. But the truth was, some part of me wasn't convinced that Red was strong enough to compensate for what I lacked. What he did have was intelligence and craftiness and patience. God knows, the man had patience. But we were talking about the kind of strength that leaders require, and Red wasn't really a leader.

For a moment, I thought Red was going to argue his case—here's why you should vote for me as alpha! Instead, he bobbed his head, as if acknowledging some correction. "Of course, that's not exactly the kind of thing you decide all at once." His face had gone unreadable, and his voice oddly formal. "Would you like me to put on some tea? Or do you want me to help you get into your nightgown?"

I gave Red a look that put an end to any thought he might have of seeing me naked again in the foreseeable future.

"Or else I could brush out your hair. It looks like it got kind of snarled there in the back."

Now, that was clever. That was one of my favorite rituals with Red; every night, he liked to sit and brush my hair. He did it with such patience and gentleness that I couldn't help but wish he'd been around to brush my hair when I was a kid, instead of my mother, who used to tear through my hair like it was the enemy. She's better at grooming animals, of course.

Taking my silence as acquiescence, Red said, "Here. Scootch on over so I can get behind you." He sat behind me, running the brush through my hair, holding on to the snarled pieces so he could work on them without tugging on my scalp. I leaned my head back and let him work, listening to the small, hungry sounds of the fire, half hypnotized by the feel of Red's hands on my hair. When the last knot had been untangled and the brush ran smoothly from scalp to ends, I felt Red's breath near my ear, his hands drawing me close. "God, I love touching your hair." Through the quilt and his jeans, I could feel just how much he loved it. I pulled back, even though it would have been so much easier to fall back into his touch.

"Thank you, Red." If he took me now, I knew that I would really be choosing him as my mate, and finding out whether or not we could have a family together. And I wasn't sure I wanted my body making up my mind for me. But more than that, I was a little afraid that his touching me would release all the things I'd locked away. As long as we talked about Red's desire for a baby, I could hold it together. If I started thinking about my own feelings, my own desire for a child, I felt I might really unravel. "I think what I really need now is a little privacy."

Red stood up awkwardly, as if someone had changed the music on him in mid-dance. "Of course," he said. "Here." He handed me the brush, then looked embarrassed. "Do you want me to heat up some water for a bath?"

"I'm too cold and tired. I'll do it in the morning."

"Sure thing. So, ah, I'll just see to Rocky and get Ladyhawke settled. If you need anything . . ."

"No, thanks." I wondered if I was supposed to be feeling guilty. I hadn't had much experience being the one fuming in a relationship. With Hunter, I'd always been apologizing for something I hadn't done. With my mother, I took the role of the reasonable one.

"All right then. But, Doc?"

"What?"

"You might want to hold on to this." He handed me a soft chamois pouch; when I poured it out, the moonstone pendant slipped into my hand.

"There's a piece of leather in there you can hold it with, so the silver won't burn your hands. I thought about trying to reset it, but since moonstone is a soft stone, it didn't seem wise to try to pry it out of its setting."

I used the leather square to pick up the pendant, which was just as ugly as I remembered. "I thought Malachy wanted to run some tests on it."

Red shrugged. "Yeah, well, a necklace that grants true sight is a valuable thing. And the fact that the silver burns you may actually give it some of its power; a lot of magical objects work that way. Best not to let Malachy tinker with it none."

I felt a surge of affection for him then, but I also wondered what I would see if I slipped it back over my neck when I looked at him. I decided I would let my neck heal before trying to find out. "Red?"

"Yeah?"

"Thanks."

He grinned at me, like a mature version of Tom Sawyer, guilty of nothing but high spirits and a taste for adventure. But he wasn't some good old boy who just happened to know a bit about the supernatural. According to his ex-girlfriend, he was a shaman. Funny how easy it was to forget that when you lived with the man. I glanced at the bandage on his arm, underneath the coyote tattoo. A blood trail, to find his way back.

"Can I ask you something, Red?"

"Course."

I twisted the chamois pouch in my hands. "That bear man . . . manitou . . . I saw. Was it . . . was he . . . real?" I swallowed. Talking about magic gave me the same queasy feeling in my stomach that talking about LSD did. It evoked bad memories of solid things dissolving into colors and colors becoming tangible.

Red leaned against the door frame, and I could feel him weighing his words. "Depends how you look at it. There's different kinds of real, I guess."

"But he wasn't even Native American. He looked a little like a young Nick Nolte. Tell me that's not a hallucination."

Red lowered his chin, trying to hide his smile. "Manitou's the Indian name for them," he said. "But they were around before the Indians got here. My guess is that the way they look depends on who's seeing them."

Annoyed at Red's casual attitude, I blurted out, "He attacked me, you know."

Red's smile vanished. "I know. Did he . . . did he hurt you?"

I looked at my lap again. "No. I sort of spat at him, and he just took off."

Red gave a whoop of laughter. I guess it was probably relief. "Did you, now? That's the perfect thing to do, you know—saliva and excrement, scares off a lot of the Liminal creatures. They're not of the flesh, not like we are, so things of the flesh can work against them. Menstrual blood, too, if you're ever in a bind."

Lovely thought. "You think he'll come back?"

Red nodded his head slowly.

"So what can we do, Red?"

Red put his arm around me, and I didn't fight it. "Hell, that's what you've got wildlife removal operators for."

I just nodded. "Okay." I wasn't going to press for more answers right now. I wasn't sure I liked the ones I'd already gotten.

Red cleared his throat. "Doc? You hungry? I could make you a grilled cheese." There was a banging sound from the kitchen: Clearly, our food-addicted raccoon had decided to help himself to a late-night snack.

"Hey!" Red grabbed the raccoon around the middle, extricating the squirming animal from the pantry closet. "Stop that. You've already eaten, you fat bastard."

Rocky chittered loudly at Red, as if giving him some passionate explanation, but Red just smiled and put the raccoon on his shoulder. "How about I take you outside for a last romp, little guy?" They left the cabin, and I sleepily thought about Rocky's addiction to junk food. We needed to get locks for the cabinets. And then it hit me: I wasn't hungry, but I should have been starving. According to the calendar, I hadn't eaten in days, but I felt as though I had just had dinner with my mother at that diner a few hours earlier.

As I got up to look for something to eat, I looked out the window, and saw Red illuminated by bright moonlight. He was hunkered down on the ground with Rocky, looking for all the world like an indulgent dad playing with his toddler.

Then, with his breath visible in the frigid air, Red stood and abruptly pulled off his shirt, revealing the howling coyote tattoo on his right biceps. He pulled off the bandage, then knelt to unlace his hiking boots while Rocky climbed up onto his head. And then he unbuttoned his jeans.

I knew what he was doing. Unlike me, Red could change at will. Well, almost at will. All it required was that he be in an ecstatic state. But that didn't look like it was going to come easy tonight. As I watched his lean, tightly muscled body, I could see the tension in the line of his arms and thighs. He was one of those men who seem scrawny until the clothes come off. Naked, he was a throwback to another age, when men worked with their bodies and became sinewy, instead of soft, with age. Red placed Rocky on the ground, and I saw that while the scratch he'd made on his arm this evening had already healed, the older manitou scratches had left scars. Usually shapeshifters heal completely. I wondered what that portended for my leg, but when I stretched it, it felt better already, almost normal.

Red threw back his head and the raccoon lifted up on his hind legs, sniffing in curiosity. Red rolled his shoulders, stretching out his muscles, trying to relax himself, and despite the lingering pain in my leg, I felt a surge of warmth that started between my legs but stretched up to my chest. The moon must be nearly full, I realized, and then I wondered how I could have missed the signs in my own body. My breasts were tender and ached, and I could feel the low cramping in my abdomen, the tension in my bones. The change was coming. The words to an old Rolling Stones song popped into my head: The change has come, she's under my thumb.

I put my hand on the glass windowpane as Red ran his hands roughly, almost angrily over himself, trying to force the feeling and the transition. I hadn't wanted Red this much in ages. I put my hand on the glass pane and half rose to join him, forgetting all about my injured leg until a sharp burst of pain reminded me. Sitting back down, I watched as a spasm seemed to ripple through Red's back. He crouched down so abruptly that it looked as though he had collapsed in on himself. I could see his chest heaving, and I stood up, thinking, Something's wrong.

And then, as if he knew I was watching, Red turned, and his eyes glowed with a strange, amber light that I had never seen before. There seemed no trace of the gentle man in that hard, assessing, feral stare. But that's ridiculous, I corrected myself. He's a shapeshifter, not a lycanthrope. He always retains full consciousness. I was about to go out to him when he broke off, swiveling so fast that the little raccoon gave a sharp squeak.

And Red snapped his jaws shut, centimeters away from the baby he had helped save. I gasped. Rocky was squeaking, but holding his ground, unable to believe his adoptive father could seriously mean him harm. He had seen Red change before. Whatever skin he wore, he was always the same.

Until now.

With a bound, Red took after the raccoon, which darted away into the woods behind the outhouse. I had my hand on my chest, as if I could calm my pounding heart. Was it possible that this was part of some reintroduction to the wild? As much as I wanted to believe that, I wasn't convinced.

I waited for an hour, fixing myself a cup of hot cocoa, eating a bowl of raisin bran. But Red didn't come back, and in the end, before going to bed, I fastened the latch on the bedroom door. Not that it would keep him out if he really wanted in, but it would buy me time.

And suddenly I remembered what Malachy had said. *He made a deal. That's how it works, I believe.*

In the morning, when I unlocked the door, I wondered what I could say to Red. Sorry, I thought you might attack me? Or, more to the point: What kind of deal? With whom?

But an hour later, when I left for the train, he still wasn't back.

And neither was Rocky.

◐○○○◑
PART TWO

FOURTEEN

◐○○ I knew that taking a trip into the city so close to the full moon wasn't exactly the most conservative course of action, but when I checked the lunar calendar, I could see that I still had a good twenty-four hours before I was out of my safety zone. Even so, I kept checking my watch, which had a little calendar window that displayed the phases of the moon. January nineteenth was gibbous, not full, but still, that moonshadow was growing awfully thin.

I don't know about other therians, but Magda, Hunter, and I all kept track of the lunar calendar with the devotion of Orthodox Jews and deer hunters. And we really hated the deer hunters, who had started clomping through the woods during the best hunting days in autumn, when the deer were in rut and giddy with lust.

Since there was a good week when the moon was full enough to keep us wolfish, and the days immediately before and after weren't the best time to schedule a major event like a wedding or a business trip, having lycanthropy meant knowing when you were safe, when you were out of commission, and when you were borderline.

I was borderline, but I knew that I needed to talk to a female friend. So even though I'd been hoping to conceal my current state of romantic chaos from Lilliana, I decided that my need for help overrode my desire for dignity.

In books and movies, women always seem to be unburdening themselves to their friends without the slightest compunction. Me, I have compunction. The way I see it, there's an unspoken agreement in most friendships, a sort of quid pro quo of emotional support. In the time we'd been friends, Lilliana and I had never made any serious demands on each other. Of course, we were work friends, which meant there remained a certain formality between us, although we knew we could depend on each other in a crisis. And that was important. I may not have known everything about Lilliana's life outside the Animal Medical Institute, but seeing how a person reacts when the surgery's not over and the dog starts waking up from sedation is a pretty good indication of character.

And, to be honest, I hadn't kept up with most of my high school and college pals, and I couldn't face the thought of trying to fast forward through the past five or ten years before explaining my current predicament. At least Lilliana knew where I was living and whom I was dating, even if she didn't know that once or twice a month, I could have been mistaken for one of my own patients.

I was already on my way to the train station when I called Lilliana on my cell phone, figuring that if she wasn't available, I'd ask to use her apartment, and if that wasn't possible, I'd get off at the Pleasantvale station and suffer through my mother's abrasive brand of kindness. But Lilliana answered on the first ring, and before I'd said more than "Lilliana, hi, listen, I know this is short notice," she'd told me that she'd been looking for an excuse to take the day off. Sometimes I wondered if she was psychic.

At a quarter to eleven, I was standing in front of her

Upper West Side apartment. Lilliana opened the door, effortlessly elegant in a maroon tunic and black yoga pants, her black hair pulled back in a French twist and her café au lait complexion flawless without makeup.

I kissed her cheek, inhaling a scent that would be undetectable to a human nose. My sense of smell was the only thing that changed before I did—hormones, I guess. This close to the full moon, my elegant friend smelled cloyingly sweet, like some overripe flower, and I had to turn my head aside to muffle my sneeze. "Sorry, Lilli. God. I feel like a refugee, showing up on your doorstep like this."

"You don't look like a refugee."

"Liar." In an attempt to make myself feel less pathetic, I'd put on mascara and blush and was wearing what I thought of as my city clothes, a pair of vaguely nautical navy trousers and a cream-colored sweater. My leg still felt a little sore, but I wasn't limping. Whatever else was changing about Red, he hadn't lost his healing touch.

I sank down onto her couch, which looked like it belonged in some upscale East Asian yurt, along with a samovar and some yak milk. The blue-tiled kitchen, however, owed more to Morocco, and none of this should have matched the wooden African chairs and animal carvings, but somehow it all came together, the epitome of boho indigenous chic.

"Now I feel like an upscale refugee," I said. "And I didn't even have a chance to explain why I wanted to see you."

"If you're worried that I had a day of museums and shopping planned, relax." Lilliana brought out a plate of fresh zucchini bread, still steaming from the oven. "You didn't sound like this was going to be an impulsive day of fun. Now, what can I get you to drink? Some juice? Coffee? Tea?" She looked at me more closely. "A double vodka?"

"Don't tempt me."

Lilliana took this in as if she had been suspecting as much. And maybe she had. She had a kind of sixth sense in dealing with both people and animals, which was why Malachy had plucked her out of the Institute's social work residency and added her to his team. Or maybe it had all been Lilliana's idea; she was pretty masterful at the art of subtle influence. "What's going on, Abra? You look like you're about to jump out of your skin."

I gave a strangled laugh.

Lilliana looked at me carefully. "Are you pregnant?"

I shook my head, and told her everything. At first, I tried to leave out the part about being a therian, because it felt both preposterous and a little embarrassing. But Lilliana kept asking me astute little questions, and pretty soon I realized that none of what I was saying really made sense when I left out the fact that I turn into a wolf once a month. Up until that moment, I hadn't realized how isolated my condition had made me. I'd thought I could just confide in Lilliana without going into the gory details, but now I saw that omitting the fact of my lycanthropy was like glossing over the fact that you'd cheated, or were really gay, or had been e-mailing an ex-boyfriend. Maybe men could be friends without divulging critical details, but it didn't work for women. "You don't seem as shocked as I would have expected," I told her when I was done.

"Abra, please. We both worked for Mad Mal, remember? I mean, he didn't exactly make a secret of his experiments." Back when I still thought of werewolves as the stuff of old horror movies, Malachy had been convinced there really was a lycanthropy virus. He'd conjectured that the virus caused regular cells to become more like fetal stem cells, able to take on any shape and function.

"Besides," Lilliana went on, "it was pretty clear last year that some seriously weird shit was going on with you and your husband."

I laughed in surprise at the unexpected profanity, then realized Lilliana had done it deliberately, the way a jazz musician might add a dissonant note for effect. "So, the thing is, Lilli, I don't know if I belong with Red or not. And I don't know if staying with him means that I'm never going to be able to have a baby." I didn't go into the whole business about my being in heat, because it felt like a little bit too much information. Despite the lasting impression made by a certain television series, most of the Manhattan women I knew kept the particulars of their sex lives between themselves and their psychotherapists.

Lilliana walked into the kitchen and returned with a bottle of chilled Pinot Grigio and two stemless Italian wineglasses. "Whoa, slow down there. Seems to me that what you're really saying is, do this man and I work as a couple? Are we strong enough as a team? All this business about being alpha—you know, it's not entirely a bad thing. If you're going to do something as big and scary as having a baby, maybe you both have to feel confident enough to say, this is my little pack, and I'm leading it." She poured out the wine and handed me a glass.

I took a sip, beginning to feel better. "I think I liked it better when I was human, and being fit to be a parent had nothing to do with whether or not you could become one."

"Yeah, and you know how well that can work out. Come on," Lilliana said abruptly, putting down her wineglass and standing up. "You know what you need now? A little retail therapy."

Despite my protestations that I hated shopping, Lilliana nagged me into putting on my pea coat and draped herself in a gray woolen poncho that would have made me look like a bag lady, but made her look like the queen of some exotic, far-off land. Then we headed over to my favorite eyeglass shop on Columbus Avenue. At Optical Allusion, the frames are arranged cunningly in the window on pillows and pedestals, as if they were jewelry. Inside, there were antique tables with artfully tarnished mirrors, and salespeople dressed in the kind of austere chic that suggested that we were in the presence of Art.

The moment I walked in the door, I felt conscious of my old, scratched spare pair of specs, drab hair, and un-fashionable clothes.

"I think these looked great," said Lilliana, who looked completely at ease dressed in yoga slacks and sil-ver sneakers, a fringed scarf looped loosely around her neck.

"Which ones?" Maybe if I let Lilliana choose my en-tire wardrobe, I would be transformed into someone el-egant, funky, impeccable.

"These." Lilliana plucked a pair of rectangular red and black frames from a display. "Let me see them on you. Oh, Abs, those are amazing. They hit your cheek-bones just right."

"Those are my favorites," said the salesman, a reed-thin man with an elfin look of amusement.

"I should have worn my lenses. I can't see myself." It was never a comfortable feeling, taking my glasses off in public. Everyone else could see me, but all I could see was a blur of browns and golds.

"You can always come back," the salesman said.

"No, I need glasses now. I can't walk around looking like this." I indicated the outdated frames with their scratched lenses. Of course, the truth was, I could. Red didn't notice if my hair was shapeless or my glasses were from the previous decade. He didn't care if I wore makeup or shaved my legs—to him, I was equally sexy in burlap or silk, furry or smooth-skinned. It was what I loved about him. And yet, if I were truly honest, there were times when I wanted him to care. I wasn't exactly the most fashion-conscious individual in the world, but like most women, I tried to express something of my inner self in the choices I made. But as far as the language of clothes and makeup went, Red was illiterate.

And then I remembered that I had more serious concerns about Red. Like whether or not he was killing the animals he used to save.

Lilliana selected a different pair of frames. "Those are nice, too . . . with the clear glass on top. You look like a sexy bohemian."

I went over to the mirror and peered into it myopically, trying to see if I had, in fact, been transformed. Unfortunately, all I could make out was a vague face-shaped blur.

"Yes, I like those, too," said the salesman, who would probably have liked a monocle if Lilliana had suggested it.

I replaced my old glasses and perused the display. "What about these, Lilli?" I pointed to a cat's eye in tortoiseshell.

"Librarian."

I squinted at my reflection. "Sexy librarian? Pull pins out of hair and unbutton shirt and you're gorgeous librarian?" The mirror was silent on the subject, and when I glanced at my friend, her brow was furrowed in concentration.

"Let's try one more look. Can my friend look at that—no, the black with the little ivory-looking inlay for contrast." This last pair was locked inside a glass case, which to my mind suggested that it was out of my price range. The salesman handed it to me as if it were a canary diamond.

"That's the best one yet," he said as I slipped the frames on.

"And coincidentally, the most expensive."

"No, he's right." Lilliana lifted my hair off my face. "Now, this is sexy librarian, Abra."

I decided to take her word for it. "I'll take them," I told the salesman. "How long will it take to get them made up to my prescription?"

"Do you want us to read the numbers off your current glasses?" The salesman took my old frames as if they were a dead squirrel and took them into the back. "Two weeks," he said when he returned.

"That long?"

The salesman's smile turned condescending. "I'm terribly sorry, you could always use one of those quickie optician's shops, but we pride ourselves on the excellence of our work. We also have a large backload of work at the moment."

I was about to capitulate and ask that the glasses be sent to me, but Lilliana put her hand lightly on the salesman's arm. "I know you do excellent work, Jeremy," she said, apparently pulling his name out of the air, "but do you think there's any way you could help us get the glasses more quickly? My friend here lives out of town." As she spoke, she tilted her head slightly, and I was reminded of a world-class violinist subtly altering the pitch of the music by the slightest alteration in posture.

Jeremy looked momentarily confused, then said that he would have to check with his manager. When he returned, he announced that my glasses would be done by the end of the day.

We walked out of the store and into the cold, bright day outside, and I turned to my friend in amazement. "How do you do that? Is it a spell? Can I learn it?"

Lilliana laughed, hooking her arm through mine. A cute young guy on a racing bike swiveled his head at the sound. "Now, how about some new clothes? I know a great little boutique on the next block."

"I think that last purchase just cleaned me out. Besides, it's probably better for me not to try on clothes next to you," I admitted, glancing down at Lilliana's willowy frame. The cute cyclist, I noticed with amusement, was following behind us now.

"Girl, you have the most amazing Renoir body. Creamy skin, perfect little upturned breasts, tiny waist . . ."

"Oh, Lilliana," I said, mockingly. "I never knew you felt this way." On the street just behind us, the cyclist grinned and then weaved his front wheel, trying not to overtake us.

"Well, it's true," said Lilliana, unaware that a construction worker had paused to lick his lips at her departing figure.

"Lilli, I appreciate what you're trying to do, but the truth is, I'm pretty much invisible when I'm standing next to you." As if to prove my point, a businessman stopped talking into his cell phone long enough to give Lilliana an appreciative look.

We paused at the traffic light, and a souped-up Camaro zoomed past, honking its horn. "Baby," called the driver, "you looking fine!"

Lilliana tilted her head to one side. "What do you mean, invisible?"

"Oh, for crying out loud, Lilli, take a look around!" I gestured at the cyclist, the construction worker, and the businessman. "You're like some kind of crazy man magnet! We can't walk two steps without some guy bugging out."

Lilliana stared at me as though I were going crazy. "Abra, those guys were checking *you* out, not me."

"Oh, please. As a general rule, I do not cause men to fall off their bicycles." I pointed to the cyclist, who had been too busy watching us to notice the taxi driver opening his door to spit on the sidewalk. The cyclist was on the street, rubbing his bruised shin, and the driver was yelling at him.

"Maybe you just don't notice," Lilliana said.

I put my hands on my hips. "Lilli, please, don't insult my intelligence. It's perfectly obvious which of us is attracting all the male attention."

At that moment, I felt a sharp pinch on my left buttock. I whirled around, and saw a young man in an anorak grinning at me as he darted out of the way. "Get me a piece of that," he said, as if ordering something from a drive-through.

"I'll give you a piece of something," I snarled back.

"You were saying?" The light turned green, Lilliana took my arm again, and we crossed the street.

"Hey," said the cyclist, holding up one arm. "Hang on."

We paused, and he came up next to us, a smooth-skinned young man a shade or two darker than Lilliana. "You all right?" she asked.

"Just scratched my knee," he said. "Thing is, I think I know you," he said, staring at me intently. "I can't remember from where, but I know we've met."

I rolled my eyes. "Lilliana, did you put these guys up to this? Is this the new ego boost—instead of hiring your own paparazzi, you hire your own stalkers?"

"No, really, I'm not fooling around," said the young man, and then he looked embarrassed. "It's just, did you and I . . . I feel this weird connection, like I'm drawn to you. I'm a great believer in listening to the heart," he explained.

"I'm a great believer in examining the head," I said, moving away from the cyclist.

Lilliana glanced over her shoulder. "So, this isn't your typical reaction from the male of the species?"

"It must be a full moon," I said, jokingly.

"Actually, it is," said Lilliana, pointing up, past the tall buildings at the translucent, swollen moon hanging in the pale winter sky.

"Almost," I corrected her. "It looks full, but it's got another couple days to go."

"Have you started carrying around a farmer's almanac? Come on, country girl," said Lilliana. "Here's the boutique I was telling you about." There were three outfits in the window, all of them variations on white shirts and slender black skirts. There were also a few shoes, sexy and clunky in the style of the 1940s. The name of the shop was The Sexy Librarian.

"You're kidding me. There's an entire store devoted to the sexy librarian look?"

Lilliana grinned as she opened the door. "You see why I can never leave the city."

It was my dream store. There were very few things in the shop, but all of them were perfect. White shirts that were nipped and tucked in just the right places, with one-of-a-kind antique buttons. There were little navy dresses that radiated an understated funkiness that was almost, but not quite, frumpy. And there were racks of 1920s silky tap pants, and stockings with seams up the back, and camisoles in pinks and peaches and russets and plums, the color of the sunset as it deepened into night.

"Oh, my God," I said. "I want it all."

"I knew you'd love it," Lilliana said happily, throwing things into my arms. "Try this. And this. Oh, and this, you have to have that on underneath."

I ducked into the dressing room, and wriggled into the camisole. I was still buttoning up the shirt when I emerged, but I thought I had the skirt on straight. "Well, Lilli," I said. "What do you think?"

"I think it's sort of like that Hitchcock scene where all the birds start roosting together," said Lilliana, and for a moment, I didn't understand what she was saying, because I was so surprised. The shop was filled with men. There were men crammed on either side of Lilliana, as if waiting for a dressing room, and other men visible behind them, checking out the sexy panties. I had seen the occasional hapless fiancé dragged into a store like this, but never a whole group of them. Huh, I thought, must be the new metrosexual fashion-consciousness I keep reading about.

And then I spotted the cyclist, and I realized something extremely peculiar was going on.

"I like it a lot," said the construction worker, who had crammed himself into a corner between the businessman, the cyclist, and a bunch of Japanese tourists.

"Go try something else on," said the cyclist. His voice sounded strained.

"Excuse me," said the saleswoman, a lovely young Asian woman who wore the sexy librarian look very well, "but you're going to have to tell your friends to leave. We just don't have room for this many people."

"They're not my friends," I protested. "I don't know who these people are. Is this some kind of mass protest thing, like when that guy was organizing huge crowds to take off their clothes in public?"

A slow smile spread over the businessman's pudgy face. "You want us to take off our clothes?"

"All right," said the construction worker.

"Oh, man," said the cyclist, who had snuck behind me to retrieve my slacks from the changing room. "I can smell her on these." He took a deep whiff of my pants and I shouted, "Hey," and grabbed one of the legs.

"Stop that. You're being weird. All of you."

"I need to be upside you," said a Japanese tourist, consulting his phrase book. "Inside," he corrected himself. "Yes?"

"I need to lick you from your toes to your ears," said the cyclist.

"You touch her and I'll kill you," said the construction worker. "That's the future mother of my children you're talking to."

"Like hell she is," roared the businessman.

Lilliana ducked under his right arm, which was holding off the hardhat, and took my elbow. "I don't suppose you're wearing some exotic new perfume?"

"I'm afraid I am," I admitted. "L'air d'estrus." Because, it had belatedly occurred to me, there was no other explanation for my sudden transformation from plain Jane to femme fatale. "Lilliana, we have to get out of here."

"Well, don't change back into your clothes—you're liable to start a riot."

Luckily, most of the men were preoccupied with jostling and insulting each other. The businessman and the construction worker were screaming abuse, while the Japanese tourists were getting very red in the face as they shouted clipped phrases at the cyclist and the anorak man.

The funny thing was, many of the guys were actually quite attractive. The young cyclist had the clean, strong jaw of a scholar-athlete; two of the Japanese tourists were flat-out handsome; and even the anorak man possessed a kind of thuggish appeal. As the tension escalated and the pushing turned to shoving, I found myself watching with reluctant fascination. There was something primitive, almost primal about this scene. Suddenly, the layers of civilization were being peeled back, and what remained was the essential, true nature of each individual. The businessman was now a large male, no longer in his prime, whose outward belligerence masked a reluctance to engage in direct battle. The construction worker, by contrast, was a splendidly muscled specimen, warily circling the young Japanese male, who was bouncing lightly on the balls of his feet and crooning to himself in a softly menacing tone.

It seemed to me, trapped as I was among these bellicose males, that there was no choice except to await the outcome. One male would emerge victorious, his skin damp with exertion, redolent of the powerful male hormones flooding through his body. He would be wounded, no doubt, and yet still possessed by all the savage instincts that had allowed him to conquer the other males. He would come to me then, his body thrumming with adrenaline and lust, his mind half-maddened by the intoxicating scent of me. But there would be no use of force. I would still have the power to turn him away, to leave him unsatisfied and burning with desire.

Now the construction worker and the Japanese tourist had removed their shirts, and their bare chests were already gleaming with sweat as the young saleswoman darted ineffectually about, telling them that she had called the police. I wondered vaguely which one it would be, and how long I would make him wait before permitting him to pleasure me at last.

"Abra? Abra, snap out of it!" Lilliana shook me, and I stared at her uncomprehendingly for a moment. "We need to get out of here before the police arrive. Especially since you may wind up affecting the cops the way you do the civilians."

I turned back to the men. "But we can't leave," I said, my heart racing with excitement as the cyclist launched himself at the Japanese tourist, who had just taken down the construction worker with a roundhouse kick.

Lilliana took a deep breath and said, "If you don't get out of here now, Abs, you're going to end up becoming the guest of honor at a gang bang."

"Mmm," I said absentmindedly, as the cyclist kicked his opponent in the balls. How much of Lilliana's distress, I had to ask, was due to her being the wallflower for once? Not so nice to be the female none of the males even notice.

"Oh, hell," said Lilliana. "I guess there's no other choice." Taking my head in her hands, Lilliana forced me to face her. "Look right into my eyes for a second, Abra."

For a moment, I thought she was going to kiss me. I think some of the men must have had the same idea, because I could feel them watching us with prurient interest.

"Abra," said Lilliana, "focus." And as if she had seized my nervous system as well as my temples, I obeyed, narrowing my focus to her dark gaze. "We must leave," she said, and I knew that she was right. If I didn't get out in the next few minutes, I'd be acting out my own personal National Geographic episode.

"Hey," said one of the men, trying to grab Lilliana's arm as she hustled me out the door. I lifted my lip and snarled at him, and he released her, allowing us to make it to the front door.

Just as we made it out into the street, the police cruisers arrived, lights flashing and sirens wailing.

"Shit," said Lilliana. I'd never heard her curse before. "How the hell are we going to get you home? If I put you on a train, you're liable to start a riot."

"Listen, Lilli," I began. "I think there's something I neglected to tell you about myself." Like the fact that I'm in pheromone overdrive.

But she was already talking on her cell phone. "Martin? Thank God. I need help. My friend's a lycanthrope and she's gone into acute estrus. Uh huh. She needs wheels and a driver, either a male with a score of less than ten percent heteroerotic on the bisexuality index, or female with less than ten percent homoerotic. Yes. Fantastic. Can it be in half an hour or less at my place?

Goddess bless, Martin, I owe you." As she hung up the phone, Lilliana caught my astonished expression and shrugged. "You know how you're always telling me I must be psychic? Well, you're not completely wrong. I'll try to explain when we're out of danger."

It seemed I wasn't the only one who had omitted a few details.

FIFTEEN

◐○○ We were racing the moon, and the moon was winning. Looking out the tinted windows of the stretch limousine, I could see the moon rising steadily in the sky. I couldn't see the light fading, but I could feel it, a low and insistent tugging at the inside of my skin.

"We shouldn't have stopped to get your new glasses," Lilliana said. She was sitting, facing me, looking worried.

"But they were ready," I pointed out. "Besides, they go with my new outfit." I was still wearing the Sexy Librarian blouse and skirt, which, I supposed, I had stolen. I was a thief. It was kind of a delicious feeling. I was a bad girl. I moved my legs in a luxurious stretch. "Do you know I've never ridden in one of these limos before? Hey, I don't suppose there's any champagne in there." I opened the mini fridge and found a miniature bottle of Chablis. "Well, this will do."

"Give me that." Lilliana swiped the wine out of my hand. "The last thing you need is a disinhibitor."

"I just wanted to relax a little," I complained, drumming my fingers on the armrest. My skin felt as if it were prickling with heat rash and I rolled the window down, needing to feel air on my face. The Saw Mill was congested with Friday afternoon traffic, each commuter hermetically sealed into his or her vehicle. The lone exception was a heavyset Labrador hanging out of a rear car window, heedless of the January chill, ears flapping in the wind. As I watched, the Lab sniffed the air, his nose twitching furiously. Suddenly, the big dog froze, then started scrabbling frantically in an attempt to squeeze his entire bulk out of the open window. I watched, appalled at the dog's inexplicable urge to jump out of the moving car, while a teenage boy tried to haul his pet back inside.

"Abra, do you need to keep the window wide open? The temperature is dropping and it must be about thirty degrees outside."

Reluctantly, I stuck my head back in. Out of the corner of my eye, I could see that the Labrador was back in his car, the windows now rolled up. "That's strange," I said.

"What is?"

I opened my mouth, and then it struck me: The Labrador must have smelled me. Dear God, I was a siren to both dogs and men. I dragged my hands through my hair. "I think this is affecting my brain," I said. "I can't seem to reason anything through."

"Abra, has the transformation ever come on this strong before?" Lilliana handed me a bottle of water from the mini fridge. I shook my head.

"No water?"

"No, it's never been this intense." I drank the water down, letting it trickle past my lips, down my throat, until it wet the material of my shirt. "Whew," I said, wiping my arm across my mouth. I caught Lilliana's startled expression. "What is it?"

"You're just not acting like yourself. I don't really know that much about lycanthropy," she said, handing me a box of tissues. "Just what Malachy taught us when we were on his team. Is this a standard progression of the disease?"

"You knew about estrus," I said, suddenly remembering that this was strange. "Malachy never taught us that."

"I wondered if you were alert enough to notice that." Lilliana uncrossed her legs and looked me straight in the eye. "I didn't know for certain, but your ex had been studying unwolves in Romania last year. I figured there wasn't much else that could account for your sudden transformation from one-man woman to agent provocateur."

"Bullshit. Right after you called for the car, you said something about almost being psychic. Care to explain that, or are you revising your story?"

Lilliana continued looking at me for a moment, as if weighing her next move. Then she glanced at the partially open partition separating us from the driver, a matronly woman who hadn't given me a second glance, even when we'd had to slam the door shut on five excited men and one enthusiastic woman.

"Jemma," Lilliana told the driver, "I'm going to close the partition completely, so that I can broadcast. You might want to put on the radio, as well." When the partition was closed and we could hear the faint sounds of a pop tune, Lilliana opened the fridge and took out the miniature Chablis. "Hand me those glasses, would you?"

I looked around and then spotted four glasses tucked into a built-in shelf near my armrest. I handed two glasses to Lilliana. "Not worried about me getting disinhibited?"

"Still worried, but I think we both need a drink."

"If you're about to tell me you're a telepath, I'm going to need all of that." I cringed inside, thinking of all the fleeting, unrepeatable thoughts that had crossed my mind while I was in Lilliana's presence. No matter how much you liked someone, there were always the things you edited a bit, or cut completely.

"I'm not a telepath," said Lilliana, pouring out the wine and handing me a glass.

"Just highly intuitive?" I said it sarcastically, but Lilliana shook her head, a wry smile playing over her lips.

"No, if I were an Intuitive, I would be able to forecast the future. I'm a Sensitive."

"Sensitive to what?"

Lilliana took a sip of her wine, hesitated, then threw back the whole glass. "How much do you know about personality testing?"

"It's big with corporate America, and I guess with corporate Europe and Asia. You take a test and it measures your extroversion or introversion and whether or not you like to analyze or work as a team."

"Most businesses and dating services use a version of the Enneagram. Some use other variants. But to a large degree, they use self-reporting and they don't test until the subjects are grown." Lilliana reached out and took my glass out of my hand. Tossing it back, she blinked back tears and then said, "Ever wonder what would happen if you had a team of experts test a child and then gear an education to that child's particular strengths?"

"No, but I think you're about to tell me." I checked the fridge and found a second bottle of wine. "And this one's for me."

Lilliana twisted a braided silver ring on her finger, and I thought with a pang of my silver and moonstone pendant. If only I could wear it without blistering, I might know what the people around me were really like. As it was, I was keeping the pendant close to me, in its little pouch inside my handbag. "You'd get some unusually talented people," Lilliana was saying. "Intuitives, Cognitives . . ." she stopped playing with her ring and met my eyes. "Sensitives."

I took a sip of the wine. "Still not getting it, Lil. I

don't know if it's the hormones, but I don't think so. You're so wound up that you're not communicating clearly."

Lilliana seemed surprised for a moment, and then wiped a bead of sweat off her upper lip. I had never seen her sweat before. "There," she said. "Now I'm expending a little less energy on broadcasting, so I can focus on what I'm saying. And not saying."

I remembered that she'd used the word "broadcast" before, when talking to the driver. But all of a sudden it seemed a little harder to concentrate. It felt as if the temperature inside the limo had risen by about ten degrees, and I took another sip of wine. "Is it me, or is it suddenly hot in here?"

"Whoops, let me adjust." Lilliana closed her eyes for a second, then opened them again. "How's that?"

I stared at her. I was no longer as warm, but I was still warmer than I had been a few minutes earlier. My skin prickled with anxiety. "Explain. Now. Using simple, easily understood language."

Lilliana reached out and took my hands in hers, and instantly, my anxiety dissipated, like a bubble bursting harmlessly in the air. "I'm what you would call an empath," she said. "Except that I can broadcast emotions as well as receive. Right now I'm radiating calm, which is why the wine was more important for me than for you."

"So the reason you knew I was in heat . . ."

"Was because I could feel it. But here's the thing, Abra, I'm not supposed to be telling you about any of this. The group I belong to—the Discipline—they don't like exposing their methods to outsiders."

Something about Lilliana's language struck me as peculiar—the pronoun "they" in conjunction with the phrase "the group I belong to" in particular. I also got the distinct impression that Lilliana was leaving out some important points. But it was getting harder and harder to pursue a logical train of thought. Outside the window, the sun was setting and the taillights of the cars ahead of us shone like bright, night-seeing eyes.

Even in the low light, even at this speed, I could sense the lives all around us: a gaunt deer, paused at the edge of a suburban lawn; a well-padded raccoon, waddling into the refuse behind a diner; a fox, carefully venturing out of its den in a half-empty office complex on the side of the highway.

"Abra?"

I continued to stare out the window, rapt at the skittering presence of rodent life in the underbrush. And then we were motoring past the immediate suburbs of Manhattan, and there was nothing but road and cars and the great glowing peach of a moon, lighting the path to wildness and abandon.

"Abs?" Lilliana reached over to feel my forehead, and I pushed her hand away, annoyed. I hated the soft, feminine feel of her fingers. That wasn't the kind of touch I craved. "Are you all right?"

"Yes, yes, of course I am. Can't you *feel* that," I added, more nastily than I'd intended. But really, that was the problem with females. Always crowding around you and sticking their noses into your business, forever whimpering and trying to insinuate themselves into your good graces. Except for the mean bitches, of course. The mean bitches like Magda would just ambush you and the only way to deal with them was to attack first.

"Abra, look at me."

I turned to look at Lilliana and it seemed she was concentrating very hard on something, because her brow was furrowed and her entire face was now bathed in sweat. Her hand was on my arm, trembling with tension. "What is the matter with you?" I shook off her arm. "No offense, Lilli, but I could use a little personal space here. I'm boiling up." I rolled down the window, and the blast of cold night air was a relief, but not enough. "God, how long is this ride going to take?" The limo stank of stale sweat and body odors and to make it worse, there was a harsh chemical stench overlaying it, the cleaning detergent that had been used to dupe weak human noses.

"We're still an hour away." Lilliana's voice was taut with strain.

"Jesus, an hour? I'm never going to make it." I started unbuttoning my shirt.

"What are you doing?" Lilliana's eyes were wide with alarm.

"I'm just so uncomfortable. Besides, we're all girls here." Irritated by the tiny horn buttons, I tugged at the shirt and it ripped in a satisfying long tear down the front.

"Abra, if you take off your clothes . . ."

"Oh," I sighed, as I unbuttoned the skirt, "that feels better." I reached behind me, fumbling with the clasp of the brassiere. "I don't suppose you could just reach that for me?"

"Abra, you have to try to exert more control over your beast. I'll help, but it's getting harder—your emotions aren't completely human anymore."

"Mmm," I said. With my breasts finally freed from the scratchy encumbrance, I bared them to the night air. There was some wild whooping and enthusiastic honking from another car.

"Abra! Come on, wild woman, let's get you back in here."

"Are you sure you're an empath?"

"I'm sure," Lilliana said as she pulled me down, away from the window.

"Then how come you don't want to show them your breasts? It's very liberating," I confided.

"Like our own private Mardi Gras," muttered Lilliana, throwing my shirt at me. "Now put that on."

"Hey," shouted a guy from the other car, pulling alongside. "Check out the full moon!"

I turned and laughed; his friend had stuck his bare bottom out of the rear window.

The driver, still scrawny with youth, leered at me. "Baby! Want to park?"

"Actually," I said, smiling with all my teeth, "I'd like to run."

"I'd run with you, baby," said a second young man. This one, presumably the owner of the pasty buttocks, was larded with the fat of inactivity.

"You couldn't keep up."

As the driver of the other car guffawed, our own driver slid the connecting partition open. "Sorry, Lilliana, I know you said not to interrupt while you were broadcasting, but what's going on here? Besides the obvious problem of these idiots, I'm getting flashes of impending disaster, and they're coming closer together now." In the rearview mirror, I saw the other woman's eyes register dismay at what she'd just revealed in front of an outsider.

"You did right, Jemma," Lilliana said, and then I felt our car slowing down.

"Accident ahead," said our driver, slowing the car down.

Lilliana leaned forward, peering out the windshield screen. "Can you *foretell* how long it's going to take?" We were crawling ahead at about ten miles an hour now, and I could see the signal flares up ahead, cordoning off the disabled vehicle.

"Hey, baby," called the males from the other car, "how about a traffic jam and penis sandwich?" They had stopped their car just ahead of us and were indicating a desire to merge—pun intended. Turning back to them, I cupped my breasts and said, "Think you can take me?"

Before they could reply, I kicked off my shoes, opened the door, and made my break for freedom.

"Wait up, gorgeous," shouted one of the men—the scrawny one, I thought. I kept running, even though I could hear the muffled curses and clumsy, crashing progress of the men behind me, and more faintly, Lilliana's anxious voice calling my name.

"Come on and catch me," I singsonged, my heart racing with the thrill of the chase. I had never really thought before about what lay on either side of the highway, but it seemed right that it should be woods, a wide swathe of silver birch and pine, with icy patches and an occasional clear-cut field littered with stumps. My feet were too numb to feel the rough stones on the ground as I ran, but I didn't mind. I felt alive at last, the sharp air stinging my lungs, the wind of my own motion making my bare skin tingle.

"Where are you? Shit," said the scrawny male's voice, and I heard a thump and a pained exclamation. "Dude," said the second, stockier male's voice, "this is warped."

"Giving up so soon?" I paused, listening as the two male forms made their noisy way to the field where I was standing, knowing exactly where they were long before they broke out into the open.

"H-hey." The stocky male was bent over and panting heavily. The scrawny one tried to strike a nonchalant pose, leaning against a tree. His gaze roamed over my naked form.

"So," he said, trying not to gasp for breath, "you're a playful girl, aren't you?" The words had a canned quality, as if he were quoting some classic porn line. The moon was so bright that I felt as if we were on a movie set. Maybe the young man felt like that, too: as if we were acting out a scene. For the first time in my life, I knew what it must have been like to be my mother in her prime.

"Ready to run yet?" I braced myself, about to take off, when the first spasm hit. I moaned and clutched at my midsection.

"Oh, yeah, you're so hot," said the scrawny male. His pale, wheat-colored hair was plastered with sweat to his head, but his slightly protuberant blue eyes were gleaming with anticipation.

"Dude, I think she's illing," said his stocky companion.

"You're illing, dude," said Scrawny. He stepped closer to me, and the smell of his lust was acrid with beer and nicotine. The pain rippled through me again, seizing my throat, and I sank to my knees.

"Oh, yeah, baby," said Scrawny. Dimly, I was aware of him unzipping his fly and taking out his erect penis. "You want to suck me, don't you?"

I shook my head, but then the liquid feeling rushed through my muscles, and I groaned out loud.

"Fuck, man, she's so into it." Scrawny grasped the back of my head and tried to push it closer to the appendage gleaming palely in the moonlight.

"Jeez, Jake, I don't know." I opened my slitted eyes and saw that the fat male was fairly quivering with anxiety and indecision.

"Please," I managed to get out, and then I had to pant, fighting to stay on top of the contractions racing up and down my spine.

"Look, Dean, she's panting for it. Open wide, baby, take it all in." And now I could see Dean's mouth opening as his chubby fingers slipped down into his sweatpants. "Oh, man," he breathed.

"Don't whack off, dude, stick it in her." Scrawny's

erection was pressed up against my nose and mouth, making it hard to breathe, and when I gasped as the next contraction hit, something fleshy was thrust into my mouth. I gagged as the second male came up behind me, his sweaty, soft hands touching my waist, but the sensations inside my body were becoming stronger than any distraction from without.

"Let's take off those glasses," Scrawny said, and when he removed the spectacles I hadn't realized I was still wearing, the last barrier to transformation was removed. There was enough human in me to perceive the irony: Remove the specs and lo and behold, the prim librarian turns into a beautiful wild thing.

Too bad the boys weren't in on the joke.

With a great spasming ripple, the pain became a rush of heat as my cells remembered what they were supposed to do. I felt the change course through me as my limbs and bones and internal organs rearranged themselves. The male behind me made a piglike squeal of horror and said, "Dude, there's something wrong!"

But it was too late. My jaws snapped shut and blood filled my mouth. I did not, however, bite down—I released my grip on the injured male almost instantly. Still, in some corner of my mind, I knew that I had done wrong. No biting—that was an important rule. Still, it hadn't *felt* wrong. It had felt quite satisfying. The constant screaming was hurting my ears, however, so I took a leap into the safety of the woods. After that, my legs seemed to do the thinking for me. They wanted to run, so I ran, sprinting ahead, then settling myself into a loping pace that felt as natural as breathing. Being human was a distant dream of complicated rules and physical limitations.

I heard another kind of raised voice calling after me, a woman's voice, my friend. But I had the sense she wouldn't be pleased about the biting—you really weren't supposed to bite, which was unfair, since they had hands and we didn't.

I ran on, guided by some internal compass, irresistibly drawn toward the magnetic pull of Northside.

SIXTEEN

◐ ○ ○ For a long time I ran, giddy with my own strength and speed as I galloped full tilt through the woods without tripping or stumbling. The pads of my paws told me everything I needed to know about where to place my weight, and even though my distance vision was vague, my peripheral sight took in everything I needed to know about the woods around me.

I paused at the tree line, just above a road, cocking my ears to make sure no car was hurtling toward me. Satisfied, I gave a massive leap that nearly carried me across to the other side and then scrambled up the slight embankment there. Above me, an owl hooted in a tree, one night predator acknowledging another.

I didn't stop to question how I knew where I was going. I was being pulled north by some urge that guided my steps and kept me quickening my pace. Given a little practice, I could have run all night without tiring. But this was new to me, and after a while, I began to break from my easy rhythm. I had no sense of how much time had passed or how much distance I had covered, but the pads of my paws were sore, and I was loping unsteadily along the side of the road when I heard the sound of a car slowing down. It was one of those cars with flashing lights—a police car, I remembered. Lifting my head, I froze when the car stopped and a man got out. He shone a flashlight over the woods, and I tensed, about to make a break for it.

"Wait."

I hesitated, because the voice was familiar, and had pleasant associations. Friend. Not pack, but not completely alien, either. As the man came into view, however, he was not exactly a sight to reassure the wary. Nearly seven feet tall, with a hawklike nose and eyes hidden by the brim of his Stetson hat, the sheriff of Northside stood as still as a statue, assessing the situation. "You're from Northside." It wasn't a question.

I took a hesitant step forward, whining a little in the back of my throat. Emmet—that was his name, I remembered—knelt down, reaching into the inside breast pocket of his uniform jacket.

"Hungry?" His voice was a low rumble, a baritone so deep that it was hard to understand him. He held out the beef jerky and I advanced, eyeing him warily. "It's okay, fella—or are you a girl?"

I lunged for the jerky, and Emmet didn't try to stop me. Safely out of his long arm's reach, I gobbled up the meat, then licked my chops.

"You Red's girl?" I stared at him, shocked that he could recognize me in this form, and then Emmet tilted his hat back and I caught a glimpse of the arcane symbols carved into his forehead. "Thought so." He seemed to think things over, then pulled his hat back down. "I will not punish you for what you did to that boy back there."

I growled at that, and began to back up.

"Got a call in over the car radio about a wolf attack," Emmet said casually. "Wondered if it might be Magda or your ex."

I growled again, because I was having trouble sorting through all my reactions. Part of me just wanted to lick

Emmet's big, work-roughened hands. Part of me wanted to beat a hasty retreat.

"But if *you* bit someone, it was self-defense." I realized there was something foreign about the sheriff's intonation, less than an accent, just the trace of something that told me English was not his first language. He reached into his jacket and produced another piece of jerky. As I grabbed it, I realized that I was no longer fully in wolf form. On second thought, maybe I hadn't been completely lupine to begin with, because I hadn't lost as much of my human consciousness as I had in the past. Maybe this was a result of changing before the full moon, or maybe it was something else.

"Want a drink?" Emmet passed me a bottle of ice-blue Gatorade and I drank it down, using my half-transformed hands. I'd never tasted Gatorade before, and was surprised at the taste—sweet and yet bitter, and so cold it numbed the back of my throat. As the cold burn of the liquid spread through my body, I felt calmer, more lucid—more human. Maybe it wasn't Gatorade. Maybe Northside sheriffs carried magic potions the way ordinary sheriffs carried guns.

At the thought of some unknown substance working in my body, I shivered with anxiety. I'm not exactly a casual drug user; aside from the one time I'd smoked a joint with Red last year, I never touched anything stronger than wine. I even debated long and hard before taking an aspirin. Red wasn't a big marijuana smoker, although he did use it ritually at the solstices—outside, where the smoke wouldn't affect me. I still wasn't sure why I'd decided to get high with Red that one time, back when he and Jackie had come to have dinner with Hunter and me. It still amazed me that I'd done it.

"Stop fretting," said the sheriff, capping the bottle and putting it back in a pack slung over his chest. "I didn't dope you up, if that's what you're thinking."

I nodded, to show I'd understood, and breathed a sigh of relief.

"Well, there was a drop of wormwood in there, just to take the edge off you. In the jerky, too."

I turned to him, alarmed. Wormwood, wasn't that the substance that made absinthe so lethal?

"It's in vermouth, too, and you don't see people dying from martinis." The sheriff's mouth remained unsmiling, but I sensed that he was amused. "Besides, you don't feel so much like biting me in the arm now, do you? Wormwood's a cerebral stimulant—your man Red taught me that."

I had to admit, he had a point. In addition to my thoughts, my hands had become more human, hours and hours before I would ordinarily shift back. Well, now I had something else to worry about: whether or not I'd stop changing before I lost all my fur. I didn't feel like being naked with the sheriff, and besides, it was cold outside.

As if reading my mind, Emmet nodded. "Snow's coming," he said, almost to himself. Then he looked at me as if I were a person and not a wolf and said, "I can give you a ride home, Dr. Barrow."

Something about the way he was deliberately looking me in the eye made me look down at myself. I squeaked, crossing my arms over my breasts, which were visible, though a fair bit furrier than usual.

"Here." Emmet shrugged off his jacket and handed it to me. "Go on and wear that."

"Thanks," I said, but it came out as a soft woof. His jacket came down to my knees and smelled of moist earth, a smell of spring in winter. My gaze flew up to his face.

"Come," he ordered, and I followed him obediently into the car.

*   *   *

As we drove, I checked myself out in the passenger's side mirror. I looked like a circus freak—Abra the wolf girl. I ran a furry finger down the bridge of my nose, feeling as self-conscious as an adolescent. And in a way, being caught midtransition was like adolescence: I never knew what new variation of me I would have to present to the world.

"Don't worry about it."

Easy for you to say, I thought, but my muzzle wasn't built for speaking.

"Want some music?" Not taking his eyes off the road, the sheriff opened the top of his right armrest and pulled out a CD. Outside, the snow had begun to fall steadily, and some optical trick of the headlights made it appear as though we were driving into a tunnel of light. "You up to something a little different than you're used to?"

I nodded, and Emmet turned on a CD that wailed sonorously to an unfamiliar rhythm. I couldn't tell if the nasal singer was male or female, or whether the song was about the glory of God or the glory of some elusive lover, but clearly this was not an easy relationship, as the chorus was a prolonged moan.

"You want me to turn it off?"

I shook my head. Actually, the tune was beginning to grow on me, and I had to fight the urge to howl along. Glancing at the sheriff's swarthy, saturnine face, I realized that he probably wasn't Native American, as I'd assumed.

Maybe he was an Arab. I'd heard an NPR radio program about Lebanese and Syrians who had settled in the American west a hundred years earlier, becoming peddlers or opening restaurants that sold kibbe and shawarma along with Texas barbecue. Then I glanced up at the amulet hanging from the rearview mirror, emblazoned with the Star of David.

Suddenly I made the connection. That tattoo I'd glimpsed on the sheriff's forehead—those were Hebrew letters. The skin on the back of my neck crawled, because I had just remembered that one of my best friends in high school had told me that it was against Jewish law to get a tattoo. And Emmet's tattoos had a tribal look. Someone had gouged a deep channel with a rough tool before applying dye.

There was something very strange about the sheriff, even by Northside standards.

"Open that," said Emmet, indicating the glove compartment in front of me.

Half holding my breath, I did as he said. There, wrapped in a white, bloodstained cloth, was a bundle about five inches long and two inches wide.

"Take it." The sheriff's voice was uninflected, without censure or compassion. "I found it on the ground next to those boys."

Oh, God. A confused memory of flesh and blood flashed through my mind. I wasn't entirely sure whether I had done what the memory implied, and I didn't want to know.

"Go on. It's yours."

I understood: What I did in wolf form was still my responsibility when I was human. Hands trembling, I glanced over at the sheriff's stony face and then unwrapped the bundle. My new glasses spilled out onto my lap, and I gasped.

The statuelike man beside me made a strange, gravelly sound deep in the back of his throat. It took me a moment, and then comprehension dawned. He was laughing. Not funny, I thought, glaring at the sheriff as I wiped the glasses clean with the cloth.

Emmet gave another dry chuckle as he turned onto the road leading to Red's and my cabin. After that, I felt almost relaxed with the seven-foot sheriff. Having a sense of humor, even a poor one, humanized him.

Emmet parked on the road, not wanting to get stuck, and as we walked toward the cabin, our footsteps were instantly covered by the rapidly falling snow. Up to four feet was predicted in the higher elevations, according to Emmet, but he said he wouldn't be surprised if it was more like six feet. Red wasn't home—no surprise, really, given the pull of the nearly full moon—and Emmet helped me light the kerosene lamps. After that, he set about building a fire in the fireplace with his dinner plate–sized hands, hunching over to avoid hitting his head on the ceiling beams. He did not, I noticed, remove his cowboy hat.

When I was dressed in sweatpants and a flannel shirt, I handed Emmet back his jacket. With clothes on my body and glasses on my face, I had pushed the change back enough to speak. "Thanks," I said, the words still a little hard to form. I ran my tongue over my canines, which were sticking up a bit too far.

"Just doing my job, ma'am." He tipped the brim of his hat, and I caught the glint of humor in his half-hidden eyes. As Emmet walked to the door in his peculiar, listing gait, I realized that the sheriff of Northside was doing a very passable John Wayne imitation, from the unusual, clipped cadence of his speech to the slightly unbalanced rhythm of his walk.

But it was only after he scraped the snow from his squad car and drove off that I realized the strangest thing of all about the sheriff. He hadn't reacted at all to the estrus pheromones that had been turning all the other men I met into slavering beasts. Which meant that he was either profoundly gay, or something else entirely.

SEVENTEEN

◐○○ After an hour, I faced it: I wasn't going to sleep. My body felt exhausted and restless, and my mind kept racing from one conundrum to another. Lying with my eyes closed, I had spent nearly forty minutes worrying about free-roaming manitous the way I used to worry about nuclear meltdowns at the Indian Point power plant. Trying to think about something else, I'd fretted about how close I'd come to being raped, and then agonized about how close I'd come to killing someone. From there it was a short jump to questioning whether I was in control of my hormones, which led me to pondering the state of my relationship with Red. At this point, I would have given anything to just go wolf and stop thinking, but whatever the good sheriff had given me had inhibited the change. It had also taken the edge off my desire, but it hadn't taken it away completely. Which made me think that what I really needed was some mindless activity to soothe my nerves and quiet my brain.

If Red did walk through the door, I thought, I was going to rip his clothes off first, and ask questions later.

Throwing off the covers, I sighed and reached for my glasses. There were times when I really missed having a television set. You could live a fairly modern life without electricity—as Red pointed out, most people in Ireland

and Wales and parts of England had been doing without it until long after World War II. But you couldn't watch television, and at the moment, I wanted the distraction of talking heads.

I picked up the biography of Jane Goodall that I was currently reading, but couldn't focus on the words. Throwing the thick hardcover onto the bed, I paced restlessly from one side of the cabin to the other, wondering where Red was, and what he was doing out on a cold Friday evening in January. Rocky the raccoon was missing, too, but of course, I'd been expecting that.

Knowing it was futile, I still checked all of Rocky's hiding places—in between the sheets and blankets in the armoire, in the cupboard with the good plates, in the bed next to my pillow. But he was gone, and there was no recent scent of him. Maybe, I thought, he'd run into the woods that night and just never returned. Maybe he'd found an older raccoon to mentor him.

Or maybe Red had caught and killed him for a late-night snack. Which made me wonder, once again: Where the hell was he?

From her perch atop the armoire, Ladyhawke watched me with one golden eye. For the first time since she'd come home, she didn't attempt to pull out my hair when I passed by, and when I glanced up at her, she cocked her head in a way that seemed almost endearing.

"Do you want me to pet you?" I'd seen Red do it, but hadn't dared attempt it myself. Yet suddenly, I felt sure that all I had ever needed to do was approach the bird without fear or hesitation. And after my night of misadventures, I felt in need of a little creature comfort. Well, what I really needed was to be held and stroked until my nerves stopped jangling, but even a soft touch would be soothing. Reaching up to scratch the one-eyed raptor's chest, I said, "You're really quite a lovely bird," just as her beak closed on my finger. We both screamed at each other, and there was a little explosion of feathers as I took a swing at her.

"That does it," I snarled. "Out! Out!" I opened the front door, and a gust of wind blew in a dusting of snow. "Go on! Fly on out!" I held the door open, but Ladyhawke just gave an aggrieved shake of her feathers and then hunkered down into herself. I took a broom from the closet and tried to shoo her off her perch, but Ladyhawke just retreated, squawking furiously.

"Fine," I said, glaring at the puffed up bird, who glared back at me just as fiercely. I closed the door on the swirling snow. "But you come near me, and I'll twist your birdbrain head off."

Ladyhawke squawked shrilly, causing me to think unkind thoughts about my absent lover. If he'd had to turn feral and kill one of our house animals, the least he could have done was go for the annoying one.

Still cursing the bird, I ran some cold water on my finger and wrapped it in a wet washcloth. Luckily, the skin hadn't been broken.

Collapsing back onto the bed, I wondered what Lilliana had wound up doing. Heading back to the city, presumably, wishing she'd never gotten herself involved in my problems. I thought about calling her, but realized that my cell phone was still in my purse, which was still in the limo, along with my new clothes.

Oh, well. At least we wouldn't lack for things to talk about when we got together again.

Reaching over, I looked through the other books on my bedside table. I always liked to have three books going at once, and in addition to the Jane Goodall I was reading *Middlemarch* and an erotic thriller that involved the Russian mafia and a lot of flimsily justified bondage. Opening up the thriller, I started to read a scene in which the anguished heroine is tied to a beam by the moody hero, who mistakenly believes she is working with the bad guys.

Impatient, I flipped back to a previous scene, burrowing under the covers as the hero dragged the heroine into a bedroom with a hidden camera. Slipping my hand under the waistband of my sweatpants, I tried to relieve some of my tension, with no success. I didn't want to be touching myself, I wanted to be touched. I didn't want the gentle knowledge of my own fingers, I wanted to surrender myself to somebody else's hands.

Maybe if I just slipped off the sweatpants. Perspiring with the effort, I managed to get myself even more wound up, but release remained tantalizingly out of reach.

Closing my eyes, I found the right rhythm and was just closing my eyes when someone pounded on the front door. My first thought was that it was Red, and my heart began pounding in excitement and trepidation. And then, as I hastily pulled my sweatpants right side out and shoved my legs back inside, I realized that Red would have had a key.

"Who is it?" The reply was muffled by the wind, but my hearing was still more acute than usual, so I knew the answer.

It was Hunter. My almost ex-husband.

I pressed my hand against the wood of the door, torn with indecision. I hadn't been alone with Hunter in over a year, and part of me wanted to speak to him again. We had dated in college, drifted apart, become friends and roommates and finally married, and nothing in our long, amicable history had prepared me for becoming adversaries. Sometimes, in my fantasies, I asked Hunter how we had come to this. In some versions, I imagined that we managed one last transformation and became friends again.

But the reality was that there was no explaining away

Hunter's betrayal, and no possible reconciliation. With Magda by his side, Hunter had broken into my mother's home and hurt her. If I hadn't prevented them from taking it further, I don't believe they would have stopped themselves. Hunter might blame his behavior on the disease—it wasn't me, honey, it was the beast talking—but I knew that he'd never liked my mother. Maybe you never really knew a man until you'd met his wolf.

From the other side of the door, I heard Hunter's voice calling my name again. "Abra, I know you can hear me."

"What do you want?"

There was no reply, and against all my better judgment, I opened the door a crack. "Hunter? What is it? Why did you come here?" Then I saw why he wasn't responding.

His sharply handsome features bestial with the nearness of the change, Hunter gazed up at me with pain-dulled eyes. He was slumped awkwardly on the ground as white flakes of snow settled on his dark head. Despite the cold, I could smell blood, thick and fresh, the blood of something wounded but not yet dead.

Crap. Just what I needed on the night my hormones went into overdrive: my lying, cheating, seductive bastard of an almost ex-husband. "So," Hunter said, "are you going to let me in, or watch me bleed to death out here?"

Red always says that when someone offers you two unpleasant choices, select a third. But the wind was whipping up the snow as it fell, obscuring the line of trees just twenty feet away, and I couldn't come up with any other options. Not bothering to hide my irritation, I dragged my former husband over the threshold.

EIGHTEEN

◗○○ "Abra." Hunter's voice was rough with pain, but he gave me a weak smile.

"What were you doing out there?" I hadn't been able to haul him into a chair, so he was lying on the braided rug by the fireplace, shivering with cold and, I suspected, shock. He'd stopped making snarky comments, I noticed as I laid a blanket over the lower half of his body. Christ, trust Hunter to wear Italian leather in a blizzard. "No wonder you're freezing. Don't tell me. You decided to go out for an after-dinner stroll."

"Attacked." He could hardly get the word out through his chattering teeth.

"Where are you injured?"

"R . . . right arm. I th-think . . . it's bad."

It had been a long time since I'd tended Hunter, I thought as I took out a heavy scissors and began cutting through the leather of his coat. He didn't say anything; he just closed his eyes, as if keeping them open were too much effort. His skin was bone white. I snapped into medical mode, trying not to think about what kind of injury lay under his sleeve.

At one time, caring for Hunter had almost been a habit. In college, he'd come down with mono, and refused to stay in the infirmary for reasons he wouldn't discuss. His mother was dead, he said, and there was no one else at home to take care of him. Another time, years later, he came back from a trip to Africa with a combination of malaria and parasites that had nearly killed him.

I had loved him then, with a fierceness that made me queasy when he suffered. And there was my triumph in his recovery, when he was too weak to do anything but look up at me with love and devotion.

The problems started when he got better, and hardly looked at me at all.

Struggling with the scissors, I managed to cut partway through the jacket before having to take a break. Thanks to the sheriff's wormwood drink, I looked and felt human, but there was a fine tremor in my hands, and I didn't have complete fine motor control. When I started cutting again, Hunter winced. "I'm sorry if I'm hurting you."

"Liar." His dark eyes met mine, and despite the pain and tension, or maybe because of it, we both burst out laughing. It was the first time in over a year that we had been in accord, and it brought back memories. But the moment passed, and Hunter closed his eyes again, his chest rising and falling with his rapid, shallow breaths.

"All right. Let's get your jacket off you before you bleed out." I gritted my teeth and sawed through the leather with as much strength as I could muster. Hunter was silent, but he slumped when I finally split the sleeve in two and could pull the sides of the jacket away from his arm. I tried to be as careful as I could not to touch the wound while cutting through his shirt, so it was a few minutes before I could really see the whole arm. Putting down the scissors, I peeled the jacket and shirt away from Hunter's arm.

"How bad is it, Abs?"

"Well, you're not going to bleed to death right away,

but it's not pretty." The blood flow had slowed, which was good, but there were jagged teeth marks on his forearm, two of them deep enough to reveal the white gleam of bone underneath. Defensive wounds, I thought, the kind you get when you bring your arm up to protect your face. Whatever had tangled with him had also crushed the lower part of his arm, and I could see the tip of the ulna protruding from his skin. Without an X-ray, I couldn't tell if the break had been a clean one or not, but I suspected there was more than one fracture.

Hunter struggled to lift himself up onto his good elbow. "Is it broken?"

"Yes," I said simply, leaving out that the break was complex, compound, and probably comminuted. "Now, lie back down while I figure out what to do next." The bleeding wasn't too bad, but there wasn't much I could do besides icing and splinting the limb, and I was concerned that Hunter might need an operation to align the bones properly. "What happened? Was it manitou?"

Hunter looked puzzled. "Bear man," I clarified. "Or I guess it could be some other kind of combination. It seems we've got new shoppers at our local supernatural clearinghouse."

Hunter grunted as I irrigated the wound with saline. "Bear. He was on our property."

"So he just attacked you with no warning?"

"Arggh—Jesus, woman." Hunter grimaced as I finished cleaning his arm. "Talk about no warning."

"Sorry, I'm not used to patients who can talk."

Hunter smiled at the joke, then winced as I cracked a cold pack and pressed it against his arm, and I felt a rush of my old affection for him.

"So Bruin didn't talk to you at all?"

"Bruin?"

"That's what he told me to call him. I've run into him, too," I said, but instead of replying, Hunter just lay there on the floor, his eyes closed. "Hey," I said, touching his face. "You still with me?"

"Hurts to breathe," Hunter said, and I cursed as I realized I hadn't really checked him over properly.

"Shit, you probably have a broken rib . . . Come on, Hunter, stay with me." I didn't say it out loud, but I was also wondering if my former husband hadn't sustained some internal injuries. His face was going gray now, and the minor blood loss from his arm didn't justify that. Shit. I didn't have the facilities to treat Hunter for anything serious here, and with a blizzard outside, calling an ambulance to take him to Poughkeepsie might take too long.

There was only one good option left.

"We're going to have to get you to change," I said, sitting back on my heels. The shift took place on a cellular level, and accelerated healing.

"Too tired."

"I know you are, Hunter, but if you don't change, there's a chance your injuries are going to kill you." Throwing the blanket aside, I pulled off his snow boots and socks, then hesitated, my hands on the snap of his jeans. "Hunter?"

He had passed out. Working as quickly as I could, I tugged off his jeans, and there he was, the man I had once loved, naked on the rug. His skin was clammy and there were livid bruises forming along his abdomen, but despite everything, he was still a handsome man, tall and broad, his chest hairier than it had been twelve years ago, in college. "Hunter," I said, lightly slapping his face. "Wake up! Look at me."

He opened his eyes. "Abs." My name was barely a whisper.

"You have to change, Hunter. I think you might have

internal injuries, and I can't do anything about that here."

Hunter lifted his good hand toward my face, then let it drop. "Sorry to disappoint," he said, then groaned.

"What is it? Is it your chest? Is the pain getting worse? Hunter!" But he had passed out again. *Shit.* And then I remembered something so basic, it seemed impossible I could have forgotten.

You can't shift without being in an altered state. Yes, the full moon was part of the equation, and so was nudity, but the final ingredient was a release of inhibitions. Usually, the release came right along with the moon and the nudity, but not always. I would have thought pain was a disinhibitor, too, but either Hunter was in too much pain, not enough, or he was holding on to his control.

Looking down at Hunter's inert form, I racked my brains for a solution. Extreme arousal, in any form, would do it. Excitement, anger—lust. Since it didn't seem smart to pick a fight with an invalid, that only left one choice. Pulling off my own clothing, I carefully aligned my body with his. I didn't feel aroused; I felt like I was trying to seduce an unconscious man. I could have tried to do this with clothes on, but sometimes one lycanthrope's change can trigger another's. I wasn't sure if the wormwood potion had worn off enough yet, but I figured it made sense to try everything. I put my hand between Hunter's legs, and gripped him.

Hunter moaned a little, and I felt the first stirrings of his response in my palm. That's it, I thought, remembering how he liked to be touched. I bit him, lightly, on the earlobe, and Hunter's eyelids flew open. "Ab," he panted. "Can't . . . hurts."

"You have to change," I told him again. "Forget the pain. Just let go, and let yourself change."

I saw his eyes change as comprehension dawned, and

then he was holding me, kissing me, and for a moment, it was strange, because it had been so long, a year of living with another man, and then it wasn't strange, because my body remembered.

I felt Hunter's erection press between my thighs, and to my surprise, I felt the warm rush of my own response. The wormwood was wearing off.

"God," Hunter moaned, "your smell . . . didn't notice before . . ."

"Yes, Hunter, let go," I encouraged him, wanting him to change now, not wanting to go any farther. This was bad enough, but to allow that final intimacy felt like a real betrayal of Red and our relationship.

"Abs . . . always . . . loved you."

I stroked his thick, dark, sweat-dampened hair back from his brow as Hunter thrust himself against my hand, again and again. With my own heat rising, I felt muzzy, boneless, adrift in my own skin, until Hunter reached around with his good hand, and brought my face in for a kiss. With that tender touch and his familiar scent surrounding me, I felt the ghost of old love brush over my skin.

And then the ghost possessed me, flooding desire through my veins. My naked skin slid against his, my breasts felt so sensitive as they grazed his hard chest that I cried out. You're going to regret this, said a little voice in my head, but I ignored it. I was on fire, and too much animal to think about what came after.

"My ribs . . . Abra . . . help me . . ."

I moved to straddle Hunter's hips and then paused. This was not my favorite position, and for a moment, I felt a flash of cold, clear thought: This is a bad idea. But then I could feel Hunter probing at my entrance, and the combination of sheer animal lust and inescapable familiarity overwhelmed me.

And then he pushed inside.

"God," Hunter moaned. It had been over a year since we had last made love, and with a little shock I realized that my body had adjusted to Red's larger size. I rocked my hips, and Hunter threw back his head again, gasping in pleasure. But my flesh felt oversensitive, aching, and even though arousal kept me sliding myself against Hunter, release—of this sexual tension, of my too-tight human skin—remained just out of reach.

Fucking sheriff and his fucking wormwood.

His hand on my hips, Hunter pushed me against him, directing me. "I can't get any leverage, you have to move."

I rocked against him, aware of a rising irritation. His words, the fit of his body, my position on top of him—everything felt wrong. *Not the right mate.* It was a body thought, straight from the bundle of nerves at the base of the spine. I was no longer aroused, I was disgusted, but having gotten myself into this, I didn't feel like I could just walk out in the middle.

"Yes, ah, Abra, yes, that's it," Hunter moaned, oblivious to my lack of involvement. "Oh, yes, Jesus, Magda's so rough, I've missed you so much, your softness, your . . . move faster now, yes, come on, girl." And then he slapped me on the ass, as if spurring on a reluctant horse.

That did it. With a burst of anger, I stood up, sliding off Hunter just as his spine began to bow and ripple with the change.

NINETEEN

◐○○ I locked myself in the bathroom, using a wash-cloth and cold water to clean myself off and wishing with all my heart for a shower. There was a whining sound from outside the door, and the scratch of claws on wood as Hunter begged to be allowed in.

"Go away," I said. "Leave me alone."

Hunter whined again and I stared at my own reflection in the mirror. In my new glasses, I didn't look like the same woman who had loved Hunter and would have done anything to keep him.

Funny, how changing eyeglass frames could change your whole look. I pulled my hair back into a bun at the back of my head. Now I looked sharp and clever and de-cisive, the kind of woman who would never be stupid enough to have sex with a man she didn't even respect. Crap, crap, crap. I couldn't believe how stupid I'd been. On the bright side, there couldn't be much of a chance of my getting pregnant, but still. I wasn't sure what dis-gusted me more: the thought that I'd nearly committed bestiality, or the fact that I'd just had sex with my bas-tard ex-husband. My only consolation was that being in estrus was like being drunk, except that there weren't any twelve-step programs for swearing off your own hormones. I scrubbed until I smelled clean to myself, but I still didn't *feel* clean.

Ugh. I couldn't believe what I'd done. I felt like divorcing myself.

"Abra? You okay in there?"

Oh, great, he was human again. The only thing worse than listening to him whine would be having to talk this thing out. Then I realized: He was human again. That shouldn't have been possible. "Hunter, how did you shift back?"

"I don't know. I found some weird-tasting jerky and ate it, and the next thing I knew, I was standing on two feet."

Ah, the sheriff's wormwood werewolf treats. "I'm assuming you're all healed?"

There was a pause. "Yes," he said.

I stared at my own unhappy eyes in the mirror. "Then please get the hell out of here."

I waited a few minutes, deliberately taking my time to get dressed in the clothes I'd grabbed off the floor in the other room. I brushed my hair out, pulling out strands as I yanked through the tangles and knots. It didn't bother me. I felt like tearing my hair out. When I finally opened the bathroom door, he was still there, wearing his jeans and looking through the bookcase in a way that made my hackles rise.

"I thought you were leaving."

"I just was looking through your books and realized that some of them are actually mine. I was wondering where the Conrad had gone to. I was just thinking of rereading *Heart of Darkness*."

"Take it."

"Actually, I think I'll leave it here." He smiled, all charm and seduction. "Gives me an excuse to come back and visit." Hunter's hand came to rest on the small of my back.

God, he really was clueless. "Move it or lose it."

In response, Hunter moved his hand in lazy circles at

the base of my spine, slipping under my sweatpants until they skimmed the top of my buttocks. "There. I'm moving it."

I took his thumb and twisted it in a move Red had shown me. "Hunter. Let me make this perfectly clear. What just happened . . . that was a mistake. I don't want to repeat it. Ever." I gave him his hand back and folded my arms over my chest.

"Aw, come on, give me a break. I was injured. But it couldn't have been that bad." Hunter grinned rakishly, and I caught a glimpse of the Ivy League boy I had fallen in love with over a decade earlier.

"I'm not joking, Hunter. Now please, you have to go. I need to clean the floor before your blood stains it." And I needed to find some way to get rid of the scent of sweat and semen before Red came home. Suddenly anxious, I bustled around, gathering up the remnants of Hunter's shirt and jacket. "Keep it or toss it?"

"Toss it. I can't see either Magda or myself getting them mended—she's not domestic like you."

"Is that supposed to be a dig?" I stuffed Hunter's torn and stained clothes into a plastic bag, then double knotted it. The plastic would mask the scent a little, so Red wasn't overpowered by it the minute he walked in the door.

"It was *supposed* to be a compliment. Sometimes I think I never appreciated all the little ways you took care of me." Hunter's face softened as he added, "I think about you, you know."

I raked my hands through my hair, feeling frantic. "Hunter, you need to go home. Now."

"In case *he* comes home? Is that what's worrying you?" Hunter gave a harsh laugh, reaching into the bookcase and picking out a Louis L'Amour Western. "Christ," he said, holding it up as if it were proof of infidelity, "how can you live with a man who enjoys this crap?"

"Because he doesn't *give* me crap." I plucked the book from his fingers and replaced it. "And instead of going on about how much I love him, he tells me how much he loves me." No way was I confessing any reservations about my relationship with Red to Hunter.

"So that's it. This time around, you get to be the one in charge." Hunter rubbed his chin. "That's why he's good for you. You're more sure of yourself. More confident of your own attractiveness." He paused, and then added, "except that you're frightened of him right now. You're terrified about how he'll react if he finds me here."

"Hunter, clearly you're having your own issues with Magda right now, but I'm not going to discuss my love life with you." I wet a rag in the sink, then walked back over to where Hunter sat by the fireplace. Kneeling down to scrub at the bloodstain, I felt a wave of dizziness. I closed my eyes for a moment, fighting the slow rotation of the room around me.

"You all right?"

I opened my eyes, swallowed, and couldn't quite answer.

"Hell," said Hunter, sounding surprised, "You're as close to the change as I am. Maybe closer."

I looked up at him. He'd knelt down next to me, still shirtless, and I saw that he'd put on weight in the past year, most of it muscle. The scent of his warm, bare flesh was familiar, and not unpleasant. "Damn." I stood up, fighting another wave of light-headedness. Opening Red's drawer, I pulled out an old flannel shirt and threw it at Hunter. "Here," I said. "Put this on and go."

Hunter caught the shirt and looked at it consideringly. "It's too small. Red's kind of on the short side, for a guy."

I gritted my teeth. "Put it on anyway."

Hunter slid his arms through the shirt, but left it unbuttoned. "I thought Red didn't want me getting my smell on his stuff."

"Trust me, he'd rather you wear his shirt than walk around half naked."

"If half naked's a problem, I could always take off all my clothes."

"God, no." I braced myself against the dresser. The thought of getting naked with him again made me feel slightly nauseated.

Hunter stood up and closed the distance between us. "You only think that from the neck up."

"Well, that's the part that makes the decisions." I didn't want to insult Hunter, but my stomach was really rebelling now, telling me in the most visceral way possible that he was not the one.

"Or maybe not," said Hunter, reaching down to cup my crotch.

"Stop it, Hunter, I said no!" Acting on instinct, I shoved him so hard that he bounced off the dresser, upsetting an oil lamp.

"Oh, crap," I said, but managed to catch the lamp and set it right before anything caught on fire. From atop her perch, Ladyhawke flapped and gave an angry squawk. I wondered if, in a pinch, she might actually come to my defense.

"Jesus, woman, what is wrong with you?" Hunter raked one hand through his floppy brown hair, a gesture I had once adored.

I crossed my hands over my chest, trying to breathe through the cramping in my stomach. "You had a fight with Magda, didn't you? That's why you were wandering around out here. What did you think, I'd take you back?"

"I figured you sort of owed me, since in a sense it was

partially your fault." The trace of a British accent was back in Hunter's voice. At one time, I thought it was a remnant of the time he'd spent in England as a teenager. These days, I felt pretty sure it was an affectation, since it seemed to come and go.

"All right, that's it," I said. "Time for you," I poked him in the chest, "to go." I pointed at the door.

"You didn't ask me to explain," Hunter murmured, curling his fingers around my hand and pulling me against his chest.

"There is no explanation! Hunter, your problems with your girlfriend have nothing to do with me. You left me, remember?" Using both hands, I started to push him toward the door.

Hunter braced his legs. "Not true, strictly speaking."

"Fine, I left you after I learned that you'd been screwing Magda *and* the cute barmaid from Moondoggie's."

Hunter shook his head, looking bemused. "You know, I don't understand your attitude about that. Magda doesn't care about my little dalliances."

"Congratulations. You're soul mates. Wouldn't want to keep you apart." I reached for the door handle.

"She's jealous of *you*, though." He said it seductively, as if he were offering me a compliment.

"Not my problem, Hunter. Although I'd appreciate it if you let her know it's not me standing in the way of a divorce."

Hunter's eyes, which had begun to lighten and subtly alter shape, suddenly went dark and human. "Don't you have any regrets, Abra? We've been through so much together. And when you were pregnant . . ."

"When we thought I was pregnant, you refused to touch me because you were busy screwing Magda on the sly."

Hunter put his hand on my shoulder. "Only because I didn't want to hurt you, or the baby, Abs. Don't you ever think, if only our transition had occurred a little closer together . . . or, hell, maybe even if they'd been further apart . . ." his voice trailed off.

"What I think is that if you hadn't become a were-wolf, I might never have noticed what a pig you really are." I opened the door, and snow swirled in. It was almost a blizzard, but Hunter could handle that. "Now, I want you to leave."

"Like this?" He indicated the flimsy protection of Red's open flannel shirt, the trickle of blood from the wound on his arm, the snow piling up in the gap of the open door. Crap. He must have reopened the cut when he bounced off the wall. Then I realized how I was being played.

"Nice try. Just step outside and take off your pants—you'll heal when you shift. And you're not going to freeze when you've got your fur coat on."

Hunter's eyes remained fixed on mine: a challenge. "Suppose I say I don't want to?"

We stood there for a moment, at an impasse. Snow blew into my eyes, but I didn't want to close the door. Hunter had his stubborn face on, and I didn't know how to convince him to leave. If we had been in wolf form, then the differences in our size and strength would not have been as great.

And with that thought, the balance of power shifted. I don't know what Hunter had seen in my face, but he suddenly reached out and grabbed my hair in a thick bunch at the back of my neck. "I've been too nice, haven't I?" His fist tightened on my hair, not really hurting, but tugging enough to control me. "I forgot the kind of games you like to play." Using my hair as a leash, Hunter brought me in closer. "My little submissive girl. I've missed you."

I struggled in his grip. "Hunter, I'm not playing anything with you."

"A little defiance—I like that. What do you say to the idea of being forced against your will, pretty girl?" He said it, not as a threat, but in a seductive whisper. It had been a long time since we'd spiced up our love life with a little role playing, and Hunter had forgotten some of the rules. Sounding like a sleazy Don Juan was definitely a deal breaker. On the other hand, real menace wouldn't have worked with me, either. The truth was, you couldn't play sex and power games with someone you didn't trust. Or at least, I couldn't. And I didn't trust Hunter anymore.

Misinterpreting my silence, Hunter grinned wolfishly. "What do you say to me having my wicked way with you?"

My reply was cut short by the creaking of the door as it was pushed wide open.

We both turned to see the snow-covered figure standing in the doorway. "I'd say you'd be making a mistake." It was Red, looking like Davy Crockett in a fur hat, his sheepskin collar pulled up against the snow and his twelve-gauge Browning automatic slung over his shoulder. Hunter had released his grip on my hair the minute the door had opened, and I nearly threw myself into Red's arms with relief. Then I saw the expression on his face, or rather the lack of one, and realized what Red's hat was made out of: raccoon fur.

TWENTY

◐○○ Red stamped his feet, dislodging snow, and then gave a doglike shake before stepping over the threshold. He held the gun angled low, but his hands were positioned so that he could easily swing it up and level it at Hunter. Or at me. "Mind telling me what he's doing here?"

"Pushing his luck."

Red kept his eyes on my face. "Should I shoot him for you?"

If there had been a hint of Red's usual wry humor in his face or voice, I would have pretended to consider it. As it was, I said, "There's no need, Red."

Glancing at Hunter, Red moved past him, toward the fire. "You're both wearing my shirts," he said, almost conversationally.

"His shirt was covered with blood, and I had to cut it off. He needed first aid," I added, trying to emphasize that this had not been a social call.

Red grunted and held his hands up to the fire, ostentatiously presenting us with his back. "And did he get some?"

I swallowed, thinking fast. If he were close to his own change, Red would be able to smell everything that had happened. Despite my attempts at cleaning up, he would be able to detect the traces of every bodily fluid that had been spilled. But Red was in human form, and he had been out in the cold for a long time, possibly hours. Maybe his nose was numb.

"I patched up his wound," I allowed, glancing at Hunter, who was grinning in a most provocative way. I made the gesture of drawing my finger across my throat.

"Yes, it was purely a medical situation," Hunter said, his tone suggesting the opposite. I shot him a warning look. Red had overlooked my moment of strangeness with Malachy, but this situation felt very different. I didn't think Red would be offering my former husband any refreshments.

After another moment, Red rested his rifle within easy reach before pulling the coonskin hat off his head. "He staying, or going?"

"Going," I said, at the same time as Hunter said, "staying."

Red took off his damp sheepskin coat and laid it over a chair. "Going would be better."

"For you, or for her?" Hunter dragged a chair closer to the fire. "Even though we're not married, I still care about Abra." He made a show of rotating his left arm as though it were still sore. "Even when she hurts me, I don't retaliate."

I didn't fall for it; if that little brush with the wall really had bruised him, it would heal within the next half hour.

"I'm not going to hurt her, if that's what you're implying," Red said, struggling to unlace his snow boots with stiff fingers.

"Here," I said, "let me help you." I knelt by his feet and pulled at the snow- and ice-encrusted laces. When I looked up, Red's face was carefully blank.

"Thanks." He pulled off the boots and I saw that his socks were soaked through. A few of his toes were white, and I sucked in a sharp breath.

"That looks like the beginnings of frostbite. We have to warm you up slowly."

Red looked past me at Hunter. "Tell him to leave, first."

I didn't hesitate. "Hunter, leave. I appreciate your concern, but it's misplaced." Placing my hands on Red's icy feet, I tried to think how best to warm them. "Can you feel anything?" I brought his feet under my shirt, against my bare breasts.

"Not yet." His voice was perfectly even, as if his feet were resting on a hot water bottle instead of against my bare flesh.

"This is going to take too long. We need to get your feet immersed in some lukewarm water." I grabbed an afghan from the back of the couch and wrapped it around Red's feet.

As I ran water in the kettle, Hunter approached me, keeping a careful eye on Red. "Is it just me, or is he acting a little peculiar? I know if you put my toes where you put his toes, I'd manage to crack a smile."

"Hunter, please get out of here." Now that Red was warming up, he had begun to sniff the air. So far, he looked puzzled rather than angry, but I didn't know how long that would last. Sex, like blood, leaves a strong olfactory footprint.

"I'm concerned. He's not exactly acting like his friendly Texan self, is he?"

Red fixed Hunter with an unfriendly look. "Don't push it tonight, Hunter." His voice was very quiet.

"Hunter, take a look at him." I put the kettle on the wood-burning stove. "He's half frozen."

Hunter jerked his thumb in Red's direction. "Ah, yes. And is that why he's glowering at you like that?"

I had to do a little two-step to get around Hunter, and Red gave a low growl of irritation. "No, I think your presence has more to do with that." Kneeling back

down by Red, I said, "Here, give me your feet again."
Wrapping my fingers around his chilled flesh, I realized
that the bottom of his jeans were wet. "Okay. We're
going to need to get your pants off."

Red's eyes met mine. "If I start stripping, I might just
decide to take a bite out of your ex over there."

"Hunter," I said, thoroughly exasperated now. "I've
already asked you to leave."

"I'm just worried about you," he said, and Red gave
a short, harsh laugh.

"I know what's worrying you," he said, beginning to
stand. "You're worried I'm going to breed her, and
you'll have missed your chance."

I put my hands on my hips. "First of all, I'm nobody's
prize bitch, and nobody's breeding me. Second of all,
Hunter doesn't even want kids. Third of all, Red, you
shouldn't walk on frostbitten feet." I might as well have
been a Chihuahua yapping for all the attention the men
paid me.

"I don't like your tone, old man," said Hunter, in his
most aggravatingly faux British accent.

"Let me rephrase it." Red pulled his wool sweater
over his head. "She's in heat, and you want her. But you
left over a year ago, and Abra's mine now."

"I rather think that depends on what the lady says."
Hunter turned to me, and I realized that for some reason, my werewolf of an almost ex was more in control
than my shapeshifter lover. Something was very wrong
here. The moon was supposed to be riding us, but Red
was a very different sort of beast.

And something else was wrong, because for the first
time since I'd met him, I felt a faint, nervous tension
building inside of me. To my surprise, Red's air of quiet
menace was giving me butterflies in my stomach.

At that moment, the kettle started whistling, and I
poured the boiling water into a big cast-iron pot that we

sometimes used to bathe rescued animals. "How about you help me bring this over to Red, Hunter, and then leave?"

Hunter lifted the heavy pot as though it weighed nothing. "Just tell me where to put it."

"By the fire," I said, filling the kettle with cold water. "Thanks."

"And now you can leave," said Red through gritted teeth as he pulled his pants off.

"Oh, I don't know—Abra might need more help." Hunter came up to me and took the kettle from my hands. "Put this on the stove?"

"Thanks," I said. "By the time he gets in, it'll probably have cooled down." I took a scissors from the drawer and began cutting through the frayed hem of Red's jeans. "I don't suppose you want to tell me what you've been up to," I said softly.

"Not while he's here." When I paused in my cutting, Red took the two sides of his jeans and ripped them clear up to the thigh.

From the other side of the room, Hunter gave a derisive snort. "Sounds familiar, doesn't it, Abra?" He lifted the steaming kettle off the stove and walked over to pour it into the pot. "Funny, isn't it, how you can start a whole new relationship with an entirely different sort of person and still wind up battling the same sorts of issues?"

"It's not the same," said Red, looking tired. "Tell him." The tattered remnants of his jeans clung to his lean, muscular thighs, the faded denim cupping his masculine bulge.

"I think she's lost the power of speech, old man."

Confused, I turned back to Hunter, only to find myself distracted by the contrast between the two men's bodies. Hunter's chest, longer and broader than Red's, was heavily furred with dark chest hair. "What?"

I tried to say something, but found myself touching Hunter's chest instead. Whatever the sheriff had given me must be wearing off.

Red took me by the shoulders and spun me around. "Abra," he said warningly, his hands tightening on my shoulders. He was angry. I had never really seen him angry before. I moistened my lips with my tongue, suddenly nervous.

"She likes playing the poor, defenseless female, doesn't she?" I opened my mouth to tell Hunter to shut up, but Red's hands pressed down, telling me wordlessly to hold my tongue. "But you're not really a very aggressive male, are you, Red? You're more like the scout, or the third in command—everybody's good old buddy in the pack."

"I'm not your buddy, Hunter." Red's eyes were heavy-lidded, deceptively casual. His arm slid around my back. "I'm not your pack."

"My goodness. Is that a challenge?" Hunter gave a mock shiver and walked slowly toward us. When he was only a couple of feet away, he stared pointedly down at the smaller man and drawled, "I'm shaking in my boots."

"Thing is, I don't challenge," said Red. "I don't announce when I'm about to attack." From across the room, the red-tailed hawk gave an agitated flutter from atop her perch. Hunter glanced at her, but Red ignored her completely. "I do kill," he added conversationally.

"I see," said Hunter, heavy on the sarcasm. "Not very sporting of you, is it?"

Red shrugged. "Killing isn't a sport."

"True enough. You know, I have an idea," said Hunter, a little too brightly.

"What?"

I glanced at the raccoon hat sitting on the floor, and wanted to tell Hunter not to push his luck. But before I could say anything, he put his hands around my waist. "Why not just share her? Then there's no need to fight."

A strange passivity seemed to have settled over me. I knew that between us, Red and I had the strength to stop Hunter whenever we wanted. But for some reason, I wasn't stopping him yet. Not because I wanted my ex-husband—I'd scratched that itch, and it had given me a rash. And suddenly I knew why I was holding my breath, waiting for Red's next move, instead of hauling back and tearing a chunk out of Hunter.

This was a test—a test for Red. As I knew from my life as a veterinarian, a person's true character comes out under pressure. Both the wolf and the woman wanted to know what Red would do if Hunter continued to press him.

"You're looking at her face," said Hunter. "Tell me, does she look distressed?"

Red's hands closed over my wrists and he pulled me against him. I put my palms against his hot chest, trying to fight for breath as my heart pounded in my breast. He was radiating heat, as if he had a high fever, and his face was flushed.

"Well, Red? What do you see?"

I struggled to break free, but found that I was well and truly caught. Red was holding my wrists against his chest, and Hunter had me around the waist.

"She likes it, doesn't she?" One of Hunter's hands slipped under the flannel shirt I was wearing and cupped my right breast. I whipped my head around, intending to say something nasty, but all that came out was a low growl.

Hunter removed his hand, but grinned. "She doesn't want to admit that she likes it, but she does."

Red was looking at me, but instead of lust, the expression in his face was almost wistful. "She's not herself," he said simply. "She's in season." For a second, I felt a crashing, terrible sadness: He wasn't going to fight for me, he was going to share me out, like a third grader offering his lunch to the class bully, hoping to hang on to part of his sandwich.

But then, with a sudden shift in tone, Red added harshly, "and so am I." Moving in one fluid surge, Red reached up, grabbed Hunter's face in his hands and kissed him forcefully on the lips.

As I watched in astonishment, Hunter reared back, his hands wrapping around Red's wrists to pry him off. But Red was stronger than he looked. His biceps bulged with the effort, but he held Hunter in place, kissing him openmouthed as Hunter tried ineffectually to shake him off. For a moment, I thought: Oh, my God, he's chosen *Hunter* as his mate.

Then, as Hunter flailed in disgust, I watched as a muscle in Red's cheek twitched and stretched, and his jaw elongated into a muzzle. He was no longer kissing Hunter; he was biting him. This wasn't love. It was Bugs Bunny, tricking Elmer Fudd. Except Bugs didn't have fangs, and cartoon violence didn't leave scars.

"Stop it," I shouted, trying to separate them. "Red, stop!" Blood was trickling from Hunter's nose and mouth, and I wondered if Red would stop himself before he'd actually severed something. Could werewolves heal from amputation? I didn't want to find out the hard way. "Red, please, stop!"

But Red wasn't paying me any attention. From the waist up, he had shifted to an intermediate form, like a wolfman from an old horror movie, only his ripped jeans keeping him from shifting fully. Which was a problem; our transitional forms are better for fighting. Using the technique for separating fighting dogs, I got behind Red and pulled hard on his legs. But I was too short, and couldn't find the leverage to lift him off his feet. I tried pummeling Red's back, even hitting his head, but his attention never wavered—I might as well have not been there.

Jesus, I was an idiot. When I'd imagined my laconic boyfriend fighting for me, I'd imagined something human—punching, wrestling, a contest of strength. But Red wasn't physically stronger. He was more cunning, and, I now realized, more savage.

Hunter gave a whimper of pain and fear, and I thought I saw Red's jaws tighten a fraction. Desperate, I jumped on his back, wrapping myself around him like a limpet.

And then the front door slammed open, letting in wind, snow, and the full fury of an enraged Magda. "All right," she snarled, "what the hell is going on here?"

TWENTY-ONE

◐◯◯ "What does it look like? My boyfriend is trying to eat your boyfriend's face off. Now shut up and help," I snapped, trying to pull Red's head back by his fur.

"Don't tell me what to do," Magda countered, punching Red hard on his snout. I winced, thinking of the pain to his sensitive canine nose, but Magda's technique was effective: Red yelped and released Hunter, who clutched his face and yowled in pain.

"Are you okay? Come on," I coaxed Hunter, trying to pull his hands away from his face. "Let me see."

"He fucking tried to bite my nose off!" At first glance, it appeared as though he might have succeeded. Bloody tissue was gushing in thick streams from both nostrils, there were bite marks all along the bridge, and Hunter's nose had already swollen up like a lopsided yam.

"I don't think he did any lasting damage, but I need to check the cartilage."

"Don't be such a baby," said Red, looking at me with clever, calculating coyote eyes as the fur rolled back from his skin and he reverted to his human form. "All I did was nip you on the nose." His feet, I noticed, were a fine healthy color again. Nothing like shifting to speed up cell renewal.

"Nip me!" Hunter pointed at his bloody face, indignant. "You nearly bit it off!"

"Well, I might've gotten a little carried away by the moment. Let me see."

Red had barely taken one step when Hunter scooted himself back along the floor. "He's fucking mad! Don't let him near me!"

"And here I thought you kind of liked the first part," said Red, a sly look on his narrow face.

"I'm not gay, you little prick!" It was hard to tell, but I thought the kissing might have upset Hunter more than the biting.

"Well, you know, maybe you liked it but just didn't want to admit it," Red drawled. A surprised laugh burst out of me; Red was quoting Hunter's words back at him.

Hunter glared at Red out of eyes that were already sporting darkening half moons. "I'll show you how much I liked it, you son of a bitch . . ."

"Stop this, all of you." Magda sounded peeved that we had been ignoring her. Like my mother, she was used to being the center of attention, and there was something theatrical about the way she had placed herself in the center of the room, in a long sable coat that gleamed like a night river and stank like a wet dog. Stalking across the floor, she knelt beside Hunter, revealing red ski pants and a pair of tall, embroidered black sheepskin boots with fringes.

"Red is right, you are being a baby," she said, taking Hunter's chin in her gloved hand. "It is not serious," she said. "You will heal when you shift again."

"You sound disappointed," Hunter muttered grumpily.

"Here," I said, taking a clean washcloth from the linen closet. "Let me see what's under all that blood."

"Give me that," snapped Magda, taking the cloth from my hand.

"Ouch. Not so hard," Hunter complained as she scrubbed at his face. When we'd been together, he'd never made such a fuss about physical discomfort, but then, I'd been the nurturing type. Maybe he thought he had to turn up the volume to get some kind of sympathetic response out of Magda.

It wasn't working.

"If you had not been sniffing around where you do not belong, you would not be in this pathetic state," Magda retorted. "What are you, a dog, to follow your nose to any available bitch?" She straightened up, presumably so she could tower over Hunter, who was still on the floor.

"Speaking of dogs," said Red, "you might want to tell your man there that wolves don't share." The red-tailed hawk gave a little squawk as Red opened a cabinet, and he absently caressed her head with one finger as he removed a bottle of Jack Daniel's and a glass. "Dogs might not mind taking turns, but a wolf doesn't take too kindly to another male going after his mate."

I felt a little leap in my pulse, and Red threw back the whiskey and gave me a look so carnal that I had to glance away. His mate. For some reason, the words gave me a primitive sense of satisfaction.

Magda's amused bark of laughter caught me by surprise. "Ah, so she's your mate now." She moved closer to me, making me conscious of something I should have noticed from the moment she walked into the cabin. I wasn't the only one emitting a scent. Like me, Magda was in estrus. And it wasn't improving her temper any. "I should have made you leave last year."

I glanced over at Red to see if he was going to offer any support, but he seemed content to lean against the counter, drinking his bourbon and observing the action. I understood why he wasn't offering Hunter and Magda a drink, but I could have used a little Dutch courage.

"Listen, Magda," I said slowly, "you can't blame me for my hormones. And I didn't exactly encourage him.

In fact, I tried to throw him out. If you're going to pick on someone, pick on him."

"You have a point," Magda conceded, turning back to Hunter, who was wincing as he examined his nose in a mirror by the sink. "Well? What do you have to say for yourself?"

"Hey, she came on to me," Hunter said. "I was out walking and I saw something outside the cabin—some kind of bear man thing—and just wanted to make sure that Abra was safe. He attacked me, Abra brought me inside—I guess when my shirt came off, she couldn't stop herself."

"You are so full of crap," I said, clenching my fists until my nails dug into my palms.

"Oh, come on, Abra, we all know you're in heat. I'm sure everyone understands that you're not in control of yourself." Turning back to Magda, Hunter said, "I didn't even intend to come inside, but she pulled me in and began tearing my clothes off."

I made an inarticulate sound of rage and launched myself at Hunter.

Hunter held me off with one long arm. "God, look, she's at me again. Red, pull your woman off of me."

Red wrapped his arms around me and whispered mockingly in my ear, "I can barely keep my hands off him myself. Maybe we should take turns."

I choked on a surprised laugh, and felt Red's arms tighten around my waist. I hadn't noticed it before, but he was exuding some faint, wonderful fragrance of smoke and woods and wild herbs.

Magda raised one imperious hand, as if cutting off an orchestra. "What is this bear man? Another kind of therian?"

"It's a Liminal critter," said Red, releasing me and re-trieving his drink from the counter. "The biggest, but not the only one. They're called manitous, and I've been tracking them, and I know where they are." A moment ago, when he'd been holding me, I had felt sure that we were on the same team. My mate. But the moment he'd stepped away from me, it had felt as though a steel door had slammed shut between us. I had been with this man for over a year, but I was beginning to suspect that I had only seen the part of him that he'd allowed me to see. "I also know where they're not. No sign of one around this cabin." Red finished his bourbon and wiped his mouth on the back of his arm.

"Maybe you missed one," said Hunter, taking the bottle and helping himself to a glass.

"That's not the kind of thing I miss," said Red, lifting the glass out of Hunter's hand before he could drink it.

"Thank you." I intercepted the glass, raising it to Red in a mock toast. "It's been a rough day." I'd had enough of changeable men. This time, nobody was going to play me. I threw the drink back, the tough dame who gave as good as she got. The bourbon hit the back of my throat and I began to choke.

Someone slapped me hard between the shoulder blades and I looked up, my eyes streaming with tears. Magda was smiling at me, amused. "Thanks," I said sarcastically, my voice still hoarse.

"My pleasure." Magda paused, her nostrils flaring. "That scent . . ." She turned, moving closer to Red, her black eyes unreadable. When she stood a foot from him, her nostrils flared. "It is not just her," she said, sounding surprised. "You are in heat as well. I have never heard of such a thing . . . in wolves. Coyotes, of course, are different."

"A woman keeps riding a man about something, it makes the man start to wonder." Red pushed his face up to hers. "You trying to get a rise out of me, Miss Maggie?"

Magda laughed, a low and husky sound. I had the

feeling it was mostly for Hunter's benefit, but something in me stiffened when she curled her big hands around Red's biceps. "I must admit, I am tempted. You seem different, somehow. Stronger." She squeezed his muscle. "Harder."

I waited for Red to tell her off, but he just raised one eyebrow. "You testing me for firmness, or looking for a rotten spot?"

"That depends," Magda began, but Hunter cut her off.

He looked almost comical in his astonishment. "You aren't seriously considering letting that . . . redneck coyote touch you?"

Magda toyed with a strand of Red's hair, and even I could feel the pull. She was a great strapping Amazon, intimidating and compelling, and if she didn't snap Red in two, she'd probably give him the ride of his life. "I've never been with a male in heat," she said in a low, seductive voice. "Perhaps it would add to my chances of conceiving. And he is a shaman, too—yes, perhaps I have not been investigating all *my* options."

I think Magda was angling for a challenge, but Hunter just shook his head in disbelief. "So you want to screw this miserable runt?"

Magda smiled, her eyes locked on Red's, her body pressed up against his. "It appears he's rather larger than I suspected."

A low growl emerged from my throat. If my horn-dog ex wasn't going to raise a fuss, then it was down to me.

"I think the missus is objecting," Red said, and I was still human enough to catch the crooked smile playing about the corners of his mouth, and the look of quiet satisfaction in his eyes.

"You," I said, jabbing my finger at Magda, "paws off my man."

"Don't be stupid, woman. I am bigger, stronger, and most important, smarter."

"Excuse me? You are *not* smarter."

"Please. You give vaccinations to lapdogs and house-cats. I research genetic mutations and their effect on behavior in the wild." Magda's lip curled. "And Hunter told me you had no real intellectual interests, which was a disappointment to him."

All right, that did it. Grabbing the glass of bourbon from the counter, I threw the contents in her face. There wasn't much left, but hell, it was a nice gesture.

Spluttering and cursing in Romanian, Magda wiped her eyes. She was furious now, hair bristling. "You must want to die very badly," she said. There was cold fury in her face, but for some reason, the adrenaline coursing through my veins wasn't telling me to run like hell. It was telling me to take her down.

"At the moment, anything that shuts you up sounds like a good plan to me."

"The last time we fought, you were not so eager."

"The last time we fought, I had just changed for the first time."

We stood there for a moment, frozen, and I caught another wave of scent from Red, earthy and aroused. The prospect of my fighting Magda was turning him on. I was trying to process how I felt about this when I caught a flash of movement out of the corner of my eye as Magda launched herself at me.

My arm came up to block her and I rolled with the movement, taking us both down to the floor. I was back on my feet a moment before her; I smiled a little, feeling superior, and Magda slammed into me in a tackle that knocked the air out of my lungs. Christ, she's strong, I thought, as her big hands wrapped around my neck and the room dimmed and began to flash with red bursts of light. Wonder why she didn't want us to shift before fighting, I thought, trying to kick my legs up so I could get her in a scissors hold. There was some clue there, something I could use. All I had to do was figure it out before I ran out of time, and air.

I didn't figure it out. The room went dark and soft around the edges, and then it went away.

TWENTY-TWO

◐○○ "I've released her. See? She's breathing. Now will you please remove the knife?"

I took a shaky breath and opened my eyes. The room was still dark, the flame from the oil lamps oddly blurred, and I felt confused and disoriented. Magda was still on top of me, but now there was a big knife jammed up against her throat. I blinked, trying to clear my eyes and my head, because I couldn't see who was holding the knife. I took another shaky breath. I swallowed, realizing how badly my throat hurt.

"Get up off her first." Red's voice was calm, and I realized that he was standing behind Magda, holding the knife pressed up against her jugular.

I watched as Magda carefully swung one long leg around. She was moving as carefully as a dancer, so as not to move her neck and effectively cut her own throat. I took another painful breath and drew myself upright, trying to take stock of the situation. My glasses had been knocked off. I felt around and located them on the floor behind my left elbow, mercifully unbroken.

Putting the glasses back on my face, I looked around the room. Hunter was lying apparently unconscious near the door. There was a dark mark, presumably a bruise, on his temple. I looked up and saw that Red had retrieved his long rifle, which was resting up over his shoulder, while his free hand held the knife to Magda's throat. Apparently, Red had used the rifle stock as a club. I had forgotten about the knife he always carried in his back pocket—it was more of a backwoods utensil than a weapon.

"Well, Virgil? Going to kill me with that knife?" Magda tilted her head back against Red's crotch. I felt a momentary bewilderment; I had never heard Red's real name said out loud, although I'd seen it on official documents.

"I'm contemplating it."

"Because if not, I would like to get up. Your erection is poking me in the head."

Red released Magda, and she gave him a measured look as she got to her feet. "I am not often mistaken in my judgments, but in your case— You are not what I expected."

With a flick of his wrist, Red folded the knife and tucked it into his back pocket. "It's not for you."

"Pardon?'

Red just looked at her with hooded eyes, as if his torn and faded jeans didn't reveal exactly what he meant.

For a moment, I thought Magda was going to attack Red, but then her gaze flicked to Hunter, who was just beginning to stir on the floor.

"Fine," Magda snapped, pushing Red away. "I would not want to breed mongrels, in any case."

"Hey, honey, I think I'm being insulted," Red said, looking at me for the first time. "You okay?" Underneath the casual tone, I detected another, more serious note.

I nodded, which made my thoat hurt. "Peachy." I pointed at Hunter, who was coughing up blood. "I'm not so sure about him, though."

"He's fine," Red assured me. "Probably just swallowed a tooth."

He held my gaze and I drew in a shuddering breath, and there was that scent again, a drugging blend of herbs and forest and the warm musk of pheromones.

"Come on, Hunter," Magda said in her commandant's voice, holding out her hand. "Let us leave them to their rutting."

"But I thought you didn't want her to get pregnant," said Hunter, allowing Magda to help him upright. He didn't sound as disoriented as I would have expected, and it occurred to me that he'd been faking unconsciousness to avoid having to fight Red again.

"It does not matter," said Magda, her voice tight with restrained fury. "Even if she does manage to conceive, it won't last." Turning to me, she added, "Have I mentioned that my brothers are coming from Romania to join our little family? You, on the other hand, are just two."

With that, Magda pushed Hunter out the door, which slammed behind them.

And then we were alone. The fire crackled behind the grate, and the windowpanes rattled from the wind, as if to emphasize just how isolated we two were. There were no constraints now; we could couple like animals. Or Red could kill me for cheating.

Red set down his rifle, and my heart began to race. As I watched him approach me, my nearsighted eyes played a trick on me, and I saw two images of my lover juxtaposed against each other, the one familiar and beloved, the other mysterious and unpredictable.

I swallowed and licked my lips, trying to think of something to say as Red stood and looked down at me. The Red I knew would have made a joke, or stroked my face, dispelling my tension. But the Red I knew should not have been able to take out Hunter and Magda. He certainly hadn't been that strong last year, which made me wonder what had changed.

"The door's over there." Red's face was unreadable. "You want to leave? Leave. I ain't going to stop you." And with that, he turned and went over to his rifle, which he started to clean with all the loving care he'd once lavished on me.

"There's a blizzard outside," I said. "What am I supposed to do, go knock on Hunter and Magda's door?"

"I didn't say I was throwing you out." Red opened the rifle's barrel and removed the bullets. "Stay, if you want."

"You're mad at me."

"Yeah. But you don't have to keep flinching. I'm not planning on doing anything about it." Red perched himself on the back of the couch and set about dismantling the rifle. I wondered if he was just doing it to keep his hands busy, or if he felt safer confronting me without a loaded gun in the room.

"I don't understand, Red."

"I haven't been honest with you." Red looked up. "And you haven't been honest with me."

I took a deep breath, forced myself to say it. "If you're referring to what happened with Hunter, that wasn't anything to do with you."

Red slammed his beloved twelve-gauge Browning down so hard that I flinched. "The hell it didn't. If you were really my woman, you wouldn't have let that bastard within two feet of you. But he got a lot closer than that, didn't he?"

"You didn't seem upset before," I said, recognizing the stupidity of my words even as they left my mouth. What was it my mother had said? Something along the lines of, he's the type who will never forgive you if you give Hunter one for old times' sake.

Red gave a harsh, humorless laugh. "You mean, I

didn't seem pissed off while Hunter and Magda were breathing down our necks? Christ, Abra, what did you want me to do—show weakness in front of the enemy? Prove that we don't have a united front?" Red looked down at his gun, and when he looked up, there was a sheen of tears in his eyes. "I can't believe you let him touch you. I can't believe you let him inside of you."

I wanted to run up to Red and put my arms around his neck. But there were cords of tension standing out on his neck, and the muscles of his arms were bunching convulsively, so I didn't make a move toward him. "I'm so sorry, Red."

"I thought you loved me."

"I do love you." I swallowed. "I'm not saying this excuses it, but he was injured, and the only way I could think of to heal him fast was to get him to change. But I guess a little bit of me must still have been clinging to the past." I watched a muscle jump in Red's clenched jaw. "I can tell you this—I'm not clinging to the past anymore."

Red's hazel eyes held mine, and there was no hint of tears or tenderness or humor in them anymore. And then, as if someone had cut something loose, he sagged. "It's because of what I am, isn't it?" He clasped his hands at the base of his neck and hung his head. "Crap. I'm not good enough for you."

"Red, no!" This time, I did go to him, putting my arms around him, trying to get him to lift his chin. "I would never think that."

"Maybe I think it. Maybe Magda's not all wrong about the Limmikin." Red was looking at me now, but with a taut, pinched expression I had never seen before. "My mother was the kind of woman men take for granted. She was always trying to fit in with some new guy's idea of the right way to live. By the time I was twelve, I was just another guy giving her a hard time."

I didn't say anything. Red had told me other versions

of this story, but I knew that he'd been leaving things out.

"I went to live with my grandfather, which was the first time I heard about being Limmikin. Mom used to say she was Mohawk, but that was like gypsies telling people they're Romanian or Spanish or whatever. Anyway, Granddad pretty much lived on his own, in a cabin out in the woods. We spent more time as wolves than we did as people. After he died . . ." Red smiled, a bitter twist of his lips. "Let's just say that I got to know the rest of my family a little too well. Tricksters, all of them. Liars without equal. Hell, they lie so well, half the time they don't even know when they're doing it." He paused. "I spent nearly two years with my grandad's clan. Moved from town to town, crossing between Canada and the States. Worked as a contractor, taking people's money and not delivering. Doing a shit job, cutting corners, sometimes just making stuff up. I bilked people, Doc. Good people. Newlyweds. Old folks." He hesitated, then went on. "One time I stuck around longer than usual because I'd met some outside girl, and I learned that one of my crap repairs killed a man. That's when I left the family, started traveling on my own."

"That's when you became a shaman," I said, realizing.

"I keep telling you and Jackie, I'm not Siberian, and that's not the right word."

I felt a stab of jealousy. "Does Jackie know all this?"

Red shook his head. "Never wanted anyone to know I was a con man and a criminal. Don't even know why I'm telling you this, Doc." He rubbed his hand through his short hair. "Guess you deserve to know, though."

I pushed my forehead against his. "You're telling me because you want to know whether I can love the real you. But whatever you did in the past . . . you left that life behind. You're not like that now." I wasn't completely sure that I believed that, but the urge to console and heal was too strong to ignore.

"I'm still guilty of the things I've done."

"You've tried to make up for them," I pointed out. "You've tried very hard to be a good man." And now I knew that I was telling the truth. Whatever his former crimes, Red was one of the good guys now.

And then I remembered the night he'd changed and Rocky had disappeared.

Red's hand came up to cup the back of my head, and we stayed like that for a moment, brow touching brow. "Then why would you let that shit you married inside your body, Doc?"

"It was a mistake."

His hand still holding the back of my head, Red drew back that crucial few inches, allowing me to see his face again. "Well, I sure as shit ain't perfect, so I got no right to blame you for slipping up. And I don't hold it against you—what happened. I do want to wipe the damn smell of him off you, though. And I know just one way to do that." He reached for me, and I tensed.

"Ah. So, maybe I'm not the only expert liar in this room." As Red half rose to leave, I grabbed his arm and pulled him back down.

"No! No, don't leave, I just . . . Before we make love, there's something I have to know."

His face was closed and hard, disbelieving. "What?"

"That new hat you're wearing . . . is it Rocky?"

I saw that this was not the question he'd been expecting. After a moment, Red shook his head. "A smart raccoon can outwit a seasoned hunting dog, sweetheart. They know how to split their trail up, lay false leads, lose their scent in running water. But if he stayed with us any longer, Rocky wasn't going to live to be a smart raccoon. I had to chase the little guy off. It was his time to

go." He went over to the hat, picked it up, and showed
it to me. "This here hat's from a bit of roadkill I sal-
vaged."

Well, that was . . . woodsmanlike of him. I shivered as
Red put down the hat and traced his finger down my
throat, trying to remember what else I should be asking.
The elusive forest smell of him had warmed until it permeated the whole room. It was so delicious, I wanted to
roll myself around in it.

"Hey, Doc."

"Yes?"

"Stop thinking so damn much."

And then Red was holding my head in his hands and
kissing me with a raw hunger that had me pulling him
down on top of me, my legs coming up around him to
press his hips down so that his erection pressed against
me through the layers of his torn jeans and my sweatpants. I rubbed against him, too aroused to release him
for a moment, but Red hauled himself up on his elbows,
grunting with the effort as he yanked my pants down
around my hips. I struggled in his grip, wanting the fric-
tion and the contact back, more aroused than I had ever
been in my life.

"Hang on, sweetheart, I'm not trying to get away."
Moving far too slowly, Red pressed his lips against my
belly, kissing his way down while I protested, trying to
pull him back up.

"You don't need to do that."

"Like hell I don't."

"I don't want you to do that right now."

Red met my gaze, and I saw that he understood perfectly. I'd washed, but I still felt as if I'd been tainted by
Hunter's touch. "Yeah, well, maybe this is about what I
want. And I want to roll around in you." Red knelt in
front of me, one hand parting me so that he could
breathe against the sensitive flesh between my thighs.

Pulling me to the edge of the bed and draping my legs over his shoulders, Red kissed me there, his tongue probing, tasting, thrusting inside, then finding the swollen bud and suckling until I cried out.

Red levered himself up and unbuttoned the fly of his jeans. I could feel the blunt head of his penis at my entrance, and stopped struggling and closed my eyes. But Red just remained as he was, braced over me on trembling arms.

"Hey, Doc . . . You better put me inside. I'm not at my best here."

I frowned at him, confused.

"My control . . . I might hurt you."

I planted my heels and said, "Hurt me." I meant it as a joke, sort of, but Red gave me a look of near anguish, and then he thrust into me so hard I gasped. He pulled out, but instead of stopping or apologizing, Red slammed into me again, and I lifted myself to meet him. "Abra. Shit." He paused, the ropy veins around his biceps standing out as he braced himself over me. "Should I . . . do you want me to . . ."

I seized him by the hair and kissed him so hard our teeth clicked together. I felt change and orgasm gathering force, and the wild scent of woods and man was filling the room, so that, with my eyes closed, I could believe that we were outside in the forest.

Red moved, his hands coming down to lift my right leg, changing the angle so he hit a place high up inside that blended pleasure and pain. I cried out, holding Red with all my strength as my orgasm flooded through me. A moment later, I felt him pulse inside me as the bones and muscles of our bodies shifted and changed.

"Hey, Doc?"

I opened my eyes. At some point, we had managed to roll off the bed, but Red had absorbed the shock of the fall. We were human, which surprised me until I realized we were still partially dressed, Red in his torn jeans, me in the sweats and ripped flannel shirt. "What?"

His hand cupped the slight feminine curve of my belly. "Just thought I should tell you: I'm going to knock you up."

I laughed, thinking he was joking. Red brought my hand to his penis, which was already beginning to stir. "What are you, a teenager?"

"I'm in heat." He moved my hand up and down on his shaft, which instantly thickened. "So you don't mind?" His sharp teeth found my ear.

"Mind what?" The scent of him was stronger now, intoxicating me. He came up on one elbow, tracing a delicate pattern over my breasts with his fingertips and making me shiver with renewed desire. I was dimly aware that there was something I should remember, some doubt or concern.

"Having my babies." His pressed a kiss to the base of my throat, and whatever I had been trying to remember floated out of my consciousness. My body was very clear about its response to the idea of pregnancy; it contracted like a fist, as if it could pull the word into the core of me and keep it there.

"Nursing my babies." Leaning down, Red pulled one nipple into his mouth and suckled it hard, sending another contraction of lust rippling through me. "Living with me as my mate." Red turned his attention to the second breast, and as stupid as it was to let my body decide this, that appeared to be what I was doing.

Red closed his teeth gently on my nipple, and I moaned. "Hang on a sec." Red gave me a last flick of his tongue. "There's something I want to do first." Red smiled, and I smiled back. Then he pulled up my sweatpants, lifted me in his arms, and carried me back to the bed.

"That was a good something." I reached up my arms for him, but Red shook his head.

"That wasn't it."

I collapsed on the bedspread, spreading my arms and legs in surrender. "So do it, already."

Red pressed his thumb to my lips. "First, tell me you want me."

That was easy. "I want you." I sucked his thumb into my mouth, and Red inhaled sharply. I pressed one foot against his erection, which was peeking out of his undone jeans. "Bad girl. Down."

I reached for the buttons of his fly. "You want me down, I'll go down."

"Hold that thought a moment." Red drew his switchblade from his back pocket and I blinked in surprise.

"What's that for?"

Red wasn't smiling. "Sounds like you don't trust me, Doc."

"I trust you," I said, with as much certainty as I could muster.

"Good." Red rolled away from me, and as I watched from the bed, he flicked a button in the bone handle, releasing the four-inch blade which had been pressed against Magda's neck. The knife, an antique, was illegal in a bunch of states, but Red always carried it, the way other men carried Swiss Army knives. Up close, I could see the symbols carved in the blade as well as the handle. Red had once explained their meaning to me: the bear claw, the double diamond shape that some called the shaman's eye, the geometric pattern known as coyote's tracks, because you couldn't tell its direction.

"Good, 'cause this would be dangerous if you didn't have complete faith in me." Red walked over to the fireplace and thrust the blade into the flames.

Oh, God, this was some kind of backwoods test of loyalty, like going out to the local tattoo shop to have your lover's name inked permanently into your flesh. I was guessing that Red had given up on my ever wearing his engagement ring, and had figured that nothing says "our love will never die" like an indelible mark of possession. Except that love still died, even when you had your sweetheart's name branded on your skin. All that changed was the emotional scarring was made visible to the naked eye.

There was a creak of floorboards as Red walked back to me, the knife's metal glowing red, then orange. Outside, the windows rattled with the force of the wind, and I found myself wishing that Red and I weren't quite so alone. As I stared at the heated metal, I acknowledged to myself that behind all my practical excuses, there was another, more complicated reason why I hadn't worn Red's ring: I had been ambivalent about getting remarried so quickly. I'd made one mistake. I hadn't wanted to make another.

And yes, I was still a little ambivalent. Maybe more than a little. Maybe that's why you used to need a blood test to get a marriage license. If more marriages involved bloodletting, there would probably be far fewer divorces. "You know," I said, hesitantly, "I'm not sure exactly what you have in mind here, but branding, tattoos—they're really not my thing."

I saw something flicker in Red's eyes, as if he were doing a rapid calculation in his head. "You don't need to receive the symbols, if you don't want to. We could just draw a token amount of blood."

I swallowed. "I don't suppose we could just make love?"

Red shook his head. "This is a sacred rite." His voice was oddly flat, as though he were disappointed in me. I realized that although Red had passed my test, I was failing his. In all the time I had been trying to decide whether or not Red was right for me, I had never considered that he might decide I was not right for him.

"What are you going to do?"

"Marry you. The Limmikin way. We mingle our blood." He stood there, self-contained, not attempting to convince me by word or touch, even though he must have known that either would have pushed me over the edge. I felt a wave of desire for him so strong that my arms ached to reach out for him, but I hesitated. My mother's question came back to me: Is Red Mallin really the man you want to father your children?

My body's answer was a resounding yes. The very thought of it made my womb contract in longing. And it was possible that we'd already made me pregnant. But as I'd told Hunter, above the neck was where I made decisions. In my head, I went through my mother's objections: *That man would do anything to keep you. Lie, steal, cheat, kill.* On the other hand, my mother had been wrong about his primitive sense of loyalty: I had, indeed, given in to Hunter, and Red had forgiven me.

Unless this was a trick, and now Red intended to hurt or disfigure me as payback. I stared into his eyes, their heated gold shading into hazel as the blade cooled and I did not hold out my arm. He remained still a moment longer, and then folded the knife back into itself while his face closed down. "It's all right, Doc," he said, his voice a little hoarse. "I don't blame you one little bit."

An image came to me, then: Red, using that knife to whittle designs into a cradle while I sat in a rocking chair by the fire, my hands on the heavy moon of my belly.

"Red."

He looked at me, his face resigned. "I don't need to hear the explanation. I get it."

I held out my left arm. "I want to do it. Marry me."

Red's eyed widened for a moment, and then he shook

his head. There were shadows under his eyes, and in them. "No, Doc, you don't. You just don't want to disappoint me, and that's real sweet of you, but it's not enough. If you do this with doubt in your heart, it won't work."

Whatever my earlier reservations had been, I was now overcome by the conviction that it was this man, softspoken and wry and capable, who should be the father of my children.

For a moment, I wondered whether I could trust *myself*. After all, I hadn't just betrayed Red with Hunter, I'd betrayed myself. Maybe this choice, like that one, could be influenced by hormones that were clamoring for mating and breeding. But after looking at that possibility directly, I dismissed it. We can never know our own minds completely, but in all my life, I had never felt more certain of the course I should take. When I had taken my vows with Hunter, I had been half-delirious with happiness while Hunter had faced the officiating bureaucrat with a bemused smile. At the time, I had thought, *It doesn't feel real.*

But this, this primitive, personal ceremony that required a drop of my blood, this did feel real.

I walked over to Red and knelt down at his feet. I knew that it was traditionally the man who did the kneeling, but hell, that was because traditionally, it was the man who had the power. In our relationship, however, I'd been the one holding all the cards. "There's no doubt in me. I want this."

Red looked down at me, and then reached out his hand to haul me up. "Abra, you can't fake your way through this." A muscle jumped in the side of his jaw. "If you're not completely certain about this bond, it's not just that it won't work, it could be dangerous."

I stayed where I was, at his feet, gazing up at him. "I am certain."

"Abra, it took you five minutes to make up your mind."

"And now it's made up."

"It's all right, honey." His hand stroked my hair. "We can still make love. It's not all or nothing."

"Why are you lying to me?"

That startled him. "I'm not—"

"Then you're lying to yourself. If we stop here, we won't just stay as we were. Okay, I admit it. Maybe there still is a fraction of a doubt somewhere inside of me. I've been burned before. But even if it won't work this way, even if it's dangerous, I want to take that chance."

Red looked down at me a moment longer, then knelt down and embraced me, rocking me back and forth. "Oh, my girl. My beautiful girl." Red kissed the inside of my wrist, then worked his way up to the crook of my elbow. "Take off your clothes."

I did, but not as quickly as he did. Naked, I gave him my left arm.

"Thank you," he said, his voice thick with emotion. "That was the key—you trusting me."

I let out a breath I hadn't realized I was holding. "So the blade . . . it's symbolic?"

"Not exactly." Red buttoned up his jeans, then drew his switchblade from his back pocket. I blinked in surprise. I felt a sharp pain and made a high-pitched sound as Red tightened his grip on my arm and made a neat, small slice on the inside of my elbow. As the blood welled up, my gaze flew up to meet Red's. He had made a horizontal cut across the vein, but before I could say anything, the knife flashed as he made a vertical slice across the crease of his own elbow.

"Are you insane?" For a moment, all I felt was the astonishment that he had actually cut me. It occurred to me, belatedly, that this was payback.

Red shook his head, then pressed his mouth against the wound, drawing the blood to the surface. I saw his eyes go wolfish with the taste of me, and my animal nature responded with a warm rush of arousal. I was not thinking as a woman, but as a wolf when I brought my mouth to his arm, filling my nostrils with the scent. I ran my tongue over the blood slowly welling from his cut, and then planted my mouth more firmly on his flesh. Red gave a low grunt, pain or pleasure or both, and then we both broke away, panting hard.

I was vaguely surprised to realize that my arm burned a little, and that the room had grown hazy. I never grew faint at the sight of blood.

"What is this?"

"Magic." With his knife, Red cut a strip from the bottom of the shirt I had been wearing and wrapped it around our arms, binding us together. Then, taking my face in his free hand, Red kissed me with such tenderness that I knew that with him, it was more than the pull of moon and scent and heat. This was intensely personal.

"I know it's probably a little late to ask, but the danger . . . does the fact that I screamed out 'are you insane' mean my hand is going to fall off or something?"

I felt Red's chuckle against the skin of my throat. "No."

"Would I know if I were still in danger, or has it passed?"

"How do you know I meant you were the one in danger?" His lips dropped to the hollow of my throat.

Realization came over me in a cold wave. "You mean you're the one who . . . I put you in danger and you never said . . ."

"Doc." His lips claimed mine, and he kissed the breath out of me.

"What?" I came up, gasping for air.

"Shut up." He kissed me again, his free hand tangled tightly in my hair, a welcome, anchoring pain.

"Please, please, please." I pulled Red on top of me, trying to undo his jeans. With my left arm tied to his right, this was a little like participating in a carnal three-legged race.

"Easy, easy," Red said, a hint of laughter in his voice.

"Fuck easy," I snarled, too wound up to play nice.

Something flared in his amber gaze, turning his eyes golden. He entered me in one quick thrust, so roughly that it would have hurt both of us if I hadn't still been moist from the last time. But I was ready for him, more than ready, and his almost violent movement sent off wild bursts of pleasure inside of me, the tensile strength of his wiry muscles as he worked himself in and out of me pushing me back along the floor with each heavy thrust. I was beyond pain, and as I crossed my ankles at the small of Red's back, I lost myself in the rhythm of his pumping hips, in the heavy, slapping sound of flesh against flesh, and Red's low, hoarse steady chant of curses or prayers. I planted my heels on the floor, rising to meet Red's thrusts, trying to get him deeper, and then I felt something shift inside, and Red's chant grew harsher. As the pleasure began to climb, I realized that whatever Red was saying, it wasn't in English. My eyes flew open, and to my shock, I saw that as Red plunged in and out of me, we were blurring together, our outlines blending and fusing. I blinked, and it appeared as though we were composed of glowing points of color and light, as if the very molecules and atoms of our being had become visible, and for a moment I thought: Maybe we're shifting. We had shifted during sex before—in fact, it was pretty usual for orgasm to trigger the change—but this felt very different. This was as though the very essence of our beings was mingling and combining and recombining. I no longer knew where Red left off and I began.

This wasn't mere chemistry drawing us together; it was alchemy, magical and transformative. For a moment, I remembered another day, long ago, when I had lost my grip on reality, and felt panic surge up inside of me. But I couldn't hold on, not to myself and not to the panic, and as the pleasure built I quit trying and just let go.

Red claimed my mouth, swallowing my cry as we dissolved into each other, simultaneously crossing over from one state of being into another.

TWENTY-THREE

◐◯◯ For the next five days and nights, I was a wolf. In the movies, werewolves revert to human with the rising of the sun, and in the beginning, that had been true for me. But now, as the moon remained visible in the winter sky, I remained a wolf. Red, who could have chosen to become human, kept to his canid form as well. I suppose it was a honeymoon, although an unusual one.

I remember snuffling my nose through the snow, searching for the scent of hibernating mice and voles, listening for their slow heartbeats under the earth. When we found one, we scrabbled at their holes with our front claws, digging them out and then jumping up and pouncing on them like cats. I remember chasing a young rabbit through the woods, Red racing alongside me, bumping me and teasing me until our prey escaped and we wound up in a pile, nipping at each other's necks and then licking each other's faces.

Our mornings and evenings were spent mating, nuzzling, wrestling, and hunting. In the afternoon, we slept curled into each other, breathing in the beloved scent of the other's fur, inhaling the aroma of the places we had been the way a human might look over photographs. It was like being very young again—the continuous sense of being cared for, touched, petted, and adored. When I moved too far away from Red's side, I had felt a slight burning sensation in my left side, close to my heart. I had known without having to ask that this was a result of our blood bond, but it was only now that I began to wonder how long this side effect would last. Not long, I hoped. Feeling the equivalent of heartburn every time I got more than a mile from my boyfriend was going to put a cramp in my working style.

Except that he wasn't just a boyfriend now. According to Red, we were now married, Limmikin style.

In our wolf forms, we wandered the borders of our territory. First we traveled up Old Scolder Mountain, where we howled in harmony with Jackie's pack, watched by a mournful Pia in human form, her pale face peeking out of the fur-lined hood of her parka. We invited her to join us, our voices rising and falling. We needed a beta in our little pack, and she did not seem to belong with her old friends, who prowled around Jackie's trailer, leaving a scent barrier that said: Keep away.

Come on, Pia, we howled, and for a moment, she harmonized. We don't care that you're human, I sang, but it was no use. In the end, she just trudged back to Jackie's trailer, a woebegone figure in snowshoes.

As we made our way through the forest, we could feel the presence of manitous, both like and unlike the animals they resembled. Around them, the air had a strange distorted ripple to it, and there was a feeling of pressure, as though they compressed the atmosphere, folding it over itself, making it dense with overlapping realities. I didn't fear it the way I might have had I been on two legs.

Still, I whined a little when we passed a large area where the air at the boundary line weighed down on me so heavily that I felt as if I were making my way through deep water. This, I knew, was the amount of our reality displaced by the great bear. I tried to think of him as a

French Canadian lumberjack, but in this form, I could only sense him as ursine, vast and powerful. Still, as wolf and bear, we were not enemies. There were old treaties between us, that allowed for us to share in some of a kill, if there was enough meat.

And there was a fresh kill. I could smell blood, and for a moment, I didn't know what kind of animal it had come from. Then it hit me: It had come from a human. I whimpered almost inaudibly and began backing up, wanting to get as far from this charged and dangerous place as possible. Red licked my ear, reassuring me, as he scent-marked along the dividing line between our woods and the Liminal. I noticed the designs scratched onto the trunks of trees, and there was just enough human in me to recognize the symbols from Red's knife: bear claw, shaman's eye, coyote's tracks. I didn't know if they were mystical wards or trail markers, but I sensed that at the very least they served as visual reminders, marking a boundary, delineating territory. For the moment, they seemed to be holding.

As we trotted away from the dead human, however, my wolf mind stopped worrying about Bruin going postal in our backyard, and what was human in me could not hold on to the thought of him. Wolves are creatures of the present.

When we reached a copse of trees, Red paused to sniff the air, then set off at a gallop as something big started from its hiding place. I followed hard on his heels, catching a glimpse of the bouncing, fatty white tail of the deer we were chasing. My heart pounding, I felt my entire consciousness tunnel down to the pursuit of this prey. She was an old doe, and we chased her through the forest and down the snow-covered cornfield on the east side of town, near the Behemoth caverns. As we tired her out, the crows and hawks and turkey vultures started circling, alerted to the prospect of a meal. Foxes

and coyotes were also gathering, but keeping a respectful distance as Red and I did all the hard work of dealing with the doe's flashing hooves and bringing her
down.

And then, just as we began feasting, we heard it: the
howling of a rival pack. At first, it was just Hunter and
Magda, telling us they were near. And then there were
two other voices, young males. These must be Magda's
brothers, come to join her. And with them, her pack was
twice the size of ours. We could not see them, but the
wind carried their scents to us, and we could tell that
these new males were not able to shift completely into
wolf form. Which made them poor hunters, but good
fighters.

When we returned home, as the moon began to wane,
we discovered that Magda's pack had scent marked into
our territory. There was a rich, oil-gland scent that had
come from someone rubbing his head and cheeks against
the bark of trees, your basic "Kilroy was here" graffiti
from a buff male in his prime. And there was also the
sharper, more acrid scent that said "Keep Out," "Guard
Dog on Premises," with a "Trespassers Will be Prose-
cuted" thrown in for good measure. It wasn't Hunter's
scent, but one of the brothers, and I realized that Magda
had chosen to claim one of her kin as her alpha, while
retaining Hunter as her mate. It wasn't unusual in the
wild for brother and sister wolves to rule as alphas, but
I had a feeling that Hunter wasn't going to be too
pleased with his new lack of status.

Red reclaimed our boundaries, and after a moment's
hesitation, I joined him. As his mate, I was also responsible for keeping our scent-fences in good repair, but I
knew from the set of Red's jaw that we were going to
have to deal with this new threat next month.

In the small hours of the night, Red and I made our
way back to our cabin. Red must have shifted to open

the door, but I was so tired that I can't recall it. I woke up in the bed, which surprised me; I was pretty sure I'd gone to sleep curled up on the floor. When I first opened my eyes, I felt a rush of disappointment at being human again. My first thought was, Holiday over, back to reality.

But some things hadn't gone back to normal.

"Good morning." Red was smiling down at me, holding out a cup of coffee. He had a towel wrapped around his waist, and he smelled warm and clean, as though he'd just bathed. "Have some coffee—it's fresh." He held out a mug, and I struggled into a sitting position. I had believed that Red was in love with me before, and I had thought I loved him back, but what passed between us now was infinitely stronger. This was love the way I had felt it for Hunter in the early days, a constant glow, a continuous sweet ache, a fierce and bone-deep tenderness. Except that with Hunter, that love had been tinged with anxiety, and the knowledge that the intensity of feeling was not reciprocated. With Red, the feeling was magnified and amplified by being returned, as if we were our own little feedback loop of power and emotion.

Red sank down on the bed next to me and watched me inhale the coffee and then take a sip. The clean, masculine scent of him filled me with the wolf-sense of rightness and belonging. As if he could read my mind, Red nuzzled my cheek and whispered, "Pack. Mate." His fingers rested on the crook of my elbow, where he had cut me in the ceremony. "How do you feel?"

"I'm not sure." My voice came out in a rough croak, and Red held the mug for me while I took another sip of coffee. I had that warm feeling of being a kid again. "Did you carry me into bed last night?"

"You were so out of it, I kind of had to."

I looked out the window. It was still dark, but at this

time of year, that didn't tell me much. And it felt like morning. "What time is it?"

"Five-fifteen. I guess our bodies are still on wolf schedule." He leaned over and kissed me, his work-roughened hand cupping my jaw, his mouth a benediction on mine. I wanted to breathe him in, all of him, and I turned into him, trying to move my legs to press against him. Red broke apart, laughing with delight. "This is one definite advantage to being human, darlin'," but I'm about to spill your hot coffee all over us." I realized that he'd been trying to balance my mug in his hand the whole time we'd been kissing.

"Oh, God, I'm sorry."

"How about I just put this down and we try that again? I kind of missed having hands, too." Red set down the mug, but before he could reach for me I swung my legs over the side of the bed.

"As much as I want you with hands, there's something I need to do first."

"Understood." Red moved aside, and I gasped as I stood up and saw the scratches and bruises all along my arms and legs. On closer inspection, Red was pretty banged up, too. There were tooth marks on his arm, and on my thigh.

"Oh, my God. What happened to rapid healing?"

"We probably overtaxed our systems a little. Do you want some of that bear ointment?"

"Ugh. Is there any other remedy?"

Red gave me a sly smile. "A warm bath, a hot breakfast, and a lovin' man." He was deliberately playing up his Texas twang, and I laughed.

"Sign me up." I dragged the quilt off the bed and wrapped it around me. I didn't feel like showing off my poor battered body at the moment, especially when I couldn't see clearly. Putting my hand up to my nose, I said, "I don't suppose you know where I left my glasses?"

"Here. I found them on the floor, but I don't think they're scratched."

"Thanks," I said, examining the lenses in the light.

"And here's your pocketbook and stuff." I put on the glasses and turned to see Red handing me my pocketbook, along with a pile of neatly folded clothes—the outfit from my Manhattan shopping spree with Lilliana. "Where did these come from?"

Red shrugged. "I don't know. I just found them on the table last night. She must have come by while we were both still out."

Still feeling groggy, I noticed a note tucked into the pocket of my folded blouse. I took a sip of coffee before opening the note, which said: *I'm leaving this at the cabin and hoping you are all right. Call me when you get back—No judgments, I promise. Remember, I'm your friend and will always be sensitive to your situation. Lilliana.* The page was crumpled and a little dirty, as if it had been trampled on. Except that it had been inserted very carefully into the pocket of the blouse, which looked pristine.

"Hey, nice specs, Doc."

"Thanks." I looked up, flashing him a surprised smile. There was something about the note that kept bothering me, and I was about to ask Red how long he'd been up and about when I realized that I needed to go to the bathroom and quickly. I would rather have used our outhouse for privacy but didn't think I could make it that far. "Excuse me," I squealed, then rushed into the little bathroom.

Funny how all the romance novels I've read don't mention the toll lovemaking takes on the female body. I winced, thinking that I needed a good week to recover—or rather, I would have, if I couldn't heal like a lycanthrope. Strangely enough, there was still a faint line on my wrist where my blood had mingled with Red's.

When I came out, Red had drawn me a bath; he helped me inside and handed me my coffee. As I soaked away my various aches and pains, Red washed my hair, his fingers so soothing against my scalp that I almost fell asleep.

"I wonder how Malachy's been getting by without me," I said, as Red wrapped me up in a warm towel.

"Worry about it later," Red murmured, lifting me and carrying me toward the bed.

"I'm too sore to make love," I said.

"Damn, the honeymoon really is over."

I laughed, then watched as Red cooked us both a breakfast of scrambled eggs and sausage. We ate from the same plate, fighting over bites of the sausage until I remembered, belatedly, that I never ate meat unless I was right before the change.

Fighting a wave of nausea, I laid down my fork. "That's weird." I took a bite of dry toast, hoping it would settle my stomach.

Red understood instantly. "You've just spent three solid days and nights as a wolf," Red said. "It's only natural that your body would need a little time to adjust. Besides, it was free range and organic, so that pig died happy."

I smiled as Red put away the dishes and opened a window to dispel the heavy smell of fried sausage. Then he lay down beside me, fully dressed, stroking my back as I sank into an exhausted sleep.

When I woke up again, the sky was light and he was gone. Ravenous again, I forced myself to stand up, fighting the peculiar dizziness that had me reaching for the couch to hold myself upright. What the hell had I done to get myself into this state?

Putting on my glasses, I hobbled over to my handbag. I knew Red might not be carrying his cell phone, but I felt such an overwhelming burst of love and need for him, that I had to at least try. My left arm was burning a path that led straight to my heart, and the feeling was growing steadily stronger, like an allergic reaction. For a second, I wondered what would have happened had I also permitted Red to brand me. Receiving the symbols, he had called it. Would completing the ritual have helped this sensation, or would it have made me burn for my lover all the more?

When I picked up the phone, I found a text message from Red: Emrgncy jb. Bk fr dnnr, MATE. I giggled to myself like a teenager, wondering whether the last was meant as a noun or as a verb. Then, when I saved the message, I saw that it was eight-thirty in the morning, and realized that I had less than half an hour to get to work. Malachy expected me to take off a few days at the full moon, but this time I'd stayed wolf for a full twenty-four hours longer than normal. No time to eat anything else, which was a shame; I was reconsidering my scruples about that sausage, as it had been delicious. I was pulling on my panties when I thought of something. Reaching back into my handbag, my fingers closed on the chamois pouch that Red had given me to hold the moonstone. Not entirely sure why, I shook the pouch out, and the moonstone pendant spilled into my hand.

The stone was cool in my palm, but I knew that the silver would burn me if I kept holding it. Acting on impulse, I slipped the necklace over my neck, thinking: I'm married. There may not have been fittings and flowers and Baroque music in the background, but I felt like a bride—blissed-out and beloved.

I touched the moonstone, not sure what I expected— maybe a pink, glowing confirmation that all was well, or at least that's what I was hoping for. Instead, the pendant began to swim with a bruised, bluish-purple color. I didn't know what it portended, but I did know that it wasn't a reflection of *my* mood. I recalled the state of

Lilliana's note, and how unlikely it was that my fastidious and elegant friend would shove a messy note into a clean blouse.

The beginnings of a faint and as yet formless concern began to take shape in my head.

PART THREE

PART THREE

TWENTY-FOUR

◐○○ "Welcome back to work," Malachy said as I came in the back door and reached for my lab coat, which was hanging in the office closet. "Have a nice holiday?"

"It was the full moon, Malachy." I pulled my white coat on, wincing as my sore shoulders protested. "It's not like I had a choice."

"Well, I hope you had fun," he said, his sardonic tone not matching the exhaustion in his face and eyes. His cheeks were sunken, and underneath the concealing layers of his lab coat, wool vest, and baggy gray flannel trousers, his body seemed almost skeletal. "As you can see, we're having a bit of a rush."

He opened the shutters so that I could see into the waiting room, which was crammed with people and their animals. All the seats were taken, and some people were forced to stand.

"What happened to Dr. Mortimer? He go on vacation?" As far as I was aware, Northside's other vet hadn't taken time off since the mid-fifties.

"I just called him," said Malachy, closing the shutters. "He's as busy as we are, if not more so."

"What's going on?" In the other room, I could hear Pia telling a client that the doctors would be right out.

Malachy opened the drug cabinet with his key and

took out a few different vials. "I'm not sure if it's an epidemic or just small-town panic as one person sets off another. But whatever it is, it's been getting worse the past few days."

"Symptoms?"

"Dogs not eating, drinking copiously, growling inappropriately at family members. Much panic over the possibility of rabies, as you can imagine."

"But it's not rabies?"

Malachy raised his eyebrows. "Of course it's not rabies. That would be too simple. Lab tests are negative for rabies and parvo, but we're still getting reports of rabid raccoons and foxes behaving aggressively toward people." Dragging his hand through his hair, Mal added, "The good sheriff and I weren't sure whom we missed more—you or that ginger rat catcher boyfriend of yours."

Well, that explained why Red had hared off so early. *Crapola*. After my interlude of running around the woods, I was hardly prepared for a regular day of work, let alone an emergency. I must have lost at least fifteen pounds on my wolfish honeymoon, and my tightest slacks, a pair of brown corduroys from college, were so loose they kept threatening to fall down. Adding insult to injury, the rapid change in hormones had made my not quite B-cup breasts so full and tender that even putting on a bra hurt. The moon might be on the wane, but it was still full enough to make me feel less than a hundred percent with the program, if the program involved wearing shoes and forming complete sentences.

But the hardest part of going to work had been leaving without seeing Red again.

Suck it up, I told myself. You're a professional.

Malachy slipped something into the pocket of his lab coat and locked the medicine cabinet. "Right," he said, a little more strongly. "You ready to face the madding crowd?"

"I've got your back," I said. The moment we emerged from the back office, we were engulfed by people and questions.

"How long is this going to take? What is going on back there!"

"I've been waiting for forty-five minutes!"

"I can't seem to explain to the receptionist how sick my Baby is!"

This last, brassy voice was familiar. Shouldering her way through the other clients, Marlene made her way to the front of the crowd, long black hair teased up in a style made popular by Elvira, Mistress of the Night. Marlene's dragon lady nails were clasped around "Baby," a snuffling, eight-week-old black Pekingese puppy wearing a pink gingham dress. The pup was Queenie's replacement, I supposed. Something small this time, so she could control its movements.

"As you can see, we're having an unusual number of clients today," said Malachy, with aristocratic hauteur, walking her back out to the waiting area. "Dr. Barrow and I will take you each in turn."

"So wait your turn, Marlene," said Jerome sharply, jutting out his heavily bearded chin. The former Manhattan businessman was wearing his usual costume of red flannel shirt, baggy overalls and workman's boots, but he seemed to have lost his folksy *Little House on the Prairie* attitude. In a classic Wall Street move, he maneuvered himself in front of three other clients, moving his animal carrier as if it were a chess piece. Whatever he had inside the carrier was making a hideous, low moaning sound, and then spitting at some unseen adversary.

"But Baby is so sick," Marlene said, sounding genuinely concerned for the puppy. "She keeps having these convulsions. And when she gets up, she seems so different—she hardly seems to know me."

"That's strange," said a young girl with purple bangs and heavy black eyeliner. "My puppy's doing the same thing." She indicated the listless black Lab sitting on the floor by her feet. "And her ears are bothering her. She keeps scratching them, and they keep standing up. Look." As we watched, the Lab puppy scratched furiously at her ears, which stood up momentarily, giving her a strange, almost wolfish look.

"Baby's doing that, too," said Marlene. "And I think her legs are giving her trouble. She keeps yelping whenever I put her down." Marlene demonstrated: The Pekingese yelped and fell on her side. Her pink gingham dress ripped along the side; Baby was outgrowing her mother's taste in clothes.

"She does have long legs for a Peke," said the young woman. "Maybe that's why they're hurting her."

"I'm sure she never used to have long legs," said Marlene, peering down at her pup. "I was told she was show quality. But now that you say it, her legs do seem to be getting longer. And so does her tail. Can tails regrow?"

Kayla, whom I hadn't noticed before, pushed herself forward. Great, all my favorite people in one place. The Moondoggie's waitress, who had gained five more pounds and was bursting out of her white-collared shirt and black miniskirt, was carrying a Maltese in her arms. At least I thought it was a Maltese. Its ears and tail looked as though there might have been some Pomeranian in there.

"It sounds to me as though there's some kind of weird dog virus going around," she said softly, as though embarrassed to speak up in front of me. "Is there some kind of disease that can change the shape of a dog's ears and tail? Because my Maltese, Bon Bon, has started to look, well, kind of wolfish."

Malachy met my eyes. "There is," he admitted slowly. "But I think it very unlikely that so many different dogs should all be affected at once."

"Are they going to be dangerous?" Marlene stared at her Pekingese. "I heard that a weekender was found dead up by her property on Old Scolder Mountain. The paper said it was a bear, but maybe her own dogs killed her!"

I flashed on the scent-memory of human blood, and thought: So that's who it was.

"What about cats? Can this thing spread to them? Because Miss Priss is acting mighty strange, and something funky is happening to her tail and hind legs."

Mal and I turned to Jerome, who was opening the latch of his animal carrier. "No, felines are not susceptible," Mal began, and then whatever he was about to say was cut off as the carrier's inhabitant sprang out, arching its back and hissing as pandemonium broke out.

Miss Priss was a bobcat in a room full of dogs. Surprising myself as much as everyone else, I grabbed the largest, most dominant dog by the scruff and knocked it off its feet. The shepherd, which had been leading the gang war against the enemy feline, stared up at me for a moment, then flattened its ears and tried to lick my face. Submission. I let him up, and then turned my gaze to each dog in turn, forcing them to lie down. A few self-groomed in an attempt to calm their jangled nerves. The puppies, which had all been barking enthusiastically, wet the floor.

When I approached the bobcat formerly known as Miss Priss, however, she arched her back, hissed, and clawed at my face. This was the first time that dogs and cats had reacted to me in this way when I was in human form, and it made me wonder. But I tried to keep my professional face on when I turned to Jerome. "Jerome, put Miss Priss back in her carrier."

"Come on, girl, there you go," he said, his voice shaking, but his hands pushing at her large rear. It was no good: In the time it had taken to avert a crisis, Miss Priss had grown too large for her carrier.

"We'll put her in one of the offices," said Malachy. Pia rushed over from behind the front desk to help us, and using a broom, we three managed to shoo the bobcat in and slam the door shut. As I listened to the unholy growling noises coming from the other side, I realized that I hadn't seen Padisha, the office cat. I turned to Malachy. "Where's Paddy?"

Mal sighed. "I let her out in the yard this morning. And don't look at me like that, I had no idea this was about to happen."

Pia turned to me. "Paddy's out there." It was the first time she'd actually spoken to me since our little scene at Jackie's. I wondered whether she'd decided I wasn't really a threat, after all.

I took Pia's hand and gave it a reassuring pat. "I heard. But he's a smart cat. I'm sure he can look out for himself." *Especially if he's turned into a lynx.* Pia left her hand in mine, and I gave her fingers a gentle squeeze before letting go.

"Do you really think he'll be all right?"

"I'm sure he will," I lied. The truth was, I had no idea whether our cat being out of the office right now was a good thing or a bad one, but I sure was getting a whole new respect for Red. Merely invoking his name in my mind made my left arm burn a line of desire straight to my heart.

"All right now, back to the asylum." Mal and I headed out to the waiting room, where all the clients were talking loud and fast. The dogs were as agitated as their owners, circling and panting and whining, and one dog that must have started out as a beagle was baying loudly.

Like the other dogs, the beagle didn't look like a pure-bred anything anymore. His odd conformation made him resemble a mongrel with a fair dose of shepherd in his mix. The dog that had started out as a German shepherd hadn't changed much at all: All that had happened to him was that his hind legs had straightened out, his muzzle had lengthened, and he had attached himself to my side as my beta. And Bon Bon, Kayla's little dog, had grown to the size of an adult arctic fox.

"Enough of this horseshit," said Marlene as she held up her Pekingese, which had already lost the characteristic pushed-in face and bulging eyes of its breed. "I want to know what the hell is going on here." The little dog now looked like one of those new hybrids—Peagle, or a Pekauser. In another half hour, I supposed, it would look like a Pekinwolf, and then it wouldn't have any Peke in it at all.

"All right, now," Malachy said, cutting into the din. "Now, have you all written down your names on the list?"

We looked at Pia, who hurried back behind the desk like a dog scrambling back to its den. "I think most of them signed in," she said in a tremulous voice.

"We need all of you to sign your name," said Malachy, and the clients began to reshuffle themselves into a line in front of Pia.

I leaned in to Malachy, who smelled of antiseptic and medicine, and, underneath, of simian power and potential rage. I touched the moonstone, which I was wearing over a layer of silk underwear that looked like a turtleneck, but under my sweater and lab coat. "What's going on with her?"

"I have no idea, the ridiculous girl won't let me take a blood sample." Malachy half turned his back to me and quickly palmed something, which he popped into his mouth.

I had a flash of her, gazing up at the full moon with

abject misery, unable to shift into wolf form. "Can't you do something for her? So that she can change, the way I do?"

Malachy narrowed his eyes. "That was never the goal," he said sharply. "We want the cells to achieve a new stability."

From the front desk, there was a yelp of surprise. The queue stared as Pia stared at Malachy, quivering with emotion. "You mean . . . you mean you did this to me on purpose?" Her voice rose on the last word, and I could have sworn that her spiky, light brown hair began to bristle. "*You* made it so I couldn't change?"

"Pia, this is not the time or the place to discuss such matters." Malachy's voice was severe, and ordinarily Pia would have cringed and acquiesced. Today, however, she narrowed her eyes.

"Just tell me this. Can you fix me? Can you give me a shot or something so I can turn back?"

The clients were listening, and I heard murmurs: What did she mean, turn back? He does terrible experiments, you know. I've heard he killed his own mother for parts.

For the first time, I realized that dogs weren't the only ones changing. It wasn't as apparent, but there seemed to be something a little more brutish, a little less civilized about the way Jerome was shouldering Marlene out of the way. Perhaps it was just my imagination, but it did seem as if Marlene and the other women were looking shiftier and more suspicious than usual. Northsiders tended to take a lot in stride, but mutating lapdogs was pushing this crowd's limits. Kayla, in particular, was looking at me with narrowed eyes. "What's this all about? What did he do to her?"

I ignored her. "Pia," I began, but Pia kept her gaze trained on Malachy.

"Tell me," she said.

Mal shook his head, so slightly that it was hardly a movement. He almost sounded regretful as he said, "No. I can't reverse the process."

With a howl of fury, Pia launched herself over the desk. Standing in front of Malachy, shaking with rage, she said. "I used to think I loved you. I thought I loved you more than my own mother. I thought you did what you did— I thought you were trying to help me. But I was just a test subject, wasn't I?"

Malachy calmly reached into his jacket pocket. If he was surprised by Pia's declaration of love, he didn't show it by so much as a flicker of emotion. "I refuse to discuss anything with you if you're going to have a tantrum, Pia."

"Please," she said, sounding like a wounded child. "Just tell me. Did I mean anything to you? Anything at all?" A single, fat tear slid down her cheek, and she brought her hand up to wipe it away, then stared at the moisture on her fingertips. I had never seen her cry before.

Malachy looked at the clients, then back to Pia. "I've already said all I'm prepared to on the subject." Despite his cool demeanor, he was nervously fingering something in his pocket; his pills, I realized. He was holding the vial the way a child might hold a favorite toy, for comfort.

"Oh, you have, have you?" At first, I thought she was going to hit him, or go for his throat. But I had underestimated how human Pia had become. With a flash, she reached out and plucked the vial of pills from his hand. "Maybe I'll refuse to let you have these, then."

"Pia!" Malachy's brows met, and his expression was thunderous. "Give those back this instant!"

"No," said Pia, and her expression was defiant and exhilarated and frightened, a classic adolescent mixture. Of course, Pia wasn't really an adolescent—not biologically, at any rate.

"Pia!" She turned on her heel and slammed into the office, and for a moment, I thought she'd run from his anger. Then I heard a crash and saw Malachy turn white and stagger. "My supply," he whispered, and then the back door slammed open and shut. Ignoring the complaints and queries of the crowd, Malachy and I ran into the back office where I'd hung the William Wegman prints and saw that Pia had opened the safe.

I turned to Malachy, who had sunk into a chair and was holding his head in his hands. I put my hand on one bony shoulder. "Do you have any more of the drugs you need at your home?"

Malachy shook his head. "I had to use them all up to get through the full moon," he said, resting his head in his hands. "I was just about to make up some more."

I felt a pang of guilt, remembering that I had left him alone while I went wolfing it up with Red. Not that I'd had a choice, but still. I gave my boss an awkward pat on the back, thinking that in one sense, this was a success for Malachy. His little protégé had cried real tears today. And she had betrayed him.

No one could argue that she wasn't human now.

TWENTY-FIVE

◉○○ An hour later, Malachy and I had secured the changeling dogs in cages and crates and closed the office. The crowd's mood had turned uglier, with Kayla accusing Malachy of seven different kinds of abuse and Marlene ranting that the virus affecting the dogs could spread to humans. I was more concerned that the lycanthropy virus had mutated so that humans could infect dogs. After all, Malachy's tinkering with the viral DNA had resulted in Pia's transformation. Perhaps the mutated virus had undergone another transformation.

But of course, I didn't say any of that out loud. Just as I didn't question why the virus hadn't manifested itself more during the fullest phase of the moon. In my opinion, that was the strangest part of all, but nobody had asked my opinion. Yet.

"If there is any possibility of interspecies transmission," Malachy had said smoothly, "your best protection is to head home now and let me run tests on your animals."

Reluctantly, the clients had dispersed. Now Malachy sank down into a chair in the waiting room, his head back, his eyes shut. "Right," he said, rubbing his temples. "First, we need to draw blood samples. Next, we need to run through the various scenarios and determine what we're looking for. Then we need to chain me up in the basement."

I gave a little laugh, to be polite, and Malachy looked at me as though I had just had an accident on the floor. "I was not joking, Ms. Barrow."

"Oh, come on, Mal, aren't you being a little dramatic?"

"Have I ever struck you as dramatic? Is that a word you have associated with me in the past?"

Okay. Point taken. At a loss for words, I realized that I had never seen Malachy in this kind of a mood; he seemed defeated. "So can't we whip up a new batch of whatever it is you take?"

Malachy rolled his eyes. "My word, what a marvelous idea! Now, why didn't I think of it? That was sarcasm, in case you failed to notice."

I planted my hands on my hips. "And may I inquire as to why you can't make more pills for yourself?"

Mal kept his eyes closed as he massaged his temples. "Oh, I can absolutely make more pills for myself. Unfortunately, by the time they're ready, there won't be enough left of me to know I ought to take them."

In the charged stillness that followed his statement, I found myself observing inconsequential things. Sunlight slanting through the window, illuminating the dust particles in the air. The flyers on the wall for stray cats and runaway dogs, left by owners who wanted them back, and the flyers for cats and dogs up for adoption, left by owners who wanted to get rid of them. Leashes and dog treats for sale, *Dog Fancy* magazine on the low table. All the trappings of normalcy, on a day that seemed headed straight into the twilight zone.

"It's still you, Mal," I said, and my voice seemed very loud in the quiet room. "It's not some other being. Just as my wolf is still me."

"It's not the same, Abra." Malachy's voice was curt,

either from fatigue or annoyance. "Maybe some essential essence of you is unchanged in wolf form. I wouldn't know. But what I become . . . is deranged." He paused. "And in that deranged state, I revel in my abased and degraded condition. I enjoy myself."

"I don't understand. What do you do that's so terrible? I've hunted deer, Mal. I've grabbed a living creature with my teeth and dragged it down. Maybe that's debased, but when I'm a wolf, it doesn't feel that way." I waited for his answer, my heart pounding. I had never talked about what I did as a wolf with Red. I had never discussed it with anybody, and I wasn't entirely sure why I was revealing this now.

"It's not terrible," said Malachy. He turned to me, his eyes pale in his shadowy face. "If you think like a wolf, and act like a wolf. But have you ever been something less than human and more than beast? Have you ever had just enough awareness to pervert those basic animal pleasures?" Malachy held my gaze. "Have you ever toyed with your prey?"

I didn't say anything, but the memory of what had happened with those young men replayed itself in my head. That had not been a clean, wolf kill. That had been me, between woman and wolf, and it had felt shameful.

"Ah," said Malachy, leaning his head back on the chair and closing his eyes again. "I see that you have. And that is why people have always feared werewolves, I suppose. Because they combine all that is worst in both species."

"Not always," I said, my voice hoarse.

"Perhaps not, for you. But I was trying to isolate the genes that control aggression. And as I said, I do not turn into a wolf. My syndrome is more akin to the one described by Robert Louis Stevenson." At my baffled look, he added, "in his novel *The Strange Case of Dr.*

Jekyll and Mr. Hyde. Honestly, woman, do you Americans even read books in school?"

"Hey, I saw the movie."

"That would be amusing if it weren't so sad." He sighed, and I realized how much I loved arguing with him. Some people have special friends for seeing foreign films, or special friends for tennis. Malachy was my special friend for arguing.

He looked old with his eyes closed, I thought, looking at him now. When he was looking at me, I was distracted from the lines and shadows on his face. But now, he seemed older than my mother, who had two decades on him. "Mal."

His hand still over his face, Malachy opened his eyes and peered at me through splayed fingers. "What?"

"Can you give me directions to make the pills?"

Malachy sighed. "And what good will that do?"

"I can make them for you, and slip them to you if you're not in the right frame of mind."

Malachy removed his hand and just looked at me. "What?"

"You're brilliant. Or I'm an imbecile. I can't decide which."

"Hey, maybe it's both. How long will it take to get the ingredients together?"

Malachy sat up. "It has to be done in stages. I can write everything down and we can do the initial steps now."

"I have one request."

"At this moment, I do believe that I would do anything you wish, Ms. Barrow."

I smiled, because it was pretty damn sweet to be hearing this. "Anything, huh?"

With a rueful shrug, Malachy amended, "If it's within my power to provide."

"In that case, as soon as we're done mixing up your

potion, I need to eat something. Let's go get some lunch."

For a moment, Malachy looked as though he was going to say something. Then he gave me a mocking little inclination of his head and said, "Lunch it is, then."

TWENTY-SIX

◐ ◯ ◯   I had always suspected that one of the key in-gredients in Malachy's little pills would be carbamaz-epine, a mood stabilizer often used to prevent seizures. Instead, he turned out to be relying on the older concoc-tion of phenobarbital laced with diazepam, along with potassium bromide, which explained why he usually had no appetite. As a vet, Mal explained, the phenobarb was easier to acquire. Besides, keeping himself so thin that his body had to break down muscle for glucose was actually part of his seizure-control plan. There was something else in there, however, that Malachy refused to explain. He ran it through the centrifuge, calling it his "secret ingedient" and telling me that it needed to be mixed after nightfall, naked, with only candles for light.

And no, he added, he wasn't joking. Yes, of course he had tried it the other way. Five times.

Half an hour later, unbidden images of Malachy as a naked witch doctor were still popping into my head and making me snicker. Mal looked as though he would have thumped me, if he'd had the strength. But as it was, he barely had the energy to walk the two blocks to the Belle Savage Cafe.

"Hey, Abra. Hello, Malachy," Penny called as we hung up our coats on the coatrack. Coming in from the cold and gray, the cafe felt wonderfully warm and bright and homey. There was a good smell of freshly baked bread permeating the room, and a faint scent of some delicious spice. An old Andrews Sisters song was playing in the background, something about rum and Coca-Cola.

"Here you go," Penny said, as she set a big bowl of beef stew in front of a young man sitting in the corner.

The young man looked up from his laptop. As he pushed his wire-rimmed glasses farther up his nose, he seemed a little startled by Penny's appearance. The youngest of the three Grey sisters, Penny clearly hadn't adjusted to the fact that she was pushing eighty. Her head seemed too large for her shriveled frame, and she wore her hair in a sleek platinum blond bob, the bangs emphasizing her blue saucer-sized eyes, the swinging sides apostrophes to the gleaming white dentures revealed by her oversized grin. All done up in a periwinkle blue dress and ruffled white apron that matched the curtains, she looked like a ghastly version of the actress Carol Channing.

It took some getting used to.

The young man cleared his throat. "But I didn't order yet."

"Smell." Penny indicated the stew, and the young man sniffed. "So? Do you want it, or not?"

"I guess I want it," said the young man, sounding befuddled. Only weekenders tried to order from the small blackboard that listed the cafe's daily specials. Regulars knew that Penny and her sisters would tell you what you really wanted, and that they would invariably be correct, even if you had an initial pang of doubt.

I glanced around the cafe. Now the young man was alternately working his way through his stew and tapping away on a laptop. The other customer was a young, expensively highlighted mother dressed in the yummy mummy weekend uniform of tank top worn over long sleeved tee and tight, faded lowrider jeans. Her toddler, who was sporting matching highlights and a Princeton sweatshirt, was refusing to eat his lovely sandwich. I knew it was lovely because the mother kept telling us all so in a carrying voice.

"But Winston, it's a lovely sandwich," she said coaxingly.

Winston turned his pout to the side, avoiding the bread. "The lady said soft bubbled egg! I wanted the bubbled egg!"

"Boiled, not bubbled, sweetheart, and it's not safe to eat soft boiled, you can get nasty salmonella germs. This is cheddar, and you always like cheddar."

Winston responded by shrieking no, no, no and trying to tip over the high chair. I looked away, trying to hide my smile. It didn't pay to ignore the sisters' advice.

"Let's sit over here, shall we?" Malachy steered me toward a table across the room from the young mother. The room was too small for us to be out of earshot, however, and even with the music playing Mal and I would have to keep our voices down. As if on cue, the Andrews Sisters began singing "Bei Mir Bist du Schon."

"All right," I said, "I think we need to talk about Pia."

Before I could say another word, however, Mal burst in with a wild laugh. "We need to talk about Pia? What is this, a soap opera? In a short time, I'm going to degenerate into a bestial state. There's an epidemic of therianism transforming dogs into wolves, and our office cat may well be prowling town in the form of a tiger." Malachy raked his hands through his woolly hair and gave another broken laugh. "And Christ, mustn't forget there's the manitou problem. And with all this going on, we need to talk about Pia?"

"Actually, I have another couple of problems to add to your list," I admitted, thinking of Magda's brothers and Lilliana's dirt-streaked note. "But I think we need to discuss Pia."

Malachy looked at me with third-degree disdain. "I have no interest in discussing Pia. She has this absurd notion that she loves me, because she has transferred her doglike devotion from Jackie to myself. This is not a matter for analysis."

"Actually, I had meant that we should talk about whether or not the mutated strain of the virus you infected her with could be affecting the other dogs."

Malachy looked chastened. "Oh. Well. Yes, that does seem a likely scenario."

Before I could follow up with another question, Penny bustled up to the table. "Well, now," she said, filling our glasses with water from a pitcher. "What will it be today, folks? I know you'll want a pot of tea, Malachy, and maybe something light—goat cheese and tomato quiche?"

Mal inclined his head, and Penny turned her attention to me.

"Coffee and . . . no, not coffee, how about some lovely fresh ginger beer for you? And I know something you're going to love: cheese fondue! Is that perfect, or what?"

"It sounds wonderful," I said, and Penny beamed at me and hurried back to the kitchen.

"So," I continued as Malachy reflexively checked his pocket for his pills, "we need to get Pia back and take a blood sample. Unless you've tested her recently."

Malachy shook his head. "No. Recently she has refused to let me monitor her condition. I have no idea what's gotten into her lately."

"She wants to be more than a medical experiment to you." And, I did not add, I know how she feels. My feelings for Malachy weren't romantic, but like Pia, I longed to have him acknowledge that our connection was more than professional. He had been my mentor, and it was only natural that now I wanted him to acknowledge me as a peer. No, more than that: I wanted him to recognize me as a kindred spirit.

Malachy looked down his long nose at me. "I sense a lecture coming on. Some treacly bromide about medical ethics and respect for individuals, no doubt."

"You did treat her like a guinea pig, you know."

"I beg your pardon. When she was a dog, I treated her like an experimental subject. When she was human, I gave her a job. What more do you want from me?"

I shrugged my shoulders. "Me? Not a thing. She, however, seems to have wanted something else—love, I suppose." Thinking about Red, I reached into my handbag, feeling around for my cell phone.

Malachy looked appalled, as if I'd suggested he try French kissing the Pekingese. "But she's barely human . . . and she's an infant."

"She's as human as you made her," I said. "And even if she's inexperienced in our culture, biologically speaking, she's an adult female. She was what, three years old last October? That's around twenty-eight for a person. Unless she's aging in dog years, of course. Is she?"

"No, of course she's not," snapped Malachy. "So what are you saying: I made her, so now she's my responsibility?"

I raised my eyebrows.

"I didn't mean I wouldn't take care of her . . . as is perfectly apparent." Malachy held up his left hand and began counting the ways on his fingers. "One, I have given her training. Two, I supervise her. Three, I feed her. Four, I pay her." Putting his hand down, Malachy said, "The only thing I do not do, in point of fact, is allow her into my bedroom."

I sat up straighter, startled by this piece of information. "She's actually told you she wants to sleep in your bedroom?"

"She's told me that she wants to sleep in my bed, but she insists she would be happy to lie curled up on the floor. Don't look at me like that, of course I refuse." Malachy reached in his pocket, remembered the pills weren't there, and then rubbed his hand over his face. "In any case, I couldn't have sexual relations with the foolish girl, even if I wanted to." Malachy pulled his hand away and said, very matter-of-factly, "The medication that controls the progress of my disease also inhibits sexual functioning."

I glanced over to see if the mother and toddler had overheard, but luckily, they were preoccupied with crust removal. "I didn't realize," I said, awkwardly, remembering our interlude in front of the cabin. Without thinking, I touched the moonstone under my shirt, and for a moment, I saw the outline of another man around Malachy; a larger, stronger, darker figure, ruled by passion instead of reason. "Did you explain the, ah, problem to Pia?"

"Of course I did," said Malachy, making no attempt to hide his growing irritation. "I thought perhaps bluntness would solve the problem, but it only made it worse. Now Pia's been after me to stop taking the meds."

I tried not to smile. "Oh."

Malachy rotated his shoulders, gazing over my shoulder at an abstract painting of circles within squares within circles. "I was going to tell her that even if I were physically capable, I would be disinclined to embroil myself in all the hellish complications of sex in the workplace."

"Maybe using simpler language," I suggested.

Malachy met my eyes, and for a moment, I saw a flare of bright green light them from within. "Although, hypothetically speaking, if I were so inclined, I would at least choose a woman with whom I could have an intelligent conversation." There was a moment of silence while I tried to think what to say, and then Malachy added, "Like yourself."

I was mated. According to Red's traditions, I was married. And up until that moment, I had been coasting on a sea of contentment. But in the long moment that Malachy held my gaze, my heartbeat quickened and my blood surged. He wanted me. I told myself that it was the surprise of hearing him say the words that was warming me. That, and the fact that I had always wanted my brilliant former teacher to recognize my intelligence and grant me special status by his acceptance of me. But despite that odd moment earlier this month, I wasn't physically attracted to Malachy. And in any case, it was a hypothetical declaration of desire.

"Thank you," I said at last. "I'm flattered that you would think of me that way. I mean, if it weren't for the medication," I continued, floundering and sinking more deeply into the mudpit of awkwardness.

"Oh, I think of you that way, even when I'm on the medication. It doesn't remove desire, just the means of satisfying it." Malachy smiled, a thin, wry smile filled with a very masculine knowledge. "But I'm not telling you anything new, although on the previous occasion, we didn't use words."

And there it was: The acknowledgment that what had passed between us that day had not been an aberration due to hormones and stress.

I cleared my throat. "But of course, I'm with Red," I said, suddenly aware of a faint burning sensation on my left arm.

"Yes, so you are," said Malachy evenly, as though I'd brought up a useful observation in class. "And in any case, I will have a very small window between becoming fully functional and losing all ability to discriminate.

Now that I'm off the meds, I have about . . ." Mal checked his watch, "six to eight hours, I estimate, until I become a danger to you or any other woman between the ages of sixteen and sixty."

I couldn't suppress a little choke of laughter. "You mean you're going to go from celibate to sex machine?"

Malachy reached for his pocket, then stopped. "There will be nothing mechanical about me. I will be a creature of impulse and aggression and lust. And from what I can ascertain, I won't be pretty, either." Closing his eyes for a moment, he said, "And I'm going to require your assistance to restrain myself."

I didn't have time to ask him to elaborate, because Penny's older sister, Dana, had come by with Mal's tea and my ginger beer. "And how are you folks doing today?" Unlike her skinny sister, Dana was a tank of a woman in a seventies-style maroon pantsuit, with the kind of breasts that keep others at a respectful distance. Her hair had the distinctive artichoke-shape that requires sleeping with rollers and liberal application of hairspray to achieve, but for some reason, she wasn't wearing her dentures today, and her mouth looked like a wrinkled, half-empty purse.

With a speed and efficiency that belied her age, Dana set out Mal's pot of tea and my ginger beer, and then set up the little burner for the fondue pot. When she was done, Dana paused and stared at me for a moment, her hands on her ample hips. "I don't know what Penny was thinking. You don't want fondue today, do you? Fiddling with bread and cheese. A nice big hamburger, that's what you need. And as for you," she told Malachy, "you don't want quiche, you want bangers and mash." Whisking away the fondue burner, she headed back into the kitchen.

"Yes, of course, English sausage is going to set me to rights," muttered Malachy under his breath. "Better

serve it quickly, before I start swinging from the chande-
lier."

I didn't question why he sounded so bitter. Even
though we had every reason to believe that I'd be able to
inject him with an initial dose of his medicine, Malachy
knew that he was going to temporarily lose his ability to
reason, and that I was going to see him in that irrational
state. That would be shaming for anyone, but particularly so for a man like Malachy, who prized reason
above all else.

I put my hand on Mal's, wishing I knew how to comfort him. To my surprise, I felt a surge of warmth at this
small contact, and then Mal closed his fingers over mine,
and my breath caught. I hadn't meant for him to interpret my touch as sexual, but I didn't know how to take
my hand back. His green eyes glowing like a lycanthrope's, Malachy slowly stroked his thumb across the
surface of my palm, sending a current of electricity right
through me.

He looked different, I realized as I watched his face.
Younger. Healthier. More vital. There were fewer gray
strands interlaced with his wiry black curls. The medicine that controlled his disease had also been poisoning
him. In its absence, his control might be weakening, but
his body was growing stronger.

I had to remove my hand. We were holding hands
now, and anyone could see, Red could see—Red—and
then I gasped and pulled away as a stabbing pain lanced
through my left arm.

"What is it, Abra?" Malachy took my arm in his
hands and turned it over, inspecting the scar. The thin
scar from the bonding ceremony looked inflamed, and it
was throbbing unpleasantly. "What have you done to
yourself?" He sounded annoyed, like his usual self.

From the table to our right, the young man looked up
from his laptop. "She has not done this to herself."

TWENTY-SEVEN

◑ ○ ○ "I beg your pardon?" Malachy said, turning to the young man seated in the corner, with his back to the wall.

"Forgive me for interrupting," the young man said in an accent identical to Magda's. "But this scar was given to her." He pushed up his old-fashioned, wire-rimmed spectacles. In his mid- to late twenties, he had a pale, narrow, serious face. In his button-down shirt and wire-rimmed spectacles, he had the look of a scholar from a previous century, but this was clearly not the case: I could see enough of his laptop's screen to make out an aerial view of our village.

I realized that he must be one of Magda's brothers, doing reconnaissance. Nodding at my arm, he said, "You are mated, yes?"

"I'm sorry, but I don't recall either of us asking your opinion," said Malachy shortly. He had the British knack for making "sorry" sound like a synonym for "deeply offended."

"Forgive me, I interrupt your conversation." The young man smiled a little wistfully, more at me than at Malachy. I had a feeling women usually forgave him anything and everything. "But I thought you should know, because you are touching her, and she belongs to another."

"Well, you should mind your own bloody business." Malachy turned his attention back to me. "So, is this boy correct? You and Red are mated?" He gave the last word ironic emphasis.

I nodded, feeling as though I'd just admitted something vaguely shameful. I glanced over at Magda's brother, wondering if I should say something, but he was back to working on his laptop.

"Well, I suppose congratulations are in order," said Malachy. "What does this mean, precisely: You and Red are setting up a den together?" Malachy's sardonic tone was what I would have expected, but there was something in the set of his face that gave the words a different emphasis. He wasn't amused; he was annoyed.

"Yes, that is what it means," our neighbor said.

Malachy glowered at the young man in a way that had reduced both interns and residents to stuttering imbeciles. "I think we can conduct our conversation without your assistance."

"At least, I believe that is what it means," the young man said, frowning as if confused by something. "But your scent . . ." he turned, looking at me with undisguised interest. Masculine interest. "You are not entirely mated, are you? There is a trace of . . . you are still available, I think."

And then I understood why Magda's brother kept interrupting, despite his mild demeanor. I wasn't exactly in heat, but I wasn't entirely out of it, either.

Malachy ran his finger over the scar on my arm, which burned at his touch. In the past, if I'd ever had a fleeting thought of what he would be like as a lover, it had involved books and conversation, a meeting of minds.

But there was another aspect to Malachy, and now I could see it staring out from behind his eyes: a darker self, raw and carnal in a way that was not wolf, but could speak wolf. "That's interesting," said Malachy. "Care to explain the discrepancy?"

If you don't have complete faith in me, this could be dangerous. I had refused the symbols, and not completed the mating, and now I was being punished. Or tempted. Maybe it was Red who was being punished. Overcome with guilt, I wondered what Red might be feeling in his arm right now.

"Well?" Malachy prompted, and I could see that the young man was waiting, as well. I was saved from having to reply when Penny came bustling over with a tray loaded with food. Whatever Dana had told her, it was clear that Penny had won the argument over our order. She set the burner for the fondue in front of me, lit the flame, and then set the food down in front of us. "Now, then," she said with a defiant toss of her bobbed blond hair, "mind you keep stirring the pot, now. And be careful, it's really hot." The bubbling cheese smelled wonderful, and my mouth began to water.

"Thank you, Penny."

"Enjoy," she replied, but as she left I thought I heard her mutter under her breath, "made a mistake, my fanny."

Deciding that it was time to change the subject, I addressed the young man, who had gone back to his satellite map. "I take it you're one of Magda's brothers."

"Grigore—the younger." Grigore nodded his head to Mal, and then to me. "Vasile is Magda's twin. And you are Abra. I have smelled your scent in the forest. Please," he said, indicating my food. "Do not let me keep you from your meal."

I speared a piece of bread with the long fondue fork and twirled it into the cheese. Despite the colossal strangeness of everything, I was still hungry. "Listen," I said, realizing that this was a perfect opportunity to make peace with my new neighbors, "I don't know what Magda has told you about me, but I don't want a fight with you, or anyone else."

"Then you should leave." Grigore spread his hands in a gesture of helplessness. "Not that I wish it. I wish, well, you are a very attractive woman, and a fertile female is always welcome. But mine is not the vote that counts, you understand. And I will support my brother, and my sister."

"Tell me, are you always such a bloody idiot?" Malachy pushed away his cup of tea as though it had offended him. "Because you seem like a bright young man. I don't know how long you've been in town, but surely you've noticed that we have a few problems that outweigh your little pissing contest."

"You speak of the Bear creature? My sister says this talk of mysterious Liminal creatures is a ploy to distract us." Grigore paused, and removed his glasses to polish them on a napkin. "But to be honest, I was intrigued. Your manitous sound a great deal like the Cabeiri— ancient Greek deities."

"Actually, I was referring to what appears to be a little epidemic we have brewing down in the office."

Grigore hesitated before admitting, "I am not familiar with this word."

"We think the lycanthropy virus may be mutating and affecting the animals." I glanced sideways at Malachy. "But we haven't confirmed it yet."

Grigore pressed a button, closing a window on his computer: We had his full attention now. "Ah, epidemic," Grigore said, giving the word a different intonation. "Interesting. So the dogs are infected? I have never heard of such a thing."

"I've been manipulating the viral DNA," said Malachy, taking a sip of his tea. "And recently one of my research subjects got loose."

That was the first I'd heard of it. "When did this happen?"

"While you were frolicking under the full moon," Malachy snapped. "And before you blame me, I should say that I'm pretty sure someone or something released the animal from its cage." Before I could ask the question, Malachy said, "And no, I don't believe it was Pia. There were small paw prints leading up to the cage."

"You think it was one of the manitou," I said, swallowing down another bite of cheesy bread. God, I was starving. Looking at Grigore, I explained, "We've invaded their space, and now they're invading ours."

"Yours, perhaps," said Grigore, shrugging. "But we have greater numbers."

There was something about this Grigore that was really rubbing me the wrong way. For a guy still in his twenties, he had an irritating way of speaking, as though he were the professor and we were the students. "Listen, Greg." I pointed a fondue fork at him. "I don't know what Cabeiri are, but I've met a manitou. It's not something you outmuscle. It's not even something you outmaneuver. It's something that gets inside your head and starts making you think that offering yourself up as a midnight snack is a swell idea. This isn't just a problem for us, or for people living near the mountain. The manitou are spreading out, and they're hungry. "

"And clever," added Malachy. "I sincerely doubt that releasing this particular subject was an accident." He took another sip of tea. "Of course, this still doesn't explain what's going on with the cats. And they're a lot more worrisome—your standard housecat is the number one killer of songbirds. If they all start growing to the size of bobcats, they'll probably start hunting anything that size and under." Malachy pointed to the toddler, who was staring at him, openmouthed. "If some grow to be as large as cougars, however, they can take down the mother as well."

From the other side of the cafe, there was a thin wail. The boy's mother was trying to gather up her toddler's things, which had become scattered all over the floor. I stood up to help her and she held up a hand.

"Oh, no, I think you've done enough!" The mother knelt down, her thong visible over her low-rise jeans as she scooped up a plastic toy. "First you start in with all this talk of S-E-X and mating, and then you go on to hungry monsters. Can't you see that you've terrified my child?"

Winston, who had stopped crying, didn't look particularly terrified as he looked up at his mother and asked, "What's mating?"

"Nothing nice," said the mother, squeezing her son's hand until he gave another sharp yowl.

"I'm sorry," I said, watching helplessly as the woman stuffed the toys into her oversized shoulder bag and stuffed the hysterical toddler into his jacket.

"You should be," snapped the woman. "Come on, Winston, we have to go!"

Winston pointed a chubby finger at the kitchen. "But the fat lady said she'd give me a magic bean!"

"Unfortunately, we have to leave, because *some* people just have no idea how to behave around children." The woman hefted the child onto her hip and left, slamming the door behind her. In her wake, a single yellow plastic top wobbled forlornly on the floor.

"My goodness," said Dana, wiping her hands on her apron as she emerged from the kitchen. "She was in a hurry." Dana gave us a flash of her impressive cleavage as she picked up the toy, but as she began to clear the woman's table, her ready smile froze. I realized that she was looking at our table as her mouth hardened into a thin line of disapproval. "Excuse me," she said sharply, and disappeared into the kitchen.

Malachy and I stared at each other as Dana returned, carrying a tray with sausages and mashed potatoes for him and a grilled hamburger on a toasted bun for me. "I'm so sorry," she said, removing Mal's plate. "I did tell Penny that this wasn't what you wanted."

"I was eating it," Malachy said curtly. "It was fine."

"And what about you?" Dana stood next to me, her cheeks flushed with anger. "Do you want this burger or not?"

"I don't usually eat meat," I replied. "But that does smell delicious."

"Well, do you want it, or not?"

"I did start on the fondue already . . ." Although now that I could smell the sizzling burger, the cheese seemed a bit too cloyingly rich. "I'm not sure."

Penny came out, saw Dana at our table, and rushed over to protect her territory. "Deinyo," she said, "I cannot believe you are pestering customers this way."

Dana set her dishes down on our table. "Well, Pemphredo, *you* didn't get the order right." I realized that the sisters must have been from Greece, originally; I had never heard the original form of their names before.

"They're perfectly happy with their food!"

Dana folded her plump arms under her generous bosom. "They're being polite."

"I know how to settle this," said Penny, her slender form quivering with outrage. "Enid!"

"Really, all we want to do is eat in peace," protested Malachy, but no one paid him any attention.

And then Enid emerged from the kitchen. The oldest Grey sister rarely left the kitchen, and I had only seen her once or twice before. Tiny and almost swamped by her ruffled blue dress and apron, her face a wizened apple topped by a few wisps of sparse white hair, Enid's eyes were covered by the milky film of cataracts. She didn't seem blind, however: Either she had memorized the layout of her shop and had really good hearing, or she had some way of seeing us that didn't involve eyes.

Looking from Mal to me, Enid turned to her sisters. "You're both right," she said, revealing a mouth almost empty of teeth. "They're in transition." Walking up to Malachy, she said, "Choose."

Looking exasperated, Mal pointed to the quiche. "This one," he said. "The one I was perfectly content eating."

Enid nodded to Dana, who removed the bangers and mash with a little disapproving tsk, while Penny shot her a victorious look. "Now you," Enid said. "Pick what you want." A bracelet of stones painted like blue eyes jingled on the old woman's wrist.

Glancing from burger to fondue, I felt completely torn. I had thought I wanted the cheese, but the wolf in me, so recently predominant, yearned for meat. Looking from Dana to Penny, I was also aware that whichever dish I chose, I would be hurting the other sister's feelings. "I don't know which I want. Both, really."

"You can't have both," said Enid, her voice so commanding that I reached for the moonstone under my sweater. As my hand closed around the stone, I thought I saw one of the eyes on the bracelet wink.

"As the old song goes, you can't please everyone," said Dana.

"So you might as well please yourself," finished Penny, sounding eerily girlish as she ended with a giggle. "Oops," she said, clapping her hand over her mouth. "Ma teef jush fell ou'."

"Oh, for heaven's sake," said Dana, leading her sister to the ladies' room. Frankly, I thought all the sisters could use the services of a good dentist.

Enid cleared her throat. "Well, girl, which one will it be?"

"I really can't make up my mind," I said. In truth, I had lost my appetite after that little incident with the teeth.

"Get a grip, Abra," Malachy said to me. "It's just lunch, and we have a lot to get done in a very limited amount of time." Without looking away from me, Mal reached over to the plate Dana was still holding and stabbed a sausage with his fork. "Ah, pig meat," he said, his eyes half closing with gustatory pleasure. He wiped the grease from his lips and I felt a wave of queasiness.

"Malachy, that's disgusting."

And then the two Grey sisters came back and smiled at me.

"Well?" That was Penny, who apparently hadn't managed to get her dentures back in.

"What did you decide?" That was Dana, smiling broadly to reveal big, gleaming white teeth.

Her sister's big, gleaming white teeth.

Clapping a hand over my suddenly roiling stomach, I bolted for the bathroom.

TWENTY-EIGHT

◗○○ Looking at myself in the bathroom mirror, I wished I had brought some makeup with me. My face and lips had drained of color, but there were dark circles under my eyes that I didn't recall ever seeing before. My stomach felt better now that I'd thrown up, but my temples were pounding with the beginnings of a monster headache.

I leaned against the sink, closing my eyes. I didn't know how much of what I'd seen was real and how much was surreal, but I did know that I couldn't just dismiss the sisters' warning. I sighed. Trust my mother to give me a gift that hurt to use but was impossible to just leave in a box and ignore.

There was a knock on the door. "Everything all right in there?" It was Enid's voice.

"Yes, I'll be out in a moment." Removing the elastic from my hair, I finger combed the sides and then redid my ponytail. On the wall was a framed photo of the three sisters in the late fifties, in front of the cafe. They looked exactly the same.

When I opened the door, Enid was holding out a fizzing glass of something that smelled medicinal.

"Here," she said. "You'll want to get this down you fast."

"Thanks," I said, taking the glass and raising it to my

lips. Then, hesitating, I asked, "Is this just some herbal infusion, or am I going to start seeing the walls breathe?"

"It's Alka-Seltzer," said Enid, her white eyes turning in my direction and a small smile playing over her wrinkled seam of a mouth. "No need to go brewing willow bark or blinding newts these days, not when there's a perfectly good pharmacy just across the road. Now, before you go wasting another question, remember that you only get three answers. Three per customer, that's the rule. And that's not per visit—folks always try leaving and coming back, but that's not the way it works."

I narrowed my eyes. "What are you?" Because right now, little old lady didn't seem to apply.

Enid sighed. "You know, with the Internet and all the resources available to you, I would think that you could figure that one out on your own. But if you insist . . ."

"No. Wait." Because I had figured it out, thanks to the extensive education I'd received in ancient Greek mythology from my mother's films. Although in *Beware the Cat* there had been a bit of confusion between the Grey sisters of Greek myth and Shakespeare's witchy weird sisters. But then again, the most pagan thing about Hollywood is the way it borrows and blends the myths of different cultures, and then twists them around to suit its own ends.

I didn't believe in anything now, but when I was younger, I believed in Hollywood movies. So I was following the *Beware the Cat* script.

"Are you trying to help me or harm me? That's the question I want you to answer, and please interpret that in the narrowest possible way."

"In the narrowest possible way? Well, in that case, I want to help you, my dear. We are all three of us of the nurturing disposition."

Now that I thought about it, maybe I should have said

she should interpret "help" in the broadest possible way. Someone needed to write an etiquette guide for dealing with the supernatural. Then I remembered that I had a guide of sorts, and reached under my sweater for my moonstone.

Enid narrowed her eyes, as if she could see what I was doing. "What's that you've got in there?"

There was something about her voice that demanded obedience. Before I could think twice, I was lifting the pendant out of my sweater and showing it to her. Even through the insulating layer of my silk underwear, the silver was irritating my skin.

"No, no, I can't see it like that. Take it off. Look at me, what do you think I'm going to do, run off with it?"

Warily, I removed the necklace and handed it to her.

"Ah," said Enid, appreciatively as she lifted the moonstone to the light coming in from the window. I wondered if she could see, or if she was relying on some other sense to examine my necklace, but I didn't want to waste another question. As Enid turned the pendant, I saw a small rainbow arc through the air between us. "Lovely. Just lovely. Las Lagrimas de la Luna. A good-quality stone, and what a gorgeous setting."

There was no accounting for taste, I supposed. "My mother said it belonged to my father's mother."

Enid looked at me shrewdly, and now I saw that like the moonstone, her opaque eyes had flashes of bright color beneath the surface, iridescent traces of blue and green and purple. "Makes it all the more valuable, doesn't it? But it's not doing you any good wearing it over silk. The stone has to be worn against the skin." As Enid closed her gnarled hand over the stone, I felt a stab of panic. "I'll pay you handsomely for it."

"It's not for sale." I didn't know why I felt so strongly about it, but I held out my own hand, palm up. "And I'd like it back now, please."

"Just a moment, dear, you haven't heard what I'm offering. If it's true vision you want, I can adorn those lovely spectacles of yours with crystals that will help you see things as they truly are, and without the itch and discomfort of silver."

"No, thanks." The true vision part sounded good, but even if I'd wanted rhinestones on my chic new glasses, there was something about Enid that made me doubt I'd get the best of this deal.

"Or how about something to help you conceive? I have a potion guaranteed to make even your great-grandmother as fertile as a fifteen-year-old."

I put my hand on my stomach, which was as flat as ever—flatter, actually, thanks to my days of living wolfishly. "I'm afraid that I have some pretty specific problems in that area."

Enid reached into the pocket of her apron and produced a small, old-fashioned bottle.

"Dear God, Enid, what is that?" The bottle appeared to contain a shriveled homunculus suspended in a pale green fluid, its pitiful mouth open in its otherwise featureless face.

"This, my girl, is mandrake root, the real kind, grown from a drop of hanged man's seed. Whatever your problem, one drink from this bottle and I guarantee conception and, yes, a full-term birth." Enid stuck the bottle closer, so that I could see that it did, indeed, contain a root, and not a tiny, malformed body. "What do you say, my dear? Do we have a deal?"

I stared at the old woman in horrified disbelief. "Enid, first of all, mandrake is part of the nightshade family, and it's poisonous. Second of all, I have no idea what kind of baby you get when you ingest something grown from a hanged man's semen, but I'm guessing not the kind of kid who grows up to be president. So no thank you, but I'll keep my moonstone." I held out my hand,

and Enid looked at it for a moment with a touch of sadness.

"You're quite right, of course. A gift given from a grandmother . . . yes, of course you don't want to sell it. But it's just not going to do anything sitting on your shirt like that."

"I have an allergy to silver," I said stiffly.

"I see. Well, may I put it on for you?"

I turned around, thinking even as I did so that this was a bad idea. But I didn't want to hurt Enid's feelings, and saying "No, just put it in my hand" felt like a direct insult. I felt the old woman's dry, cool hands against the back of my neck.

"I see now that you really do need this necklace," Enid was saying as she fiddled with the clasp. "That's half the trick, you know, finding out what it is that people need. Some need a dress, just to get them the interview, say, and some need a skill, like software programming or spinning straw into gold. You need to be able to use your instincts, even when you're not running around on all fours. Now, then." Enid stepped away and I faced her. "Now you'll be able to face what's coming with your eyes open."

"It feels a bit tight." I put my hand to the necklace and discovered that she had fastened it around my neck like a choker, so that the silver was touching my naked flesh. "Enid, what did you do? I told you, I'm allergic to silver!" Looking into those unspeakably ancient eyes, I wondered how I could have put my faith in her, even for an instant. Trying to remove the necklace, I found the catch impossible to open. "How can I get this off again?"

"By removing your head, of course. Oh, dear, and that was your last question, too."

I tried yanking at the chain, then growled and grabbed

Enid by the spindly arms. "Old lady, if you don't show me how to get this off . . ."

Enid was unruffled. "You want me to remove your head? Don't be a dolt, girl, can't you see I've done you a favor?"

I was about to shake her when there was a crash from the other room.

"My word," said Enid. "I do believe your friend might be in trouble." With a frustrated grunt, I released Enid and ran into the other room to find Malachy lying on the floor, unconscious. Grigore, Dana, and Penny were crouched beside him, Grigore holding down his hands, the two sisters each pinning an ankle to the floor.

"What's going on?" I reached for his wrist, and Grigore shook his head.

"He's having a seizure."

As Grigore said the words, Malachy began to vibrate as though some giant hand was shaking him. His eyes rolled back in his head, and I had a moment to grab a pencil from Penny's apron pocket and cram it into Malachy's mouth before his jaw snapped shut.

"Malachy. Mal. Can you hear me?" Kneeling beside my boss, I pulled back his eyelids and examined his pupils. For a moment, they remained fixed on some distant horizon, and I thought: He's gone. I felt a sudden hollowing in my stomach. Whatever had been unexplored and unresolved between us would now always remain so.

But then Malachy's pupils dilated and he was looking at me. "What happened?"

"You collapsed, and started to shake," said Grigore.

"Did I?" Mal looked befuddled, and so unlike himself that I found myself wrapping my arms around him.

"Are you all right?"

Malachy opened his mouth and another seizure took him. I replaced the pencil and held on to him, waiting it

out, wondering what this was doing to his brilliant, sin-
gular mind, hoping it wasn't irreversible. And then
Malachy went limp, and I stroked his sweat-dampened
hair back from his high forehead. "Mal, can you hear
me?"

Malachy stirred and opened his eyes. He began to
flail, as if fighting. I removed the pencil and said, "Easy,
easy. You're okay."

For one unguarded moment, I saw a flicker of uncer-
tainty in Malachy's green eyes, and then his lids lowered, shuttering his gaze. "Well," he said, "I do hope
you're not going to start fussing over me." He glanced at
his watch. "We need to get back to the laboratory and
finish compounding the medicine. I believe we have less
time than I had first estimated."

Gee, I thought, no kidding. "Can I help you up?"

"I'm perfectly capable of standing up without assistance, thank you very much."

Ignoring this, I put my arm around Malachy's waist to
help him up, ignoring the burn of the silver moonstone
around my neck and the dull throb in my left arm, along
the scar Red had given me in our mating ceremony.

I knew better than to touch it, though. I figured love,
magic, and poison ivy had one thing in common: The
more you scratched the itch, the more you were affected.

TWENTY-NINE

◑○○ Along the way back to the veterinary office, Malachy and I saw signs that Northside's dogs were not the only creatures behaving strangely. A young moose, seldom seen this far south, ambled down Church Street, its head down as if it refused to even acknowledge our presence, before veering off into the wooded thicket behind the funeral parlor. The new moon was invisible in the afternoon sky, and after the days of seeing it full in the sky all day as well as night, I found myself missing it like an absent lover. Red. I flipped open my cell phone and tried him again, but the phone indicated he was out of range.

There was a mocking sound, almost like laughter, and I turned to see five crows flap heavily down to the ground, where they hopped around like paparazzi, waiting to catch some big name in a moment of weakness. A massive red-tailed hawk gave a low screech and sailed over the telephone wire, and a turkey vulture landed on a split rail fence opposite.

I nudged Malachy with my elbow. "Are you thinking *The Birds*? Because that looks very Hitchcock to me."

"I am wondering what fresh kill they anticipate," Mal responded. "And hoping it is not us."

A moment later, as we turned the corner onto Main Street, a group of ten-to-twelve-year-old boys swarmed past us, whooping and hollering. This would not have been remarkable, except for the fact that it was the end of January and the boys were naked from the waist up and using jump ropes to drag a grown man in a suit and tie behind them.

After a moment, I recognized the school's principal, Mr. Glynn. "Boys," he kept pleading, "boys, please. Don't you realize that this will go on your permanent record?"

Clearly, this was not quite the deterrent Mr. Glynn intended, because the boys merely laughed and jeered at him in response.

I wanted to run after them and help, but Malachy put his hand on my arm, stopping me. "We need to figure this out, first. Look up."

Obediently, I looked up at the blue sky. "What am I supposed to be seeing?"

"Look at the clouds, Abra," said Malachy, sounding impatient. "Look to the east."

"It's getting dark," I said.

"A storm is coming. But not a winter storm. That sky, those clouds—I'm not an expert, but does that look like a January sky to you?"

I shook my head, and realized that the quality of the air had changed. There was something subtle in the angle of light, in the smell on the breeze, that felt more like March than January. But the heavy, dark clouds that were gathering in the east were from another season entirely: July, perhaps. The season of wild shifts in weather, when clear skies could abruptly turn to thunderstorms, or hurricanes and twisters.

"And look there," said Malachy. "The birds are coming back."

I turned to see a dark swarm of shapes flying toward us: Canada geese in their deep V formation, swallows and robins, and many others I didn't recognize. It was a mass migration to our unnatural spring.

"I'm guessing this isn't just global warming at work," I said, taking off my coat.

"I suspect this is a bit more localized." Malachy held his coat over his shoulder and took my elbow, as if we were out for a stroll. I tried my cell phone again. "Still no reception," I said.

"Is that usual?"

I shook my head. Northside had an unusual number of dead zones, but Main Street wasn't normally one of them. I punched in Red's number again, and this time there was a faint signal. "He's not picking up," I said.

Mal nodded, quickening his steps. Now that the seizure had passed, he seemed energized. Maybe the misfiring of his neurons had worked as a kind of autonomic electrotherapy. Hurrying now, Mal said, "We'll try again back at the office."

I nodded and lengthened my stride to keep up with him. I felt a slight cramp in my side and began to slow down again.

As clearly as if she were standing there beside me, I heard my mother's voice in my head, saying: *Abra, this is no time to baby yourself.*

Hearing voices. That couldn't be good. On the bright side, however, Malachy had been reporting that he saw the same things I did, which meant moonstone wasn't a hallucinogen. I didn't know why it had given me that strange vision of the three sisters, Malachy, and Grigore, but maybe the longer the stone touched me, the more I got used to it. I tried not to think about what the silver was doing to my skin. When I thought about it, I began to itch.

"Stop scratching yourself," Malachy said, and I put my hand down.

As we passed old man Miller on his porch, the town's

former mayor suddenly stood up and leaned on his cane, his long white beard trembling as he began to prophesy in a quavering voice. "Heed me well, O Children of iniquity, the whole nation shall be punished for thy sins."

"I thought he was an atheist," I said, looking back. "And when did he grow that beard?"

"About the same time Jackie turned professional." I turned in astonishment to see that Jackie was sitting in the gazebo in the little village square where Santa greeted the village children at Christmas. Like Santa, Jackie had a long line of people waiting to meet her, but unlike Santa, her bright-eyed devotees were all men. The men were wearing long-sleeved shirts, and some of them were carrying chickens, and one or two were holding a rope tied to a goat or a pig.

Up on the gazebo, Jackie was wearing a silky purple nightgown. And reclining on a huge pile of furs and blankets, her wolfdogs arranged in a semicircle around her.

"Hey," said a local farmer as I cut through the line, but I ignored him.

"Jackie," I said, "what on earth are you doing?"

Jackie didn't get up from the improvised bed. "What does it look like I'm doing?"

There was no polite word for it. "Are you feeling all right? Why don't you get up from there and come with Malachy and me." Inspired, I added, "We'll call Red for you."

Jackie smiled, and it was her old, familiar, wry smile. "Honey, Red will find his way to me. Today I am high priestess here, and the goddess inhabits me. All the men must worship me. Even yours."

I shook my head, trying to find a way to reason with her. "Jackie, I don't know what's going on here, but this isn't you. And when you come back to yourself, you're going to regret the hell out of this."

"But I am not myself, Abra," said Jackie, and for a moment, behind her faded blue eyes, I saw a flash of fire. "I am the goddess. Come," she said, holding out her hand to an eighteen-year-old with a gigantic Adam's apple that kept bobbing up and down in excitement. "Worship me."

I hightailed it back to Malachy before I could witness the service. "Malachy, we have to stop her. She's turning herself into the village whore."

Not the village whore, said my mother's voice inside my mind. *The temple prostitute.* And I remembered that in my mother's film *El Castillo De Los Monstres,* the virgin daughter of Don Carlos had been transformed into the high priestess of Baal, and offered herself to all the men in the village.

And Malachy was joining the line of men.

"Whoa there, Boss. Wrong way."

His face was slightly flushed, and he dabbed at his forehead with a handkerchief. "I think I ought to just speak with Jackie for a moment. Ask her if she's seen Red."

"Maybe we should stick to the original plan."

"Really, Abra, I should think you would see the logic of consulting with Red's former girlfriend." Malachy took another step toward the line, and seeing that someone else had taken his former position, was about to tap the man on his shoulder.

"Come on, Malachy." I grabbed him by the arm, and he shrugged me off, intent on reclaiming his place in line. "Malachy, this is wasting time." Malachy didn't even glance at me. I looked off, past the field behind the gazebo, into the tree line at the edge of town. Bruin was there. I couldn't see him, but I could feel the heaviness in the air, the density of overlapping realities that marked his presence.

Unless Bruin wasn't there, and he had simply marked off this whole town as his territory.

"Malachy, please," I said, tugging at his arm. Red, I thought, where the hell are you? This morning felt like a hundred years ago.

"Pardon me," Malachy was telling the man in front of him, "but you're in my place."

"I didn't see no one standing here," the man replied. He was wearing a Tractor Supply cap and carrying a jar of honey, either as gift or lubricant.

"I stepped aside for a moment, but that was my place."

"Buddy, I am not letting you in front of me. And you don't even have an offering."

"It's you who have stepped in front of me, buddy," said Malachy with cold fury. Seeing that there was no other way to get his attention, I stepped in front of Malachy and slapped his face. Hard.

For a fraction of a second, I thought he was going to slap me back, or worse. But then Malachy touched his face with a wry smile and said, "Thank you, Abra. I think we had best move directly to the office. Whatever is influencing the people and animals of this town . . . without my medication, I am far from immune to it."

No shit. As I took Malachy's arm again, I could feel the heaviness of the air, the electrically charged atmosphere of a summer storm, the heat-distorted shimmer of buildings in the distance. Every instinct told me to take cover, except that I was pretty sure that getting inside wasn't going to protect me. I'd felt this wrongness before, although last time it had ruffled my fur, and I hadn't had words to describe it.

Now, with moonstone certainty, I knew that this storm was metaphysical, and it wasn't just going to change the weather. It was going to redesign reality.

As we walked away from Jackie and the queue of men

in front of the gazebo, I could hear the man in the Tractor Supply hat tell the man in front of him, "What an asshole. I hate line jumpers."

"Stop breathing down my neck," the other man replied.

I had to literally drag Malachy by the arm to keep him from turning around.

THIRTY

◐◉○ As I secured the sleeve to the straitjacket, I asked Malachy, "Are you sure this is really necessary?"

"No, but it's so much fun. Of course I'm sure it's necessary. Did you fasten it securely?" Malachy craned his neck to check himself in the mirror.

I tested the strap. "I think I did it right. This is my first time putting a guy in a loony suit, you know."

"I think you need to pull it tighter."

"I'm afraid your arms are going to lose circulation. We can always tighten it later." Despite the fact that Malachy had hours left before his medication wore off, he'd decided that we needed to put him in restraints, just as a precaution. And deep down, I had to agree with him. Something about the town of Northside had always amplified the effect of any preternatural weirdness, but thanks to the manitou, we were all in weirdness overdrive.

"Later I may not be so cooperative. Pull it one more time."

With a grunt, I gave one last hard yank. I was sweating from exertion, and when I glanced down, I could see nipples through my long-sleeved white silk undershirt. I had dressed for winter, in layers, but it was too hot for sweaters now. Unfortunately, I hadn't thought to wear a brassiere, and my breasts were still swollen and tender.

Never mind. Focus on the present dangers. I took out my cell phone and tried to reach Red again. Again I got a signal but no response. I was about to close the phone when I saw that I had two new messages.

"Abra," Malachy said, sounding annoyed. "You've made this too tight."

"One minute," I said, trying to listen to my voice mail. To my disappointment, the first one wasn't from Red, but from my mother, who wanted to know if I'd been trying to call her. This, of course, was her way of letting me know that she was pissed off that I hadn't been in touch.

"Abra," Malachy said sternly. "Can you please put that phone down and come help me?"

"Just wait a moment," I snapped, going on to the next message. This wasn't from Red either. Instead, it was a woman named Galina Michailovna. Just my luck, I thought; she's probably selling something. When I listened to what she had to say, however, my chest tightened with anxiety. "Ms. Barrow, this is a friend and colleague of Lilliana Kadouri. I was expecting to see Lilli at supervision today, but neither she nor her driver were seen since they dropped you off over a week ago."

Malachy was watching me, his eyes shrewd and watchful and touched with a faint, manic light. "Who was it? Is it Red?"

"No," I said, closing the phone. "Not Red." A wave of grief began to rise up, ready to crash over me. Lilliana and her driver hadn't been seen for a week. I thought of the dirt-stained note she'd left at the cabin along with my pocketbook and clothes, and the strange, heavy places where the manitous' reality overlapped with our own. I remembered the scent of human blood, and the dead weekender. But that woman hadn't been the only one to die while I ran around the forest, enjoying myself. And then, just as I began to press my nails into my palms and bite the insides of my cheeks in a burst of self-loathing, I knew with an intuitive flash: Lilliana wasn't dead. She was a sensitive, a broadcaster as well as a receiver. She could play men like instruments. If anyone could keep Bruin from selling his sacrifice scheme, it was Lilliana.

"Bad news?" Malachy's voice was soft, almost kind.

"Lilliana brought me back last week. She's been missing." Back when we'd both been working for Mal, I hadn't really understood why he had plucked her from the Animal Medical Institute's social work program. Now, of course, it made sense. Lilliana's empathic gifts would have been a great asset in diagnosis—and in political maneuvering within AMI.

"That woman is too resourceful to wind up mauled to death by a spirit bear," said Malachy. "So what we have to do now is locate Red and begin searching." He sounded so much like his old self that it seemed a bit peculiar that he was wearing a straitjacket.

"You're right," I said, drying my eyes on my sleeve.

"Of course I'm right. And now, if you're done dabbing at the old mascara, I've lost all feeling in both arms. You've got to take this blasted thing off and do it again."

"All right." I had started to unfasten the strap when Malachy began cursing. "Bloody hell, Abra, what did I tell you about listening to me?"

I paused, feeling sweaty and tired and sore. "You said not to pay attention if you started to contradict yourself. But you didn't . . ." I looked at Malachy. "Oh, crap. I almost fell for it."

"Very good. You're learning." Mal's eyes dropped to my breasts for a moment, then lifted. "Now, loosen the straps. We have to check on the animals and finish preparing my medicine."

"Very funny." I went to the closet and pulled out my

lab coat. I didn't like the way Malachy's eyes kept dropping to my chest. Or, rather, I didn't like what it implied about his deteriorating condition.

"No, I'm serious, Abra. Obviously I can't work while I'm in a straitjacket."

I pulled my arms into the sleeves. "You'll tell me what to do, and I'll be your arms."

"This was meant to be a test run, Dr. Barrow. Now, let me out of here—we don't have much time left."

"Sorry, but nice try." I opened the door to the room where we kept the animals, and there was a wild sound of howling and whining. It didn't take a genius to figure that our canine patients had just switched from the toy and sporting groups to the hunting category.

I held the door and gestured to Malachy. "After you."

Malachy gave me a familiar look of irritation. "I'm not playing around, you stupid girl. At least let me take a piss first. Unless you'd like to give me a hand with that, as well?"

Shit. We hadn't discussed this. "All right," I said, coming around his left side.

"Thank you from the bottom of my bladder," Malachy said sarcastically.

Ah, the British. None of this euphemistic "going to the bathroom." At least he hadn't informed me he needed to take a . . . my hands stilled on the straps. "Wait a minute. This is another test, isn't it?"

"You're testing my patience, all right."

I still didn't undo the strap. There was some quality of tension and alertness about Malachy that wasn't quite right. And the image of myself, lying dead in this office, was a useful reminder to be cautious. "On the other hand, Mal, why don't I help you undo your trousers?"

"Now, there's an idea," said Malachy, and his eyes were burning with a fierce green light.

Uh oh. "Mal, I thought you said we had hours left before you changed."

Malachy frowned as if I were losing my mind. "We do. Hours and hours. Now, let's go see about the dogs."

I held the door for him, just like before. As he walked through, I said, "You know, Mal, something just occurred to me."

He turned and looked over his shoulder. "What?"

I slammed the door in his face and locked it behind him.

This isn't Northside, I told myself. It looks like Northside, and it's laid out like Northside, but this is a brand-new town, with brand-new rules. What looks familiar is what's going to trip you up, so use your intuition.

I really wished I'd worn a brassiere today.

There was a pounding on the door as Malachy flung himself against the wood. "Abra! Let me out of here!" The dogs were racing around, too. Somehow, he'd gotten his shoes off and unlatched their cages with his toes.

"Don't get your panties tied in a knot," I said, trying not to get flustered as I took out the large office scissors and cut the legs of my corduroys off at the knee.

I had wasted two of my questions, but at least my fairy grandmother had managed to give me the ability to know what I knew. No more questioning my instincts. No more waiting for Malachy to give me permission or hoping Red would come to the rescue. I knew what was behind all this, and I knew what I had to do.

"Let me out now," Malachy said in a perfectly reasonable tone, "and I won't fire you."

"I'm just changing my shirt," I replied. "Give me a sec." Working as quickly as I could, I used two wide dog leashes crisscrossed over my chest to create a makeshift bandoleer over my silk undershirt.

"Come on, Abra," Malachy said, coaxingly, but with

just the right hint of impatience. Whatever was behind that door had some of Malachy's cunning, and without the moonstone, I wasn't entirely sure that I wouldn't have fallen for it.

"One more minute." The tone was right, the words sounded like ones Malachy would have chosen, but the voice was a full register deeper, as if the chest around the larynx had expanded.

"Abra!!!" The door shook and the wood began to buckle as Malachy kicked it, hard. Looking at where the wood was buckling, I swallowed a lump in my throat. Crap, he was big. For a moment, I just stared at the door, mesmerized, waiting to see if the next impact would break through the wood.

You're not watching a movie, kid. Keep working.

Ah, the small, clear voice of my intuition. Even if it did sound a bit like my mother, I was getting pretty damn fond of it. Using a thin rope leash, I secured the waistband of my baggy corduroys. Next, I stuck the scissors in the bandoleer on my right side, so I could pull it out quickly. I grabbed two syringes of phenobarbital, still missing the secret sauce, and then quickly mixed up four syringes of Telazol, inserting one into each boot and two into my crude ammo belt. The two syringes of phenobarb went up, closer to my shoulders, because it was less dangerous if something went wrong and it went into me instead of whoever I was aiming at. I added one more rope leash, in case I needed to lasso a stray or garrote someone, and, remembering at the last minute that I preferred Rimbaud to Rambo, I stashed a bunch of doggie treats into my pockets.

I was loaded for bear.

And then Malachy kicked the door one last time. There was a loud crash as the wood gave way, and the wolfish dogs came hurtling out, snarling and circling as they tried to divide their attention between me and the guy who had torn the door off its hinges.

"Oi," said the creature as he stepped over the threshold. "I got a bone to pick with you."

He didn't specify which bone, but I was guessing something large enough to count as one of my favorites.

THIRTY-ONE

◐○○ My first impression was that there was a definite market for Malachy's new version of the lycanthropy virus. A lot of guys would give their left testicle to achieve the kind of hulking, muscular physique that Malachy now possessed. He was still fully human, or at least he wasn't part wolf, but his massively muscled arms looked a bit long for his body, and there was a demonic light in his heavily lidded eyes that didn't bode well for my immediate future. The remnants of the straitjacket clung to his thick neck and heavy shoulders like a bizarre poncho, but he carried himself like a street fighter, on the balls of his feet, and as he approached me, his white teeth showed in a feral smile.

"That was very naughty, tying me up like that," he said in a thick Cockney accent. Typical upper-middle-class English class prejudice, I thought, giving his savage alter ego a working-class burr.

"You did ask me to do it," I pointed out, taking a step back and trying to calculate how long it would take me to get out the door.

"Me? I didn't ask you, love—that was fucking Malachy, the junkie wanker. You can call me Knox."

Oh, perfect. I didn't know much psychology, but I figured that this kind of splitting wasn't a sign of mental health. "I'm sorry, Knox, I made a mistake," I said, trying to remember everything I knew about multiple personality disorder. I'd seen a TV movie once, *Sybil,* about multiple personalities. Sally Field had played the title roles.

Turns out I didn't really know anything about the disorder. "Sorry, Knox," I said.

"It's all right," said Knox, shrugging. "Happens all the time. What I don't understand is, how can folks confuse us? It's not like we look the same. I mean, do I look like that fucking nancy boy? Do I?"

I shook my head, but Knox did look like Malachy's younger, healthier, lunatic brother. His hair was still the same wild mass of black corkscrew curls, his nose was still a sharp blade, but his brow ridge seemed more pronounced, and his eyes glowed the way wolves' eyes do at night. Still, the intelligence that filled them was unmistakably human, although there was an element of animal cunning and impulse in there as well.

Ah, the ability to think in the abstract without any conscience to direct it. The definition of a sociopath. I was so glad that I had a moonstone necklace welded around my neck, so that I could really understand how badly I was screwed right now. "I must have made a mistake," I said.

"Indeed you did. And you hurt my feelings, see? Because Malachy is a sick old fuck. I don't like being confused with a sick old fuck. You can understand that, can't you?"

I nodded. Maybe if I just kept going along with whatever he said, it would all be all right.

"The way I sees it, you need to make it right."

"What can I do to make it right, Knox?"

"Let me think . . . ah. Got it. You can let *me* tie you up."

So much for going along with him. "Sorry," I said, wishing I could have laid my hands on a tranquilizer gun. "I can't do that. Listen, Malachy, I don't know how much of you is in there, but I don't want to hurt you."

"Already told you, darlin'—not Malachy. And how about being on the receiving end of some hurt?" said Malachy, smiling a very unpleasant smile. His canines were very sharp. "How does you feel about that?"

"I feel pretty negative about that, Mal."

His green eyes flared with fury. "Call me that again," he said, "and I'm going to make you very sorry."

Shit. He sounded so much like Malachy, and I was used to being with a man who looked like a beast on occasion. It was hard to believe that we couldn't work this out in words.

Then that's the role you have to play, said my mother's voice. *It's your only advantage.* And even though I had never tried to manipulate a man in my life, I realized that this really was the only way I'd get close enough to use my weapons. In a straight fight, Tall, Dark, and Hairy here was going to beat me.

By rights, I should have been able to go at least partially wolf, because the moon was still more than three quarters full. But something was wrong; either I was too nervous to access that part of me, or something else was interfering with the usual lunar cycle. But with the moonstone around my neck, I knew with certainty that there was almost nothing of wolf in me. I felt the way I did during the darkest day of the month, when the moon was entirely in shadow.

I was going to have to rely on my human talents, such as they were.

"I don't think you really want to hurt me," I said optimistically, as if I believed it.

"Of course I don't *want* to hurt you," said Knox. A wolfish dog made a sudden lunge for him, and he knocked it aside with a careless flick of his wrist, sending it crashing against the wall. "But, you see, I seems to lack a little fine motor control."

Crap. He could lie in this form. That was one thing even half-formed lycanthropes couldn't do: When the animal is predominant, it's almost impossible to use language to describe things that are not true.

Scattering the remaining dogs with a glance, Knox turned back to me and asked, "How's your threshold for pain, little girl?"

Forcing myself not to focus on the whimpering dog picking itself up and limping away, I met Knox's gaze. His eyes were still green in this form, but they glowed with an odd, phosphorescent sheen, like something that lived in the darkness of the ocean depths, drawing its prey. "I might not mind a little pain, if there were pleasure with it."

Knox cocked his great, shaggy head to one side, the gesture so familiar I had to remind myself that this was not truly him. "Go on," he said.

"Well," I began, and then he was across the room in a single bound, his great hand shot out, grabbing my ponytail and pulling until my head came back, baring my throat. "This, for example," Knox said. "Is this what you calls pleasurable pain?"

"No," I said, keeping calm, trying not to panic at the sheer size and strength of him. "There's only one kind of stimulus going on, and nothing to make me recontextualize it as pleasure."

There was a spark of something in the creature's eyes, as if I had reached something within. "Explain."

And then I knew exactly what to do. Because I'd watched this scene a hundred times, with my mother playing the mousy librarian turned sorceress. Hell, I'd been named for this character; it was the role I'd been born to play. "I need to feel you against my body," I said. "Don't let go of my hair, but don't break my neck, either."

Knox's massive arms closed around me, lifting my feet clear off the floor as he lowered his mouth to mine. One hand still gripped my hair so tightly that my scalp burned, but now I could feel his rapid heartbeat against my breast, and feel the enormous length of his arousal pressed up against my belly. "Like this?"

"Uh huh." The bonding mark wasn't burning this time, probably because I would rather have been fondling a shark.

"You don't smell like you like it," said Knox.

I kept forgetting how much animal there was in him. I was going to have to lie with my body, or this wasn't going to work. "Let's try this," I said, and kissed him with everything I had. Ignoring the strangeness of that great, shaggy form, the sharpness of the canines against my tongue, I conjured the memory of our other encounter, when I had sensed Malachy's beast rising and felt desire for it, and him.

Wrapping arms and legs around Knox, pulling against the hand that held my hair, pressing myself against him while his hand came up to hold my rear.

I could feel his huge fingers cupping me, one finger stroking the crease between my buttocks. Don't panic, I told myself. This is working. I reached my hand up, trying to reach one of the syringes.

"Boring," said Knox, breaking free. "When do we get to the pain part?"

Okay, this was not working. And then it hit me: Malachy is inside there. This is a version of the man you know. "You tell me, Mal."

"I already told you," growled Knox, "not to call me that."

"But that's what I find stimulating," I said. "The

thought that my cool, aloof professor has finally un-
leashed his beast."

The big hands dropped me so that I landed hard on
my ass. "I ain't nobody's beast, woman. I've got nothing
to do with that gormless weakling."

"You don't have his inhibitions," I responded, standing up and brushing myself off. "But what about his
intelligence?"

"There's an idea," said Knox. "Maybe I should per-
form one of his old experiments. He always wondered
what would happen if he used a human instead of a
monkey."

"But I'm not purely human, any more than you are,"
I said, making myself step closer. "Like you, I have a
wild side."

"Huh. If you do, I don't see it," said Knox. "You look
like a plain old bit of fluff to me. Human. Timid. Nervous." He put his face down, closer to mine. "Break-
able."

There was nothing I could do about the smell of fear
coming off me. All I could do was stare into the eyes of
the beast and say with utter conviction, "Look deeper.
There's more to me than meets the eye. I've got a lover
who adores me, and I'm supposed to be bonded to him,
but when we were in the cafe and you told me that you
wanted me, Mal, I wondered what it would be like between us."

Knox's neck and shoulders tightened and his face
turned almost purple with rage. "That sick limp-dicked
fuck was not me!"

"The hell it wasn't," I retorted. "It was you," I said,
poking my finger into his chest, "Malachy Knox, doctor
of veterinary medicine, and now that you're not fucking
impotent, don't go telling me that it was someone else!"

"I'll fucking sort you out," said Knox, grabbing me
around the throat.

"Because you're too scared to admit that you want me," I said, as calmly as if we were arguing a diagnosis. "Malachy."

"Say it again and I'm not fucking responsible," said Knox, his fingers tightening around my throat, pressing the moonstone into my skin.

Say it again, whispered the moonstone in my mind.

"Malachy," I said, risking everything. "Mad Mal."

With a roar, he was on me, and I couldn't breathe because he was kissing me that hard, with desperation and a passion so fierce that it shook me. His hands crushed me against his massive chest, and he moved his mouth over mine like he meant to devour me. *Air. I needed air.* I pushed at him, trying to make some space between us.

He raised his head then. "Change your mind?" His green eyes were glowing more softly now, and his voice was a rasp, a whisper.

I took a deep breath, then pulled his head back down to mine. "No."

With a low growl, Knox took one massive paw and closed it over my left breast. I gasped, steeling myself for a brutal squeeze, but instead, the creature touched me with surprising delicacy. "Your nipples are hard," he said, sounding astonished. "I thought this was some kind of trick."

"No trick, Mal." This time, as he kissed me, there was something touchingly tentative about the way he explored the shape of my breast. Then, just as I arched my back in response to that maddeningly light caress, he pinched my nipple hard enough to make me gasp.

"Pain?"

I shook my head. "Pleasure."

"Abra," he said. I looked up and saw that Malachy's eyes were no longer glowing, and the expression in them wasn't sadistic or cold. In the midst of that harsh, stranger's face, Malachy's eyes were looking out at me with anguish and desire and something else that I could not quite put a name to. "I can . . . Christ, I can think again. I don't know how long I can . . . if you don't want to do this, Abra . . ."

"Malachy," I said, "look in my eyes. I want to do this."

He looked in my eyes, and I shot him full of both syringes of phenobarbital.

THIRTY-TWO

◐○○ I was lost. It was ridiculous, but I had to admit it; for the past half hour, I had been trying to get back to the Belle Savage Cafe, but either I was becoming disoriented, or the town was rearranging itself. There was a small field that had stretched between Orchard and Main, and I had made the mistake of cutting across it to avoid Jackie and her men. Granted, I'd never had much of a sense of direction, and I'd been known to get lost in November when the leaves fell off the trees. But this was ridiculous. None of the usual landmarks were visible. The earth was reclaiming the town. I wiped sweat from my forehead, wondering what to do next.

From here on in, I was using a car, even if I only had to move two steps from one store to another. There were worse things than becoming obese from not walking. Like dying in the wilderness just behind Orchard and Main.

Baby, the young black wolf that had been Marlene's Pekingese, sat down and cocked her head at me as I tried to get my bearings. She and Hudson, the Lab, were sticking close by me. The other wolfish dogs were ranging on ahead, but I knew that they were within earshot. They weren't quite a pack yet, and I wasn't their leader, but they had a dim sense of me as alpha from their pre-transformation memories of the vet's office. I wasn't sure how long it would last, but I was glad of the company.

I tried not to think about Malachy, and what I had done to him. I tried even harder not to think about what he would do to me if he woke up before I got away.

I wiped my face on my arm, wishing I'd thought to bring a bottle of water with me. "I don't suppose you can smell where we are, can you, Baby?"

Baby whined as I turned in a slow circle, trying to see past the rapid growth of trees and vines obscuring the street signs and hiding the houses and stores from view. At this rate, I'd be standing in the middle of a forest by nightfall.

There was a low, hoarse cough from somewhere in the distance, and then a sound like an old woman screaming. Great. Cougar. Knowing that there was no way to hide from a big cat, I figured I'd have to bluff this out. Throwing back my head, I howled for all I was worth, and after a moment, Baby and Hudson and the other dogs joined in. Bon Bon and the former shepherd appeared in the high grass, but some of the other dogs never showed. Maybe the former dachshund and pug hadn't survived the full transition. Maybe they'd just gone off on their own. Or maybe they'd become cat food.

We howled a little while longer, and then Baby cocked one ear higher than the other, and I scratched her head. I couldn't read the signs myself, but watching the others, I thought the cougar had moved off. In the wild, Red had taught me, most animals don't go angling for championship matches.

He explained that people were always worrying that coyotes would attack them or their pets, but most of the time, they didn't need to worry. Since small injuries can become serious without medical help, wild critters know that it pays to pick your battles carefully. They prey on the weak, but if the weak turns out to have a bunch of pals, they give it a pass. Most of the time, at any rate. The same goes for leadership challenges. Leaders are politicians, even if they go around on four legs. And no one with even a drop of political savvy wants to go head-to-head unless they've exhausted all the other options: making aggressive noises, narrowing eyes, frowning, baring teeth, using dominant body language.

With a little luck, Red had said with a smile, you get to figure out who's tougher without actually tearing each other to shreds so that neither of you wins.

Oh, Red, I could sure use some advice right around now. I took out my cell phone again and tried his number, but as I suspected, he was still out of range. I touched the little scar on my arm, but it no longer tingled. I tried not to think about what that might mean. Had my fooling around with Malachy broken our bond, or was he injured, or worse?

He's not dead, said my intuition.

All right, then. I checked that all my weapons were still in place and then whistled for the dogs. "Okay, guys," I said, "let's get going." If I'd expected an eager response, I was sorely disappointed.

My ragtag pack of former lapdogs were already sniffing around, exploring the scents around them. As leader, it was up to me to pick a direction, but the others weren't going to sit there, waiting for me to make up my mind. If I hesitated too long, they would follow their own instincts.

I held the moonstone, trying to get an intuitive hunch, but it didn't seem to work as a compass. As I dithered, the grass continued to grow around my feet, the bushes filled out, and the weeds and puffballs sprang up until they obscured my view. Bees buzzed around the purple heads of clover, and the scent of honeysuckle was so intense that I felt as though I could get drunk off it.

Once, when I was in college, my mother told me not to hesitate too long over major life decisions. My roommates had nicknamed me "Our lady of perpetual fretting" because of my penchant for analyzing every option, and when it came time to declare my major, I became paralyzed with indecision.

When I called my mother for advice, all she said was, "Don't let the grass grow under your feet." Well, the grass was growing, all right, and if I didn't walk, I was going to drown in it. And then I remembered that I could use the sun to orient myself. It was late in the afternoon now, and so the sun had to be dipping toward the east. The town's center was east of our office; all I had to do was walk toward the sun.

"Baby! Bon Bon! Hudson! Come!" I couldn't remember the shepherd's name, so I just added, "Shep!" I broke out into a slow jog and the dogs fell in alongside, tails waving, tongues lolling.

I ran until the breath was sawing in and out of my chest, and the dogs started to give me funny sidelong glances, as in, Hey, remember, we're not regular army. I had begun to worry that I'd screwed up somehow, but as I slowed to a walk and checked that all my hypodermics were still in place, I saw the familiar shape of the Stagecoach tavern. I'd overshot the cafe, but I didn't care; at least I wasn't lost.

As I walked past the tavern's gray clapboard facade, I saw a white face peering out at me from a high window for a moment. Shivering, I quickened my pace, and then screamed and nearly jumped out of my skin when someone tapped me on the shoulder.

"I'm sorry," said the tapper, who was wearing chef's whites. "I didn't mean to frighten you."

"I thought . . . thought you were someone else." Like my boss, whom I just seduced and left unconscious on the floor of his office.

"I get a little nervous, too," said the chef. At least I thought he was a chef, because of his outfit; on the other hand, he might have been on leave from a mental asylum. He had an anxious grimace of a smile, purple shadows under his eyes, a wild frizz of orange hair, and he looked as though he had recently lost a great deal of weight. Not exactly the man you wanted touching you without permission. "I just needed to ask you if you'd heard anything about a storm."

"No, I'm sorry, what have you heard?"

"The others keep telling me that a storm is coming," said the man, whom I now recognized as Abel Tasman, the mischievous Boston chef who had taken over after Pascal Lecroix had committed suicide last year. I'd eaten at the Stagecoach once, and he'd asked me how I liked the new menu. I had lied and said I liked it. I guess a lot of people must have lied to Abel, because he'd kept the same menu, even though fewer and fewer people actually ate there.

"The others?"

"Pascal and Gunther and Elias," said Abel, glancing nervously at the wolfdogs. They looked spooked, and I didn't blame them. I knew Pascal was dead, and I had my suspicions about the other two. "They say I should get down in the cellar," Abel went on, "but I don't like it there. Would you like to come with me?" He looked a bit more hopeful as he added, "I like to have other living people around me when I go down there, but lately none of the staff will keep me company. I'll give you some wonderful chocolate and cactus soup, and some tomato and goat's milk ice cream I just whipped up."

With food like that, the place really didn't need a curse. "Sorry," I said, walking away as quickly as I could. "I have to get to the Belle Savage Cafe."

"That's what they all say," muttered Abel as he looked after me. It might have been my imagination, but

I thought I saw two pale figures by his side, one a hawk-faced man in an eighties baggy linen suit, the other a short, bald fellow in a Victorian frock coat.

I was casting anxious glances at the sky as I reached the cafe. Maybe Abel had no idea what normal people liked to eat, but he hadn't been wrong about the storm: The clouds had spread into a solid layer and were darkening as though someone had left a deep bruise across the heavens.

"I think we made it just in time," I told the dogs, and then realized that they couldn't come inside with me. "Sorry, guys," I said, and then my cell phone rang. I flipped it open. "Hello?"

"Hey, Doc." It was Red. His voice sounded as though he were standing in the middle of a hurricane, or as if he were on the other end of the earth, instead of just a few miles away.

"Where are you? Are you all right?" I looked out at the town, and now the clouds were black and the wind had picked up, bending the trees back.

"I'm okay," he replied, and then there was a burst of static, drowning out the rest of his words. "Red? Red? Talk louder, I can't hear you."

"Where are you?"

"In town," I said, nearly shouting, as if that could make me hear him better. "I know about the animals going feral. And Pia stole Malachy's medication, and he's gone all Mr. Hyde." I stopped talking and listened to the crackle on the other end. "Red?"

"Just listen." The phone was going in and out, swallowing every other word. "Stay. Don't. Home."

"Don't come home?"

Another voice came on the line, and even though I'd only heard it once before, I didn't have to ask who it was. "That's enough," Bruin said in his nasal Quebecker English.

I heard Red say something, and then there was a sharp sound of something being hit, and a grunt of pain.

"Red! Red," I screamed into the phone. "What's happening?

"What are you doing to him, you bastard?" I moved two feet to the right, and suddenly the line was clear. There's a difference between magical force fields and cell phone range, but not a big one.

"I just remind him who is in charge, cherie. He's pretty tough, though—I been hitting him a lot, and he don't complain much."

"Why are you doing this?" Stupid question, but it just popped out. When you're really in crisis, that's when the clichés come out. Nuance, originality, subtlety—those are luxury items. As if to prove my own point, I added, "Please, can't you just leave him alone?"

Bruin laughed. "But Red, he would not leave me alone, would he? *Non*, he put wards and shit all over the damn place. Also, I notice you don't ask about your other friend, eh? You don't mind what I do to her."

Lilliana. Oh, God, how could I have forgotten? "Is she all right?"

"She is much better than all right; she is delicious. Now, why don't you come on home and you can see them both?"

In the background, I heard Red say something. Bruin laughed. In the distance, the sky flashed light, then went dark, and a few moments later, there was a thunderous boom. I held my phone a little farther from my ear, thinking that with all the supernatural activity going on, it would be ironic to be electrocuted during a lightning storm.

Suddenly, I heard Red's voice; somehow, he'd managed to wrench the phone from Bruin. "Don't come home. Lilliana's fine—he won't kill her, he's half in love with her. And as for me . . . I don't need your help."

Tears stung my eyes, and I was suffused with a feeling of such love and admiration that I could barely speak. "I understand," I said, choking a little. I understood that he was in trouble, and being brave, and that I needed to gather help and go and rescue him. And Lilliana, of course.

"No, Abra, you don't understand."

I looked at the phone for a moment in confusion. "Red?"

"I don't want you around here. Go fucking help Malachy if you want."

My stomach clenched. He knew. Somehow, he knew. "Red, I can explain . . ."

"Yeah. I know. But guess what? I'd rather have Bruin here beat me up a few more times. At least with him, I can see it coming."

And with that, the line went dead.

"Well," I told the dogs, who were lying on their stomachs, looking nervous, "I finally reached Red."

As if on cue, the skies opened up and the rain lashed down. I put my hand on the doorknob, and turned.

It was locked. "Hello!" I pounded on the door, and then gasped as I saw the shape of the dark clouds. "It's Abra. You have to let me in, I think there's a tornado forming!"

"Sorry," said a voice from the other side, "but we're closing." I thought it might be Penny.

"Please," I begged. "I just need to get out of the storm."

"It's dark," said Dana. "We always close before dark."

"But it's only dark because of the storm!" I looked over my shoulder and had to squint, because the leaves and dust were blowing into my eyes. "Enid, please! Let me in!" I tried to think of something to bargain with, and came up empty. "I swear I'll be in your debt forever, just please, please open the door." The minute the words were out I knew I'd probably made a mistake, but then I heard the sound of locks turning.

"Here." The door opened a crack and something was thrust into my hands: a cheap red rain slicker and a cloth bag containing something heavy that clinked. "Now get you gone, girl."

I tried to jam my foot in the door before it closed completely, but I was a half moment too late, and then I heard the sound of locks being fastened. For a moment, I was so mad that I swung my arm back, intending to smash whatever was inside the cloth bag against the door. But I couldn't bring myself to do it; whatever else the sisters were, they were powerful beings, and I didn't want to squander their gifts.

I slipped the red rain slicker over my head, and then, glancing at the rapidly approaching funnel cloud, I made a split-second decision; Stagecoach Tavern or Moondoggie's. Stagecoach was closer, but I didn't have a good feeling about being trapped with a bunch of suicide ghosts.

With my red hood obscuring my vision and the cloth bag slung over my back, I ran toward the edge of town. My wolfish pack of former lapdogs ran alongside. I had nearly reached Moondoggie's parking lot when I tripped over something lying on the sidewalk and fell on my face.

At first, I thought it was a tree. My second impression was that I'd stumbled over a corpse. But it was neither. I'd fallen onto the sheriff of Northside, except that he seemed as lifeless as the clay sloughing off his face and body in the driving rain.

THIRTY-THREE

◐○○ Logically, I knew the sheriff had to be dead, but I tried hauling him toward safety anyway. Without much success. As anyone who has ever taken a pottery class can attest, there is nothing heavier than wet clay, and that was what the good sheriff looked like: a statue made of wet clay. But the minute I'd seen him, I'd touched the moonstone locked around my neck and known I had to try to rescue him. Even if he did look like he belonged in the Pottery Barn.

"Emmet!" Nothing. I tried slapping his face, yelling in his ear. Okay, so he couldn't be roused. I called the dogs, and pulled at the sleeves of Emmet's jacket to see if they would get the hint.

After a moment, Shep grabbed the corner of the sheriff's sleeve and started tugging at it. Working together, we dragged him about a foot before collapsing.

This wasn't going to work. I estimated we had about two minutes before the storm reached us. Pulling his hat back from his forehead, I saw that the last letter of his tattoo had been smudged. Or maybe it was the first letter; I'd read that Hebrew ran right to left. Since the rain couldn't have reached the tattoo under Emmet's hat, it seemed logical that the smudging had come at some earlier time—maybe even before the good sheriff had turned into a big heap of dirt.

I needed something sharp—the hypodermic needle. Using the largest size I had, I carved out the letter as best I could, following the faint lines and trying to remember how it had looked the last time I'd seen it.

"If that doesn't work, I'm going to have to leave you," I said, squinting up at the sky. The rain was falling so hard that I could barely see the shape of Moondoggie's twenty feet in front of me.

"It worked," said Emmet. He dragged a hand over his face, and loose clay came off, but what was underneath sure looked like human skin. "I owe you one."

"Hey, I owed you. Now we're even." I helped the sheriff to his feet, and then we took off in a lumbering, staggering jog, the dogs racing at our heels, giving agitated yips and casting nervous glances behind them as the storm drew closer.

I was heading for the front of the restaurant, but Emmet tugged me toward the side of the building.

"Not the front door," he yelled, "we need the storm cellar."

I'd never really paid attention to the sloping white cellar doors before, and if it hadn't been for Emmet, I never would have gotten them open. Even for him, it was a bit of a struggle.

"Go on," he said, and the wind half blew me inside, the dogs' claws scrabbling on the cement stairs as we went down into the dark. Emmet was in a moment later, his massive arms trembling as he pulled the doors closed behind him.

"Jesus Christ, that was close," I said, pulling the slicker's hood off my head. I just sat there for a moment with my back to the door as I drew in air with great, gasping pants. The floor underneath was dirt, and I could smell cool, moist stone. I didn't know how big the room was, but I could feel a draft against my cheek. Heaven.

"You can't stay here," said an unfriendly voice, and then my eyes adjusted enough to the gloom for me to make out faces instead of just rough shapes.

Now that I could see, the cellar had roughly the same dimensions as the dining room upstairs. There was an old couch down there, and a few wooden chairs from upstairs, along with a broken table, some ashtrays, and a fair number of empty wine bottles.

I recognized a few of the waitstaff seated around the cellar, including Kayla, who had a cut on the side of her face and dirt stains on her white shirt. A few of the other waiters looked equally rough, and I figured that, like me, they'd had one hell of a long day.

"I said you can't stay," repeated the owner of the un-friendly voice, whom I now recognized as Marlene Krauss. "And neither can the dogs." Baby, Hudson, Bon Bon, and Shep had arranged themselves around me in a black, white, and brindle pattern of panting dogs. The rest of the cellar's inhabitants were regarding the wolfish canids with varying degrees of alarm.

"Marlene," I said, "you're talking about Baby there." I pointed to the smaller of the black dogs. "Don't you recognize her?"

Marlene narrowed her eyes, as if trying to see the out-line of her little Peke in Baby's large adolescent form. "That's not my Baby, not anymore. As far as I'm con-cerned, that's a dangerous and diseased animal. And you're a werewolf—maybe you've got it, too."

There were excited murmurs and whispers as the oth-ers took this in. In Northside, nobody ever mentioned people's supernatural status—it was as gauche as walk-ing up to a movie star and announcing that you knew they were famous. You pretended they were normal, and they pretended they were normal. The unwritten rule of Northside.

"Please," I said, "it's not even a full moon."

"That didn't stop you from nearly biting my head off a few weeks ago!"

"Marlene," said Emmet in his steady, John Wayne drawl, "I think you're letting your emotions get the better of you."

Marlene's leathery face creased with displeasure. "Sheriff, you're okay, of course. But there isn't enough food and air down here for everybody."

It was hard to tell, but I thought Emmet might be amused. "How about I only breathe once every other minute," he said, "just to make up for Abra."

"Very funny, but who knows how long this storm is going to last? And look at the town. By the time we get out of here, it's probably going to be a jungle." Marlene shook her shopping network turquoise bracelet watch farther down on her wrist and assumed the manner of a bank officer refusing a loan. "I'm afraid we need to husband our resources."

"She's right," said one of the waitstaff.

"No, she's not," said Kayla, as the wind rattled the cellar doors. "She can't go out in that."

The doors rattled again, this time harder.

"She has to go now," shrieked Marlene, pointing her dragon lady nail in my direction. "Before she turns on us!"

With a whimper, Baby scurried over to my side and cowered between my legs.

There were murmurs of agreement and others of dissent, and I instinctively stepped a little closer to the sheriff.

The doors banged this time, and someone gave a startled shriek. "Oh, my God, we're all going to die!" It was one of the waiters; Kayla slapped him.

"Get a hold of yourself," she said, and then put an arm around his shoulders as he started to cry.

"Wait a minute," I said, "that's not the storm—that's

somebody trying to get inside." I could hear it now, the sound of someone's fist pounding against the door.

"Don't let them in," bellowed Marlene, and Kayla told her to shut up and sit down. I was liking the waitress better all the time.

"All right, listen up, everyone," I said. "I'm going to open these doors, because we are not just going to let someone die out there."

"Don't listen to her!" Marlene, of course.

"This isn't just about survival," I said. "This is about surviving with our humanity intact." Granted, I was probably not the best person to lecture anybody about intact humanity, since mine had been showing some definite wear and tear of late. But for some reason, nobody called me on it. "Okay," I said, trying to make eye contact with as many people as possible, "everybody grab hold of something and brace yourselves." I turned to Emmet. "Sheriff, can you help me with the door?"

Emmet gave me a little tip of his hat, which I thought might have been ironic. Then he grabbed the door handles, and I grabbed on to him, and we pulled hard.

Just like in the cartoons, the door opened with no resistance whatsoever, sending us both flying backward.

And as I looked up into the clear, warm summer night outside, Magda stepped out of the shadows. She was dressed in black commando gear, with a knife strapped to her thigh, a gun at her waist, and a rifle slung over her shoulder.

"The storm is over," she said in a low, authoritative voice. "But that was just a burst of fireworks intended to shock and awe us. Now the enemy is going to send in the ground troops." She surveyed us, as if sizing up our willingness to fight. "Some of you may have heard about bear attacks. Some of you may have heard about a new kind of rabies. The truth is that our town is being invaded by creatures that don't belong in this dimension."

Magda's Romanian accent made this speech sound uncannily like one of my mother's less successful movies. In the dramatic pause following this last remark, Marlene and Kayla began to chatter until Magda silenced them with one upraised hand. "There is no time for debate. The threat is real. And you may think you're safe down here, but once you step out of this cellar, you're just collateral damage."

Of course, once Magda had said it, it seemed perfectly clear to me. The Manitou were trying to take over our reality, and the storm had just been their first salvo. I stood up. "Magda's right," I said, about to launch into a little spiel about banding together against a common enemy. Unfortunately, no one paid the least attention to me: instead, they all streamed up the ladder, peppering Magda with questions and suggestions. The sheriff tried to wait for me, but Magda beckoned him over and told him she needed his advice about the layout of the town.

I should have been glad that we were all teaming up. But as I climbed up out of the cellar, I couldn't help thinking that my delusion that I was going to be a kick-ass heroine had just been cured. I was being relegated to bit player, and once again, Magda was taking the lead.

THIRTY-FOUR

◑ ◯ ◯   "So what are you supposed to be," Magda said as we trudged along Route eighty-two. "Little Red Riding Hood?"

"Very funny." I'd taken the slicker off and shoved it into the cloth bag, which was slung over my back. I had to stay pretty close to Magda or one of her group, since they had all the flashlights, and without them, the sidewalks were so dark I could hardly see my feet.

I tripped and Grigore caught me by the elbow. "I thought you looked cute in it," he said in a conspiratorial whisper.

"Please keep up and try to be careful," said Magda, sounding exasperated. I wasn't living up to her vision of werewolves as a kind of superior race. She had a lot of rather unpleasant theories about how humans had weakened the species by introducing antibiotics and messing with the survival of the fittest. Well, I might be a weaker specimen, but I was the one who had come up with the idea of where to find the manitous.

Magda had wanted to climb up Old Scolder Mountain, where most of the manitou sightings had originated. I'd said that the cavern that ran underneath the cornfields to the east of town was a more logical choice. According to Red, there was a nexus of power formed by the mountain, the cavern, and the woods just behind our cabin. If I were a big spirit bear, and I was leading an attack on a town, I know where I'd put my headquarters. So we voted: Magda, Vasile, and the sycophantic Hunter had raised their hands for the mountain, while Emmet, Kayla, and I had argued for the cavern. Grigore, to Magda's annoyance, had broken the tie by siding with us.

"How far away are we now?" asked Grigore, who looked more like a graduate student than a warrior, despite the rifle at his waist.

"Not far. I think. I'm a little directionally challenged. And I was only there once, last summer." The truth was, I wasn't sure exactly how to find the cavern on my own; we were all following Emmet.

"By the way, I like the necklace." He gave me a raffish smile, and I couldn't help but smile back. "Moonstone, yes? A powerful tool. But doesn't the silver pain you?"

"Not so much now." I touched the pendant at my neck, realizing that the silver had stopped irritating my skin, but I didn't know if that meant I had gotten used to it, or if it had just burned away my nerve endings.

"And how is your boyfriend?" asked Grigore. "The one who collapsed in the cafe."

"He's not my boyfriend," I began, and then I heard heavy footsteps coming up beside us.

"Grigore," said Vasile, the older brother, chidingly. I wouldn't have needed to ask if this one was related to Magda; he looked like the masculine version of his sister, down to the streak of white in his black hair. There was a thin scar bisecting his left cheek that lifted the corner of his mouth, making him appear as though he were half sneering. "Flirtation is not appropriate. While we fight the common enemy, we are allies. Afterward, we will have to sort out our own differences." He gave me a look that suggested that he would be the one doing the sorting.

Grigore protested, saying something in Romanian that probably translated as, You're not the boss of me. Vasile responded in the same language, and with a curt nod, Grigore turned to Emmet.

"Will you come with me to scout ahead?"

Emmet looked at me. I guess he figured he was my only reliable ally. "That okay with you, Abra?"

"I'll be fine."

"Go as silently as you can," instructed Magda, as the two men headed off into the tree line that separated the road from the cornfield. Earlier today, the corn had been nothing but snow-covered stubble; now it stood nearly shoulder high. "And the rest of you, remember, when I give the signal, we must stop talking entirely." I wasn't sure how, but she'd wound up taking charge of our combined bands, even though the sheriff seemed a more logical choice.

Who was I kidding. Growing up, she'd probably played Resistance while the other kids were playing house.

"So, what exactly is the plan?" Kayla asked, quickening her pace to catch up to me. There was a fine sheen of sweat on her face, and she was struggling with the pace. It was petty of me, but I was glad that there was someone here more out of shape than I was. I got most of my exercise as a wolf. As a person, I'd been neglecting my cardio.

"I'm not exactly sure," I said. "I think we're probably going to try to get the drop on them." I felt silly, saying it, but it was hard not to get swept up in the whole adventure film feel of this thing. Even if I wasn't a kick-ass heroine, I was a guerrilla fighter, wearing a bandoleer and marching off to save my boyfriend and my friend and the town.

"We're probably going to get killed, then," said Kayla, with surprising matter-of-factness.

"Oh, I don't know about that," I said. "Magda and her brothers look like they know what they're doing."

"I didn't say *they* were going to get killed. They have guns and rifles. But I've got a kitchen knife, and you've got hypodermics."

"And a scissors."

Kayla gave me a sidelong look before going on. "I'm assuming that none of you can change—oh, stop, of course I know about all of you having lycanthropy, I had to have a test myself after, you know." She didn't mention Hunter's name, but she self-consciously tucked a strand of fair hair behind one ear. "In any case, I don't think the odds are stacked in our favor."

I trudged along, not saying anything. I realized now why Magda was in charge instead of me. I was a coward.

"Hey, girls," said Hunter, who was conspicuously on the outside of Magda's inner circle. In his khakis and blue oxford shirt, he looked like he'd headed out for the country club and accidentally grabbed a scythe instead of a golf club. "Never thought I'd see you two getting so chummy."

Kayla just gave him a withering look and strode on in her white tailored shirt, little black miniskirt, and sensible shoes, a zaftig waitress on the warpath.

When all this was over, if we were both still alive, I was going to buy that girl a drink.

I indicated Hunter's scythe. "What are you planning on doing with that, anyway? Going to landscape something to death?"

"Something like that," said Hunter, with a grin. "I figure we might need to hack our way out through the undergrowth."

Actually, that made sense. "I have to admit," I began, but Magda held up her hand and shushed me. Grigore had returned, and he gave his report in breathless Romanian. In the hushed silence, I could hear all the night insects and frogs trilling and chirping. What do you have to be so happy about, I thought.

"They are at the cavern," Magda said, without acknowledging that I had been correct. "All right. I think we have to have a plan. The best fighters—Vasile, Grigore, Emmet, and myself—will circle around through the woods. The rest of you should approach directly through the corn. Abra, perhaps you can make a diversion?"

I looked over at Kayla, remembering her estimation of our chances for surviving this night. "I have sedatives," I said, "but they're only good at close range. And all Kayla has is a knife. Maybe you want to give us at least one gun?"

"We can't waste the ammo," said Magda brusquely.

"Wait a damn minute," Hunter broke in. He looked as though he were about to throw a major fit, and I thought, He isn't a total prick, he's going to argue against leaving Kayla and me defenseless.

"What's all this about the best fighters?" Hunter moved the scythe from his shoulder and planted it firmly in the ground. "Magda, I think you and I need to have a little talk about what exactly my role is in this relationship."

For a moment, I was so pissed off that I really thought about stabbing Hunter with one of my needles. The rush of anger gave me a strange pang; I missed my wolf. I hated these dark, moonless nights when my sense of hearing and smell were at their poorest.

But we ought to be able to see the moon tonight, I thought, as Magda launched into Hunter, telling him that he was not working as a team player.

The moon should have been just past full, and Hunter and Magda and her brothers and I should have still been feeling its pull. Of course, it was also supposed to be winter, so I hadn't been paying attention to the particular way reality had been distorted.

"Kayla," I said, "do me a favor."

"Sure." She looked at me a little suspiciously. "Unless you're going to tell me to drop dead or something."

"Come on, Kayla, really."

"You have to admit, you've been pretty harsh. And I've been trying to show you that I'm sorry for how I was with you."

Oh, for crying out loud. "Look, if we survive the night, we can hash out all our differences. But what I need right now is for you to look at the moonstone around my neck." Because it was a choker, I couldn't lift it up to look at it. "Can you tell me what color it is?"

"Sure." Kayla leaned over to look at it more carefully. "Sort of a murky grayish blue. Why?"

"Because it started clouding over this morning," I said, beginning to put things together in my mind. Up until this morning, the manitous had only been able to affect things and people in their immediate vicinity. Something had given them a far greater power. Or rather, something had enhanced their natural abilities.

Lilliana. But Lilliana didn't have the capacity to change reality. What she could do, however, was impact people's perceptions. A sensitive, she'd called herself, able to broadcast as well as receive. Either because she'd been coerced, or because she'd been co-opted, Lilliana was aiding the manitou.

"Wait a minute," I said, "I think I have an idea."

"Abra, no offense, but this is not exactly your area of expertise," said Magda. "Vasile, Grigore, Sheriff—let's move out."

"I think we ought to listen to what Abra's got to say," said Emmet, tilting his hat back to show the bottom of the tattoo on his forehead. "She was right about the cavern."

"Yes, but now we are about to engage in a fight with the enemy," Magda snapped. "We are all going to be killed unless we are very clear about who is in charge."

"You may be in charge of them," Emmet said, jerking his thumb at the brothers, "but Abra's in charge of me, and I'm not budging till I hear what Abra's got to say."

"What do you mean, Abra's in charge of you?" Magda gave me a squinty-eyed look.

I shrugged. "I have no idea what he's talking about."

The sheriff placed one cowboy-booted foot up on a rock and rested his elbow on his thigh. "Let us just say that I am in her debt. Now, Abra, what did you want to tell us?"

"The bear manitou, the guy I call Bruin, is holding my friend Lilliana. And I think he's using her psychic abilities to cloud our minds."

Hunter frowned. "In what way?"

I pointed up at the sky. "I think they're keeping us from feeling the moon, so that the five of us can't shift at all. And as for the weather . . . it feels like it's at least eighty degrees out, which is another strike against us."

"Of course," said Magda. "Wolves are not at their fighting best in high summer."

"But January is naptime for bears, so he's at a disadvantage." I pulled the cloth pack off my shoulders.

"What's in there?" asked Hunter.

"I'm not sure. It was a gift from the Grey sisters." I reached into the bag and pulled out a small bottle of what appeared to be homemade wine, and a gingerbread man, wrapped in wax paper. "I think it's magic. I guess what we need to do is divide this up into equal portions and see if it breaks the spell."

Vasile said something sharp to Magda, and she replied with equal heat. After a moment of rapid-fire Romanian, Magda cleared her throat. "Vasile says that even if you are right, we cannot all sit around drinking wine and eating cookies."

"Besides," added Grigore, "if the old women gave the food to you, perhaps it is only intended for you. If we all eat a little bit, there may not be sufficient magic to change anything."

"I suggest we keep to the previous plan," said Magda, hefting her rifle onto her shoulder.

Emmet shook his head. "I ain't leaving Abra."

I was touched by the sheriff's loyalty, but even I had to admit that Magda was right. "It's okay, Emmet. You go with Magda's group."

"I resent the implication that I am not one of the better fighters," Hunter said, and Kayla and I exchanged looks.

"Just go with them, Hunter," I said. "Kayla and I have the dogs. We'll be all right."

To his credit, Hunter did look a little abashed when he realized that he was leaving his former wife and lover alone. "If you want me to stay," he began.

We didn't, and Hunter trotted off with the others. He wasn't even beta in that pack, I realized; Grigore had taken that position.

"Okay," said Kayla, slapping at a mosquito that had landed on her bare thigh. "So what do we do now?"

I unwrapped the gingerbread man and prodded it slightly with my finger. It didn't giggle or protest or attempt to run away, so I brought it up to my nose and sniffed it. "I guess we eat it." I broke the cookie in two. "Heads or tails?"

"Tails." Kayla took the gingerbread man's feet and sank back down on her heels. With her high forehead and her perky nose and her apple cheeks, she looked absurdly wholesome. "You know, I never really understood the point of the whole gingerbread man story. Is it pro-cannibalism? Anticookie?"

"Maybe it's about tricking the trickster," I said. "You know, like in the end, when the fox tricks the gingerbread man into jumping onto his back?"

"That's good," said Kayla approvingly. She swatted a mosquito on her arm and took a bite of the left foot. "Not bad. A little damp from the heat, but still."

"Here's the problem," I said. "I'm terrified of doing this."

"Of eating gingerbread?" Kayla took another bite.

"Absolutely. I'd rather be shooting at things. I'd rather be shot *at*."

"Never taken drugs, huh?"

"No, I ate LSD by mistake when I was a kid." Even talking about it made me nervous. I lifted up the gingerbread man's head. "If this makes me feel anything like that, I don't think I can do it."

"So give me the cookie." Kayla held out her hand. "Listen, this isn't laced with acid. It might be magic, but so far, it hasn't done anything for me. But if it freaks you out too much, don't do it."

"No, no, you're right." I lifted the cookie to my mouth, then hesitated. I didn't even like gingerbread. Cookies that made good dollhouses didn't necessarily make good eating, in my opinion. Closing my eyes as if I were eating some loathsome reality TV challenge food, like maggots on toast, I took a bite of the gingerbread man's head.

The lapdogs whined, begging for a taste, and before I could stop her, Kayla threw four crumbs to the dogs, which gobbled them up and sniffed the ground for more.

"See?" Kayla popped the last bite of gingerbread into her mouth. "That wasn't so hard." She gestured at the bottle of wine. "Let's crack the vino."

I took another nibble of the gingerbread man's head and took a look at the bottle. It had one of those old-fashioned stoppers that's attached with a little wire, and I had to use my thumbs to get the mechanism open.

Or not. "Can you do this?" I handed the bottle to Kayla, and she opened it easily, then offered it back to me. "No, you go first."

She took a long swallow. "Not bad," she decided. "Kind of tastes like communion wine."

I sniffed the mouth of the bottle. The sisters' wine smelled fruity and sweet, and a little like plums. I took a swallow, and the taste brought back a very old memory, one I hadn't thought of in years and years.

When I'd been very little, three or four, my father's mother had once made wine in the bathtub at our house, and I remember helping her mash the grapes. My *abuela*, whom I recalled as a very old woman in a black dress, had given me a little taste and then she'd gotten silly and started dancing around the bathroom in her bare feet, which were calloused and cracked like old leather. I had thought she was being very odd, with her face all serious, as if she were in pain. I hadn't known about flamenco. "Wine and dancing," she'd said in her thick accent, as she sat down to catch her breath. "They are both ways into the magic, *comprendes*?"

I hadn't thought of that in ages. *Abuela* had died when I was six or seven, and although Dad had gone to her funeral, my mother and I had remained behind. I think my parents were having some pretty serious problems by that point. Still, I wished I had gone.

"I think we need to dance," I told Kayla.

"Man, are you a cheap drunk."

"No, I think it's part of what we need to do—a kind of chase the clouds away dance so we can see the moon."

Kayla quirked one eyebrow. "O-kaaay." She got to her feet and pulled off her heavy waitress shoes. "But don't we need music?"

"We can sing," I said, unlacing my sneakers. "Pick something."

"It's a wonderful night for a moondance," Kayla sang, swaying back and forth. Despite her recently acquired plumpness, she moved with the grace of someone who had studied ballet. Then she stopped. "I feel like a prize fool."

"We could sing that sixties song, about moonbeams and peppermints. If we remembered the words. Or the tune."

"Or that Cat Stevens song, 'Moonshadow.'"

"I don't think I can dance to that," I said. "Oh, wait, I have one! 'Dancing in the moonlight,'" I sang, snapping my fingers.

"Oh, oh, I love that one," Kayla said. "Dadum bark and dada bite," she added in her musical contralto.

"I don't remember any more words," I chimed in. We stopped swaying and dancing. "This isn't working."

"Maybe we need to get dizzy," said Kayla. "That's what I do with my daughter."

"You have a daughter?" I stared at her, and Kayla laughed.

"She's six, Abra. Not Hunter's. Dan's."

"Oh." Kayla must have been a teenager when she had her baby, I realized. And Dan had left her because of Hunter. "I'm sorry. That must have been hard, losing him."

Kayla shrugged. "It was the thing that scared me more than anything else—being without a man. I thought there was no point in living if there wasn't a man around to constantly tell you that you were gorgeous and he was crazy about you. But you know what? I'm happier like this. Fat and on my own."

"You're not fat."

"I'm heading there. But like I said, I don't care. I may not be gorgeous and I don't have a man, but I'm okay with it. Hey, I have an idea." Kayla held out her hands, crossed at the wrist. "Remember how to do this? You just grab hold and spin around."

"Now, that I can do." We spun and spun, and it was like being six again, when getting dizzy was like getting drunk, and we laughed as the wind picked up and whirled like dervishes with our heads tilted back as the clouds moved off.

"I have to let go," said Kayla, and we both collapsed on the ground, staring up at the full moon. There was a coolness in the air that hadn't been there before; the temperature was dropping. I thought that right now, I felt closer to Kayla than I did to Lilliana.

"I can't catch my breath," said Kayla.

"But we did it." I reached out for her hand and squeezed it. I could feel the moon's pull on my skin. I was no longer smell blind.

"Whoa," Kayla said. "Did you feel that?" She had pressed her hand to her chest, and I lifted up onto one elbow to look at her.

"Feel what?" The ground was growing colder under me, and I sat up.

"My heart. Feels like a bird trapped in my chest. Here," she said, putting my hand just over her left breast. It was fluttering.

"Maybe you ought to lie down," I said, just as I watched Kayla's eyes grow round with alarm.

"There's something in there," she said. "There's a bird in my chest, trying to get out!"

"You're panicking," I said, holding her hands. "Your heart is racing because you're panicking. Just take deep, even breaths." She tried, but her eyes were bulging with panic, and her plump face was red and swollen. Swelling. Where was that coming from? I started to worry about her airway closing down.

But then I started to feel it, too. Not my heart, beating

in my chest like a bird's wings, but the sudden feeling that I had lost connection with my body. My consciousness felt as though it had receded back somewhere in my head, and I couldn't recall how to make my hands and legs move. The panic I'd warned Kayla against took hold of me: I couldn't remember how to breathe.

I had become untethered from my body, and it wasn't like the experience from my childhood that had haunted me. It was worse. I could feel myself drifting away, lifting out of my body like a rising mist. I could see my body on the ground, and I had the strangest sense that I was looking at a favorite outfit that I had thought I couldn't live without, an ensemble of skin and bones and hair that I had thought expressed the very essence of who I was in the world. I looked at my long ponytail, and realized how much sense of self I had invested in my hair. When I wore the wolf skin, I thought, I had more sense.

I might wear another outfit someday, I thought as I began to drift higher. I looked up and I could see the moon, now, a small island in a vast and alien ocean. Dancing in the moonlight, I thought, and I could feel myself ripple in the breeze.

I drifted farther up. I could see a few headlights on the roads, but there were no lights on in any houses. The electricity was gone, knocked out by the storm. That wasn't so unusual, in the summer, but something told me that this time, the Con Ed guys wouldn't be around in the morning to fix the lines. I was so far up now that I could see a sort of hazy ripple in the air all along the boundaries of Northside. It looked as though there was a wall of mist, but I knew that if I passed through that wall, I would feel the heavy density of realities folding in on themselves.

The manitous were annexing the town. They weren't

just going to take back their old routes. They were going to pull the whole territory into the Liminal.

I guess we were going to become the new Bermuda Triangle. I could see the stars now, and hear them, too; they were ringing like celestial bells, in a register just at the threshold of perception. This was the Liminal gateway to the universe, the road of the manitous. I had to admit, I was more than a little excited to find out what lay ahead.

Still, I couldn't help but wonder if my mother would be able to find my body, or find out what had happened to me. I wondered if Red would miss me. I made myself look down one last time, to the world I was leaving behind. As if I had adjusted a pair of binoculars, I zoomed in closer on the cornfield.

My body looked peaceful, but right beside it Kayla was in acute distress. She was clutching at her chest, drawing her knees up, whipping her head back and forth.

Quick diagnosis: I couldn't leave her like that.

With that thought, I plummeted back down into my body. It felt like jumping from a height into a cold lake. Or maybe it felt like being pushed, since I hadn't actually made the choice to jump. With a gasp, I rolled over and crawled up to Kayla.

"My clothes . . . choking . . . help me." Pulling out the scissors I'd brought along as a weapon, I cut Kayla free of her clothes. I'd already guessed this wasn't a heart attack, but my suspicions were confirmed when her eyes were wide with fear and pain and something else, something that made them go impossibly round as her nose seemed to shrink in her face.

I didn't have time to watch, because I had to slice through my own shirt and pants. A moment later, I felt the twist and pop of bones rearranging, the slide of fur over my skin.

When I looked up, I saw that winter had returned to the land.

The Grey Sisters had released my wolf. My lapdogs had each grown to the size of small ponies, and whatever had remained of dog in them seemed to have vanished. But when I looked around for Kayla, all I could see was a little barred owl, hooting softly, as if in astonishment, at all the sudden changes.

THIRTY-FIVE

◑○○ I still had the moonstone around my neck, and maybe that was why, for the first time since I'd become a lycanthrope, I could think ahead to what I was planning to do. With the moon a shade less than full, I was also not completely wolf, although this time, the difference seemed to be mostly psychological.

As Kayla flew soundlessly with low, heavy beats of her wings, I raced with my pack across the cornfield toward the opening of the cavern. She was a silent flier, and I could tell she was more than a little pleased with herself. The wolfdogs were excited as well. This felt like a chase, and they were wild now and lived for the chase.

The tall summer corn had vanished, and I was relieved to feel snow under my padded feet, and reassured beyond words by the presence of the moon. A little of my reality had returned, although I could feel the presence of the misty boundary.

I wished I had a sense of how long it had been since we'd eaten the cookie and drunk the wine. It felt like hours, but that didn't mean it really had taken that long. For all I knew, Magda and the others might be still biding their time, waiting for us to create a diversion. Or maybe the fighting was over, and they were all dead.

As I spotted the mouth of the cavern, I paused, listening as Kayla lighted down by my feet.

"What do we do," she said, except that it sounded like the hooting of a barred owl. It was easier to understand than Screech Owl, at any rate. Wolves understand most owls and ravens, but screech is a pretty strange dialect. "What do we do," Kayla repeated. Or maybe she was saying something else entirely; the truth was, I've never been very good at languages. The wolfdogs were walking cautiously around the mouth of the cavern, sniffing it and leaping back, as though it could bite them.

I whined, telling Kayla that we needed to figure out what was going on before we stormed in. But in the end, coward though I was, I realized we were going to have to just make our way cautiously into the entrance.

Like a lot of caverns, the opening of this one was deceptively small. It appeared to be a narrow hole, barely even a cave, and it was easier going in on four legs than it would have been on two. For a few feet, it was claustrophobic, and then the walls and the ceiling opened up and we were in a huge natural amphitheater. It was dark, but owls and wolves have excellent night vision, so that wasn't a problem. The ceiling of the cavern was an inverted cathedral of stalactite spires and steeples, and they would have been pretty if they hadn't looked so much like spears aiming down at our heads. Kayla hopped onto my back and I started to pad across the smooth, slippery stone surface, sniffing the cool stone scent that permeated the place. The wolfdogs followed more hesitantly, Baby and Bon Bon daintily picking up their paws on the slick stone, while Shep and Hudson moved more deliberately ahead.

There was a faint breeze in the cavern, and I sniffed again: Beneath the minerals were other, familiar odors. Magda, Hunter, the brothers. Red.

"You're too late, Doc." I turned, and Red was walking up out of the deeper recesses of the cavern. I moved toward that beloved voice in a low crouch, my ears pressed flat against my skull, my tail wagging in the low, submissive circle that is canid for *I adore you*.

Except that all that came out was whimpering and puppy eyes, as is so often the case, even when the guilty party walks on two legs. He had a wistful look on his face, and he was wearing old jeans and a soft leather jacket that clung to his lean form, and I felt I had to smell him, really smell him, so I stuck my muzzle into his face and breathed him in, all the clean, kind, goodness of him, the animal scents that told me where he'd been, the level of stress in his sweat.

Red reached up and gently pushed my head away. Something was making him very tense. I shoved my muzzle closer, wanting to read him some more. "That's enough, girl," he said, and there was a note of steel in his voice I hadn't heard before.

He was still angry with me.

Kayla hooted again, and hopped onto Red's arm. He looked at her, his solemn expression cracking into a smile for a moment.

"Good lord," he said, "what happened to you?"

Kayla ruffled her head feathers and turned her head nearly 360 degrees to look at me.

I gave a low woof, the best I could do under the circumstances. I was relieved to see that Red looked unharmed; after hearing Bruin was using him as a punching bag, I'd been braced for the worst.

"And I see you've got some new friends, too." Red nodded to the gigantic wolfdogs, and they looked on in curiosity as Red put his hand out onto the ruff of fur at my neck. "I guess we'll save the big speeches for later," he said, and I felt such a wave of relief and love that I wanted to roll over and over, the dog pantomime that said, if happiness were a scent, I'd be covered in it.

But Red's hand held me in place, moving to the scruff

of my neck. And then he did something so unexpected that I had to fight the urge to shy away.

He pulled the belt out of his jeans. Seeing my reaction, he gave a dry chuckle. "Aw, you know me better than that," he said. Then he looped his belt through my neck-lace as though it were a collar, and led me deeper into the recesses of the cavern as though I were a dog.

Or a prisoner.

When Red had showed me the cave last fall, he hadn't taken me all the way into the room people called the Chapel, because I hadn't liked being so far under-ground. But as we walked along the subterranean river formed by the dripping stalactites, I knew that was where we were headed.

What I hadn't been expecting was light. As the path sloped steeply downward, there were torches planted along the path, but they glowed a phosphorescent green. I thought of Malachy for a moment, and Red glanced at me as though he could read my mind.

And then we reached the Chapel. It was a large, bowl-shaped room, with stones that seemed to have been carved into seats. The torches illuminated this room so that I could see a stone that looked like a face hanging over a large slab of rock that looked like an altar. The face was the kind of thing people always claim looks like Jesus. It didn't look like Jesus to me.

"Well, well, look who's come to join the party," said a short, muscular, sloe-eyed boy lounging on a rock. If I hadn't been wearing the moonstone, I might not have realized that this was Rocky. He had a clever, predatory face and thick, bristly hair that looked as though it had gone prematurely gray. He was playing with Red's silver switchblade, flipping it open and shut with a mischie-vous smile. On second thought, maybe I *would* have guessed that he was Rocky.

It would have been harder for me to identify the lovely young woman with the straight, proud nose and shoulder-length auburn hair artfully falling over one eye. As I watched, she lifted her chin and arched her back, as if showing off the scoop-necked black dress she was wearing. Which was mine. She'd gone into my clothing, goddamnit.

I would have figured out how she felt about Red, since she made no effort to hide it, tracking his every movement and giving me dirty looks. I curled my lip at her, and Red gave a sharp tug on my leash.

I hated to repeat something Hunter had said to Magda, but we were really going to have to discuss my role in this relationship.

And speaking of Hunter, where was he? I caught the scent and sniffed, straining at the leash as I realized that he and Magda and her brothers were tied up and gagged in a corner of the room. Unlike me, they hadn't shifted; maybe they'd been too close to the manitous when the moon had reappeared. Or maybe they'd been distracted by the fighting.

As far as I could figure, you had to tend your reality like a lawn around these guys, or else they would take over like a bunch of dandelions.

There was no trace of Emmet anywhere in the Chapel. Of course, he smelled kind of like wet stone himself, so it was hard to be sure.

"I still don't understand what you ever saw in her," said the auburn-haired woman, glaring at me. "And who's that new slut on your arm?" she added, pointing at Kayla. "She doesn't even know how to tuck her wings properly."

Kayla hooted at her and adjusted her wings so they fit more smoothly at her sides.

"Just lay off it, would you?" Red brushed past the woman, who reached out and tugged at my tail. I turned and snapped at her, and Red tugged my leash, hard. "You leave her alone, too," he told me. I felt crushed.

Then I heard a low, rasping growl that was almost a laugh, and saw a great, honey gold bear standing at the entrance on two legs. Bruin. He landed heavily on all fours and as he lumbered in, I saw that Lilliana was walking by his side.

She was wearing a pair of men's jeans and a button-down collared shirt two sizes too large for her slender frame. Her hair, normally worn in a sleek French twist, was frizzing a little at her temples, but she still looked as regal and composed as an ancient Egyptian queen, not like my image of a hostage. She met my eyes for a moment, a cool, level look that I could not quite read, and I reminded myself not to go by appearances. She might not be on my side anymore.

Bruin looked at me, grunted, and gave a little shrug, and his bear skin slid off, revealing his human form. Unlike lycanthropes, he wasn't naked after the change, which I thought was a real advantage. Running a hand through his thick, golden brown hair, Bruin crouched down beside me, putting my nose level with his calf-high moccasins.

"Your woman, she is persistent," said Bruin.

"She ain't my woman." Red looked at me with what I thought might be sadness. "But she is a fighter."

"It seems a shame, my friend," said Bruin. "After all you sacrificed to get her back, too." His smile was unpleasant. "Agreeing to trade your own long life for a measly mortal span of years, throwing away your position and power—and all for a woman who does not remain faithful. *Quelle dommage.*"

"Knock it off," said Red, clearly annoyed. "You don't need to grandstand."

"But I think it's amusing. She doesn't even know what

you've gambled and lost, does she? You didn't want to influence her decision."

"Just shut it," said Red. I had never seen him so angry. But underneath, there was something else; embarrassment, I thought. Maybe even shame. I was beginning to get an idea why; clearly, Red had never been Bruin's prisoner. He had tricked me, that much was clear. What I didn't understand was the reason why.

"Bruin," said Lilliana, touching him gently on the arm. "There's no need for all this," she said, and her voice was a balm, soothing and soft.

"I would think your friend might want to know why Coyote decided to betray the town, after all." Walking over to me, Bruin crouched on the ground beside me. "You do want to know, don't you? Because it is curious, after all Coyote did to negotiate for your town, why he handed everything over."

"I'm not Coyote," said Red, just as he had told Magda so many times. He was a red wolf, and it drove him crazy when people confused him with a coyote.

Bruin frowned, then nodded in acknowledgment. "Not anymore." Eyes slitted, Bruin reached out and grabbed me by the muzzle, pinning my jaw shut. "You know what he traded for you that day? What he gave up so he could find you and take you to safety?" Bruin gave my head a shake. "Do you have any idea?"

"Let her go," said Red, sounding more tired than angry.

"Bruin, please." Lilliana's voice was pitched so low I had to angle my ears forward to hear it better.

Bruin looked over his shoulder at her, and this time, the anger in his voice was tinged with anguish. "He is— he was—Coyote. Of all of us, he has always been the one to walk easily between our worlds. Because he is a Trickster, *tu comprends*? He has no way of his own, so he can borrow any way he likes. And unlike the rest of

us, he can die and be born again and again. But what he
does not have, cherie, is an immortal soul." Bruin's hand
squeezed my muzzle, hurting me. But his words were
hurting worse. "He sacrificed that existence for you. Because he thought you loved him truly. And if you mated
with him, pledging yourself completely and remaining
faithful, you would have given him the protection of
your soul. You would not have lost your soul, but a
piece of it, a fraction of it, would have grown to become
his soul."

"It's not her fault," said Red. "She didn't know."

"That you are dying because of her faithlessness?"
Bruin released my muzzle. "So now she does know. Perhaps you think it is amusing, to play the femme fatale in
truth. Ah, wait—I want to hear your response, so here."
Ignoring my low, warning growl, Bruin grabbed me by
the scruff of the neck and shook.

And just like that, I was human again, and naked.

THIRTY-SIX

◐○○ *Red was dying.* I was struggling to process this thought, but it was hard to concentrate on whether or not I was being lied to and manipulated while I was standing in a cold room, surrounded by enemies and covered by nothing but gooseflesh. I squinted to bring Bruin into better focus, wishing like hell that I hadn't left my glasses out in a field somewhere, along with my clothes. From now on, I really was going to have to switch to contacts, no matter how much they irritated. Or maybe Lasik. "Could I please get some clothing?" I asked, shivering.

"I vote no," said Rocky.

"Here," said the manitou woman who had been Ladyhawke, handing me a blanket. "I've seen enough of you naked with that one," she added, pointing at Hunter.

"And I've cleaned your crap off the floor, Birdie," I retorted.

"Good," she said, with a toss of her auburn hair that momentarily revealed the scarred skin where her eye should have been. She looked like a woman, but when she opened her mouth I realized that she was a teenager. "You never deserved him, you know. I can't understand what he ever saw in you."

Wrapping the blanket around me like a sarong, I felt

a little better. "Maybe I didn't deserve him," I said. "I came right out of a bad relationship, so maybe it took me longer to recognize what I had." I went up to Red, and I realized how pale and thin he was. There were mauve shadows under his eyes that I did not recall seeing before, and it struck me that he looked older than he had just a few moments before. "Are you really dying?" I felt my throat close up.

Red nodded. "Don't blame yourself, Doc."

"But can't someone do something? What if I take those marks now?"

Red smiled sadly. "It's not the kind of thing you can do out of pity. And you can't mostly want to do it, either. It's kind of an all or nothing deal. I guess I should've explained it better, but I fucked up."

I put my hand on his cheek, and my blanket slipped, forcing me to grab it. "You didn't fuck this one up, Red. I did." I swallowed hard. "I'm sorry about what happened with Malachy. If it makes any difference, I know now that I would rather be with you. When the town started changing, I kept trying to get back to you. And every time something happened, I thought about things you had told me or taught me. And it finally became clear to me that if I had to live in a stone-age world, there was only one man I'd want living in my cave. *You.*" I took a breath and let it out as a choked laugh. "Take away all the trappings of the modern world, and it's easier to see what's really real."

Red swallowed hard, like he was fighting back something bitter. "That's nice, Doc. But you still don't get it. I wasn't off trying to save the town. I was busy handing over the keys, and trying to make it look like I wasn't involved."

"But why? What changed your mind?"

Red gave me a hard, direct look. "What you just said. Take away the electricity and the supermarkets, and I figured I'd look pretty good to you. Because you didn't receive the marks. If you'd gone all the way, then I would never have . . ." He broke off. "If it makes any difference, Doc, I regret the hell out of it."

"How charming. But it changes nothing," added Bruin.

I pivoted and walked up to him, my heart pounding so fast it was difficult to speak. "Maybe not. Maybe I can make a deal. Can't I ransom Red? I wasn't ready to complete the bonding ceremony before, but I am now."

"It's too late," snapped the hawk woman.

"But why is it too late? Doesn't it mean more now that I understand what's at stake?" I moved toward Rocky. "I don't think it's too late for anything. You don't want the manitous to lose their ancient pathways. I understand that. I don't know when you decided that it was all or nothing, but we don't have to be enemies. We can work together."

"Bullshit." Bruin's voice shook with rage. "You think I don't know how it works? We make a deal with you, the next thing we know, someone new is in power and the old deal don't fly no more."

Rocky and Ladyhawke moved around to stand beside Bruin, and I looked past them, at Lilliana. A bead of sweat was running down her forehead; she was broadcasting. But was she working for me, or against me?

"What about Lilliana? She belongs in this reality. You can't just hijack this whole town into another dimension, with all the people here inside it."

"She loves me," said Bruin smoothly, running his hand over her arm. "For me, she make this sacrifice. Don't you, cherie?"

Lilliana looked up at Bruin, putting her slender, dark hand against his cheek. "I don't want to lose my world," she said. She called him a name I hadn't heard before, something long, with little pauses in it. "I don't want to live in permanent exile any more than you do."

Bruin looked thunderstruck. "But you said . . . I thought . . ." His expression was almost comical.

"But there is another way," I said. "You could trust us. Work with us."

"Trust you," sneered Bruin. "Do you know how many times I have trusted? How many treaties I have made?"

"I don't know," said Rocky, flicking Red's switch-blade open and shut. "I think she might be telling the truth."

I held out my hand. "Let me have the knife, Rocky."

He looked at me for a long moment, and there was mischief in his face, and seriousness as well. He was Red's adopted son, all right. He threw the blade and to my shock, I caught it. I was doing pretty well without glasses.

"Here," I said to Bruin. "Take it." And then I went over the stone altar and clambered awkwardly on top of it. "You guys like sacrifice, right? Well, I'm ready to give up whatever it takes to make a deal." Taking a deep breath, I reached out and pulled the ponytail holder out of my hair. Then, with only my long hair veiling me, I spread the blanket. This was high-stakes poker, and I figured naked sacrifice counted for more than sacrifice with a woolen blanket.

Bruin loomed over me. The knife glinted in his hand.

"What are you bargaining for?"

"For another chance. For the town. Here's the deal. We keep your old paths open, and tear down anything that was built and we don't allow anyone to build any-thing new."

Bruin looked at the knife, considering. "And you would trade your life for this?"

"I will let you spill my blood." But if my heart kept

pumping like this, I could wind up spilling more than I intended. I tried to take deep breaths, slow my racing pulse.

Bruin took a step toward me. "Bleed you but not kill you? Interesting."

I put my hand up. "Wait," I said, my voice squeakier than I would have liked. I had given up trying to slow my heartbeat, but I wanted a little more insurance that Bruin wouldn't go carving me up. "There's one thing more. I get another chance to bond with Red."

Bruin touched the tip of the knife to his thumb, testing it. "That is not up to me." He hesitated. "I do not know if it is too late or not. You can try."

"Okay, then."

Bruin raised his hand high. Lilliana gasped but she didn't say anything: Maybe she was expending all her energy on broadcasting peaceable emotions. Or maybe she was in shock. I was hoping for the former.

Red's hand grabbed Bruin's before it could come down. "No," he said. "I'll do it."

"Are you sure?" Bruin hesitated.

Red just held out his hand.

Their gazes held for a moment, and then Bruin handed over the knife.

This time, the hand that held the knife over me belonged to my friend and lover. "You sure about this, Doc? It can't just be a scratch, you know. Not for this."

"I understand." In the past few minutes, he seemed to have aged years. In the flickering light of the torches, he looked like a cancer victim, or a prisoner of war.

Red turned my head to the side and raised the knife. And a horrible thought occurred to me. There was something familiar about the story Bruin had told me. Which wasn't really strange. We were in the realm of myths and fairy tales now, where themes and motifs crossed the borders of different cultures.

At the end of the original fairy tale of *The Little Mermaid*, which my mother used to read to me at bedtime, the mermaid stands over her faithless love, the prince. Like Red, she had bargained away her long, magical life for a chance at an immortal soul. But the prince had married another, and the mermaid was doomed to die— unless she traded the prince's life for her own, and sprinkled his blood across her legs, transforming them back into a fish's tail.

With the moonstone still around my neck, I knew this was no fairy tale. If Red killed me, he could become Coyote again.

"I'm so sorry to do this," Red said, and his voice had tears in it as he brought the knife up in a swift motion.

"Not as sorry as you're going to be," said a voice coming from the entrance to the Chapel, speaking in a low, flat, John Wayne drawl.

I turned to see the good sheriff, leveling a rifle at Bruin. Malachy, bringing up the rear, was covering the rest of the room with a gun. And it *was* Malachy, gaunt and sardonic, and not Knox, who took in the sight of Magda and the others hog-tied while I lay naked on an altar, covered only by my long hair.

"Thanks for the assistance, guys," I said, "but I'm here of my own free will."

"How embarrassing," said Malachy. "And here we thought you were about to be filleted *against* your will."

"Somehow, Mal, I ain't convinced of the veracity of her statement," said Emmet.

"It's true, Emmett."

"You know, that's what my name means in Hebrew," said the sheriff, giving me a level look. "Emmett means truth. Take away the first letter—you get death."

I nodded, remembering how I'd recarved that first letter into his forehead. "He's not going to take anything I can't stand to lose."

"If he does, he'll stand to lose something of his own," said Emmet.

Bruin growled. "Then it does not count as sacrifice."

"Okay," I said, sitting up. "Listen, everyone. Whatever Red does to me, nobody is to retaliate. Understand?" I looked up at Red. "I'm ready."

Red shook his head. "Not yet." Then he took my hair and gathered it in his hands, as if he were going to brush it, leaving me totally exposed to everyone in the room. "Lie down," he said. I did, with my hair hanging down over the stone table, feeling a little less sure now that my whole body was revealed. I knew lycanthropes were supposed to be casual about such things, but I wasn't. And then, at the last moment, I realized what Red was intending to do.

I sat up on the stone altar, shouting, but I was too late. Red had plunged the knife into his own chest. He seemed to fold in on himself as he collapsed to the floor, and I slid down beside him, desperately trying to assess the damage. God, there was blood everywhere, bubbling up from my hands as I held them pressed to Red's wound. Glancing up at his face, I saw Red's lips move, forming a word. But no sound came out, and as I looked in his eyes the light went out of them. Not all fairy tales end with happily ever after. Like the little mermaid, he'd chosen to sacrifice himself.

Screaming Red's name, I checked for his pulse, and then frantically began doing chest compressions. I knew it was futile, but I ignored the voices telling me to stop, and fought the hands that tried to grab my wrists.

Until I realized that my patient wasn't just alive; he was *smiling*.

EPILOGUE

◖○○ A month later, I came home to find origami hearts and birds all over the cabin and a delicious smell of burning meat in the air. I'd hoped my carnivorous appetites would wane with the moon, but these days I was ravenous for animal protein all the time. I guess I was a lapsed vegetarian now—one more change to add to my list.

I took off my hat and fluffed out my hair. I was surprised at the feel of my bare nape, and sometimes it felt as though I had removed a limb instead of just cutting off four feet of hair. Still, I was glad that Bruin had decided I didn't actually need to spill blood to seal our pact. I guess Red had spilled enough for both of us.

Of course, it would have been nice if the tricky bastard had let me know he actually had one more life left in him. Especially since I nearly had a heart attack when he sat up and pulled the knife out of his chest.

But I don't really hold it against Red. He'd possessed one last chance to gain a soul, and he had been willing to trade his very last life for it—the one he'd kept up his sleeve, as it were. So I couldn't blame him for making sure that I wasn't holding anything back.

And I think Red had really believed that he could keep me from sacrificing anything. He hadn't looked happy when Bruin had insisted that I take the knife and complete the bargain.

I touched my shorn hair again. In any case, Marlene had done a fairly decent job of making the ragged ends look like a deliberate style. Red even claimed he liked it, saying he thought it made my eyes look bigger, and that the nape of my neck was his new favorite body part.

My mother said it would grow out and look better in a year or so.

I touched one of the origami hearts. "What's this for?"

Red came up behind me to take my coat. "Let's warm you up first. How is it outside?"

"Cold." Four weeks after the manitous had plunged us into an unnatural summer, and I was so sick of winter I half wanted to ask if they could do it again. But then I thought of the paperwork involved.

Being town supervisor, as well as being a veterinarian, didn't leave me a lot of free time. And that was what I had become: de facto mayor of Northside. It turned out that reviving Emmet had made me his boss, and then the town board had decided to make it official.

"How did the meeting go?" Red knelt down and pulled off my wet boots.

"Long. The council is still arguing over the zoning issue. But we have agreed to fund the Brownies' Maypole festival, and there's an agreement on the table that will protect the sacred ground on Old Scolder Mountain."

"Bruin must be pleased." He'd attended the session to ensure that the manitous' interests would be represented.

"Bruin looked preoccupied, actually. I think it's because Lilliana went back to the city last week."

Red rubbed his palm along his jaw, considering. "Or

maybe he's just not supposed to be awake in the middle of February."

"I guess you're right, but. . . ." I stopped, looked around at the origami decorations, and realized what they meant. "Crap. It's Valentine's Day, isn't it? I bought you a card, but I haven't had time to write in it yet."

"I don't care much for cards, anyhow," said Red, his hands moving up my ankle and around my calf.

"How can I make it up to you?"

Red paused, his hands halfway to my thighs. "Now, there's a question."

"Mmm. Speaking of questions, where are the dogs?" Now that we had been adopted by four enormous wolfdogs, Red was getting more serious about building our canid dream house.

"I sent them out to play while I cooked the flank steak." Red stood up and I wrapped my arms around his neck.

"How did you know I felt like meat tonight?"

"I've got a piece of your soul growing inside me, remember?"

I did remember, because when I spent too long away from Red, I felt a hollow ache in my chest. What was harder for me to bear in mind was that the same man who sometimes ticked me off by leaving the toilet seat up was actually Coyote, the most Liminal of the Liminal creatures, who had passed back and forth between worlds until he belonged to both and neither. As far as I could tell, Red had been honest about his family history. He'd had a rebellious mother who had left her clan, and he'd been taught by his grandfather in the ways of the Limmikin. Red just hadn't mentioned that he'd had quite a few other lifetimes, or that Coyote was all about dying spectacularly and then being reborn. Red was hard to pin down on the subject, but it seemed that Coyote was always born to the Limmikin—they were his special children, his tribe. I wondered what would happen to them now; maybe some other trickster god would adopt them. But when I was with Red, I got caught up in the seductive normality of day-to-day life, and forgot about his mind-bendingly long and checkered past.

I nuzzled Red's neck. He smelled delicious, clean and woodsy, with a faint, musky tang. "New aftershave?"

"Uh-uh. You smell pretty good yourself." He trailed his fingers over the moonstone choker. Red was looking in my eyes, a knowing, masculine smile curving his lips. And all of a sudden, I felt a rush of arousal so strong Red broke out into a broad grin.

"You look a little too smug, Buster."

"I have to admit, I'm feeling pretty smug."

"You know, this isn't exactly natural. I'm not in heat anymore."

"I guess I'm getting domesticated," Red said, grasping my wrists and pulling me closer. "Dogs do it all year long, don't they?"

"You don't feel domesticated. But the dog part sounds about right." Ever since that day in the cavern, Red had revealed a more confident, mischievous side. Maybe it was because I knew his big secret. Or maybe it was because of the marks branded into my arm, and his, that marked us and linked us more closely than we had ever been before. I couldn't read his mind, thank God. But I did know what he was feeling, and vice versa.

It had given us both permission to play with more of an edge. "Listen, Redneck, I haven't even had a glass of wine yet." I twisted my wrists free of his grasp. "Besides, I don't think I'm really ready yet." I walked over to the wine cabinet and pulled out a bottle of merlot.

Red pounced on me, taking me down to the ground, his arms stopping me from hitting the floor. "You smell ready."

"Get off me or I'll bite you."

"Bite me."

We thrashed around, rolling on the floor, until Red had me pinned again, my wrists held over my head. "Now, where to begin . . ." He bent his head to my right breast, nipping me through the fabric of my blouse.

"Oh, Red," I said, suddenly on the verge of tears. Red smiled, his body lean and hard against mine, his calloused hand soft as he reached under my skirt to cup my abdomen. I didn't look pregnant yet, I just looked like I'd been eating too many doughnuts, but neither of us cared. We were going to have a baby, and even the fact that Magda was pregnant as well didn't bother me. The only thing that did niggle at the back of my mind was my desperate promise to the Grey sisters the night when reality got a little porous over Northside. But there were so many things to worry about when you were pregnant. I was just relieved that I wasn't whelping a litter.

I tugged at Red's hair to stop him from kissing my belly. "Hey. Coyote. You have any idea how much I love you?"

"I was hoping for a demonstration."

"What about the steaks?"

"Darlin', I put those in the warmer the minute you walked in the door."

My phone rang, and Red stiffened against me, so I bit his chin to get his attention. As he kissed me with real concentration, the message machine clicked on and Marlene began nattering on in her nasal voice about some kind of building variance. I ignored it. A little while later, while Red was kissing his way down my belly, the phone rang again, this time my mother, wanting to know about whether we'd come any closer to deciding on a venue for the wedding.

We got into a laughing fit, but recovered. The third time the phone rang, Red threw my phone against the wall.

In nature, coyotes are among the most adaptable of animals. They can live in mated pairs like foxes, hunting mice and voles, although when they yip and howl, they can throw their voices and fool you into thinking there are many more of them. But when conditions are right, coyotes can live like wolves, forming large packs and taking down big game.

They are opportunists and con artists, and are notoriously difficult to destroy. In the old Native American myths, Coyote died a thousand ignominious deaths, only to rise again. But despite his reputation as a trickster, I knew that Red had made his choice. He had only one life left to live. And that one would be with me.

For my part, I had made my peace with loving Red, and with the knowledge that I might not have chosen him if I'd never become a lycanthrope. If I'd been human and living in Manhattan, I might not even have gone out on a first date with him.

Which would have been a shame, because I would have missed out on the kind of man you wait a lifetime to find. But then, humans work at such a disadvantage when it comes to selecting their mates. They get distracted by clothing and hair texture and skin color, by age and accent and, most of all, by the enchantment of words and the illusions they can conjure.

Red and I had a more fundamental connection, and once a month, we were reminded that love, like territory, needs to be maintained. There's a lot to be said for being human, but if you want true loyalty and undying passion, let a wolf be your guide.